INSIDE THE BUBBLE

INSIDE THE BUBBLE

Noga Niv

Translated by
Riva Rubin & Sharon Niv

INKSHARES
SAN FRANCISCO

Written by Noga Niv

Edited by Anne Horowitz
Translated by Riva Rubin and Sharon Niv

Design by MacFadden & Thorpe
Cover Art by Ben Rotman

This novel, set in California's Silicon Valley, is a work of fiction. With the exception of WIZO and the Jewish Federation, real organizations used fictitiously, all other organizations, events, and characters are entirely fictional and are the product of the author's imagination. Any resemblance to real persons or events is purely coincidental. All of the psychological material in this book is based on established scientific and professional literature.

Published by Inkshares, Inc. in San Francisco, California

Printed in the United States of America

First Edition

1 2 3 4 5 6 7 8 9 10

Library of Congress Control Number: 2014958997

ISBN 978-1-941758-04-5
(Paperback)

To my family, Israel, Sharon, Yonatan, with love

and

To the memory of Galit, my friend, who was one of us. She died at age fifty-two after losing her battle with cancer.

The artist is the creator of beautiful things...

Those who find ugly meanings in beautiful things are corrupt without being charming. This is a fault...

There is no such thing as a moral or an immoral book.

Books are well written, or badly written. That is all...

Thought and language are to the artist instruments of an art.

Vice and virtue are to the artist materials for an art...

All art is quite useless.

—Oscar Wilde, preface to *The Picture of Dorian Gray*

Preface

Daniela

Five years have passed since I wrote this book about my life and the lives of my friends in Silicon Valley. This collection of anecdotes could have come from any place in the world. Nonetheless, it came from a specific time and a specific place.

So what was it all about? It all started with a website called Hevreh. com—Hebrew for "the gang." This Facebook precursor brought us Israeli expatriates back to our yesterdays, stirring us and reconnecting us symbolically to our roots. It was like the unexpected stir that occurs when an old flame emerges and brings us nearer to a lost, distant youth, returning to us something that had been seemingly forever lost. Hevreh made us feel that sort of nagging longing, irrational and unceasing, a longing that came from afar and that crossed the oceans that divide the here from the there and the now from the then.

What else is this book about? A group of Israeli women who found themselves connected to one another out of the necessity brought about by isolation and distance from home. Born in another part of the world, we followed our husbands across continents and oceans and found one another by chance. We were all married to more or less successful entrepreneurs, and we played second fiddle in the technological symphony. We all knew, however, that without our support, their ventures would never have blossomed as they did, and the dazzle of success would never have burned as brightly. Nevertheless, while the men in our lives were sprinting along the fast track, we remained out of the limelight, did not appear in *Business Insider*, and were never interviewed on MSNBC. But we had a presence. I have tried to capture that presence in this book.

Since I wrote about Gabi, Mika, Gila, and Anita, our worlds have changed. My gang has disbanded. When I think of our group now, it feels as if I am gazing at an old photo album of a family gathering—we have all dispersed to continue our respective journeys. Our story is not uncommon: sisters for a moment, sharing a common reality. We were a group within a changing dynamic, subject to forces that pushed and pulled us and inevitably separated us.

Over the years, Hevreh seems also to have lost its magic. These days, everyone is sharing and liking on Facebook. The PalmPilot has disappeared and been replaced by the iPhone and Android. These technological innovations alter only the means, however, not the essence of our lives.

What else is this book about? A bubble that burst. A bubble that gave birth to thousands of millionaires and left many more frustrated. The bubble burst, but the promise remains. Silicon Valley continues to be a magnet for those who thirst for success, and every year the scene lures new dreamers who strive to find riches and happiness in the Valley of Promise. Most arrive for a year or two, only to make a sudden exit and immediately return home. ("Immediately" is an elastic term describing an undefined period ranging from two years to life.) The characters change, but the dream persists, and the events recounted here repeat themselves almost unchanged.

I approached my friends Gabi, Mika, Gila, and Anita, the protagonists in this book. I shared my manuscript with them and asked for their response. These are their words:

GABI   Dear Daniela, greetings from Jerusalem.

I read the book and liked it. You succeeded in capturing the complexity of life in Silicon Valley, even the pain. You have no idea what a relief it's been to return home, back from the uncertainty. The transition wasn't easy. As you can imagine, we each had to struggle to find our place in this tough country, but at the end of the day, there is nothing like coming every Shabbat to dinner at Grandma Yael's. It beats gourmet restaurants anywhere in the world. I'm sitting in our cramped little dining nook, so different from that huge dining room we had in California. I'm looking at the small garden, drinking coffee, thinking that I'm quite alone, but not lonely. You, Daniela, are an email away, and life in Jerusalem has a dynamic of its own.

Now that it's behind us, I'm glad that the adjustment period has ended. The children know who they are now—they don't ask me anymore, "Mom, am I American or Israeli?" They have many friends and are much more independent. They don't even need to be driven around.

As for me, I admit that at times I miss the carefree Californian life. Next year, Yaniv will be drafted into the army. For me, this means the beginning of nine sleepless years of worrying and ironing uniforms. The three boys will go on consecutively, one after the other. But there's no question that on the whole, things are good. Being back at work is wonderful: I teach and create. My studio is full of new sculptures and paintings, and I feel so busy and full of energy. Danny, as usual, is traveling all over the world, and as far as he's concerned, the difference lies only in the direction of flights and in the names of the travel agents.

Roni has finished her army service and has started her university studies. I'm happy to say she has an Israeli boyfriend, a good guy from an elite unit in the army, and he's been accepted into the MBA program at Harvard. They're getting married in the summer and will leave for Boston in August. Roni will manage easily—after all, she's familiar with the American way of life. So, that's it, Daniela. All's well. Come for a visit. I miss you, and Keren misses Maya. And don't forget to bring me the tablecloths from Bloomingdale's and the perfume from Tiffany.

Love you,
Gabi

MIKA   Darling Daniela,

I'm writing from Grindelwald, in Switzerland. I've rented a wonderful cabin with a piano and a view of Jungfrau Mountain in the distance. Every day, I walk along green paths, listening to cowbells. I eat healthy food, play the piano, and write my music. In short, I'm enjoying life, because life is music.

I've read your book. Daniela, you've written a book about creativity. I hope many will read it and identify with it, perhaps even find the inner strength to overcome their mental blocks and, like me, connect with the creative world. Your book reminded me of Jung and his approach of sublimating one's inner repressed substance in order to grow and develop. I read your description of my obsession, with its painful connections to my youth, and I'm horrified. I can't believe that this nonexistent relationship with Yaron ever threatened my sanity, my marriage to Shaul, or the rest of my life.

Daniela, one of the reasons for my stay in Switzerland, apart from the views that inspire me, is the psychoanalytic institute in Zurich. I visit at least weekly, continuing my therapy of connecting to the sounds from within that emerge only with age and life experience.

Thank you for this gift. What are your thoughts about a reunion of our gang? This time in a cabin in Grindelwald? I plan to be here until the end of summer, after which I'll spend six months in Israel. Plan for August? I'll email Gabi, Gila, and Anita.

Till we meet, kisses,
Mika

GILA   My dear Daniela, I'm writing from Berlin.

I read your book and laughed, cried, and yearned. I also enjoyed myself. I tip my hat to you. I didn't know you had it in you—the ability to write about all of us with such honesty and to delve into the messy guts of it all but emerge smiling.

The book you've written is about women in the middle of their lives. You've described all of the uncertainty we faced, as well as the inner strength we found, the way we fell in love, and the way we held our heads up high, no matter where we were or what life threw our way. There's something ineffable that happens in the middle of life. An inner something. Here and there, you brought tears of regret and recognition to my eyes. I admit it. Even Yigal's story moved me, as if I didn't know him, my own husband. On second thought, I don't think Yigal would recognize himself in the book, and maybe that's for the best.

I still haven't given up the theater. I think it may be worthwhile to work on a stage version of the story you've written. I'm prepared to direct and even act in it. I have some close friends who can help. I've really thought about this. If you decide to publish the book, I have contacts among the big publishers. They recently published a book by a friend of mine. Give it some thought, Daniela. Talent is one thing, contacts are another. Contacts are just as important. That's it, good luck. See you soon in Mika's cabin.

Hugs,
Gila

ANITA   Daniela, I'm writing from Denver, Colorado, from Hillary's campaign. I'm sorry. I tried to read, I really did. I even slogged through fifty pages before giving up. I stopped for a few reasons: First, you're not giving credit where it's due. You wrote a book about the Israeli community in Silicon Valley, and I'm sorry to say you're way off base. You don't reflect things accurately. There are top-notch people there who just don't get a spotlight in your book. You're not giving them the respect they deserve. You make it seem like we're all just a bunch of adulterers. What would my mother say?

Second, if only you had some talent for writing, it might be worthwhile. People have to recognize their limitations. Why don't you hire some Stanford doctoral student in literature to ghostwrite your memoirs? Yossi Giladi did it, and he's a success. You could reach a broader audience that way too, Daniela, in English. If you think small, you'll never make it big.

Third, and this is the main reason I stopped reading, I'm up to my ears in work for the Hillary campaign. She asked me personally to join, because of my various connections with philanthropic organizations and worldwide charities. I couldn't turn her down, nor did I want to. And I believe in her with all my heart. I'm so busy with organizing women's meetings across the continent. I suggest that you too join, Daniela. We could use so many more hands from women who care. Forget this book, and come invest in something that really matters.

Yours regardless,
Anita

PART ONE

LATE AUTUMN

Chapter 1

Lori rose from the couch with the agility of a dancer. Her heels drummed on the floor of my office as she extended her bony hand to the door handle, fingernails glistening with fresh polish. She smiled broadly in my direction, batted her false eyelashes, and purred at me, "See you, Dr. Oren."

As I watched her leaving, I mumbled, "See you next week." After the door closed, I sank into the chair by my desk and buried my face in my hands, distressed and short of breath. I'd been seeing patients daily for more than twenty years, but not once had I come upon a case like this. Hoping to find some logic in the sordid story I had just heard, I reached for Lori's file from my cabinet.

I had met Lori about two years prior. She'd been referred to me by Dr. Warner, an attending psychiatrist at the nearby psychiatric hospital, after she had grown obsessed with Dr. James, a resident in the outpatient clinic. Lori would sit all day, every day, in the waiting room, anticipating the moment Dr. James would leave his office, and harass him with endless questions. She flooded his voice mail with long, tiring messages, bought him expensive gifts, and refused to give him a moment's rest. Attempts to refer her to other therapists in the department met with failure. Lori clung doggedly to Dr. James. The department head, Dr. Warner, explained that he had decided to send her to a private clinic in order to take the load off the unfortunate Dr. J. He warned me that she was a difficult case and rather hesitantly wished me success.

Lori then presented herself at my office in the psychology clinic where I worked alongside several other therapists in Palo Alto. Young, in her midtwenties, with exotic features that revealed her Japanese heritage, she had an alluring figure, highlighted long hair, slanted eyes adorned with fake lashes, and a wide, sensuous mouth that glistened with lipstick and flashed indulgent smiles in every direction. Lori seemed like the sort of woman who would have a constant row of drooling admirers in her wake. Her low-pitched, caressing voice reminded me of Shirley Bassey's. When I asked what she did, she answered in childish slang that yeah, like, she was a singer who wasn't singing right now and, actually, she'd never sung for an audience, professionally. And, yeah, she was bulimic, binged on huge amounts of food, and immediately needed to throw up. This happened three to five times a day. And yeah, she got depressed and sometimes cut herself with a razor blade to feel that she existed. Yeah, like, she got married about a year ago to a guy twenty-five years older than she was; met him in Las Vegas when she was drifting from bar to bar with her drunk friends.

She didn't elaborate on the subject of her marriage.

Lori confessed to a little quirk: she bought clothes from mail-order catalogues. She bought dozens of items to be delivered. When they arrived, she would try them on, decide to keep a few of the items, and return the rest by mail. Sighing heavily, she explained that the problem was that she opened everything at once and then got confused between a red bra from one company and black panties from another. With a bashful smile, she admitted that she never received refunds for the items returned to the wrong store. When her credit card reached $20,000, her husband canceled the card. Lori protested angrily, cried, and cursed the man. "I hate him, hate him, the dumb retard!" she shouted in the clinic, her face scrunched up like that of a little girl who'd been wronged by life.

I arranged a meeting with the husband, to size him up. I found a pleasant, well-spoken, intelligent, meticulously dressed man who was a senior executive in a respected company. He spoke about his wife's hospitalization in a psychiatric ward in the short course of their marriage, her outbursts of rage, deep depression, constant vomiting, and uncontrolled behavior. He was compassionate toward her, as if to a beloved, wayward child.

A complex case: comorbidity of borderline personality disorder with obsessive-compulsive tendencies, bipolar disorder, and an eating disorder. I decided to begin treatment by putting her on medication, then regulating her eating disorder. The rest of the plan remained to be determined.

In the first year of treatment, Lori found a young lover, Steve, in one of the bars she frequented drunkenly on her own. He was a guitar player who barely made a living from freelance performances. He was impressed by her sweet voice and asked her to join the little group he had formed with another guitarist and a drummer. They spent many romantic hours of endless rehearsals together and did a few performances in San Jose bars. During this time, Lori seldom went home and stopped coming to sessions with me. "I'm well," she told me about a month after she had met Steve. "My life is just amazing."

A year later, only a few weeks before the tragedy, she called and asked to come back for therapy. She complained of depression, insomnia, and unexplained stress. I tried to understand what had recently changed in her life, but she was incoherent.

Then, four weeks later, at the end of a weekend, my home phone rang. It was Lori. In a tearful, broken voice, she told me that the police had come knocking on her door. The burned wreckage of her husband's car, they told her, had been found north of San Francisco. The body inside was unidentifiable. They wanted to know when she had last seen him. He'd left the house early on Saturday morning before she had returned from a night out with her lover, so she'd last seen him on Friday night.

I went to Lori's house on Monday, the day after her phone call. I found a disheveled, inconsolable woman without a trace of makeup. Her eyes, devoid of the false eyelashes, were red and swollen, her lips pale. She wept bitter, heartbreaking tears and moaned like an abandoned kitten seeking solace.

To my surprise, Lori pulled herself together in only a few days. The hair, the eyelashes, the red lips, the high heels, and the miniskirt entered my office. I, who had been expecting a woman in mourning, was in shock to recognize the same old childish demeanor, the familiar eyelash batting and seductive smiles.

It was the same old Lori, speaking of the compassionate phone calls and the adoring attention she was receiving from her late husband's friends. "Wonderful people!" she said, clasping her hands as one does while enjoying a place in the spotlight, and not quite recalling the tragic nature of the situation. With a joyful, confident smile, she described the ceremony she was planning to commemorate her husband. She'd chosen a beautiful church with a romantic view overlooking the sea.

She'd decided who would read a serious, moving poem and who would deliver a eulogy. No, she was not going to speak, she explained piously. She was going to sing her husband's favorite song. In his honor, she said while batting her heavy eyelashes, she had ordered tons and tons of white lilies and narcissus to fill the church with their scent. There would be tiny black caviar sandwiches and classical background music. She had bought herself an elegant black suit for the occasion.

Lori's excitement reminded me of a bride preparing for her wedding. Or, perhaps more accurately, of one of my friends, carried away with the enthusiasm of planning a son's bar mitzvah. There was not a trace of sadness in Lori, nor any sign of mourning. I wondered if her meteoric recovery indicated an antisocial personality, in addition to the staggering string of diagnoses she already had.

Today, Lori had turned up at the clinic even more radiant than usual. She had just been informed that the insurance company would be depositing two million dollars into her bank account. Her husband's life insurance was all hers. "I knew he was insured," she said, beaming, "but I didn't know it was for so much money!"

In the same breath, she sailed into farfetched, grandiose plans. She would invest the money in real estate, in bonds, in high-tech shares. She was thinking of starting a business: import-export, maybe a designer fashion store. "So many possibilities," she sighed with satisfaction.

I was troubled. Before me sat an infantile woman, suddenly playing her hand at a substantial sum, and not unlikely to lose her livelihood in one ill-advised move. I asked Lori if there was someone whose judgment she trusted, who could be asked to give her financial advice. "Sure." She nodded energetically. "Steve and I have been discussing it for ages."

My blood froze. For the first time, the suspicion crept into my heart that there had been a murder and not an accident. I searched my memory as to whether I was obliged to protect my patient's privacy or report to the police. No. I had never heard Lori planning or threatening to commit murder. I had no cause for suspicion. But why had she returned for treatment four weeks before the accident? I mulled over this distressing question. Surely, Lori's request for treatment four weeks before the accident was merely a coincidence and not an alibi prepared in advance to prove that she suffered from a serious mental condition. I debated with myself in an effort to reject subversive thoughts. After all, I'm not a police investigator, not a detective, I repeatedly told myself. Best leave the investigation to the professionals who had examined all possibilities connected to her husband's death.

I had to admit that I had lost my empathy for Lori. I would have to consult my colleagues. I decided to raise the matter at the coming professional meeting. But still, I was troubled by the fact that I no longer saw Lori as the wayward child, so loved by her late husband and in need of protection.

I put the matter aside until I could think more objectively and returned Lori's file to the drawer. The weekend was approaching, and I remembered that it held a promise of adventure. I had to get into a different frame of mind: lighter, more personal, and more feminine. Taking off my professional tailored suit, I quickly slipped into jeans, a loose sweater, and clogs and shoved the high heels and suit into my overnight bag. I turned off the classical music in the waiting room and locked the file cabinet that contained my patients' files, in keeping with California's laws of confidentiality.

I took one last quick look around to see that everything was in place for work in the coming week and returned the box of tissues to the shelf under the coffee table and the DSM-IV to the bookcase. I smiled affectionately at the statue of Freud that sat upright and earnest in a sexy chair shaped like a woman's curvy legs in cancan dancers' boots and garters. It was the work of the sculptor Frank Meisler and my husband Yoel's gift to me for my fortieth birthday, five years earlier.

As I locked the door, I glanced at the plaque I had earned through so much toil and sweat: DR. DANIELA OREN, PSYCHOLOGIST.

I strutted to the parking lot, slung the bags onto the back seat of the car, and, opening a map of Northern California, studied the roads that led to Lake Tahoe. Four hours of driving ahead of me. Onward to Dumbarton Bridge, Interstate 880 north, from there to Oakland and then Interstate 80 to Truckee.

It had been some time since I had driven such a long way on my own. I was usually in the passenger seat on longer trips and relied on Yoel to get us where we were going. Normally, after a day's work, I rushed to pick up Maya from elementary school and Alon from high school, glad that Ayelet, my sixteen-year-old, now got around on her own. With the two younger ones sitting quietly in the back seat on good days or quarreling loudly on not-so-good days, I would stop at the supermarket, fetch the dry cleaning, dash home, and prepare dinner. Then I did the dishes, walked the dog, and collapsed in front of the television.

That day, with a sense of great freedom, I broke the routine. They'll get by without me, I thought. Yoel will take over, and nobody will feel my absence. In my mind's eye, I saw him handling the kids. There would be no arguments when he allocated tasks. Nobody would sing the familiar tunes: "Why me?" "It's not my turn today." "Not now." Somehow, with Yoel, they were happy to cooperate, like swimmers on a relay team. Whereas when I was in charge, they tended to relax. Even the dog, Oscar, named after the writer, would obey Yoel's commands. He routinely ignored me, even though I was the one who fed him, petted him, and attended to all his needs. It seemed that I lacked the necessary charisma.

I inserted *Crime and Punishment* into the CD player to fill a gap in my education. Mika had suggested it. A long journey seems shorter when one listens to a story. I stepped on the gas, and off I went, down the road that led to a dream cabin in a forest in the mountains, where my four friends were waiting to spend a weekend with me.

A moment before Raskolnikov took command, Daniela the psychologist transformed into just Daniela, and I let my thoughts roam freely among the day's patients, starting with Helen, the anorexic Orthodox Catholic, angry with God for withholding suitable opportunities from her, despite her tremendous effort and sacrifice; Ryan, the physics doctoral student, a narcissistic depressive who found no purpose in life once he realized that his research would not change the world order; Nicole, whose soul was scorched by childhood traumas and who lived from one crisis to another; young Michael, taking his first steps with the fair sex, paralyzed by panic, his hand in mine as we paced virgin territory. And the last one of the day: Lori. I have to consult one of my colleagues, I told myself, and the sooner the better.

I turned my attention back to the tape, ready to listen to the shocking psychological encounter between the interrogator and the murderer. I left Interstate 880 for Interstate 80, as the skyscrapers of Oakland's downtown passed on my right and mellow waves struck the shore of San Francisco Bay on my left.

The road from Oakland to Sacramento stretched over three tapes, and I decided to postpone the fourth and final one and leave the remainder of Raskolnikov's torment for another time.

I took the winding road up the mountain toward Truckee. The sky turned from blue to pink and then was covered in dark purple before finally becoming black. A full moon hung over the mountains and in the reflected light the sharp, snowy peaks gleamed a brilliant white. I couldn't remember seeing anything so beautiful since our family trip to Emerald Lake in the Canadian Rockies with Gabi Gonen and her family, some five years ago. There too, nature had been revealed to me in its full splendor, a copper-green lake surrounded by stark white ancient icebergs that were reflected in its water as in a mirror. Exactly like Yoel's green eyes. I had a moment of sadness at not sharing the beauty of this moment with him. I missed Yoel.

There were fifteen miles to Truckee, according to the sign on the right of the road. I retrieved a slip of paper from my pocket with precise directions from Mika. Right, left, straight for two miles, sharp turn right to a side road leading into the forest. There was a stream to the right of the path. One last turn, and the new cabin that belonged to Mika and Shaul Navon appeared on the mountainside.

The girls' weekend at Mika's was actually a farewell party for my closest friend, Gabi. She was a beloved friend to all of us and a painter who had promised us a creative workshop before she packed her belongings and her five children and left Silicon Valley, where she'd lived for the past fifteen years, to go home to Jerusalem in the coming summer, while her husband continued his constant world travel for work.

I slowly maneuvered the Toyota into a parking spot next to the double-storied cabin. I recognized Gila's Jeep and Anita's Jaguar. A cold breeze stung my face as I got out of the car. I stretched my tired legs and loosened my joints, which were cramped from four hours of driving.

Mika opened the door, her brown eyes brilliant, her pale features chiseled like those of a Greek goddess, and her short hair like ripples of honey. Regal in a black velvet dress, she gave me a warm hug and showed me into a huge salon pleasantly warmed by a fireplace in the center. A white Steinway stood in a corner of the room, just like in her house in the city and in all the houses where she'd ever lived. Mika was a talented pianist.

On the coffee table, there sat a plate overflowing with fruit and cakes. I hugged each woman in turn and handed Mika the gift I had brought: a shallow Japanese vase filled with pebbles, which I was pleased to note complemented her cream-colored carpet. Two purple velvet couches and three black armchairs adorned this elegant living room, in which sat three lovely nymphs, their legs wrapped in wool blankets that resembled mermaids' tails. My girlfriends.

Gabi had invited all of us to the painting workshop. Nira was the only one who hadn't turned up. Nira, the wife of Yoel's business partner Rami, was a serious runner who wouldn't miss a marathon, this time in Boston. Not even for the unique occasion of this sorority gathering. Nira never, ever broke her ironclad rules.

Generally, neither did I, which is why I hadn't joined the others when they set out for the cabin early that morning. I felt that despite the warmth of my girlfriends, something was missing. It was a naked feeling. Yoel and the children, who usually clung to me like the clothing on my body, were back at home.

I looked at the women. Gabi was my best friend, but the others were also dear to me, each in her own way. I loved Mika's noble spirit, her generosity, modesty, and talent. Her empress persona reflected her inner beauty. Mika was wise and experienced. She was the "older sister" in our small crowd; I often consulted with her regarding my children because I knew she had been there, in my shoes, years before.

Gila was a woman of the world. From her fashionable looks, you could easily learn about the trendiest designers in town. In fact, from Gila you could learn about almost any trend that mattered. She was witty and charismatic, sweet and warm. She always had something astonishing to share, which meant that in her company there was never a dull moment. To me, she represented a glamorous world like Alice's Wonderland.

And then there was beautiful Anita, who, with all due respect, had forgotten that not long ago we had all waded in the same swamp from which her husband, Ido, had emerged as the prince of high tech, kissed by Lady Luck. Anita had also placed a crown on her flowing hair, spread her wings, and flown high. While I remained in that old swamp surrounded by the croaking of frogs, Anita, like Eliza Doolittle, had transformed her voice. Since the moment she'd taken flight, I had been relegated to the outskirts of her social network. My former spot was now occupied by far more influential, glamorous folks.

Mika served me mushroom quiche with cheese and salad. I devoured it. I recalled that I hadn't had a bite since morning.

"Mmm, could I get your recipe?" I asked—in Hebrew, of course; we spoke Hebrew among ourselves.

"No problem," she answered. "I'll send it to you."

Nothing was a problem for Mika. She was a woman for whom everything was easy, who browsed through life with no particular effort. She was a successful musician, a piano teacher at a conservatory in Palo Alto, and occasionally she made an elegant appearance as a concert performer. On top of all that, she was the beloved mother of four and the wife of a glowing husband, and that she would excel in those roles was taken for granted. Apparently, taking it easy was a mark of her childhood.

I, on the other hand, did not take anything easily; cooking, in particular, was a special challenge. I'd grown up in a home where food carried no importance. My mother was the sort who hoped that someday pills would be invented that would serve as a replacement for breakfast, lunch, and dinner. It was not only that my mother hadn't cared much about her family members' taste buds, it was my own nonexistent appetite that limited my interest. As a child, I was called the fisherman, as I fished out the onion from the salad, the cabbage from the soup, and the olives from anything set before me. I grew up mainly on dinner rolls with chocolate spread and toffees. No wonder I entered my adult life with scant culinary knowledge and skills. This lack was only one among many aspects of myself that seemed undeveloped. I always felt that I was missing out on the latest architects and designers, the trendiest music and places to visit, the finest gourmet food and wine. I never knew if I should blame the small, provincial town where I'd grown up, or if it was just something inherent in me, that I missed out on the general wisdom and lacked polished manners. All I remembered of myself as a child and young adult was that I'd been very studious. "A good girl from a good home"—that was me, a description carrying the most boring connotations. However, in my adult life, my friends helped me change. They were my sources of information, my agents of transformation, even my agents of socialization into the unknown public social arena. Although I had the credentials and the formal education, they were my informal educators. And I was a willing and dutiful pupil. I looked around with open eyes and an open mind, observing as much as I could.

Most of all I admired friends who were socially at ease, and who could whip up delicious, exotic dishes. I envied Gabi, who deserved a culinary medal of honor. Everyone in the Israeli community of the Palo Alto diaspora knew that Gabi's dining table was always loaded with quiches, salads, stuffed vegetables, omelets, roast beef, fish, and irresistible desserts. Everyone knew that diets and resolutions were useless in the face of Gabi's delicacies. Her guests feasted on the cornucopia and licked their fingers as Gabi melted with pleasure at the sound of chewing and compliments and completely forgot the three days' work she had put into preparing the heaps of food.

With my quiche on elegant china, I joined the group, which was in heated discourse over the obvious topic of conversation for any group of women of our age: status updates on our children. Gabi, whose five children were born over the course of ten years, served as the glue for our little group. Every one of us had at least one child whose age matched one of Gabi's.

There was nothing as efficient as motherhood for forming deep ties among women in the Valley. Everyone participated in driving the children to school, extracurricular activities, and play dates. We made plans for the school holidays, exchanged educational advice and babysitters, and put out one another's little fires when necessary. Back home, we had enjoyed the help of mothers, sisters, and sisters-in-law, but as foreigners in America, we sought out ethnic warmth and came to regard one another as family: blood sisters.

"They expect children to act like little trained sheep! Do you have any idea what the kids will do to Yaniv in Israel if he shows up acting like a polite little American boy? The kids will eat him up alive. How do these Americans expect such discipline from them? They're only children," Gabi lamented. Yaniv's natural chutzpah had been drawing fire from his fourth-grade teacher. Gabi shifted her plump body, her black curls in disarray on her forehead. From behind her thick glasses, she focused her blue eyes on us like a belligerent lioness. "Whenever a little problem arises, the teachers send the kids to the school psychologist and call the parents without making the least effort to handle the situation themselves."

Anita, in her expensive jeans and stylish jacket, rose from the couch and sat on the floor, crossing her legs. On her left hand, she wore a glistening rose diamond ring worth more than the Jaguar she had parked outside.

Recently elected to the board of the Albert Einstein School for Gifted Children, Anita now rose to the defense of the establishment. "Albert Einstein is a small, private, high-quality school. The teachers are carefully chosen to foster excellence, and they are not there to handle problematic behavior," she said with a rigid glance at Gabi. "Anyway, since when do parents come with complaints against the school? In Israel, did we even think of interfering or going to see a teacher?"

"You'd be surprised," Gila flung back at her. "Things are changing everywhere. Nowadays, parents are involved in the curriculum and have influence. After all, he who pays the piper calls the tune, here and in Israel, too."

The jab was directed at Anita. Ever since a few—some say a few hundred—million dollars had come her way out of a clear blue sky two years earlier, with the sale of Ido's company to Oracle, her life had been transformed. She had been appointed chairperson of all sorts of things, including the West Coast chapter of the Women's International Zionist Organization and TechnoKid, a nonprofit organization that sought to provide a computer for every child in the Middle East in order to create amity and hasten the peace process. Recently, when a huge amount of money from Ido and Anita Eitan flowed into the building of a new swimming pool in the local community center, she had become a member of the executive board in charge of planning future programs for the center. From the platform at the "crowning" ceremony, she had declared that her itinerary was packed and her plate was full. Her friends would testify to the fact that it was high time she learned to refuse invitations to head this or that organization, she said. However, she confessed with a million-dollar smile, she still had not learned to do so. Since then, Anita walked shrouded in mystery, looking important, networking, known and in the know, presenting and representing, but mainly meddling in politics, both local and within the Israeli community. Nothing escaped her, and she devoted herself wholeheartedly and dynamically to every task.

"What do you expect, when Israeli kids are thrown into the American school system?" asked Mika, whose children had passed through elementary school and were now trudging through high school. "We Israelis aren't suited to the American mentality. Their ways are foreign to us. They worship academic degrees from the right universities," she said with a consoling smile in Gabi's direction. "They live in circles that exclude those who did not have a bourgeois American upbringing; it's hard for us to make any real contact with them."

"And some families can be suspicious of outsiders," Gila added. "You can't imagine the interrogation I had to endure when Netta invited a friend to sleep over. And Netta's almost seventeen! 'Full of shit'! I believe that's what they call it."

"What does *that* mean?" Gabi stared at her, taken aback.

"Pretentious, condescending behavior. Something smelly." We laughed.

"Still, we have a lot to learn from the Americans," said Anita, who, thanks to her financial circumstances, was now in the midst of a hot romance with American high society. She was Cinderella at the ball, dancing with San Francisco's aristocracy, who had no idea that the ball gowns in her closet had been acquired only recently, when her husband became a rich man. "Last week I was a guest at the home of Sylvia and Gary Goldin. Do you know them? They own that jeans brand that's gotten so popular. Believe me, I've never seen anything like Sylvia's hospitality in any Israeli home. Amazing." She dropped a few more big names to prove that she rubbed shoulders with the right people.

Anita ignored the fact that for the second time that evening, she was hurting Gabi, our very own hospitality queen, and the main reason for our get together this weekend at Mika's.

"I hope that there's actually something to eat at the Goldins'," said Gabi ironically, "but you have to search for the food when you're sitting around the table of an average American family."

We laughed. We roared with laughter, remembering our own embarrassing encounters with the local culture.

"I realized long ago that American Jewish culture is very different from our Israeli culture. We don't fit in at the synagogues. We can understand the language they read but we don't connect," Gila said, plucking a juicy red grape and sucking on it as if it were a lollipop. "Also, we were raised on theater, music, and a unique sense of humor. And I miss it so much! When I watch entertainment shows on television, I don't get the point. I can't believe they call that garbage entertainment. Not that there's any shortage of garbage in Israel," she amended, "but somehow it's a different sort of garbage. And the real dilemma is how to educate our children while we're here. In terms of which culture? Which identity are we shaping for them? And in a much more concrete sense, which youth groups should we send them to? The Israeli Scouts, or the American Jewish organizations?"

"Sorry! My kids won't go to Israeli Scouts," Anita declared. "When in Rome, do as the Romans do. You can't raise a child with a split personality. We don't live in Israel and there's no point in insisting on preserving a culture that separates us from our environment." I couldn't help thinking that Anita was an Israeli in personality and an American when it was convenient.

Gabi stretched in the armchair and pulled her dark curls back from her face. Her beautiful face became serious as she fixed her blue gaze on a hidden point in the distance. "That's the main reason why I've decided to go back to Israel," she said quietly. "Roni's about to be called up for her army service and, afterward, she'll go to university. Eventually she'll get married and I'd prefer that it be to an Israeli, who speaks our language and likes our food." She looked at us for reassurance. We all laughed. Who wouldn't love Gabi's food? "The rest of my children are standing in line. Now," she stressed, "we have to go back. We can't delay it. Danny's always been full of excuses and good reasons to go on living here. This thing's dragged on for fifteen years. But I've decided that we've run out of excuses. It's now or never."

Her decisiveness made us uncomfortable. We all lived in the shadow of the decision to stay or go, now or who knows when. We were all worried and indecisive about our children's future. I tried to suppress those questions. My children were a bit younger than Gabi's kids and I knew I had a few more years to avoid dealing with the question of their cultural and national identity. I admit, it was easy to suppress these dilemmas, but they were always there, popping up and floating over my head.

"There are no easy solutions," Mika said. "My daughter once said, wisely, 'You know, Mom, you don't have to move to wherever I happen to be living.' Since then I wander around, hopping back and forth."

Mika, who had raised four children, two of whom were already adults, split her time between three continents. Her eldest son was in the army in Israel; her daughter, already out of the army, was studying at the Sorbonne; and her twins, who were sixteen, were in high school in California.

"She's right, your daughter," loyal Gila backed her up. "The young generation, they are citizens of the world. Netta's meant to have a career as a professional musician, and I don't think she'll find her place in Israel," she added, referring to her own daughter. "The country's too small for her."

Gila was ageless; her long hair was streaked with silver, and she had feline gray eyes and a Julia Roberts smile. Her body was as slender as a ballerina's in her black outfit. She was always wearing black. That day she wore a short, classy cashmere sweater that revealed the tiny navel on her firm stomach, tight pants, and high-heeled cowboy boots. She had been acting in avant-garde theater in Israel when Yigal, an outstanding medical student at Haifa Technion, lured her off the stage. They were married several years after her brother was killed in an air force pilot-training accident. Gila's parents never recovered from the loss. Her brother had been the pride of the family, their hope and joy. Gila tried in vain to take his place, to grant her parents a pinch of pride and satisfaction. But as far as they were concerned, she remained in the shadow of her dead brother, in spite of being something of a celebrity, performing on stage and even as a repeat guest on a television sitcom in Israel. She could never match the son who was no more.

It was hard to detect sadness in Gila, who, in her real life, played the role of a perfect wife. Her picture-perfect husband Yigal was a professor at Stanford and a senior neurosurgeon in great demand worldwide. Netta, their picture-perfect and only daughter, had been born destined for greatness. Gila's home had two grand pianos, back to back in the middle of their living room, their hearts exposed to declare the order of priorities in the house: piano above all. Gila's collection of famous friends and her wide network of connections were as perfect as she was. Only her gnawed fingernails and some unexplained aches and pains ever betrayed a touch of disquiet.

Five years ago, Gila had pressed Yigal to leave Tel Aviv's Ichilov Hospital in favor of a secure job at Stanford, in order to advance and enrich Netta's musical education, because she'd heard that the music department at Stanford encouraged gifted children.

"My girl studies piano with an a-ma-zing teacher." Gila emphasized each syllable. "He won the Rubinstein Competition years ago and now devotes his time only to brilliant students," she said with a level look at Mika, who comprehended the subtle distinction between talented and brilliant. "It's only a shame that there aren't any violin teachers here, to complement her piano training. Too bad Itzhak Perlman doesn't live in Palo Alto anymore."

Gila consoled herself with the hope that when she finished high school next year, Netta would study with Daniel Barenboim in Berlin. She had a good chance of being accepted. In any case, the Academy of Music in Berlin was far better than Juilliard, Gila told us, and presumably Netta would find a suitable violin teacher there.

"They've already offered Yigal a position at Humboldt University," she reminded us. "Berlin will be exciting for all of us."

Gila hungered for the rich artistic culture of classical Europe. In her opinion, America's East Coast was likewise culturally far superior to Silicon Valley. It was well known, she informed us, that to see excellent theater, one must head to New York, or at the very least to Los Angeles.

On her periodic visits to Israel, Gila caught up with the latest developments in theater, as well as with local celebrity gossip. When she returned to California with a slew of "Page Six" news, we—her girl-friends—feasted on the delicious info like pigeons on breadcrumbs, like devotees of some venerated *rebbetzin*.

Our conversation was interrupted by a phone call. It was Ido on Anita's mobile, asking where their first aid kit was. Ma'ayan was hurt. She'd hit her bare foot against the wall and he was afraid she had a fracture. Anita had left Ido at home with their three kids: Ma'ayan, their six-year-old, and their two middle school boys. Ido could be a devoted husband and family man, but only when he was around. He'd had to cancel a flight to Taiwan at the last minute to accommodate

Anita's weekend with her girlfriends, and I wasn't sure he was happy about his involuntary gesture of generosity.

"Should I take her to ER?" he asked Anita.

Taking advantage of the pause, Mika went to the kitchen and came back with long-stemmed glasses and a bottle of Cabernet. Gila stood up to help, and the two of them began whispering to one another. I guessed that it was about Netta's audition for a junior piano competition. Mika was trying to calm Gila, whose veneer of perfection was suddenly showing signs of cracking. Gabi took the opportunity to phone home and check what was going on in her absence. Danny, as usual, was on a business trip. Roni, the eldest, was looking after the little ones. I imagined Gabi's fridge bursting at the seams, as always, and knew that Roni, who was blessed with a serenity she didn't inherit from either of her parents, could easily cope with her four siblings. But Gabi was worried. Anxious.

Anita navigated Ido to the first aid kit in the second drawer on the right of the sink in the children's bathroom. "And take her to have an X-ray. It can't hurt, honey," she commanded. After a few comforting words to the tearful Ma'ayan, she returned to us.

"It's amazing how a successful businessman like Ido loses his cool when confronted with children's tears. I'm surprised he didn't phone to ask where the cups are kept in the kitchen," she grumbled. "It's like he's a houseguest! I should have kept the nanny over the weekend. I knew Ido couldn't handle it."

Once, years before the sale of Ido's company to Oracle, and before the pink diamond ring adorned her finger, Anita had complained to Ido that all the other Israeli couples found the time to go shopping together, to furnish the house together, to watch the children's baseball games and attend PTA meetings together, whereas she and Ido just slept together and, actually, never saw each other outside the bedroom. Anita had told us that with a gentle, accepting smile, Ido had answered, "Isn't that better than the other way around? What if we went shopping together, shared a laugh at the baseball games and the PTA, and didn't sleep together?"

Almost twenty years had passed since they met at the air force base. Ido, a quiet, confident F-16 pilot, was made for success. He lost his heart when Anita was posted to the squadron, equipped with long legs and a jaunty smile—beautiful in that Audrey Hepburn way. Her short stint in the army ended when she became pregnant. It didn't initially occur to Ido, a nice boy from Tel Aviv, to do the responsible thing and marry Anita, but he couldn't resist her tearful outburst, her hurt feelings, and the pressure from her family. Her parents made it clear to her in their native Romanian that she was not welcome back into the family home unless she returned with a ring on her finger. Immediately. That was how the intellectual family of Professor Michael and Dr. Amira Eitan of Tel Aviv and the working-class family of Marga and Yosef Berkowitz of Bat Yam came to be joined.

Shrewd, capable Anita understood that there was much to be gained from the intimate connection with the Tel Aviv elite. She would observe and learn their ways. She made up her mind to distance herself from her parents, dampening their hopes of close family ties with the Eitans.

Pressure from her family increased when Ido became rich. With the sale of the company, Anita and Ido received a long list of demands from the Berkowitz family. These included the purchase of an apartment for Anita's divorced sister, as well as a monthly allowance to support her children; settling the grandmother in a luxurious home for the aged; a seven-figure sum, in dollars, to enable Anita's parents to retire; and an additional assortment of demands that Anita and Ido met as a loveless obligation, despite the knowledge that there would be no end in sight.

Mika poured a full glass of wine and handed it to Anita.

"You know, men are like little children. So dependent, they can't manage without us. We're the ones who actually make sure the home goes on functioning," she said, handing us each a long-stemmed glass of dark wine with an earthy bouquet. She spoke in a soothing, sweetly authoritative voice, like a big sister. She didn't push, she didn't project frustration, and she didn't hunger for success. She was comfortable with her gracious, feminine image. Only if pressed would she speak about her latest concert performances or her respected place in the world of music.

"Maybe they behave like children," Gabi remarked, "but let's admit, we live in a man's world. Look around. How many women make it on their own merits in the high-tech world? I can count them on one hand." She was quiet for a moment before adding, "Nor do they really excel in other fields, not financially, anyhow."

"What are you talking about?" Anita bristled. "Is there a shortage of successful women? Women move mountains!"

An embarrassed silence ensued. Gila sided with Anita: "It's just a matter of choice. If they wanted to, women could build even better careers than men. I know some American women who've made millions."

"And what, are those successful women married? Have they got children and husbands who support them?" Gabi cross-examined her.

"No, most are single," Gila answered, "but that's also a matter of choice. Usually women need to juggle many more chores. I wouldn't give up raising my child; I wouldn't want to stay in the office for long hours every day or fly on endless business trips." We looked at her in agreement.

"There's a lot of research," I intervened, allowing myself to showcase my professional expertise, "that finds low self-esteem among adolescent girls. The males are so much more aggressive due to all their testosterone, and the females are left marginalized, assuming a social role of self-deprecation. I'd guess that successful women have a comparatively high level of testosterone," I said. Pursuing my train of thought, I added, "They also probably have more satisfying sex lives, because testosterone is responsible for sex drive and sexual pleasure in both sexes."

"Really?" said Anita, amazed. "I didn't know I had testosterone!" She snickered.

"Oh, definitely," I answered.

"Whatever the case, I wouldn't trade places with any man," said Mika. "Look how nice it is, among women. The men are too busy achieving goals, whereas we enjoy a more stress-free life. If women ran the world, it would look much better," Mika sighed.

We nodded. At that moment, my associations ran far. I remembered the recent collapse of the Twin Towers and wished for a better world.

"There's nothing like a reunion with high school friends. Last time, we had a psychic tell us we had a wonderful future ahead of us," she added.

We laughed.

"Apropos long friendships, I have something important to tell you." Gila sounded as if she were getting ready to reveal a secret. "We should keep this to ourselves." She hesitated, seeming to wonder whether it would be better to maintain privacy. Maybe she was testing us again, asking herself if we could be trusted not to spread her private matter. Finally, it seemed that her need to get her secret off her chest overcame her doubts.

"Tell me, have you heard of Hevreh.com, the website?" Tech-savvy Gila didn't pause for our response and proceeded to tell us that anyone could sign into the site and search for old friends.

"In Israel, it's the rage—everyone is reuniting virtually, and there's immense excitement," she said "Thanks to Hevreh, I found Talma, my best friend from childhood. She was a year older than I and lived two floors above me. I always admired her—beautiful, brilliant, an amazing athlete. On the way home from school we used to dawdle for hours talking about absolutely everything. I'd wait for her at the gate every day. Those talks with Talma were the best part of my childhood. We spoke about the other girls, the boys, our bodies, our dreams for the future. We made a pact of sisterhood. We swore oaths, got lost in fantasies together. Every summer, she went to visit her grandmother in Belgium, and I was alone, counting the days until her return. And she always came back radiant, wearing the latest European fashion. And her stories! Some of them she probably made up, but they always left me with my mind blown. At one of our sleepovers, she even showed me her nipples after they first started swelling."

Gila's eyes shone with nostalgia. Ours too. Suddenly faced with our own nostalgia for our childhood friends, we listened to Gila, moved and longing.

Gila continued, "We parted ways in our teens. Talma began dating young, and at that point I still had no idea what the boys wanted from me. She got married so young that she didn't even go into the army and moved to a small agricultural town in the south. Her parents moved to another city, we lost contact, and, in fact, we never saw each other again.

"When I was surfing the site, I looked for her name on the list of my classmates. I emailed her, and we arranged to meet in Tel Aviv. That was a month ago, on my last visit to Israel. My life changed from the moment I saw her. At that moment, we both knew we were meant for each other. We couldn't restrain ourselves. We just devoured each other. Talma is fantastic!"

Gila delivered her dramatic monologue slowly, emphasizing each word, using her acting talent to hypnotize us, her captive audience. Gila. She loved words that were larger than life—words meant for the stage.

"She's breathtakingly beautiful." Her voice shook a little; a blush covered her usually placid face. "Blue eyes, coal-black hair, and always wears white. It turned out that she divorced her husband years ago and left the small town with her three children. She's now an event planner in Tel Aviv. Our love for one another is stronger than anything I've ever felt. She connects with me in places nobody knows and nobody else has reached. We discovered that our strong childhood bond has never unraveled. The seed that was sown is now blooming. We simply could not understand how our paths had not crossed until now. I'm torn with longing every moment we're apart. Life flows by, and we must find as much love as possible, as much as we can."

Silence. The bomb Gila had dropped stunned all of us except Mika, who never looked surprised. As if there were nothing new under the sun, as if she'd heard everything that was to be heard and nothing could shock her.

"So, are you lesbians?" Anita broke the silence.

"I always have been bisexual. When Yigal met me, he knew that I had one-night stands with women and that I was an unconventional girl. He chose me anyway and accepts me as I am. That's the beauty of Yigal. He's a wonderful person. When things are okay with me, he's okay too. I won't give him up, either."

"So how does this triangle work?" I asked, trying to digest the news.

"Look, Yigal is open-minded. He puts his heart and soul into his work, and golf is the love of his life. He loves me in his own way, which is accepting and not stifling. He's not shocked that I'm in love with Talma. He knows I'll find a way to combine my two relationships without anybody getting hurt." Her words sounded convincing in their simplicity.

"Talma and I have decided not to make any changes in our lifestyles. I want to keep my family life intact for Netta as well as for Yigal, who is a wonderful person and doesn't deserve to be abandoned. Talma wants to raise her children until they leave home. Until then, we'll go on living apart and get together from time to time in one part of the world or another."

Profound silence. Gila's experiences always carried an aura of glamour and adventure. Her lesbian affair took on the glow of an enviable adventure that exceeded the emotional capital of ordinary people. When confronted with Gila's glamorous lifestyle, I often reverted to feeling like a provincial village girl who didn't know what she was missing. Now, too, as I took in the loud drama of her life, the grayness of mine seeped into me. A perfect story! Even the colors of the two women—Gila in black and Talma in white—complemented each other, like queens on a chessboard. There was no limit to Gila's passions or experimentations. She had no guilt; she allowed herself to shed all conventions and experience her life and love with intensity.

Actually, I mused, it was the sort of emotional intensity I had seen only in my bipolar patients. For these patients, the superego is weakened during the manic condition, and they allow themselves to behave in ways healthy people never would. Was Gila one of these? Not likely. But could Gila's drama turn into tragedy in an instant if this fragile romantic threesome shattered?

Gabi sat in uncomfortable silence throughout Gila's monologue. It occurred to me that Gila's romance was rubbing salt in some of Gabi's old wounds and scars, particularly when Gila described the ecstatic heights she reached in her affair with Talma—heights a run-of-the-mill marriage could never attain. Gabi kept her distance from Gila, an obvious distance. Maybe she was afraid her silent shout would break free and sound itself if she dared admonish Gila and accuse her of irresponsibility.

Mika looked pensively at Gila. "Someone should outlaw reunions like that. Something strange happened to me, too. Since I met some of my high school classmates on my last visit to Israel, I've been having trouble sleeping at night. It isn't healthy," she said, not elaborating. I wanted to ask her what she meant, but her expression communicated to me that she wasn't willing to elaborate.

"It's late," Gabi yawned, implying that she'd had enough. There was too much electricity in the air; we needed to pause and take it all in. "We have a long day of creative work ahead of us tomorrow."

The canvases, paints, and brushes packed in the trunk of Gila's Jeep awaited our hands and inspired spirits. After swiftly clearing the glasses and plates and loading the dishwasher, we went to our rooms, only to meet and wait our turns outside the bathroom. Eventually, we emerged in our nightgowns, our faces smeared with colorful creams.

Good night, friends.

I was in Mika's son Yuval's room, not accustomed to a twin-sized bed. I contemplated Gila's dramatic confession, seeking hidden meaning. I wondered if I was surprised to hear her coming out of the closet. Apparently not. I thought of my patients, how painful it was for some of them to come out. In this, too, Gila was unusual; it was clearly not at all painful for her.

Gila's confession was just another episode in her colorful, flamboyant life. Almost a bohemian life, I thought. Something I'd always felt was out of my reach. I examined the excitement I'd felt after her confession. I was mesmerized by her story. Was I a latent lesbian on some unseen continuum? I played with that idea for a moment. But I knew that as much as I enjoyed women's friendship, there was no substitute for the excitement I felt toward men. It must be something else. Yes. Gila had revealed her multilayered self, and for a moment I'd lived vicariously in a world of endless opportunities, released from the trap of my tedious routine. I sighed.

I thought about the bonds we'd formed amongst ourselves, women living on a cultural island in the heart of California. We were all married to Israeli men who were constantly on the move worldwide. All of us had families in Israel, an identity we longed to reclaim. We all lived on the edge, visiting Israel a few times a year for a breath of love, a portion of culture, and a recharge of our batteries. We all returned stocked with newly released books and suitcases bursting with clothes, shoes, and jewelry. As if there were nothing to wear in the States. In this way, we tried to dislodge the here and now and reinforce our ties with the there and then. We were all up to date on new plays and new restaurants in Tel Aviv. We all had our favorites—Israeli hairstylists, fashion and furniture designers—and we took pride in how our Israeli tastes and touches distinguished us from our American neighbors. We all celebrated the Israeli holidays and festivals in a kind of modernized kibbutz style. At times I thought that we'd just relocated ourselves and our families to a new settlement in a different part of the world, maintaining our Israeli mental territory. We lived in a land where people spoke a different language, but we didn't. We might have moved far from our families back home, but the change was only geographical. In our mentality, we had not changed a bit. And, I asked myself, why should we?

ೋ

A strong smell of coffee woke me from a deep sleep. I stretched like a cat, indulging in the bed for a few more minutes, enjoying the pale sunbeams that came through the big window to flicker on the dark wall opposite me. I lingered in the bathroom, intent on privacy, preparing to go out and meet my friends once again.

My hair still wet, I wandered into the country-style kitchen, where I found the group already convened, each of them attached to a cell phone, talking to loved ones. Mika was talking to her daughter at the Sorbonne. Anita was asking about Ma'ayan's foot. Good, good, so it's not broken. Gabi, smiling into the phone, was checking what her children had eaten for breakfast. Yaniv hadn't forgotten to brush his teeth, and Roni gave a report of her four siblings' itineraries for the day ahead. Gila was dictating a detailed list of groceries for Yigal to pick up at Whole Foods, reminding him to make sure to get only organic products. And yes, he must wake Netta and make sure she prepared for next week's audition. After Gila finished her call, she went for a morning run around the cabin.

Unlike my friends, I wasn't in a hurry to check on what was going on at home. The separation from my family didn't worry me. On the contrary, I knew everything was running smoothly. I asked myself if this was denial, but I didn't feel guilty. I was pleased that this time I was giving myself a break and leaving Yoel with the youngsters. After all, things were usually the other way around: I stayed behind while he circled the globe like a satellite, back and forth, taking off and landing. Always returning to our bosom, but all the while our lives ran smoothly without him.

Suddenly, my thoughts clouded over. Out of nowhere, I recalled Lori's precarious life, and my distress returned. What was happening to the young woman? Maybe she was in trouble. I checked my office phone for messages and was relieved to find no messages from Lori. However, there was one unexpected voice mail that sparked my curiosity: I was pleased to hear Gilad Levy asking for an appointment.

Rapprochement, I thought. This was a term coined by Margaret Mahler, a psychologist who observed a clear behavioral pattern in one- to two-year-old babies. They repeatedly distanced themselves from the parent but returned in order to reinforce their self-confidence. Infants who have a secure attachment to a parent tend to be stable and confident and may dare to move farther away than those with an insecure attachment. A similar phenomenon occurs at later stages in life, particularly in adolescence, when teenagers practice separation and try to distance themselves physically and emotionally from their parents but always return to the family nest until they are ready for the final parting. The process is the same when a couple separates and, quite often, also when a patient leaves psychotherapy.

I had treated Gilad a number of years earlier when he was going through a period of emotional turbulence. He was about to embark on an impossible marriage to Kimberly Anderson, the daughter of a Texas oil tycoon. Impossible, because the relationship between the two families was similar to that between the Capulets and the Montagues. He'd stopped therapy soon after the birth of his first child, but two years later he resumed it, complaining of frustration in his professional life—a burning envy of his colleagues' success—and a persistent feeling that he was riding the wrong wave. During that period, he'd joined forces with Ido Eitan, Anita's husband, and together they'd built a data analysis company, one of several projects that Ido was involved in.

But I hadn't seen Gilad in a few years, and I was curious to know what brought him to ask for an appointment now. What could it have been?

I couldn't share these thoughts with my friends. I needed privacy. I left the babble of phone calls and went out to the deck, which was constructed from thick, oil-painted wooden beams and featured a large Jacuzzi. A big wooden table and carved chairs stood in the center. I leaned on the railing and looked at the breathtaking landscape. It was magnificent.

The snowy mountain peaks touched the sky. High creamy clouds, as if taken from a Rembrandt portrait, adorned their throats. They were enfolded in a cloak of thick forest green, with little islands of snow that glittered in the sunlight. A swift river flowed over pebbles in a winding channel until it broke into three waterfalls: a high one by the nearest peak and two lower ones that scattered down the slope, spraying foam and filling the valley with a pleasant bubbling sound. I stood motionless, astonished by the beauty, with my arms wrapped around myself in the chill morning air. I shivered with cold, refusing to part from this grandeur that stirred strains of pathos in me. I breathed deeply. My teeth chattered in the bright late October morning. I cast another glance at the mountains, apologizing for deserting them by going inside to get warm.

"How did you sleep, princess?" asked the queen.

"Wonderfully, Mika. If you secretly hid peas under my mattress, I must not be a princess," I answered.

I poured some coffee for myself, thinking of Yoel, who woke me every morning with a cup of coffee in bed. I missed him, my Yoel, but only for a moment.

"Tell me, Mika, how did you choose this charming spot?"

"Shaul always dreamed of a house in the mountains, and I have always been attracted to water. Any source of water—river, lake, sea—makes me happy."

A shiver of longing went through me, as I remembered the view of the Mediterranean Sea from my childhood room. I would wake up every morning to sea—calm blue with white whipping edges on a summer day, or raging gray waters in the winter. The Mediterranean had been the backdrop of my childhood. Not to mention my social life, which was so deeply connected to that same beach. My entire childhood had happened right there, on this blue landscape. I flashed back to adolescent boys and girls in swimsuits playing badminton on the beach. My first boyfriend, my first kiss, even my first breakup had all happened on this very sand. Suddenly, Mika reminded me of my childhood friend Nehama, whose name meant "comfort" in Hebrew. Everything Mika said brought me a measure of comfort and also reminded me of my lighthearted childhood friend.

Mika went on, "When we heard about this plot, we bought it that very day and decided to build the cabin. That's Shaul. He's like a natural magician—he really knows how to make dreams come true."

Shaul and Mika complemented one another like a pair of clasped hands. Shaul also had an invisible regal halo, in addition to great charm. He usually wore jeans, sandals, and a loose shirt, as befitted a kibbutznik from Nahal Oz. From his humble appearance, a stranger would never guess the string of dazzling successes Shaul had had.

Mika and I set the table for breakfast. Our ten practiced hands, which knew how to get things done, took vegetables from the fridge and washed, cut, and spiced them. We sliced bread and arranged a platter of cheese, olives, and salami. Within minutes, we were seated at the round table, facing the glass doors that allowed the landscape into the room: snow-covered peaks, fir trees, and flowing water. The delightful meal lasted for hours. We took all the time in the world to chatter without pressure from the men in our lives and to giggle like teenagers.

The shrapnel from the bomb Gila had dropped last night was gone and mostly forgotten. Only Anita shot embarrassed glances at Gila now and then, checking to see if she was changed in any way by proudly coming out of the closet. As usual, we spoke about our lives here in the States, as well as about the latest news from Israel. The conversation that began with the Atkins carb-free diet, whether it was sound or a little dangerous, moved on to our parents' health: one's backache and another's failing memory. All of us nodded in agreement about the difficulty and anxiety of caring for our parents from a distance, via modem. Then we shared stories from friends in Israel about living in the shadow of the Intifada and terrorist attacks—a matter of grim fates, guilty feelings, and distressed sighs. Here we were in the States, safe, while our families and friends in Israel were living under constant threat.

At some point between our third and fourth cups of coffee, Anita jumped up and went to her room. She returned with a batch of elegant envelopes. "I'm organizing a charity evening for an organization in Israel to help needy youth and their families. It's going to be at the Fairmont in the city, with a gala dinner and speeches by the consul and hopefully some Israeli celebrity—we're still working that out. I've made lists of people who can allow themselves financially to attend and ones who can't allow themselves socially not to. I don't know them personally, but I'd like you to help me contact them."

She distributed the envelopes among us. The lists were meticulously put together, in keeping with the skills Anita had acquired as an air force squadron's operations clerk back when she was nineteen. They contained the names, addresses, and telephone numbers of famous people. Asterisks next to each name indicated who was asked to make the contact. The asterisk beside Rami and Nira allocated them to me. That suited me. I'd be glad to help. But that was only the beginning. The list contained people who were hard nuts to crack and some who were a waste of time. Whatever the case and however unpleasant it was to get involved in the *shnor* industry, we knew that, like it or not, we would be bound to help, just like the good fairies in *Sleeping Beauty*. It had something to do with the way we all lived, as a kernel of Israelis abroad, motivated by a trace of group pride.

Time passed. More time passed. We finally cleared the table, which looked as if it had been hit by a hurricane. Together, we tidied and cleaned. I mused that there were ten hands in my house, too, but they were usually occupied with more important things in life, like checking email. In my house, I was left to cope with life's trials on my own, because I'd given up asking for help.

What is happiness if not routine broken by a pleasant revelation—a delightful passing moment, something refreshing, a lovely surprise? If happiness were permanent, it would become predictable, taken for granted like the air we breathe. The value of happiness increases with its absence. There's nothing like routine to blur happiness, and there's nothing like breaking routine, even just once, to bring happiness. That is the kind of delight I felt that morning. If we met regularly for creative workshops on the banks of Lake Tahoe, the specialness of the moment would be lost.

We were happy. Buoyant and full of expectation, we crowded into the Jeep. Gila was at the wheel with Mika, who knew the lay of the land, on her right. The rest of us sat closely together in the back seat.

Armed with sunglasses and tracksuits, we were like excited kids on a field trip. The path led down the mountain alongside a swift, frothy stream. The lake came into view in its entire splendor at the foot of the mountain. Gabi was pleased that it was a calm day; there was no wind to blow down easels and canvases. We drove on a narrow road that circled the huge lake. In the middle of the lake, we saw a little island with a neglected old structure on it, which Mika informed us had been built in the previous century by a romantic who intended it to be a grand castle for his beloved, like the one Napoleon had built for Désirée on Isola Bella in northern Italy.

Gabi said the observation point on the cliff was ideal for connecting with the landscape. We unloaded our gear, laid out brushes and paints, and angled the easels in various ways to face the lake, according to Gabi's instructions. Anita and Gila immediately revealed their apathy. They extracted folding chairs from the Jeep and stretched out, getting some sun.

"The art of painting," Gabi began with an air of drama, "is like a mirror for the soul." She took a deep breath and closed her eyes with missionary zeal. "The final figure on the canvas is the product of the processing of external visual stimuli by the artist's internal interpretation. The final form is entirely subjective. In simple words, artists paint what they are feeling and not what they are seeing. Think of Picasso's paintings, which mainly reflect his inner world and not the figure or object before him."

Gabi's weighty and well-intentioned words were wasted on me. So was the reference to Picasso. For me, only her words about the importance of color in expressing emotion were meaningful. What could spring from the mirror of my soul, I asked myself. I imagined five little imps shaped like the members of my family and tugging at a *tallit*—a virtuous prayer shawl—symbolizing my soul. Each in turn quoted the Talmud, saying *kula sheli*—she's all mine, she's all mine. As if with each child's birth I had to find another part of myself to distribute; like a fertilized ovum that divides and redivides to create life, my soul would never again be a single unit. I wondered if, at the height of creativity, I'd find a chance to reunite the parts to recreate the whole, original me— the core of myself that was usually shoved aside by the force of life's demands, sidelined by the routine of grocery shopping, rides to school, laundry, cooking, and even by my work, which left no room for the essential Self within, since psychotherapy is aimed at healing the Self of others. There was no room for my essence. Maybe here, facing Lake Tahoe, the Self would be reborn in the Gestalt manner, according to which the whole is greater than the sum of its parts.

I surveyed my surroundings. Mika and Gabi were engrossed in their work, Gabi wielding her brush with precision and Mika with charismatic abandon. Apparently, they knew something I didn't know. I must admit that I hadn't held a paintbrush since kindergarten, and I'd never painted in oils. I considered joining Anita and Gila, who were taking it easy nearby. No. If I took on a mission, I didn't let go. I hung on by my fingernails and, if necessary, by my teeth. On second thought, I decided to try my hand at an abstract painting. I remembered Miró, who painted from the subconscious.

I dipped a medium-sized brush into deep blue and painted. Wild splashes of brown dotted with black within my blue lake symbolized the island with the abandoned castle. My soul in its five divisions blistered from the painting in the shape of five little red imps. I added the sun as four crossed white strokes splattered with gold dots, like the sun I had seen in one of Miró's gigantic paintings in Barcelona.

I took a step back and examined the result. My effort bore not the slightest resemblance to a work by Miró. If anything, it was more like something my daughter had once brought home from kindergarten. As for soul, I returned to my brush and canvas, added two parallel yellow waves, on which I superimposed wild black zigzags in the manner of Kandinsky. I thought, this is the expression of my general feeling, freedom, and liberation. The result was disappointing. I wanted to fling the painting into the lake, so that nobody would know, no eye would be damaged by it, no soul offended, heaven forbid.

I put down the brush and turned to look at what Gabi and Mika had painted.

Gabi had painted the green frame of a Mediterranean window with its shutters wide open. A stylized vase of flowers, the strong colors reminiscent of Matisse, stood on the windowsill. Beyond the window lay a view of a lake in the middle of which was a small island surrounded by boats and overhung by large, dark clouds. Gabi was absorbed in mixing colors to achieve the right shade of blue. "The background must be painted in a mutable shade," she explained when she noticed me watching over her shoulder. "That way, we emphasize the variegated shades of light in the sky so as not to bore the viewer."

"Gabi, why the cloud? Where did it come from?" I wanted to know.

"It's an inner cloud," she said thoughtfully, continuing to mix the blues.

Mika's painting reflected a lake surrounded by hills, a little island in the middle, surrounded by boats. An embracing couple reminiscent of couples in Chagall's paintings hovered above the water. I liked Mika's idea. The romantic element suited her. I consoled myself with the fact that her technique, like my own, could have used some improvement.

"I find it hard to imagine Shaul hovering in the air," I said, winking at Mika.

"What makes you so sure I painted Shaul?" she hinted broadly, making me rather curious. With a veiled glance, she added, "And maybe the female figure isn't me."

For the second time that weekend, I felt that Mika was revealing and quickly re-concealing a secret.

As friends do, Mika, Gabi, and I showered compliments on one another's work and dismissed the compliments paid to our own. I honestly didn't believe what they said about mine.

"I wish I had the spontaneity and boldness to make such wild, uninhibited brushstrokes," Gabi remarked.

I tried to agree that my painting came from some bold place within me, but that just wasn't the case. Lack of talent, yes. Mika stated that if she had a color sense like Chagall's, she might have managed to produce something worthwhile.

"A painting isn't done in a day," Gabi, our kind instructor, summed up the workshop. "You have to return to the painting time and again in order to modify the colors and add elements that you missed in the beginning. Like a child, the painting grows and develops before our eyes, and we have to pay attention and listen in order to do what's necessary for it," she said, drawing on her experience as a mother of five.

"Look at that scribble!" Anita laughed mercilessly when she saw my painting.

I wanted to explain that the five prancing figures represented my family and that the dancing on the island symbolized my soul afloat on the sea of life, but she had already turned her attention to Gabi's dramatic colors.

"What's with the big cloud above the island?" Gila asked.

"Apparently an inner cloud," replied Gabi. "I'm distressed about going back to Israel—the instability of moving. The distress took me by surprise. I wasn't aware of it until now."

We stood looking at the painting, silently studying Gabi's heavy, menacing cloud. It all comes out in the painting, I thought. Gabi's right. Art really is the mirror of the soul.

"I'm hungry, girls," Anita announced, having apparently spent a great deal of energy sunbathing.

That was the signal. We packed our gear in a hurry, including the canvases, which were dry already. Then we considered our next move—which restaurant to choose for lunch. Anita was dying for a hamburger and fries. Gila flatly refused to put such garbage into her mouth. Gabi's phone rang, putting an end to the argument.

"Mom," we heard. It was Gabi's eldest girl, Roni. "Keren's sick. She's got a fever and stomachache. Can you come home?"

Gabi, who never missed an opportunity to eat, lost her appetite as well as her interest in the outing and her friends. With no further discussion, she made up her mind to return to Mika's cabin and leave. I offered to go with her back to Palo Alto, where we lived in the same neighborhood. Mika, Anita, and Gila decided to spend another night at the cabin and leave in the morning.

We parted with hugs and kisses and many thanks.

"And don't forget about the meeting with Luigi Fracassini, at his gallery. Remember? My wonderful professor from San Francisco Academy of Art. The event is in two weeks," Gabi reminded everyone, before closing the car door.

I started the car, Gabi already on the phone giving Roni long-distance instructions: "Give her Tylenol drops. If the fever doesn't go down, put her in a lukewarm bath and make sure she sits there until she cools down. And remember to give her plenty of tea."

As we drove off, even before the cabin was out of sight, Gabi sighed and lunged into a sad monologue. She felt guilty about leaving for the weekend without making sure that Danny would look after the children. She said she could never make plans that relied on his presence, as something urgent always came up and placed him on the first available flight to Southeast Asia. She said that since she'd given up on including him in the family's day-to-day lives, they'd all grown happier. Actually, she mused, she wasn't sure Danny would have handled Keren's sickness more competently than Roni, because Roni was so wonderfully responsible.

Gabi paused. Her face became somber as she resumed her train of thought, and her voice seemed to emerge as if from a deep dream. Roni was the main reason for her decision to return to Israel, apart from worry about her parents who were growing old alone. She was, after all, her parents' only child. Roni was in love with Nick, a football player from her high school who had energetically courted her. She didn't buy Gabi's insistence that he wasn't right for her, and that it would be a good idea for her to date someone from the family's Israeli circles. Nick was a popular, handsome boy with a reputation for driving the girls at school crazy. Roni's relationship with Nick was the envy and excitement of all of her friends and caused her to float dreamy-eyed with happiness. Even Danny had been raising eyebrows at Nick's frequents visits to Roni's room and didn't hesitate to refer to him as "Nick the prick" in her presence.

"Danny can be really hard on Roni, you know. He's not very subtle," I said, interrupting Gabi's torrent of words.

"Years ago," Gabi persisted, "Danny and I discussed the possibility of our children growing up in America and marrying someone who was neither Israeli nor even Jewish. It scared me, but Danny was indifferent, as if he had no control over it. Even now, he reluctantly agrees with me, but it's difficult for him to leave his business and go home. For me, as a child of Holocaust survivors who lost their entire families in the Nazis' incinerators, the possibility of my daughter marrying Mr. Nick McCormick and ending the family's Jewish genealogy is unthinkable."

Her blue eyes sparkled with tears. She removed her glasses and dried her eyes with her sleeve, replacing the glasses in the little dent they made on her nose. "My own relationship with Danny demonstrates that long-lasting relationships can begin at a very early age. That's why I take it so seriously and why I'm so scared. We may not just be talking about some passing romance of a frivolous teenager."

I knew their history as a couple. Danny and Gabi were born and grew up in Beit Hakerem, Jerusalem. In the family album, black-and-white photographs taken nearly half a century ago on the outskirts of Jerusalem showed their mothers pushing prams from which Danny and Gabi peeked at one another. They had been together all their lives, but gossip around Silicon Valley cast doubt on Danny's fidelity, hinting that on his frequent trips, he tasted from many a forbidden fruit.

"How do the children feel about going back to Israel?" I inquired.

"The children live in total denial. They don't seem to think about it at all. I take comfort in the fact that they feel at home in the house in

Rehavia; we're there at least once a year. I think their familiarity with the surroundings will make it easier for them to adapt. It's hard to carry the whole family on my shoulders. I hope they don't think they'll see their father less often only because of a whim of mine. I hope Danny finds himself an interesting job in Israel." Gabi stretched her legs. "Some sort of proposal is taking shape in Israel for Danny to direct a company. It sounds perfect for Danny and his professional strengths, but it's still under wraps. Too complicated. And he hasn't found anyone to replace him here."

"You'll leave a gap in the Valley's landscape," I said, anticipating the pain of parting.

Gabi and her family had lived alongside mine for a long time. Together, we raised our children, celebrated the holidays and, in fact, created a substitute extended family for one another. She had been there for me when I arrived in California with my husband and the two kids who'd already been born, some ten years ago. She'd helped me find my way around in every possible respect. She'd helped me locate our rented home, find schools for my kids, and even connect with other psychologists in the Israeli community. She'd been there for me when I enrolled at a graduate program so I could practice as a psychologist in California (I had already practiced for years in Israel), and she'd babysat for me when Yoel was not around and I needed a moment for myself. I'd never forget her gesture, about ten years prior, when I traveled to Europe with Yoel, and she offered to look after four-year-old Alon, two months after she had given birth herself. Throughout those eight long days, when I called to ask how Alon was, she never told me she was counting the minutes until my return. She admitted her exhaustion only after I rushed from the airport to collect my son. "I'm half dead," as she put it. The perfume I brought her was certainly inadequate to express my profound gratitude. Nor did it erase the guilt I felt about failing to consider the burden I had dumped on her.

Our conversation was cut short by another phone call from Roni. Yaniv and Itai wanted permission to go with friends to a PG-13 movie, and they were still underage.

I thought about Nitzan, a therapist who had recently started to work in my clinic. She told me through a veil of tears that she was miserable despite her lovely new house, and would rather live in a small old flat in an apartment building in Israel; she was ready to pack her things and leave the minute her husband Oded agreed. Oded, on the other hand, was happy in America. He had high hopes and thought that life over here offered golden opportunities that didn't exist in Israel. She knew Oded would be miserable if she imposed her will on him and made him return home. Since they'd come to live in California, she felt as if she were in a tug-of-war between his misery and hers. Although Nitzan came to the States only a few months ago, and Gabi had lived here for fifteen years, I perceived the two of them as a single entity. They complained about permutations of the same problems, as if the years couldn't blunt the pain of their disconnection from Israel but only slightly rearrange the circumstances. Gabi ended her phone conversation, and my train of thought was disturbed. "We're near San Francisco, still an hour away from home," she said. "Can you stop for a few minutes?"

I stopped the Toyota at the nearest gas station and before I could pull on the hand brake, Gabi jumped out and dashed for the toilets, reminding me of Oscar, who waited for me to open the door every morning so he could dash to the nearest bush to empty his bladder. Gabi came back with packets of chips and popcorn and was soon busy chewing. We quickly covered the distance to Palo Alto on the open road. Half an hour, and we were home.

Maya and Oscar welcomed me at the door. Our family lived in an Eichler home, one of many in Palo Alto. It was a wooden one-story house with large glass windows. A brick path led to the front door, dividing the small lawn, which was planted with red and yellow seasonal flowers on both sides. The dog was wagging his tail, while Maya jumped up and down as if we'd been apart for at least two weeks. I took her in my arms, feeling her delicate bones against me as I hugged her sweet body. She chattered away, telling me about Jessica's birthday party and the picture she had drawn there. She ran to her room and came back with a watercolor painting of a lake full of boats, surrounded by high mountains with the sun overhead. In the forefront stood a girl with her back to the lake. She had a broad smile and eyes like Maya's—one green and the other green with a brown fleck—gazing into the distance.

"What were you thinking about when you painted the lake?" I asked her.

"Daddy said you went to paint a lake, so I also painted a lake. For you."

"It's so beautiful, we should frame it and hang it on the wall." I kissed her soft cheek. It was true. Maya's painting was more beautiful than mine. Apparently, girls of all ages enjoy doing the same things.

A few steps later, I was in the kitchen. One look at the stove revealed the menu of the past two days. The ceramic tiles on the wall were covered in cooking oil. The remains of fried eggs next to a spurt of ketchup were splattered on the marble counter, with leftover spaghetti dangling on the steamer. The pots patiently awaited me in the sink, next to a pile of cutlery.

Ayelet drifted by, blowing a kiss in my direction. Her attention focused on the telephone tucked between shoulder and ear. Speaking English, she fired a rapid volley of sentences, the meaning of which I couldn't catch, but I assumed she was encouraging a very depressed friend. Ayelet believed that, as a psychologist's daughter, she had a genetic right to advise her friends. After all, she was ahead of her mother in most respects, hence the obvious conclusion that the skill was in her blood and, if permitted, she could successfully manage her mother's practice.

Two more steps into the den, and there was Yoel's back, hunched over the computer. He stood up and gathered me close, my lips level with his neck; I kissed the skin that used to be taut and was now softened by the passing years.

"You're back early!" he exclaimed happily.

"Keren is sick. I volunteered to drive Gabi home."

"It's good you're back. I have to prepare a presentation for Monday and time's flying."

His happiness at seeing me was secondary. "Rami and I are starting a round of fund-raising next week," Yoel explained. "We're hoping to raise twenty-five million from the Japanese investors and a smaller amount from VCs. If we succeed, we'll buy Tom Jenkins's company in San Diego, and then we'll have no competition in the field. Do you understand what that means?"

I nodded. I understood but wasn't carried away by his enthusiasm. I knew it was a long way from vision to fulfillment, and that many tough moments lay ahead for Rami and Yoel on their climb to the peak of their dreams.

"So, we need to pick up Alon from scouts and prepare dinner." Yoel reinstated me in my role as general manager, lightly tossing me back into domestic chaos without allowing me a moment of transition.

Being the disciplined pet that I was, accustomed to Yoel's total dedication to his career, I didn't even try to initiate a discussion about splitting chores in the home. I had come to terms with the fact that I had married a tireless, pious worshipper of the institution of work, who regarded his labor as a self-appointed mission. He was not to be disturbed with matters of no importance, such as dirty dishes. At times, I imagined Yoel and Rami wearing the traditional Hassidic fur hat and long coat, their peyos swaying as they bowed in prayer before the computer. I envisioned them successfully developing a new product or raising funds, then dancing on the table like orthodox Jews celebrating a festival in the synagogue.

"Have you heard of the website called Hevreh?" I asked as I headed toward the door.

"Sure." His face lit up. "I got a lot of messages from high school friends. Even Orly Bergman sent her regards—according to her, I was the class hunk." He blushed.

"Who's Orly Bergman?" The name wasn't on Yoel's list of ex-girlfriends.

"Orly was a very sexy girl in my class. A tall, skinny blonde with big boobs." He mimed their shape on his own chest. "I never thought I had a chance with her; she was always surrounded by upperclassmen. Boys her own age didn't count, as far as she was concerned."

His tone revealed a longstanding, deep hurt. I looked at him in amazement, trying to sound pleased for him. "How nice that you were the class hunk."

"You also used to be very sexy," he said, trying to pacify me.

I gave him half a thanks for half a compliment.

"Should I list you on the site? You can get in touch with your old classmates, if anyone even owns a computer in your Podunk hometown," he mocked.

I remembered the anxious girl I was in high school. My face covered in pimples, I was scrawny, and the breasts that budded overnight looked awkward and gigantic to me. For years, I tried to conceal them in tight bras and loose shirts. And that wasn't all. I wore ugly glasses and thought my shoulders were too broad, my hips too narrow, and my legs too thin. One day, in a fit of anger, I cut off all my hair. What would my old classmates remember about me? I shuddered at the thought.

"No, thanks, Yoel," I said.

Chapter 2

Copenhagen. Danny boarded the plane and picked up the *New York Times* on his way to his seat in first class, where he settled down with a self-satisfied grin. He'd been upgraded from business class; his week's visit had been a definite success. Life was good.

The company's European branch was performing well beyond expectations. Mike Jacobs, who had been chosen to set up the sales team, was showing initiative and leadership and had prevented the company's sales from falling behind competitors' sales in several critical situations. There were signs that the present quarter was going to be much more successful than the last, according to the number of orders already signed and those expected to arrive soon. If we go on like this, we'll capture the market in a year or two and wipe out the competition, Danny thought, occupying himself with devising a long-term strategy.

He rubbed his hands in satisfaction, noting that the bulk of the week's commercial success could be attributed to Margot. Who had enlisted her to manage the finances in Copenhagen? He searched his gray matter but couldn't remember. Whoever it was, bless them. His smile spread, and he restrained himself from licking his lips as he recalled her long legs and the honey between them. How could he refuse her invitation to come to her office late at night to "go over the accounts"? He lingered over every detail time and again, losing count of the trysts over the past week, which had continued until moments before he boarded the plane. Such a sweet cherry would oblige him to make more frequent visits to the Copenhagen branch, he admitted to himself with a helpless sigh.

He opened the newspaper and leaned back. By mistake, his elbow bumped the arm of the blond flight attendant as she passed by. She was carrying a heaping bowl of smoked salmon covered in Russian black caviar, which spilled onto his head. Alarmed, she rushed to the kitchenette and came back with an armful of towels and a breathless flow of apologies. It was all her fault, she said, and offered to wipe Danny's head, on which the little black globules of caviar blended with his black hair. When she bent over him, Danny had a close view of the orbs of her breasts in front of his face. He controlled a sudden impulse to nibble on them and drag her to the kitchenette. There was a limit even to Danny Gonen's gluttonous impulses. After all, he'd been greedy enough over the past week. He took the towel, thanked her, and rubbed the caviar out of his hair. Like Milan Kundera's Tomas, Danny recalled uncomfortably that he had not showered properly or washed his hair after parting from Margot. He consoled himself with the fact that his neighbor's seat was some distance from his and put the matter out of his mind.

When Gabi walked in the door, her five children pounced on her in excitement, each according to height, clinging to her like puppies begging to be stroked. Keren nestled her head between Gabi's knees and clasped her mother's broad thighs in her plump little hands. Gil and Yaniv hugged either side of her round belly. Itai was chest-high, and Roni embraced her shoulders. At moments like these, Gabi cherished the weight she had gained after her pregnancies, because there was nothing she enjoyed more than being able to provide a soft, warm surface for five heads to nestle. Long before she bore children, Gabi had dreamed of becoming the larger-than-life mother of many children. She had hoped to be the opposite of her own mother, who was gaunt and bony, with hardly any space to hug one skinny child.

Gabi felt Keren's forehead. The fever was down. She opened the fridge, removed pots and plastic boxes and skillfully stirred, warmed, cut, arranged, and briskly served a hot meal to her children. They crowded around the table and updated her on their last two days as they chewed and swallowed with the appetite of children relieved to discover they haven't been abandoned.

Gabi and Danny's couplehood, which had begun in their childhood, had its ups and downs. Sometimes Gabi felt that Danny was her own flesh and blood, that she had no life without him. Other times she could hardly wait for him to disappear off on one of his business trips, so that she wouldn't have to see his face, hear his roaring voice, or put up with his outbursts of rage that came without warning. At such times, she wanted to send him on a never-ending journey, and her imagination ran wild as she built herself a quiet new life in her mind. One without Danny. Except that Gabi was a guilt virtuoso. Very quickly, compassion overcame her, and she forgot the insult and forgave him. She always forgave him.

Gabi was the only child of a mother carved from ice and a father lacerated by the war. Her mother was born in Salonika, during the war. From the age of ten until she was fourteen, she was hidden from the Nazis by a peasant family. Her parents, who promised to return after the war, had paid money and jewelry to the peasants, who used her as a servant. After the war, when she was fourteen, the Youth Aliyah sent her to Israel, where she discovered that she was alone in the world.

Gabi's father was also a Holocaust orphan. At thirteen, he was sent from the Warsaw Ghetto to Auschwitz. He jumped from the train that took his family to the camp but climbed onto another train when he realized that his father had not jumped with him as planned. He never found his father or the rest of his family, and the two years of confinement in the camp left him with scars that never healed.

In spite of the atrocities he had endured, her father was the life and soul of the house during Gabi's childhood. He loved his daughter and encouraged her with all his might. He saw her as a ray of light and the extension of a broken life. Her mother, on the other hand, was always somber and complaining. Her mother thought that Gabi's life was unfairly easy compared to her own childhood. She accused Gabi of being lazy, selfish, and inconsiderate. She made her work hard, hang and fold laundry, scrub pots and pans, wax the floor, cook and shop for groceries. Household chores were all assigned to Gabi in order to "prepare her for life," said her mother, who mercilessly taunted and insulted Gabi while she worked. It was only when Gabi grew up that she understood that her mother, in raising her tender daughter so coldly and with such toughness, was merely repeating the treatment she had endured from the peasants. It was as if the cold that had blown through the rooms in Greece had frozen all memory of the warmth of her early childhood with her parents before the war.

Gabi's parents clung to one another like a pair of abused puppies licking their wounds. They felt guilty that they were each the sole survivor of their respective families. Each took comfort in the other's pain. Gabi was named after her father's mother and was meant to be a living memorial candle for all the family's dead. The endless anxiety and pain that her parents felt over their loss seeped into her until she was inundated by it.

"Anxiety is my middle name," Gabi often said in jest, "if not my first." That summed up her personality. My friend Gabi, the constantly worried and pessimistic one. She had no faith in Danny's success or in that of her children, and certainly not in her own. She was afraid that the future would be bad, that Danny's shares would fall because the stock market would collapse, that they'd lose their assets, that the children would fail, that they wouldn't choose suitable friends, that an incurable disease would strike, a fatal road accident would occur, or a plane would crash and the whole family would be wiped off the face of the earth. When Danny left on a business trip, he had to report his safe landing. When one of the children was late in coming home, Gabi went into emergency mode and expected the worst. Sometimes she was afraid that she or Danny would end the marriage and leave the children to grow up sadly in a single-parent household.

Gabi and Danny had grown up next door to each other. Unlike Gabi's dismal house, Danny's was cheerful and lively. Yael, his mother, had three children and taught art at the local elementary school. She loved Gabi and gladly took her in. Gabi's long braids, her big blue eyes behind round glasses, and her permanent sadness touched Yael Gonen's heart. Gabi was drawn to Yael's warmth like a moth to a flame, and through Yael she developed a profound inclination toward art. She liked studying the many art books on Yael's bookshelves; at first, she furtively paged through them with a sense of trespassing. She stroked the glossy pages of the *Great Painters* encyclopedia, attracted to the glowing colors and abundance of images. In time, encouraged by Yael, none of whose children showed any interest in art, Gabi learned to identify artists from the Renaissance, Baroque, and Impressionist periods. She particularly liked the Impressionists Monet, Matisse, Pissarro, and Gauguin and returned to look at their paintings again and again.

Yael was impressed by Gabi's artistic talent and, to encourage her, hung her pictures on the kitchen wall.

Gabi's mother, however, did not approve of her daughter's love of painting. Smiling sourly, she rebuked the girl, "What will you do with it? What? In life you have to have your feet on the ground, not your head in the clouds." Gabi, abashed, promised herself to hide her drawings from her mother's hawkish eyes.

She spent most of her time at Danny's house. The ball games of their early childhood later became board games and cards in their latency, and then came more daring games. When hormones were running wild during their adolescence, impelling them to discover the mysteries of the body, the bond between Gabi and Danny was sealed. Their wedding was a mere formality. Nobody doubted that the two, who had never been apart, were meant for each other.

As an adult, Gabi chose a lifestyle that was as different as possible from the one she'd known in her childhood home. To escape from the silent gloom of her mother's house, she made up her mind to fill her own with children, so that it would be in a state of constant turmoil. Cleanliness, the ideal her mother pursued down to the last speck of dust, was a thing of the past. Since Gabi had suffered from endless sermonizing and bullying with regard to her cleaning chores, she refrained from making any demands at all of her offspring, so that they would never see her as a hateful, nagging mother. Between the biweekly visits of the cleaning lady, the mess in Gabi's house mounted steadily, augmented by the mud and dirt carelessly tracked indoors by their many friends and visitors. A festival of trash.

In order to get from room to room, it was necessary to forge a path through satchels, books, notebooks, toys, clothes, shoes, and scraps of food. The cleaning lady asked for a special rate for cleaning the Gonen household, because there was so much more work than in any other house. The Afghan rugs with their geometric designs in breathtaking colors, spread on the polished wood floors, and the original oil paintings on the walls were clearly visible only twice a week, in the short time between the cleaner's departure and the arrival of the children like five stampeding horses. The whole house teemed with piles of objects that provided scientific evidence for the laws of entropy time and again.

In their youth, Gabi and Danny had been living in a small apartment in Beit Hakerem, Jerusalem. Gabi was studying at Bezalel Academy of Arts and Design and Danny, at the Hebrew University of Jerusalem. Gabi, lacking motivation and goals, was in no hurry to complete her degree and took five years to finish. In the fifth year, she and Danny were apart for the first time in their lives. Danny went to study business administration at Fontainebleau, near Paris. Gabi was in an advanced state of pregnancy and remained in Jerusalem. She didn't join him because of her anxiety: How could she give birth in a foreign country? How would she raise her first child without Grandma Yael? How would she communicate with doctors in French? And she wasn't too sure about French medicine, anyway.

The temporary separation from Gabi opened Danny's eyes to a new world. Like the ugly duckling, he discovered a new reflection of himself. No longer the suburban adolescent joined to Gabi and who knew no other girl, he was an attractive and charming young man. In France, he discovered French women and noticed that they melted before him. They admired his height, his black hair and blue eyes, his high cheekbones, and his dark complexion. Danny jumped delightedly from bed to bed, at first with a certain amount of guilt. Later, he built defensive walls based on his own inner logic and convinced himself that there was no harm in it. If Gabi didn't know, she couldn't be hurt. If nobody was hurt, what he did was all right. His moral reasoning condoned whatever measures he took to keep Gabi from knowing. In the end, he was protecting her. Therefore, in her interest, he could use any means: faking and concealing facts, inventing excuses, and, mainly, denial. The lies came naturally to Danny. They were so convincing that he even grew to believe them himself and claimed emphatically that he never lied.

Over the years, Danny became a practiced hunter of women. He perfected a sidelong glance, which he directed at women who entered his sensitive radar zone. If he was rewarded with a coy look, he conjured a particularly disarming expression, one intended to convey amazement at the splendid beauty he was beholding. As though he were figuratively rubbing his eyes in disbelief, it was a look that expressed, "Such stunning beauty, wit, and perfection, I have never yet seen." That admiring gaze allowed him access to most of the women who liked his appearance, status, Lamborghini, and, above all, his performance in bed.

More than once, he was accused of sexual harassment by women whose charm had soured for him. There was no cause for concern, however. Danny had a lawyer who took care of such things in a bona fide legal manner.

Gabi, who had always longed for a large family, was delighted by each of her five pregnancies and gained some ten pounds, layer upon layer, after each delivery. This weight increased her waistline but decreased her libido nearly to nil. Thus a new dynamic was created in the bedroom. Gabi evaded sex with many excuses, and Danny evaded any mention of his other women—a balanced arrangement for both bed and home.

On the night after I dropped her off, Gabi went to bed as usual after doing the dishes, putting the children to bed, and watching her favorite program on television. Danny came home from his business trip after she'd fallen asleep. He sank into bed beside her and was soon sound asleep. Shortly afterward, a strange smell awoke Gabi. She sniffed at Danny, who was gently snoring next to her, recoiled in disgust, and wondered if her husband had fallen into a sewer on his way home. After a while, she approached him again and sniffed his hair and face, like a puppy. She suddenly paled. The intimate smell of a woman wafted from the man in her bed. Nausea. Who was this bitch, and what had he been doing between her legs? She was furious. She tried to imagine the position: Lying, kneeling? Perhaps he had been sniffing her from behind, like a dog. Suddenly it became clear. That whore must have sat on top of him after he withdrew from her, rubbed herself against his head, and smeared his hair with the cocktail of their juices. Gabi could almost hear her groaning, "More! More!"

That was it. That was the source of the stink. The mental image became increasingly clear in her head. She convulsed with the force of her disgust and ran to the bed in the den, where she lay awake for the rest of the night.

Yes. Everything was clear: all the late-night conferences, the dinners with "customers," laconic telephone calls, and, now, the smell. She had incisive proof that there was another woman between Danny's thighs. Reason enough to get him out of here and back to Israel. Maybe with his mother nearby, he would finally begin to behave like a father of five children.

In the morning, she got out of bed to get the children ready for school. She was bleary-eyed and still in her nightgown. Her hair was wild, and her breasts were shaking with fury. After wrapping the last sandwich, she poured cocoa, cleared the cereal bowls from the table, and sent the children on their way. Danny came into the kitchen, washed and polished, reeking of aftershave, wearing a suit and tie like a bridegroom, and showering her with smiles. He approached her seeking a hug. Gabi slipped out of range.

"Where were you last night?"

"My flight landed at midnight." He looked at her with surprise.

"Did you come straight home?"

"What else?"

"You came to bed stinking as if somebody peed on you." She stared accusingly at him.

Danny rolled his eyes to the ceiling. "I don't know what you're talking about...Wait. Now I remember! I sat in first class on the plane from Copenhagen. The stewardess served smoked salmon and Russian caviar appetizers. I leaned back and bumped her elbow, and she spilled a bowl of caviar on my head. She brought me a towel and I tried to rub the mess from my hair, but apparently the smell remained. I'm sorry."

Gabi hadn't expected a plausible excuse, which left her confused and at sea between his logical explanation and her own reasoning. She hesitated for a moment, at a loss for words. Perhaps her suspicions were groundless. She was almost apologetic.

"What's happening about the offer from Israel? When are you going to start working on our return to Jerusalem? There's not much time until summer."

"I'll have to postpone it until I find someone to replace me. I can't leave a public company without a CEO. The board of directors won't permit it; the excuse that my wife is pressuring me isn't really going to convince them. After all, you don't want me to burn all my bridges. Besides, Gabi, are you sure you want to move this year? What about the buses getting blown up in Jerusalem and the cafés going up in flames? You won't even let the kids get on a bus in Palo Alto, because you're scared it will explode, so how will you cope with the terrorist attacks in Jerusalem?"

He didn't wait for an answer. He took a spoonful of leftover cereal and a sip of cocoa from a colorful plastic cup, gave wild-haired Gabi a quick, not quite convincing, kiss on the cheek, and left.

Gabi took a deep breath, aired the rooms to clear Danny's presence, and asked herself what she should do. She wanted to share her feelings of anger and insult and wondered who best to turn to. She thought of me. She knew I was accustomed to hearing hair-raising confessions. It stood to reason that I wouldn't be shocked.

Gabi went to the bedroom and sniffed the sheets. Last night's disgusting smell was now mixed with the smell of sweat and maybe alcohol he'd had on the plane. In the end, she did what any woman would do—she shoved the sheets into the washing machine.

That afternoon, Gabi and I sat close to each other on high chairs by the counter in my kitchen. The kitchen was not small—there was a large table and chairs on the side of the room that faced the back garden—but we preferred to sit close, our shoulders almost rubbing. While Gabi opened her heart and shared her story, Keren was playing in Maya's room. I poured coffee into our mugs and listened to my friend. Despite what she had expected, I was shocked. I was inclined to believe Gabi. I wondered if Danny, the snake, had invented the caviar story in an inspired moment, desperately grasping for an explanation. Although I'd reminded myself a hundred times never to act in a professional capacity outside the office, I assumed the poker face of the psychologist who has heard everything under the sun and could never be shocked.

"The source of the smell isn't important, Gabi. You feel that there's a bad smell between the two of you, and the atmosphere needs to be cleared. You're losing your trust in Danny, and you need to address the core of the matter."

Gabi sighed deeply and nodded. "He evades serious conversation and leaves me feeling that I'm bothering him and burdening him with trivialities; I'm all alone in this. I don't know what he really thinks or feels. This morning, he casually informed me that this summer isn't a good time to go back to Israel, as if I hadn't yet heard about the terrorist attacks all over the place."

"You need to have a serious, heart-to-heart talk," I said.

"We're walking on parallel paths that never meet. Each of us thinks the other has to change their mind," Gabi remarked sadly.

"Don't forget you have children in the middle of all this. The moment they discover that their parents aren't on the same wavelength, they'll take over and then, Gabi, you'll really lose control."

Gabi took off her glasses and rubbed her eyes in despair. "Roni complains of stomach pains and nausea and sometimes of breathlessness. I thought she might be pregnant, but the doctor can't find a physical cause for any of it; he thinks it's a psychological reaction to stress."

"Sounds like panic attacks," I said, worried. "Is she getting therapy?"

"She meets with the school counselor."

"If the symptoms recur, I can refer her to a psychiatrist friend of mine. There's very effective therapy for anxiety and panic attacks." Gabi was on the brink of tears. I stroked her shoulder. "Perhaps Roni is reacting to the tension between you and Danny. You have to initiate a real discussion with Danny. When was the last time he paid intimate attention to you?"

"Do you mean when was the last time I slept with him?"

"That, too."

"I don't remember any sexual contact since Keren was born."

"If so, Gabi, you've got a project. Arrange a romantic weekend somewhere beautiful. Leave Keren with me. Pack some sexy underwear and wake up your sleeping Aphrodite. I'm sure Danny will be glad to come home."

I suggested the idea, although I knew it might not be welcome, but Gabi's thoughtful expression indicated that she was considering it.

"A romantic weekend sounds like a good idea, if Danny would be good enough to take some time off, for my sake. But I promise you, Daniela, nothing will stop me. Not even Danny's persuasiveness, because I'm determined to return to Israel this summer, whatever the cost!"

Unlike her usual self, Gabi was decisive and unhesitant. I recalled her father's determination, when he jumped back onto a train to Auschwitz, to be with his parents; I wondered if Gabi was subconsciously repeating this pattern by insisting on rejoining her family in Jerusalem with a stubbornness that endangered her marriage, which was already hanging by a thread.

"You know, Daniela, my parents have never asked me to come back to Jerusalem. After every terrorist act, I anxiously phone them to make sure they're all right, and it's as if they're living in total denial, as if nothing can shock them after the atrocities of their childhood. They calmly travel around the country with their environmental preservation volunteer group, as if nothing dangerous is happening around them. They even tour the Old City and outlying areas of Jerusalem. But I feel that if I don't live close to them in their old age, I'll be betraying my basic values. Danny doesn't have those strong feelings. His parents are younger than mine and didn't go through the Holocaust. Also, he has siblings, unlike me, and isn't solely responsible for taking care of his parents."

"It's unhealthy to act out of guilt, Gabi. Some feelings can't be changed, and there's nothing you can do. For one thing, you know that you'll never get a kind word or compliment from your mother, nor an expression of pride in you or in the children you're raising."

Gabi sighed. I'd hit upon her sensitive spot, and touched unresolved issues from her childhood. She admitted that her desire to return to her parents wasn't rational, that the move to Jerusalem could leave her with nothing. Danny would feel that he had sacrificed his lifework for her, the children would have to cope with big changes, and there was no assurance that her parents would even appreciate the effort she would be making for their sake. Mainly, she missed Grandma Yael, Danny's mother, but that was another story.

Gabi was silent for a moment. In her eyes, I saw a new insight seeping into the remains of her morning's anger.

"I like the idea of a weekend together to work things out. But we need to do it before the evening with Luigi Fracassini. Have you made a note of it, Daniela?"

"Yes." I wouldn't miss an evening with the famous professor.

We stood at the door, two mothers and two little girls. We hugged and kissed as if Gabi and Keren already lived in another country. When they left, I sat with Maya, staring at the television. Gabi's turmoil raised questions and speculations in my mind. Had I ever doubted Yoel's faithfulness? I remembered when Nira came to our house to invite Yoel to go cycling in the mountains. She was carrying a tray of stuffed cabbage that made his mouth water. I remembered how she stood at the door and kissed Yoel, chatting with him in Bulgarian, their mothers' native language. On the way to the kitchen, she put her thin, tanned arm around my shoulders and whispered, "Tell me, Daniela, is he good in bed? I bet he fucks like a stallion."

I was dumbstruck with astonishment. When I recovered some long seconds later, I responded as if I'd just heard the best joke in town. In the same so-called joking manner, Nira suggested a partner swap. She proposed snatching Yoel for a weekend and magnanimously offered Rami in exchange.

It's obviously a hot issue for Nira, I thought, but Yoel definitely wouldn't be tempted. His trips abroad were something else, I told myself with a sigh. But I'd never know what really happened there.

I was brought back to the present by Yoel, who came in and proudly announced, "I brought you some tomatoes," as if he'd carried out a difficult mission.

The semantics irritated me. I wanted to point out that the tomatoes were not meant for me, but for a salad for the whole family. I wanted to say that stocking the fridge was not my sole responsibility, and what sort of example was he setting for the kids in declaring that the tomatoes were for me. I wanted to say it, but said nothing. I remembered similar arguments from distant days, when I was a young, feisty chick ready for battle. In those days, we'd mount the barricades and get stuck there. We'd sharpen our swords, send up sparks, and in the end I'd surrender, tired. I'd grown sick of quarreling. Perhaps I'd simply matured and put things in perspective. After all, not every little thing justified taking up arms. In the clinic, I sometimes met couples who exhausted each other in a power struggle about housework, each of them fanatically resisting being the sucker.

"Each side has to make sacrifices in favor of the relationship," I told them, like John Kennedy encouraging the nation to "ask not what your country can do for you, ask what you can do for your country," even though I knew that one side sometimes exploited the good-heartedness of the other.

In the case of Yoel and me, it was not about exploitation or, heaven forbid, nastiness; it was about my husband's wholehearted belief that the existing order must not be changed. That was how he was raised, and that was how he raised his children. In theory, he was in favor of equal rights and opportunities for all. He liked to say that some of his best friends were successful women (such as the Columbia University math lecturer who'd written him a love letter that I found among the pages of a book from his bachelor days). But in reality, splitting housework was, in his opinion, simply impractical. Specifically, how could one share the ongoing responsibility for child care, rides, grocery shopping, cooking, and laundry with someone like him, who simply wasn't around? If he were at home, he would gladly have taken an active part. But he was not. So he brought me a cup of coffee in bed every morning, feeling that in doing so, he fully met his obligations, expressed true love, and symbolically participated in our couplehood. And me? I settled for this gesture of goodwill. I suppose this meant that I had become an old hen who knew how to appreciate what she had.

"Nice of you to remember, thanks," I said with a sweet smile, pointing to the tomatoes.

He reminded me that the next day he was embarking on a business trip that would take him to three continents and said he had to pack.

And I accepted it, maybe even viewed it as an advantage. When he flew around the world, as often as twice monthly, there was nobody to bicker with over tomatoes. When he came back, like Martin Guerre returning to his love sevenfold more passionate, all anger was forgotten. My heart opened in anticipation of his return. Ido once remarked that business trips around the world were a tried and true recipe for the preservation of couplehood. Maybe he was right. Apparently most of the Israeli men in the Valley also rigorously adhered to the theory. Perhaps even Danny.

"You'll miss Alon's concert and Maya's ballet recital," I told him, setting off little waves of guilt that didn't last long.

"You'll represent me admirably," he responded.

What else is new? I thought. I attended most school events on my own. I came to terms long ago with the fact that I was raising my children almost like a single parent. However, there was some consolation in knowing that I was not alone; in the Valley, we were all grass widows. Business trips around the globe were an integral part of the high-tech lifestyle, the travelers citizens of a small, borderless world. The same code language was spoken, and the same technological god was worshipped in Asia, Europe, and Israel. Everyone worked around the clock, under pressure, in the race to beat the competition. An Israeli sociologist who visited Stanford concluded that among the high-tech community, a new culture was emerging, with norms and values that transcended nationality and ethnicity, and rendered its members part of a brotherhood of creativity. The women, who rarely jet-setted to the same extent, were passive sisters within this maddening creative brotherhood.

A poster in Yoel's office at his start-up company in those days portrayed a lion chasing a deer, with the caption: "High-tech is like the jungle. It doesn't matter if you're a lion or a gazelle: when you wake up in the morning, you'd better start running." This nicely summed up the normative principles and values of the glorious techie culture.

"I'm going to Japan, Korea, Singapore, and Hong Kong, with two stopovers in Europe. Then the week after that, we're headed to the East Coast, only for a few days," he informed me in a conciliatory tone. "With this VC fund-raising round, I have to mobilize the big guns on all fronts."

Yoel spoke in military terms. In his mind, the start-up war of survival demanded strategies straight from the war room, which is what his home office resembled. All three telephone lines and the fax would often ring all at once, and I knew better than to touch a telephone when he was around, because all calls were for him. His inbox was bursting at the seams, and wherever he was, he was connected to a mobile phone that never stopped ringing, even in the late hours of the night, weekends, mealtimes, drives, and visits to the bathroom. In fact, on his throne in the bathroom was where it appeared that most critical decisions were made. Seemingly, I was the only one disturbed by the noises that emerged from the bathroom in the midst of heated telephonic discussion. When Yoel set off on his journeys, there would be a temporary quiet in our house, broken only when those who were more in the know than I informed me that our perpetual traveler was about to return.

That evening, after the tomatoes had become a salad, and the children were in bed, I lay alone listening to Yoel talking on the phone in his office. Through the doorframe, I could see his back bent over the computer. The lateness of the hour and his deliberately oversimplified and slow English indicated that he was talking to a colleague in Asia. In a few hours, he would begin speaking with Israel and in the early morning, he would talk to the company's representatives on the East Coast. When we lived in Israel, and the calls from the States continued late into the night, I hoped that the situation would ease after we moved overseas. But it didn't; it grew worse.

I listened with longing to his voice, as if it were coming from a distance. I yearned for the warmth of his body against mine, feeling him inside me. It was only a few hours ago that I had encouraged Gabi to reawaken her sleeping Aphrodite; what about my own goddess of love? I awakened her in my imagination. The faceless Aphrodite rose with alacrity and entered the office. Naked, she stood behind him, tenderly kissed his neck, pulled off his T-shirt, and drew delicate figure eights on his back with her nipples. In my imagination, I saw him turn slightly to show there was life in him, reaching to touch her-me with his left hand, his eyes fixed on the computer screen displaying imperative real-time information. Covering the mouthpiece with his right hand, he whispered to Aphrodite, "Later."

Aphrodite came back to my bed with her eyes lowered. "I've lost my magic," she said sadly, "I don't stand a chance against the Japanese." And I remembered how at one time that ploy would reliably drop the pen from Yoel's hand, shut down the computer, and disconnect the phones. As for poor Aphrodite, the magic of the rabbits she pulled from her hat was defeated by Japanese enchantment. I held defeated Aphrodite close. It was all a matter of timing, I told her. Soon we would sail toward distant worlds.

And sail I did. Lying in bed, I reviewed Gabi's confession. I thought about her powerful need to return to Israel and remembered that I'd also had such plans. They never materialized, hadn't withstood the test of time. My family resisted, my children informing me through their tears that they were not suitcases to be packed up and dragged from place to place according to my wishes.

I thought of Gabi's parents and my own, who also never complained and never said a word about the great distance that separated them from their grandchildren. The distance wasn't only physical, but also cultural and mental. The children could hardly speak Hebrew. They knew nothing about the hardships endured by generations of their ancestors, and they were growing up in the States like green, happy plants with weak roots.

In the twilight between waking and sleeping, a scene unfolded in my mind, perhaps a dream, perhaps a memory. I was marching in military uniform along a sand path that led to my Grandma Batya's house in a small village in the center of the country. Weeds grew in abundance on either side of the path, a reminder that there was nobody to clear them. The yard was also wild since Grandpa Baruch had died more than a year earlier. There were deep cracks on the outside walls of the little Jewish Agency cabin, Grandma Batya's house, because the clay soil had shifted the foundations. Grandma had vehemently opposed renovations to the house, because she "couldn't stand workmen under her feet" and, more important, because she was afraid they'd steal her meager retirement pension from deep inside her closet. Since Grandpa's death, her mental state had deteriorated, and she'd become suspicious and withdrawn. From time to time, she wrongly accused her sons of various misdeeds, although they took devoted care of her. She accused the doctors of negligence, and they sent her on her way with only a bottle of aspirin when she was certain she had heart disease, if not a rare form of cancer gnawing at her. The doctors said she was as strong as an ox and would live another ten years, well into her nineties. She fired her housecleaners and caregivers, saying they "didn't know how to work." She was afraid they would rob her of her few worthless possessions.

My khaki shirt sweat-stained and creased, I knocked on the door and stood inhaling the hot air of a steamy August evening. The shutters were closed and all that could be heard was the sound of television inside the house. Some minutes later, I heard the flapping of slippers and the hoarse voice of an old woman: "Who's there?"

"Daniela," I called. Grandma repeated the question several times, because she was hard of hearing. She opened the door a crack, keeping it securely chained on the inside, and peered at me with green eyes dimmed by cataracts. Grandma Batya would not allow some *pisher* of a doctor to cut her with a scalpel.

"Daniela, what a surprise! Wait a minute," she said in her heavy Yiddish accent and locked the door, leaving me standing outside. She came back after a while and let me in, having improved her appearance. Her dentures were in place. She was now wearing a bra, so that the front of her torso, which had previously looked like a lump of jelly, was better arranged and, as befitted a religious woman, a kerchief covered her hair. I kissed her, and she gripped my arms.

"What a surprise, what a surprise," she mumbled. "Come, sit, eat something. What shall I make for you to eat?"

"I'm not hungry, Grandma. Do you have some juice?" I said, to please her without putting her to any trouble.

Grandma staggered to the kitchen on her thin, bowed legs and returned with two glasses, a bottle of orange juice, and a plate of home-made cookies on a tray.

"Do you like butter cookies?" she asked. "They aren't pretty, but they have a good heart." That was how she used to personify cakes and food she made herself. We sat in the dining nook at a table with an old, stained tablecloth scattered with crumbs.

"Lovely that you came, lovely that you came," she mumbled rhythmically. "You know, just a few minutes ago, I came home from a Torah lesson with the rabbi's wife. We studied a chapter from the *parasha*. It's so good to study, it refreshes the soul. And the rabbi's wife is an educated woman. So clever. It's a pleasure to listen to her. Daniela, always study and study! Never stop! There's so much to learn in this world," she sighed. Grandma lectured me, perhaps because she thought she herself didn't have much time left to satisfy the curiosity that still burned in her. "And never, never pay attention to what people say. Listen to me, I took so much to heart, and that's not good." She passed her withered, age-speckled hand over her chest.

"You're so pretty, bless you," she said with a proud smile. "Like my little girl, Rivkale. Do you know that you are also called Rivkale?" I nodded. I remembered the story—delegations of aunts and uncles came to bless my parents after my birth, as the first baby born to a family that had suffered so much loss in the war. They all asked to commemorate lost mothers, sisters, and daughters. My father, a mensch, couldn't turn anyone down and bestowed upon his eldest baby daughter three names. One of them was Rivka, chosen for the sister he lost in the war.

"She was such a happy, smiley baby," Grandma recalled. I felt Rivka becoming so tangible that I expected her to appear and join us at the crumb-covered table.

"To this day, I remember how she danced with joy in a new dress and ran to show it to everyone." Grandma's hands were still dancing while her gaze turned inward to the gray matter of her memory, atrophying with her old age. A little smile spread on her lips, her hands danced on the tablecloth. "She died in my arms." She cleared her throat, her eyes sad and dry. "Daniela, may you never know sorrow." She straightened the kerchief on her head and sighed.

"What did she die of?" I asked.

"Dysentery and hunger. There was nothing to eat. The Ukrainians, may they rot in hell, were worse than the Nazis. They ripped out Grandpa's beard, killed his parents before our eyes, and made us march all the way from Bessarabia to Transnistria in the Ukraine. It took many days in cold and hunger. We had three small children. Grandpa carried Meirke; I carried Rivkale until she died. And Shloimele, your father, who was healthy, walked on his own the whole way without any help. He was only six years old. He didn't complain. He knew he had to walk. Such a hero, your father. You should know. What a wonderful boy, your father. Even your grandfather lost the strength to walk. One day he said to me, 'Bassa, I've got no strength left, I want to die.' And I told him he couldn't die, because of the children. The Ukrainians killed anyone who walked slowly." She looked far into her memory, her head shaking. "They didn't want sick, slow people. I pushed your grandfather to make him keep on walking, to make him stay on his feet. One day, they wanted to take him aside and kill him. I begged them not to. I had blond hair and green eyes, and I said I wasn't Jewish, that I was a *goya*. That I was married to this Jew, and they should let him live. So they listened to me and let him live. It was God's gift to us that he was allowed to live. You should know it. Lots of times God came to me and saved me. One day I prayed to God to give me food. So God heard me and sent me an angel."

"An angel?"

"He sent me an angel who looked like a goy. A peasant who gave me bread. And if we stayed alive, it was only thanks to God." She choked back a silent cry. "It was so cold that I had to hold the children between my legs all night to keep them warm. Like this." She showed me. "When we came to Transnistria, they put us in a stable, but it was better, because we could cover ourselves in hay. Just imagine, Daniela, how people lived. Every evening, the Ukrainians, may they rot in hell, came and took the men and whipped them. Again, your poor grandfather wanted to die. It was only by a miracle from God that we are here. And a great miracle that I lived to see grandsons and a beautiful granddaughter like you. Better you shouldn't know any of this. But we must not forget. And the most important thing is to believe in God.

"So, Daniela, have you got a bridegroom yet?" she asked, moving from there to here, from then to now.

"No, Grandma, I'm only nineteen, still in the army."

"Army? Who needs the army? It's not for a nice girl like you. A nineteen-year-old girl should have a bridegroom. Look how big you are, bless you. Not good to be alone. Must have a bridegroom. Listen to me," she said scraping breadcrumbs into her bony, age-flecked hand.

On the brink of sleep, with my eyes closed, I contemplated the paradox. My grandmother, the Holocaust survivor, believed that she had been granted her life by God, and therefore she worshipped Him. Unlike his mother, my father, who had survived the same atrocity, said that because his childhood had been annihilated so cruelly, there must not be a God. Who knows. My father erased the suffering of the Holocaust from his memory, grew up like the salt of the earth, commanded soldiers, and fought in all of Israel's wars. And his daughter was raising her children in California. What a shame.

Chapter 3

Lori was due to knock on the door of my office at any moment. The suspicion that had arisen in me during our last session persisted. I hadn't managed to consult my colleagues in the interim, but I told myself there was no firm basis for my suspicion that Lori had planned her husband's death. On one hand, I had a strong desire to shake off Lori and refer her to another therapist; why get involved in a murder story? On the other hand, I feared that a sudden referral might adversely affect her already vulnerable condition. I decided to act with caution at this stage and make no hasty decisions about continuing the therapy.

I used the few minutes before the session to refresh my knowledge of California's laws and ethics concerning patient-therapist confidentiality in cases where the therapist had knowledge of a patient's involvement in a murder. In cases where a patient threatened to murder an identifiable victim, the law was absolutely clear, stating not only that the therapist's obligation to confidentiality was waived, but also that the therapist was obligated to report the information both to the police and to the victim. This law was named after an unfortunate victim, Tatiana Tarasoff, murdered by a therapy patient who had disclosed his plans to a therapist who did not take immediate action to protect Tarasoff. However, the legal literature contained no information regarding any obligation to report a retrospective confession to committing a crime, or being an accessory in planning a crime. Hence, the secrecy of such information, if disclosed while on the couch, was protected. I decided that if Lori confessed to being involved in murder, I would encourage her to turn herself in to the police.

Lori arrived fifteen minutes late. Her appearance shocked me anew. She looked as though she'd spent the previous few nights roaming the streets as a homeless vagrant. Her left forearm revealed fresh and gruesome razor cuts, her clothes were filthy, and her red T-shirt blared: TOUCH ME I AM HOT. Her ragged jeans were covered in soot and her feet, in simple flip-flops, were black with dirt. Under her uncombed, tangled hair, she bore no trace of makeup or fluttering false eyelashes. Lori's face was blank, and a smell of mold and smoke wafted from her. I dreaded the filth settling on my pale velvet sofa.

"What's happening to you, Lori? Looks like you've been neglecting yourself lately."

Lori burst into heartbreaking tears that flowed down her cheeks and lasted for long minutes. I offered up a box of tissues, but she didn't notice. She had sunk into her profound sorrow, and my presence was neither comforting nor even relevant. Her tears wet the T-shirt and stained the surrealistic inscription on her chest.

I asked what I could do to help her.

"I'm guilty, I'm guilty," she sobbed bitterly.

"Guilty of what?"

"I'm guilty of my husband's death." She looked as if she were mourning on the edge of a grave, writhing and gripping her hair as if she would pull it out by the roots.

"What did you do?" I asked gently, fighting with myself. On one hand, I didn't want to know; on the other, my curiosity persisted.

"I killed him." She sobbed into the handkerchief I put in her hand.

"How did you kill him, Lori?" I spoke quietly, hiding my emotional turmoil.

"The fact that I had a lover; it killed him. I caused him so much pain. All because of me, it's all because of me..."

I was relieved. I recalled her complaints about her older husband. "He's fat, he comes too soon, he doesn't know how to satisfy me," she used to pout. She had been her husband's pet, the beautiful woman beside him at events and celebrations. He had given her emotional and financial support and seen to it that she lacked nothing.

"Feeling jilted hasn't killed anybody yet." I tried to console her, but she refused to be consoled and stared at me, her eyes blank.

"Have you harmed yourself, Lori?" I pointed to the deep red cuts on her left arm.

The cuts were signs of self-punishment common in people with borderline personality disorder. Lori cut herself to substitute physical pain for the deep pain that cut her to the core, distracting herself for a moment by inflicting a pain that was easier to bear.

"Have you been eating and sleeping?"

"I'm back to puking five times a day, and I can't sleep at night."

"You've had a hard time, Lori." I caressed her with my voice. "Where is Steve? Have you seen him in the past few days?"

"I kicked him out and told him never to come back." She shrugged and wiped her tears on her sleeve.

"Why?"

"He doesn't love me. He's only interested in my money. He keeps pressuring me to transfer the insurance money from my husband's account to our joint account. He's angry; he said I betrayed him."

I was amazed at the ease with which Lori had brushed Steve out of her life. I wondered if this had to do with delayed grief over her husband's death. My pity for Lori returned, and I was glad to find my suspicions were pushed aside. The look of the grieving woman sitting across from me at the moment contrasted sharply with the lighthearted figure from the week before. The self-injury, the constant weeping, the dreadful neglect, the eating disorder, and the insomnia suggested that her depression had hit the sinusoidal low of manic depression.

"Have you been thinking of killing yourself?" I asked quietly, trying to get an accurate picture of her condition.

She shook her head in denial.

"Is anyone in your family supporting you at the moment? Can someone come and stay with you, to look after you?"

I immediately wished I could retract the question. I couldn't expect a positive answer. Lori's family background was one of the most difficult I'd ever come across. Her great-grandfather was a Polish immigrant, a drunkard and a fornicator who sexually abused both his daughters. Her father was the son of one of them. His cousin, who was also his half brother, committed suicide. Lori's father suffered from depression, obesity, excessive drinking, and health problems all his life because of the stigma of his disgraceful birth. His attempts to support his wife and daughters ended in failure when he was still young, and the family survived on welfare checks and food stamps. He spent every day sprawled on the couch in front of the television, bemoaning his fate, the injustice of the world, the exploitation of the poor by the rich, the rotten capitalist government, the sick educational system, and so on and so forth. In his distress, he harshly berated and beat his wife and daughters. Her mother, a spineless woman, died young of an alcohol-related disease. Lori said her mother abused her as much as her father did. She used to lock the children out of the house on snowy nights, shutting her ears to their cries, ignoring their desperate banging on the closed shutters. Apparently this was an accepted educational method where she came from. Lori's sister, older by two years, earned a living as a stripper and call girl in Las Vegas. Since Lori's marriage, the contact between them had weakened, because Lori's late husband considered her sister a bad influence.

In answer to my question, Lori shook her head and burst into tears again, mumbling that she missed her husband, who had been so good to her, and that now that he was gone she had nobody left in the world.

I thought it would be best to convince Lori to be voluntarily hospitalized in a psychiatric ward. The cuts on her arm and the vomiting indicated a strong possibility that she might harm herself and were sufficient reason to commit her involuntarily, if she refused hospitalization. Unfortunately, it seemed like an essential move at that stage, because her safety was not guaranteed were she to be sent home in the state she was in.

I mustered my most gentle voice and asked her if she'd agree to be hospitalized for observation and reassessment of her medication. I explained that she should not be alone at home and that in the psychiatric ward, they would ease her suffering.

Accustomed to hospitalization, Lori did not like the psychiatric ward, which robbed her of her freedom to do as she pleased. She couldn't get alcohol there or vomit her food. She tried to resist. She promised to eat and not vomit, to bathe herself and sleep, and take proper care of herself from that minute on.

I looked at Lori with skepticism. We both knew there was no chance of her precipitously emerging from her profound depression.

After a few minutes, I showed what I hoped would be my trump card. "If you don't agree to voluntary hospitalization, I'll be forced to commit you against your will, which will mean that your stay in the hospital will be longer than necessary. In the meantime, with your permission, I'll get in touch with your sister and ask her to come when you are released from the hospital and take care of you until you're stronger."

Lori gave me a weary look. She realized that she wouldn't talk her way out of this one and resigned herself to my decision.

I called Dr. Warner, director of the psychiatric hospital in Woodside. The nurse recognized Lori's name and guaranteed that an ambulance would be sent to my clinic. While we waited, Lori signed the release form waiving confidentiality so that I could discuss her case with Dr. Warner and her sister. I promised to contact her sister urgently and ask for her help.

Two muscular and smiley male nurses in blue uniforms arrived within minutes. Lori parted from me with a weak smile and entered the ambulance with an air of importance, as if it were a grand limousine waiting to convey her to a VIP hotel. Feeling sad, I watched her leave. Even the two million dollars from insurance, now padding her bank account, did nothing to improve her wretched state. In the best-case scenario, she would have to use the whole amount to pay for psychiatric care for the rest of her life. A more realistic, less fortunate, possibility was that she would spend the lot on one huge party that would leave her destitute for the rest of her life. I made a note to refer her to a financial advisor when she was released from the hospital, in the hope of saving her from self-destruction.

Once the ambulance carried her off, I opened the windows of my office to clear the air of the remaining stench and cleaned the sofa with a damp cloth. Then I contacted Dr. Warner and left him a message notifying him that Lori was on her way to him for hospitalization and also to inform him of the death of Lori's husband and her depressive state. I described her vacillating moods, self-neglect, and the guilty thoughts that led her to believe she had murdered her husband. I requested that he check whether these guilty feelings were normative and connected to the mourning process, or if perhaps they were based in reality.

I put down the receiver, relieved to share responsibility with Dr. Warner's respected professional authority in the treatment of this complex case.

Then I phoned Las Vegas. Lori's sister's recorded answering machine message was delivered in a sexy, intimate whisper promising to return the call. I briefly notified her of Lori's hospitalization, requested her help, and left my telephone number.

I was exhausted. Weariness spread through my body and slightly dulled my senses. The hospitalization of a patient was not a daily occurrence and demanded considerable effort. Maybe there was an additional reason for my exhaustion. It had to do with the dynamic between me and Lori, the way I was affected by her vulnerability and restlessness. I looked at her as my complete opposite. My life was so protected; I was never alone. I knew my way around the world I lived in, and I was never lost. And yet I knew there must be a thread of connection between us. She represented a part of myself that I disowned, a part of Daniela that I would never allow to emerge. I would never allow myself to spiral so low, to hurt myself or others, to lose track of my inner compass. But what if I *did* lose track of my inner compass, I asked myself.

I knew I had ten minutes in which to recuperate before my next appointment, which would require my full, fresh attention, so I dragged myself around the corner to Starbucks, to revive my spirits with a double espresso.

Gilad was in the waiting room. As he smiled at me, his eyes squinted tightly, creating a thin line of lashes behind his round glasses. As always, his pupils darted about with the panic that had stricken him in childhood, the day his sister was run over by a truck. He held out his hand when I entered. I shook it warmly and invited him into my office. He sat on the white leather armchair facing me, next to the gray sofa where Lori had sat a few minutes before, and nodded a greeting to the statue of Freud, as if to an old friend. I opened a window, still detecting a whiff of Lori. Trying to stall for a moment, I asked Gilad if he'd like something to drink and was pleased when he accepted: black coffee, two spoons of sugar. In the kitchenette next to the waiting room, I took a deep breath. I needed a break. I felt like someone who had walked out of one movie theater directly into the next, not getting a moment to really process the first film before delving into the second.

Making the coffee allowed me to clear my head while doing something trivial. While I waited for the water to boil, I reviewed Gilad's history in my mind.

I recalled the session when he told me, with tears of joy in his eyes, about the birth of his first daughter, as if it were a miracle, as if divine powers had united in the cosmos, joining parts of his life together with magical ether to bring a real, living and breathing child into the world. His open, tangible happiness brought tears to my eyes, too, as if I'd had a hand in joining the parts, in the miraculous birth itself.

Gilad was living with a trauma he had suffered at the age of ten, when he was responsible for his four-year-old sister on afternoons while his mother worked in the neighborhood store, and his father drove a fuel truck. On the afternoon in question, Gilad heard his father's huge truck approaching, but failed to notice that his sister had run out of the house to greet her father. The truck reversed and ran over the little girl. Gilad heard his father's shouts of distress and dashed outside. He saw the small crushed body, a great pool of blood, and his father screaming and tearing his hair out. That picture had pursued him ever since, his sorrow mixed with feelings of guilt over the loss and the subsequent disintegration of the family.

His father sank into deep depression, took to drinking, stopped working, stopped talking, retired from life, and turned into a limp, senseless vegetable, madness in his gaze. The only thing that occupied him was reading newspapers. He hoarded them meticulously until his little apartment became a moldy, dusty storeroom full of paper, empty tin cans, and bottles. The stacked newspapers reached the ceiling, filled the hallway, the kitchen, and the stairs leading to the attic. For most of the day, his father crouched in his bed, and Gilad had to force his way through the piles of paper, tin cans, and bottles in order to get to him.

His mother, who was a bad-tempered woman before the tragedy, became even more furious afterward and never forgave her husband or her son. Both of them served as a constant reminder of her loss. She banished her husband from the family house and heaped a fury of abuse and humiliation on Gilad.

"You useless failure." She reminded him day and night of his sin. "You'll never amount to anything. That's your punishment for not looking after your sister—you're a curse!"

She berated him in spite of his impressive athletic accomplishments and even though he had the highest GPA in his grade every year. Although he served in an elite unit of the intelligence corps and, later, studied at the Haifa Technion, and although he went on to study at the Stanford Graduate School of Business, she thought it was all a fluke and adhered to her opinion that Gilad would "never amount to anything." These two parents inhabited him: his mother, who made his life miserable and reminded him unceasingly of his "sin," and his father, who was drowning in the sea of his guilt and refused to return to the world of the living. With both of them hanging like millstones around his neck, Gilad struggled to keep his head above water throughout his youth. Fighting valiantly, he managed to refrain from sinking into the waters of his father's hopelessness and his mother's bitterness.

Only his darting eyes bore witness to his restless inner struggle.

While at Stanford, he met and fell in love with the daughter of a wealthy Texas oil tycoon. In Gilad's eyes, Kimberly Anderson was a fairytale princess—not only beautiful, rich, and successful, but also a supportive, loving woman he could lean on. In contrast to his mother, Kimberly admired Gilad and viewed him as a treasure. For him, her love came as a gift, a sweet surprise, an indescribable joy. Uniting the two families, however, was an impossible undertaking. The effort to bridge the gap between the dysfunctional Levy family and the Anderson family planted in the oilfields of Texas exposed a wide abyss. Kimberly had grown up ensconced in happiness and wealth, whereas Gilad had not the faintest idea of either. Kimberly's parents expected a son-in-law of their own sort, and Gilad's separated parents were unable to understand what their only son wanted with a wife who had no intention of converting to Judaism. "At least, you owe me that consolation," his mother railed at him when he told her that Kimberly did not intend to convert, just as he did not intend to convert to Christianity.

With a bitter smile, Gilad had described their wedding. In the end, he'd told me, a compromise was reached, and it took place on the vast lawn of the Andersons' estate. A rabbi who was flown from Brooklyn and a local priest jointly conducted the ceremony. The bride's aristocratic family was seated at one long table, while the groom's parents were placed at two separate, demeaning little tables alongside the main one. In the background, their many friends from business school let down their hair and ate, drank, and danced with the bride and groom until dawn.

The water boiled. I poured and stirred, then carried the coffee back to my office, where I sat facing him.

I asked my usual opening question. "What brings you here, today?"

"Can I talk to you about sex?" he asked, as if seeking permission to undress in front of me. I nodded, trying to conceal any trace of embarrassment. Gilad was seven years younger than I was, and I hoped the age difference would negate my femininity, leaving only my professional image intact. It occasionally happened that a male patient's glances pierced the conventional professional barrier and his eyes, seemingly of their own volition, scanned my body. Most were embarrassed by this and looked away, fixing their gaze on a point behind my chair, as if looking for a fly on the wall.

But of course, there were the ones with chutzpa, like the student from New Zealand who was half my age and seemingly twice my height, who took pleasure in letting his eyes roam up the length of my leg and higher, shamelessly lingering at various points on my body. When I went to my desk to look for a form in one of the drawers, I could feel his eyes measuring and assessing my buttocks. I remarked to myself that when the Italians won the international competition for lasciviousness, the New Zealanders must have been absent. I was pleased when he calmed down after a few sessions, having satisfied his curiosity and ceased to see me as a sex object. Only then did he begin to focus on his problems and take the therapy seriously.

And then there were the ones who were starved, like the NASA engineer who had not been with a woman in ten years and, in spite of his obvious embarrassment, looked at me in a way that made me feel like a freshly baked roll in front of a hungry man. His deep-seated hunger frustrated him constantly, causing him to salivate secretly during our sessions. The analytic therapy focused on this hidden salivation.

With my twenty years of therapeutic experience, I learned to conceal my embarrassment and accept male curiosity with understanding. Nevertheless, in spite of the years, my momentary discomfort following those fixed glances was always there. Only the increasing gap between my age and that of most of my patients lessened the intensity and alleviated my discomfort to some extent. And seeing as Gilad had never looked at me with chutzpa or hunger, my discomfort this time was only very slight.

"Yes. We can discuss sex," I said. "I'm listening." Gilad spoke rapidly, shooting a high-pressured jet of words into the room while I tried to follow what he was saying, but it wasn't about sex. Instead, he spoke about his job as the manager of the start-up launched by Ido Eitan.

"We developed this particularly clever mechanism for a search engine for data storage," he reminded me. "It seemed like an idea that just couldn't fail, but our project is dying, because customers don't need such a high level of sophistication. Also, the cost of using our product can't compete with simpler search engines, and the expense of our development doesn't allow us to lower the cost. In retrospect, it turns out that this project was before its time, and it won't manage to survive." He rubbed his forehead, gazing at the floor.

The last time I'd seen him, Gilad had told me that Ido had personally invested millions of dollars, in addition to the millions he raised from investors. However, the bubble had since burst. Gilad now explained that when Ido realized the project was heading for failure, he asked all of his employees to take salary cuts.

He shook his head and spread his hands, "So, of course, all of my big dreams of success are totally shattered right along with this dying project. I'm looking around, and I see everyone making it except for me. Like always, I'm on the wrong track, outside the inner circle, even though I bet on someone like Ido, who's already struck it big in the past."

I remembered that in recent years Gilad had drifted among several start-up companies that had made no progress despite the large sums of money invested in them and that he had joined Ido in the belief that his salvation lay with him.

"If you don't make at least twenty million dollars, it's hard to believe that you're succeeding in the Valley," he said to me, and I couldn't help but think that life in Silicon Valley distorted proportions entirely. People were no longer satisfied with a good income that supported their family—they looked for success measured in millions, numbers taken for granted in the era of the bubble, when every week brought news of a new prince galloping on the horse of success with hundreds of millions of dollars bundled in his saddlebags.

"In the year 2000, twenty thousand new millionaires emerged in Silicon Valley, and I'm not one of them," Gilad said.

I thought to myself that he'd hit upon the core of the Valley's intoxicating appeal. Nowhere else on the face of the earth did frogs routinely turn into princes.

"It's unfair to compare yourself only to those who are more successful than you, without comparing yourself to those who are less successful," I told Gilad. "Actually, you shouldn't make comparisons at all. You must look at your achievements on a personal scale of success and failure without keeping an eye on others."

Gilad considered this for a while and then returned to his previous line of thought. He was frustrated at work, whereas Kimberly was doing fine. She had begun to withdraw from him as soon as she was on the executive track at a successful company. She was swiftly promoted and was managing a department of hundreds of workers. As a result, she was engrossed in her job and had lost interest in him and their two daughters. She came home late in the evenings after the girls were already in bed and immediately got busy on her computer. In her free time, she talked on the phone to her boss, who apparently was not immune to her feminine charms. Recently, she had taken to dressing in very sexy clothes and spending large sums on regular visits to beauty salons and hairdressers. She bought herself a sports car at a time when most of her friends—like her, mothers of young children—were driving SUVs or sedans. She also frequently flew to professional conferences.

"All signs point to the fact that Kimberly has forgotten that she has a family," he said, clearly pained. "I don't want to accuse her of having an affair with her boss, but I can't rule it out. I don't understand what's going on. I'm not a psychologist."

He glanced at me for a moment and then proceeded in a rush, "And it pains me to say that's not the end of the story. It's just the beginning. One day I received an email from an old friend of mine, Nirit. She'd searched for me on Yahoo and reached out. I was so happy to hear from her. We grew up in the same neighborhood and went to the same high school. We were friends, but there was no romantic connection between us. She got married straight after high school and soon had three children."

Gilad spoke with increasing emotion. Nirit was married to a senior executive who worked late hours and traveled often. She was a nurse by profession and worked in the orthopedic department at Tel Hashomer Hospital, near Tel Aviv.

"Since my wife is busy with her work and doesn't have time for me, I was living in a vacuum, and Nirit filled it. Enthusiastically. In the beginning, we just emailed, but we pretty quickly moved on to phone calls." He paused, his expression grim. "I gave her my cell phone number, and now she calls me a few times a day at work. I like talking to her, so I neglect the pointless projects I'm supposed to do. I've tried to set limits, but it's failed. All of a sudden, life's interesting, like I'm having a torrid affair; I'm being drawn in, and I can't resist."

"What do you talk about?"

"Everything on earth. She remembers my parents. We talk a lot about them and about her parents, who were also divorced when we were in high school. We've analyzed my mother's personality, dissected her into bits. We've made a salad out of her," he said with a satisfied smile. I noted that the profound, unforgiving anger that he felt for his mother was still simmering. "We've spoken about her marriage and mine, about decisions we've made, about the children and the professional issues that end up taking precedence over family. She told me how her husband was losing touch with the family and sinking into his work, which has caused her to become depressed. She's still in therapy."

"It seems like you're treating one another through these phone conversations," I remarked. "What does her psychologist say about this romance of yours?"

"Her psychologist has advised her to end the connection, but we both feel that our talks give us the strength to carry on with our regular lives."

"You are ambivalent. On one hand, you say the phone calls disturb you and interfere with your work; on the other, you say you don't want to put a stop to them. So, what help do you want from me?"

"I disturb her as much as she disturbs me. I encourage her to call, and she calls. I feel myself waiting for her calls. It's physical. I'm impatient for them. They make me feel young again, and desired, for the first time in ages. Like I'm back in high school. I've been drawn into a telephone romance that's hard to end. I want to understand what's happening to me. I need help to get out of this whirlpool, before it sucks me under."

"At the beginning of the session, you asked if we could discuss sex. Is there sex in your talks with Nirit?" I asked, feeling my way.

"Good question. As long as I don't go to bed with Nirit, my conscience is clear. But since Kimberly has grown so distant from me, something has happened. I lost my erection last time I tried to have sex with her. She didn't help, and I haven't even tried to approach her again. That was over five months ago," he said, angry and offended.

I asked if he was impotent under other circumstances, too, and his quick answer confirmed that he frequently had a morning erection, which proved that his masculinity was intact, unlike his spirit. He was like a hurt bird, hunching its wings and dispossessed of a song.

"You feel as if you're knocking on Kimberly's door, uncertain if you're a welcome visitor."

"Exactly!" Gilad looked me in the eyes. "I feel rejected, unloved, and sexually unattractive to my wife, whereas Nirit shows a lot of interest in me. I love and want my wife, but it's hard to resist the temptation."

Toward the end of the hour, the true crux of the problem became obvious. I advised Gilad to separate his two burdens, in spite of the intricate connection between them. I suggested that he take a good look at his marriage and figure out what he could work on. On a practical level, I suggested that he lower the frequency of his conversations with Nirit and try to understand why they excited him so much.

We parted with a handshake and arranged to meet in one week.

At home, I wore a different hat. Like Marcel Marceau, whose expression flips instantaneously from happy smile to sorrow and back again, I had resumed my motherhood persona, standing at the ironing board, ironing a white shirt and black pants for Alon's concert later in the day. The sounds of his clarinet coming from his room mixed with the *Nutcracker Suite* coming from Maya's room, where she was prancing around in a pink tutu with a huge flower pinned to a ribbon on her head and was swaying like a heavy branch in the wind. She was practicing for a ballet performance at the end of the week. In my house, everyone was practicing for one thing or another, for life.

I'd also been practicing all my life for something that was as of yet unclear. I was a sort of eternal student—a diligent student in the college of life. I kept my life precisely organized and perfectly timed, apart from the wild daubs of paint that had taken me by surprise at Gabi's workshop, and which reminded me of Lori in their erratic nature.

Again, she appeared in my mind. Why she, of all my patients? Again I thought that maybe it was because of the vast difference between my orchestrated life and her life, filled with its chaos and unbridled abandon. As if she were a negative of me, my exact opposite. Lori had never practiced anything, never made an effort, but her borderline personality had infected me with restlessness, causing me to walk on eggshells and navigate carefully between her deceptive words. No, I don't think she murdered her husband, I persuaded myself with a relieved sigh, taking comfort in the fact that she was now confined in Dr. Warner's ward.

And Gilad...Why was he suddenly intruding upon my thoughts? His story converged with mine. He was a high-tech person like Yoel. Like many of our acquaintances, he was a frontline fighter in the start-up companies' war of survival. I thought about his unfinished war on all fronts and his feeling that success evaded him—that it was slipping through his fingers. His work and marriage were both uncontrollably disintegrating—collapsing systems. And what about his wife, running on her own competitive track? Did the tracks have to collide? It seemed that Gilad was in a double competition. Outside the family, he was frustrated in the high-tech race, and inside the family, he was competing against his wife. And in both realms, he found no peace of mind.

Like him, most people in the industry found themselves in a race that infected them with constant restlessness. Scores of companies had risen and fallen, each of which had had great hopes of soaring, but only a few ever succeeded. Still, the fact that a handful had made it was enough to encourage others to enter the long-distance race. The entire Valley was clinging to the promise that inspired many good people to join that endless marathon.

I thought about Yoel and his struggle on the path to success. Gilad and Yoel came together in my mind, but they weren't alone. They all waded in the high-tech melting pot—Rami and Yoel, Ido and Danny,

Shaul, Ami Mandovsky, and Yossi Giladi—all hustling forward in a never-ending race to the top. As soon as they summited one mountain, they got busy tackling the next one, the next goal.

Gilad fought against his mother's voice: "Nothing will come of you," whereas Yoel's mother had imparted to him the mantra that he had long since internalized: that no man in the universe could surpass her dear son's success. This was also a kind of pressure. It seemed that in the craniums of all the high-tech addicts working around the clock as though more adrenaline than blood surged through their veins, sat a competitive and agitated collective Mother, pushing them forward in the achievement marathon; it was she who fanned the flames of the gold rush blaze that compelled them forward.

This panic had turned Silicon Valley into an end-of-the-millennium Renaissance Venice. Full of revolutionary ideas and thirsty for the success flooding the Valley, people flocked from all over the world, and many talented Israelis also fell prey to the Valley's charm. Housing prices rocketed; competition was fierce. Everyone was convinced that a historic revolution of great magnitude was underway, and they wanted their share of the prosperity that would inevitably follow.

And what about me? After all, I was also part of the phenomenon. It could be said that I was watching from the sidelines, happy to have a roof over our heads yet feeling no real sense of belonging to the madness. Yoel and Rami, yes. They belonged to the circle of believers who were convinced that the Internet would change the face of humanity. I doubted it. In retrospect, now, two years after the bubble burst, it seemed to me that nothing had actually changed. My life was no different, with the exception of email. I just couldn't imagine life without it. And of course, Google, which gave me whatever instant information I craved. Except that, in my case, before turning to Google, I asked Gila, who was generally the one to keep me up to date on all major news as well as inventions and innovations of any sort. Only then did I turn to Google to supplement the depth of my knowledge. It was really the Gila-Google combination that had changed my life.

Beyond these two, the cultural revolution that had been prophesied to change humanity hadn't reached me yet. My personal user interface still resided in my leg muscles and fingertips. I still preferred to feel material—books, cloth, tomatoes—between my fingers rather than to choose them on the Internet. I admitted this truth bashfully, shying from the disapproval of my tech-savvy friends. I felt I represented a lost generation, because my children behaved differently. They had been born with mouse in hand and used it like an extension of their own digits.

"Mom." Maya interrupted my reverie, demonstrating a pirouette and a curtsy. I put down the iron and applauded enthusiastically. Cultural revolution or not, there was no replacing the institution of motherhood.

As though to echo my sentiment, Ayelet and her best friend Katie walked over and stood in front of my ironing board.

"Katie's Mom is getting a divorce," Ayelet said, looking down at the floor. This was news to me. I knew she had gotten married for the second time only five years ago, and since then she'd had a little boy.

"We're selling the house," Katie said sadly. "Because my brother's moving to Oregon to live with my stepdad, and I'm moving to New York with my mother." She looked at me and then back at Ayelet. Her eyes were full of tears.

"You look sad." I left the iron on the board and approached Katie with a hug.

Katie rubbed her eyes. "I'll miss my brother and my friends," she said, weeping now. Then, adding to the gloomy picture, she said, "New York is too cold in the winter."

"Can we invite her to live with us, Mom?" Ayelet asked. "Just until she knows where she's going to live." I couldn't resist her pleading. Katie stood beside her, peering at me, her eyes red and a pleading expression on her face too.

Statistics suggested that in 2000, 50 percent of marriages in California ended in divorce, and 60 percent of those who married a second time got divorced again. Lo and behold, the statistics were supported in my house, with Katie's red eyes as proof.

"I'll phone Katie's mother and ask if she agrees." I hoped Katie's mother would absolutely refuse, because in my world, mothers didn't separate from their children.

But apparently Katie's mom lived in a different world. A proud, well-groomed lawyer, she had once asked me, "How can you Israeli women live with Israeli men? They're the worst of all chauvinists!" as if I were an anthropological throwback from the Middle Ages.

Honestly? I was hurt. My pride was hurt. The woman had adjusted her Jackie Kennedy Onassis sunglasses, her French tips attesting to the fact that she never washed dishes, mopped the floor, or did the ironing. I answered with a forced smile that chauvinism was a matter of interpretation—a state of mind, maybe even geography.

Her expression had made clear that Katie's mother, unlike us, the Israeli wives, would never have found herself at the beck and call of her family. She wouldn't compromise on the slightest aspect of feminism, meaning that it was hard to live up to her standards. It now appeared that her second husband had also failed to live up to her standards.

Now, Katie's mother sighed on the other end of the line. "You know how it is, when you don't find happiness in a marriage, you have to stop and look elsewhere. We only live once, and we can't forget the self that gets lost in child care and career. Without true love and true understanding, there's no point to a relationship."

The emotional speech was intended to justify the importance of that self, to explain herself a bit. The woman who had lost her independence and freedom in her first marriage was unwilling to pay that price again in her second. She would not compromise on freedom. She said she didn't mind if Katie stayed with us for a few days until things settled down. She had tons of things to do—running around, meetings with lawyers; she hoped Katie's psychologist would handle the emotional stuff, she said, laughing sarcastically.

"You're also a psychologist," she remembered all of a sudden.

"Sure. No problem," I answered without making a fuss. After all, the lawyer had a great deal on her plate, a list of urgent tasks to take care of. And so not only did I take in a teenage girl named Katie while her mother was off in pursuit of her happiness, I also appeared to have gained myself another patient.

It won't be a dramatic change, I tried to reassure myself. After all, Ayelet was already constantly on the phone with Katie—the only difference now would be her flesh-and-blood presence. Indeed, in no time the two girls were like Siamese twins—inseparable, chirping away to each other, their movements amazingly harmonized. As for me? I willingly buckled the collar of motherhood around my neck, wagged my tail, and took an abandoned pup into the kennel.

Chapter 4

Yoel returned from his travels on Friday, landing directly into our nest, which was decorated with flowers and imbued with familial warmth. The house smelled of Shabbat, with fragrant garlic-paprika chicken in the oven, just as he liked it. He beamed with happiness, like a homecoming soldier, embraced us, showered us with kisses, and savored our longing for him. The children clung to him and I also found myself in his embrace, like a lump of metal irresistibly attracted to a magnetic field. He tossed Maya up in the air, horsed around with Alon, and joked with the Ayelet-Katie duo. His deep bass voice filled the house, and the children's delighted laughter rolled through the rooms to combine with it, creating a pleasing symphony.

Yoel told me about the sights and smells of remote places: the exotic fish market in Tokyo; the incredibly fast trains from Tokyo to Kyoto and Nagasaki; the grand hotels in Seoul and Singapore; gourmet dining in Antwerp and Paris. I told him about Alon's concert at school, Maya's ballet performance at the dance studio, and about Ayelet and Katie, who were as one. I thought about the two of us, how we lived under one roof, sharing one bed, yet had absolutely different lifestyles, as if we were on different planets, with different status. And he thought I should pity him a little because of his mobile existence, the tiring flights, the meetings that sometimes did and sometimes did not succeed, the suffocating cigarette smoke in Europe and the Far East—and his longing for us, his beloved family for whose sake he endured so much in silence. I caressed him, wishing with all my heart that I could go with him, to ease his suffering. Just a little. As if!

The next morning, Yoel's allocation of family time ran out, and he was back in the familiar tumult of phone calls.

᧠

Around noon, we set out for Rami and Nira's house in Los Altos Hills. Rami had invited Yoel "to settle some urgent matters" about the start-up and added, to entice, that Nira would make some of her stuffed vegetables for lunch. I went along, pleased to have the opportunity to interest Rami and Nira in Anita's charity project. Yoel and I had known the two of them for many years, since before we'd left Israel. Both families had relocated to California together, some ten years ago, when Rami and Yoel had worked for an Israeli start-up, which had been sold to a larger American company about five years ago. Since then, Rami and Yoel had continued their professional journey together, starting a new company that had almost crashed before being sold at the last minute to a competitor, and then yet another company, making their current endeavor the third time they'd worked together in a start-up.

We left Palo Alto and drove toward the hills that separate San Francisco's South Bay from Santa Cruz on the coast. The landscape changed on the outskirts of Palo Alto. Feathery clouds drifted in the blue sky, and the sun painted the sloping hills yellow. Rows of oaks marked the seams of the hills, climbing around peaks and creating curls of green around bare patches in the forest. A golden nimbus hung above the crests, and scores of brown, black, and white horses grazed on the grassy patches among the trees. Groups of cyclists in helmets and phosphorescent sports outfits moved along the road. An unwritten law in California required sportsmen to wear the right uniform. The cyclists pedaling on the side of the road were wearing cycling shoes designed to grip the pedals and special cycling pants padded to lessen friction. They blended with the landscape, lending the illusion of a spring festival.

This pastoral atmosphere was invaded by the voice of an NPR announcer delivering a special report about the separation fence in Ramallah. The journalist was interviewing a long line of Palestianian locals who were protesting against the confiscation of large tracts of agricultural land. A woman, speaking Arabic, complained that the fence separated members of her family. In order to visit her sister, she would have to travel for an hour to get around the fence. Her children, who were used to walking between the villages, would now have to make a tiring detour. Not to mention the checkpoints. The occupation army was making life difficult. "They don't let us live," the woman cried over the radio. "We stand for hours without water, waiting at the checkpoints!" The journalist ended the interview and expressed subtle words of empathy and support for the villagers. Indeed, their lives were miserable and intolerable under the Israeli occupation. They had no rights and were subject to a regime whose army showed no restraint.

"Not one word about the reason for putting up the fence," Yoel grumbled. "As if, one fine day, the Israelis woke up and decided to build a fence, because they were bored. Where's the Israeli information authority?" Like Yoel, I was frustrated that there was no mention that the fence had been built to prevent suicide bombers from entering Israel. No mention that seven hundred Israelis—women, children, civilians—had been killed in buses, restaurants, and night clubs.

"They're not in the least interested in balancing the picture with pro-Israeli information. It's NPR, remember? They're often accused of left-wing reporting. Some people say they support any and every underdog, right or wrong!" I raged. "They call suicide bombers 'fighters.' When there's a terrorist attack in Israel, they count the number of dead; they hardly bother to mention that these were children on the way to school or a dance club, and they include the Palestinian terrorists in the number of casualties."

"Something must be done about the weakness of Israel's information structure," Yoel asserted. "Last week, the consul asked the Jewish Federation to pressure San Francisco's wealthy Jews to stop supporting the local press and public broadcasting stations if they persist in slandering Israel."

"Meanwhile," I said, "the ones really carrying the weight for Israel are the Jewish students at Berkeley. They hold their own against the overwhelmingly anti-Israel, pro-Palestinian sentiment on that campus."

"Anyway," Yoel said, trying to change the subject and lighten the mood, "got any good gossip for me?"

"Actually, yes. I have something juicy for you, if you promise to keep it secret. Promise?"

"Promise," he said, crossing his fingers.

I told him about Gabi's visit and the smells that woke her in the middle of the night. "So, what do you say, Yoel? Was it the smell of Russian caviar or the smell of debauchery?"

Yoel smiled to himself, hardly believing his ears. Out of male solidarity with Danny, he said the story was probably the fruit of Gabi's fertile imagination. "Russian caviar or not, there's enough oxytocin between them to keep them together for another hundred years," he said, and we smiled in mutual agreement.

The previous year, after much begging from me, Yoel had agreed to accompany me to a psychology conference in San Diego. Among the abundant lectures we attended, the one delivered by biological anthropology professor Helen Fisher was deeply etched in his memory. A short, gaunt woman dressed in a gray suit, her silver-streaked gray hair in a bun, Fisher spoke about the chemistry of love or, in her words, "what happens in our brains when we are in love." She spiced up her talk with references to scores of studies from which she concluded that there are three unrelated networks in the brain that are responsible for the love experience: the sexual attraction, the romantic love, and the emotional attachment networks.

The first network, related to sexual desire, is hormonally activated by testosterone. She explained that in the case of men, the excretion of testosterone focuses them on a single goal—achieving sexual satisfaction. This factor is prominent in mice. The male is absorbed in the sexual act, and nothing can distract his attention. The female, however, looks from side to side, her mind on other matters in the middle of the sexual act itself. "Maybe the grocery list," Fisher said, and the audience gushed with laughter.

"The second network represents romantic love and is characterized by two neurotransmitters: dopamine, which is released at a relatively high level, and serotonin, released at a low level. As we know, a very high level of subcortical dopamine creates psychotic conditions such as schizophrenia, whereas a very low level of cortical serotonin is connected to depressive conditions. Hence, romantic love as reflected in the brain's nerve activity is a borderline psycho-depressive condition." Citing love poetry written by poets of various nations and eras, Fisher proceeded, cynically, to illustrate the extent to which romantic love is a reflection of a disturbed mental state. She pointed out that the common denominator among the romantic poets was the sweet, tantalizing illusion created by the love object. As an example of the light psychosis that afflicts lovers, Fisher quoted the following lines written by a ninth-century Chinese poet: "I could not take my eyes off the mat your feet had touched, nor could I relinquish the comb that had passed through your hair."

"The good news about romantic love is that one can fall in love at any age, and the feeling can be renewed endless times throughout life," said Fisher. "The not-so-good news is that the phase of romantic love is only the initial stage in the couple relationship and does not last forever. It reaches its height during courtship, when the love object is not completely won, and loses strength when the relationship changes from courtship dynamics to couple dynamics. In other words, the romantic stage exists as long as there is uncertainty that the emotion is reciprocated by the love object. When the emotion is reciprocated, the romance fades. People who seek only romance find themselves hopping from one such relationship to another, and when the romance disappears, their search for a new love object begins. In cases where the love is not reciprocated, the romantic connection with the love object continues. In spite of the dismay and disappointment of such people, they never break the connection and never seek love that is less romantic, but more realistic."

There were murmurs of agreement from the audience as people remembered their own heartbreaking experiences of unattained love, because dopamine had been running wild in their brains. Perhaps there were those in the audience who recalled the love addicts they knew, people who were still hopping from one love object to another to get the "high" brought on by too much dopamine and too little serotonin.

Fisher continued to fascinate the audience. "The third network of nerves in the brain is related to ongoing love relationships known as 'attachment.' This is the stage we all aspire to reach, the stage that characterizes long-term couplehood. The hormone released in long-term love relationships is called oxytocin and, unsurprisingly, it is also the hormone released during birth. The oxytocin forms the mother's love bond to the newborn baby and stimulates the breasts to produce milk." She went on to say that fathers of newborn babies also show a high level of this hormone. "Apparently, it enables the connection between father and baby. This precious oxytocin is the glue that unites couples over a long period of time."

Our hands, Yoel's and mine, automatically sought each other. The oxytocin flowed between us like a hermetically sealed electrical circuit.

"The main problem of too much oxytocin," said Fisher, spoiling the fun, "is that oxytocin suppresses the release of testosterone. Think of breastfeeding women, whose oxytocin level is overflowing. They don't have much sexual desire, do they?" Everybody nodded in agreement. "Likewise, we find a decrease in sexual desire in couples who have been together for a long time," said Fisher, tossing the cruel information into the auditorium. "But this doesn't necessarily mean that the testosterone level is suppressed with regard to other people, since, after all, the three networks are not at all dependent on one another. You can continue relating sexually to one person, have a romantic connection with another, and have an emotional attachment with yet a third, all at the same time."

The audience laughed in recognition. We all left feeling as though we suddenly understood how the chemistry of love worked in the brain. Indeed, an enlightening and unforgettable lecture.

Yoel and I continued to smile and warm ourselves with thoughts of oxytocin until we reached the electric gate that blocked the entrance to Rami and Nira's house.

Nira, wearing a sporty cycling outfit, her cropped hair wet, was setting the table for four in the dining nook with brisk, efficient movements. She'd finished her morning swim of a hundred laps in the half-Olympic-sized pool in their backyard and was planning to cycle forty miles in the hills after the meal. If she managed to feed the cats in time, she would join her friends in an easy ten-mile run, thus ending another day of training for the Ironman race due to take place in Honolulu at the end of summer.

She needed our visit like she needed a thorn in her ass, but Rami had invited Yoel for a work meeting, and she had already made stuffed vegetables, because Rami had to have something to eat, and, besides, she was always happy to see Yoel. She'd have to cut her conversation with me short, because her training schedule took top priority.

Nira's identity had become wrapped up in her athletics. Since her only son, Tomer, had enlisted in the Israeli Defense Forces the previous summer, she'd poured her heart and soul into arduous training for the Ironman. Either way, she found herself sleepless with worry, so instead of sitting idly and letting the anxiety gnaw at her, she decided to focus on activities that would give her a certain control over her life, her body, and her thoughts. As long as she was covered in beads of perspiration, her anxiety over her son's life was kept at bay.

Her training companions, sports addicts like herself, became her sole companions. They met twice a week for a breezy ten-mile evening run and on weekends, they combined running and cycling. Swimming was the only training they did on their own. After training, they conversed online, swapping stories about their successes and failures, encouraging one another to make a bit more of an effort, not to break.

Since Tomer's enlistment, Nira had found an additional channel of activity. Her heart, shrunken from anxiety, swelled once again for the neighborhood cats. The previous summer, she'd begun taking in stray cats and keeping them in her backyard. She gave them food and water and allocated spaces to separate the friendly ones from the schizoid loners. At first, there were seven cats in her yard; in no time, the number increased to seventy. Some came of their own accord, as if they'd heard through the grapevine about a communal arrangement in Nira's yard. Others were brought in by neighbors in the know.

She employed construction workers to build pens out of beams. The pens were scattered over half an acre behind the pool and blocked the view of San Francisco Bay and the San Francisco skyline in the distance. But Nira had no time for the view, because her cats received not only food and shelter, but also quality time with her. She would free them in groups of ten and let them indoors for ten minutes at a time. Since Tomer was in the army and, hence, the television was dormant, the more well-behaved cats were allowed inside to play with toys she scattered on the floor of the television room.

Nira's busy day was divided by the hour. An hour for swimming. A second hour for tending to the cats and cleaning the litter boxes. Two hours on the bicycle. Seventy-seven minutes for playing with the cats. Half a marathon run with the friends, and back to the cats. Once a week, she found a narrow window to prepare the stuffed vegetables

Rami liked so much. Then, at the end of the day, she joined her cycling and running friends again, this time online, to talk about successes and failures. When she went to bed at night, she hoped her eyes would close and her mind would not submit to troubling, distressing thoughts. Most of the time, it did submit, and she gave in and swallowed an Ambien.

Nira and Rami, looking like the Marx Brothers, received us at the front door. Both were short and skinny, with short, curly black hair. Rami had a prickly moustache and Nira, an untended lawn of black grass on her upper lip; grooming was not on her list of priorities.

Near the entrance was a simple, narrow oak table, purchased some ten years ago when they'd come to the Valley "only for a year or two," to represent the Israeli company that had employed both Rami and Yoel. An unattractive collection of dried leaves and thorns was a permanent fixture on the table. Their home was functional and modest, with no superfluous or luxury items. The walls were bare of what Nira called "scribbles." In the spacious living room, a beige sofa and two armchairs stood on a drab gray carpet. A glass-topped coffee table completed the furnishings. The only art object in the house was an oil painting of flowers, by Gabi, given to Nira on her birthday. They'd bought the house in the hills of Los Altos after selling the second start-up, with the aim of installing the half-Olympic-sized swimming pool for Nira.

"Come in, the food's getting cold." Nira kissed Yoel, and pecked me on the cheek. Rami, who saw Yoel in the office daily, wasn't excited to see him again. He greeted me with a reserved nod and then proceeded to ignore me as usual for no apparent reason.

We sat at the round table in the dining nook. Nira served the stuffed vegetables, rissoles, and salad and urged us to eat. Yoel needed no encouragement to take large helpings of the food, which reminded him of the taste and smell of his mother's cooking. I nudged him under the table to remind him to restrain himself before he emptied the dish. Polite conversation soon gave way to a vociferous duet by Rami and Yoel about work. They were like children, interested solely in their own narrow world.

"So what's happening with Tom Jenkins?"

"The negotiation is going quite well."

"But it looks like Jenkins Sr. is suddenly resisting selling us the company. It's his life's work."

"Listen, he spent years developing his company. It's hard for him to sell it to a young start-up."

"Even if we are offering good money."

Rami couldn't understand why Tom Jenkins was allowing nostalgia to affect a business negotiation. Rami, who was guileless, was ready to go the limit. He had already explained to Jenkins that the sale would not only benefit him financially, it would also stabilize the shaky company. It was true that the Jenkins company had a product with potential, but it was badly managed.

"That's obvious, isn't it? I don't understand why Jenkins is being so stubborn!"

"Look, Rami," Yoel said, "you've already given him a detailed explanation of the improvements he needs to make to merge his company and ours—how to tap into a huge wave of success. Maybe it's something personal?"

Yoel had worked with Rami for years and was well acquainted with his abilities and weaknesses; their familiarity with each other had allowed them to establish a balanced division of labor between them. They complemented one another: Rami, the creative one, conceived the ideas for development and, of equal importance, Yoel was responsible for their implementation. They had cycled through three start-ups together; Rami was like the minister of foreign affairs expanding the client market and consolidating relations with investors, while Yoel was responsible for handling the development teams and sales in the field.

"So what do we do?" Rami asked.

"We need to approach him with a different strategy."

"Different how? More money?"

"It's not about money this time," said Yoel. "It's about the life's work of an old man. We have to think creatively, outside the box. If we promise him we won't dismantle his company, or fire workers, that we will leave him a certain amount of control over the group after the acquisition, maybe he'll listen and be satisfied."

To Rami, this sounded really irrelevant. Business was business, as far he was concerned: numbers, procedures, graphs, columns of expenditures, and income. Mainly income.

Nira and I listened to their agitated dialogue. Differences of opinion were frequent in their time-tested union, and they always managed to bridge them, like a married couple. I had learned from experience that it was best not to interfere with their tactical moves, and I preferred to express my opinion only when asked. However, I often observed from the sidelines, as if I were watching moves in a game of chess. Of course, Rami and Yoel had also had some failures over the years, but who was counting? In my opinion, the key to their success lay in their incorrigible optimism and their bold moves.

"To me, Jenkins sounds like an old crybaby who refuses to acknowledge that his time is up," Nira said, reflecting Rami's opinion, as always. She stood up and began clearing the table, and I joined her in the kitchen. Rami and Yoel continued their discussion, speaking in high-tech jargon: acquisition, revenue, time to market, and so forth—portentous, weighty words.

When we rejoined the men, with coffee and cake, I exploited the short silence that ensued while Rami and Yoel investigated the cake to raise the question of donation to Anita's project.

I took a deep breath. "Anita is organizing a WIZO fund-raising dinner to aid distressed families in Israel," I said, referring to the Women's International Zionist Organization. Before they could brush me aside, I continued, "The event is scheduled for the end of summer, at the Fairmont Hotel in San Francisco, and there will be representation from the Israeli government. Anita wants to know if you want to participate and, of course, donate a few hundred dollars?"

Silence.

For the first time that day, Rami looked me in the eye. "Let me tell you something," he said in an ominous voice. "If Anita is interested in donating to distressed families, she has my blessing. Let her donate. If Anita is interested in organizing a party for her friends, let her organize. But I don't understand what one thing has to do with the other. What is the connection between a donation and a party? Tell me, hasn't Anita heard of giving without publicity?" The veins in his neck swelled with anger.

"Rami, you know that's the accepted way of raising money here. Not a month goes by without an invitation to an event with money on the side," I said apologetically.

"Raising funds to help distressed families is something else. It's an internal matter of the Israeli government and its priorities. I'm not prepared to go into it."

"What's wrong with it?" I asked. "Why is donating to poor families different from other donations? The money is the same money; you just decide where it goes." I felt rebuked and needed to defend Anita.

"I want you to understand something," he said condescendingly. "As a rule, such events are intended for donations to public bodies like universities, hospitals, or AIPAC. But for God's sake, how can you have parties to raise money for hungry children or needy families? The food would stick in my throat if I were expected to chew a gourmet dinner at an event for hungry children." He looked at me as if he'd proved his point.

He was right in what he said. I regretted having broached the subject. A visit to Rami's temple of justice usually made me feel that I was a leaf in the wind, as far as my principles were concerned. I never stopped to ask why or what and just allowed myself to follow the herd. Sometimes I thought that his principles bordered on the extreme. He didn't participate in the Palo Alto Israeli community's annual memorial ceremony for the soldiers who fell in Israel's battles, because he wouldn't listen to sorrowful songs or watch high school pupils dancing in ballet costumes in order to remember his comrades who'd dropped like flies in the Yom Kippur War. He didn't waste money on expensive restaurants, because Nira's cooking was "excellent." He mended torn trousers ("So what?"), even though he had millions of dollars in the bank. He had educated his son according to the values of thrift and modesty.

How could I convey Rami and Nira's negative response (they always spoke in one voice) to Anita, who expected the community's total participation? She was so enthusiastic and had invested so much of herself that any refusal would take the wind out of her sails. I sighed. I would not spoil my relations with Rami over a difference of opinion. I knew from our long acquaintance that he weighed his actions and usually contributed generously and discreetly, but not this time.

Nira supported her husband's view throughout the conversation, the two of them barricading themselves behind a solid, resolute opinion. There was no room between them for disagreement or, heaven forbid, emotionality. Everything was intellectual, clear, and absolute. Even Tomer's enlistment had been met with their acceptance and mutual support. Tomer had spoken to his parents in their language, producing an inarguable principle in favor of his goal, which was to volunteer for an elite unit in the IDF. If he deferred his army service until he completed his studies, he would be twenty-two and too old to serve in such a unit. In any case, they had raised him as an Israeli in every way and, as such, he would serve in the army and that was that.

Nira, pressed for time, invited me to visit the cats and dashed outside without waiting for an answer. She skipped among the cages as I trailed behind her, worrying that she would trip or accidentally overturn one.

"Daniela, let me introduce you. This is Shahori and next to him is Sheleg," she said, using the Hebrew names for Blackie and Snow. "They're both energetic, aggressive males. And here"—she moved to a small, tidy cage—"we have Mitzie, a refined lady aged about five."

I smiled to myself as Nira explained what each cat did to win her affection. She was like a little girl playing with a dollhouse. She also had a well-conceived educational philosophy. "Like children, they have to learn what's acceptable to me and what's not. A cat that doesn't behave itself will be grounded until it knows better!"

However much I tried, I couldn't foster an interest in her cats.

I tried to change the subject. "Nira, how is Tomer? How does he feel in the army?"

"Tomer is fine," she said with a little smile. "Handling it."

Pursuing her subject, she said, "The Los Altos municipality owes me. They should thank me day and night for caring for homeless cats. I save them at least one and a half fully paid jobs."

"When was the last time you heard from him? What does he do in the army?"

"He's on a course at the moment. He gets in touch when he has the time," she said. And back to the cats.

"But those clueless municipality workers don't think they owe me anything. On the contrary, they want me to get a special permit to care for animals. Have you ever heard anything so rude in your life? Instead of helping me!"

"Who does Tomer stay with when he's on leave?"

"My mother. Sometimes my sister." I read the distress in her eyes. It was as if she were saying, one more word about Tomer, and I'll burst into tears. Lose control. Which I can't allow myself to do, not in front of you.

I became tense. I saw in Nira a reflection of my future. My Alon had admired Tomer from the time the older boy was his scouts instructor. Tomer was Alon's model; the younger boy followed the older's footsteps like a duckling after its mother. I would have four years of grace until Alon went into the army, as he planned; then I would find myself in Nira's shoes, a marathon runner, going on crusades for cats to maintain my sanity, I thought sadly.

"I'm founding a nonprofit organization for Los Altos cats," Nira continued. "I've already collected sixty signatures, and I need another sixty people to support me in getting a license to run a nonprofit organization and receive tax-free donations from the public. You've no idea how much I spend on these cats. Will you join?"

I nodded, again feeling that my principles were lax. Except for my principles about supporting my friends, each of whom had her own burning agenda. I could already see the envelope that would arrive in the mail asking me to donate generously to the cause of Los Altos cats, if only to meet the obligation I'd signed before Nira.

"I have to hurry to pick Maya up from a birthday party, I'll come back later to get Yoel," I said, to get away from Nira and her cats.

"Oh, I can drop him off on the way to my evening run," she said, happy to have a chance to be alone with Yoel for a few minutes.

I began to object but restrained myself. Why spoil it for her?

Chapter 5

A week later, Gilad returned to sit in the armchair facing me, a tortured look on his face. The words burst from his mouth so fast that I had to make an effort to catch them, as if I were chasing soap bubbles. He was doing his best not to contact Nirit by phone, a task that was as agonizing as breaking an addiction. He was experiencing a physical pain that cramped his muscles and shook him to the bone. He tried to cope with it through intense activity, such as playing soccer with friends, initiating projects, and conducting business meetings late into the night. But the pain persisted. In the end, he gave in and made the call to Nirit, to which she appropriately responded with anger: all of a sudden, he had disappeared, without a word of warning, leaving her feeling rejected, in the dark, not understanding what was happening to him.

He explained that he needed to distance himself—that he didn't want to threaten his marriage. To which Nirit retorted that he had nothing to fear; after all, she was also married and had no intention of breaking up her family. "I need our talks, though," she said and persuaded Gilad to resume their regular phone calls.

And Kimberly? Gilad had found the courage to confront her with his feelings. He complained that she was cool toward him, and she responded with a shower of insults: he was selfish, had no feelings for her, was inconsiderate toward her and her work and, in fact, was jealous of her success. She resented him for needing her the way a baby needs a comforter, and she was certainly sick of being harassed by him.

"Make something of yourself, of your life!" she shot at him. "We're both Stanford graduates! Instead of being pleased with my success, you make petty comparisons and spoil things for me. I don't have any more energy for you and your crap."

"How do you think it happened that you didn't know until now how angry she was with you?" I asked, surprised by his seeming obliviousness.

"Kimberly claims that she tried to suppress her anger."

"Maybe her recoil from sex with you has something to do with passive aggression toward you. Have you tried asking her about this?"

"She says she's got no more energy for me and that she hasn't even got the energy to try to be nice or inviting."

"Have you thought of couples' counseling?"

"Our couplehood isn't her first priority, since she invests her whole being in her work. I only hope that while she's busy establishing her professional status, she doesn't ruin the family we've built together." Gilad looked sadly at me.

Lowering his eyes, he told me that Kimberly had turned her body into a shrine. She nurtured it and pleasured herself with all kinds of massages and spa treatments. She removed her body hair with a laser, including the most intimate areas. As he told me this, Gilad's eyes burned with pain and jealousy; he was aware that she wasn't doing so with him in mind.

"Perhaps Kimberly's anger, which has been passive and hidden until now, pushed you into the relationship with Nirit. You have to try to understand why she's angry with you. Keep talking to her, Gilad. You have no alternative but to try to understand her anger fully," I told him calmly, trying not to interpret his words to mean that Kimberly was being unfaithful to him.

It was obvious, however, that their relationship was in danger. During this session, Gilad's concern for his family's stability, his reason for seeking therapy, had been replaced by fear. The picture had shifted and sharpened. The severity of the situation had gotten through to him, and he was suddenly afraid that Kimberly would decide to dismantle their union. He now realized that she perceived married life as a trap from which she had to escape. She had penetrating questions about their future and saw no point in continuing to try to save the life of this sacred beast called marriage, a beast that was dying before her eyes. With tears in his eyes, his voice shaking, Gilad told me that he did not want to continue courting his wife, begging for a bit of warmth only to emerge rejected. He wanted an intimate, pleasurable relationship with his partner, and he was afraid that Kimberly, kicking in fury, would never be able to give him that warmth.

"Your needs are reasonable," I told him, looking for soft, supportive words. "A sexual relationship is a dance for two. When you sense that your partner isn't interested, it's difficult for you to keep dancing. Your need to feel that Kimberly is attracted to you is perfectly understandable. But don't lose the hope of reviving your sex life. Tell me, Gilad, have you always felt rejected? Has Kimberly acted disinterested from the beginning?"

"I suppose we have had ups and downs, like most couples," he said, looking at me for confirmation. "But to be honest, she always seemed cool. If sexual relations are a dance for two, then I've never had a fully present dance partner to have fun with. I've always had to initiate, persuade, and plead."

Gilad sounded bitter, perhaps a little envious. Maybe he felt that the neighbor's grass was greener, more inviting. Maybe the reassurance I gave him about his need to feel loved and wanted in his wife's bed stirred unrealistic fantasies about other couples. Maybe my words about the dance for two made him think I was a great dancer who was waiting for an invitation from him to the dance floor. Maybe not. Maybe my sex life was of no interest to him at all, but his envy was tangible, and it increased his frustration.

I remembered the advice of George Oliver, my first instructor in the therapeutic arts. He taught me to use my feelings as a therapy tool: "Listening to your inner emotions can give you a lot of information about the patient. The tunes you hear are parallel to those your patient is hearing." Taking his advice, I decided to use the strong feeling of envy that pervaded the room by confronting Gilad with it.

"You feel rejected by Kimberly, and it brings up a deep sense of deprivation, as if everyone around you is happy with their lot while you are left out in the cold."

Gilad nodded, confirming that I understood his feelings.

"I haven't turned forty yet. I feel that life still owes me something."

I listened to Gilad's frustration and into my mind came a vision of his pitiful father, drowning in a pile of yellowed newspaper, that same pathetic figure that Gilad was horrified by, and was terrified of becoming. He wanted to be different from his father. He did not accept the misery of his life as an inevitable fact. He would try to find the happiness he deserved. Unlike his father, he would not allow his family to disintegrate.

"You're not prepared to accept less than what life has to offer. You won't settle for next to nothing, like your father."

He nodded in agreement.

"Last time we met, you told me that you loved Kimberly, that she was clearly the woman of your life. Do you still feel that way, in spite of the difficulties?"

"Yes. At all costs."

Gilad was professionally competitive with his wife. She was more successful than he and was highly valued, whereas he was wobbling in a start-up company that quite recently had seemed extremely promising but was now on the verge of obscurity. Gilad felt that, compared to his wife, he had "caught the wrong wave."

Envy is a painful emotion connected to a profound sense of deprivation at an early age. A constant, nagging hunger, like a deep pit that can never be filled. It is a hunger that affects various aspects of life. Making notes at the end of the session, I told myself that further treatment needed to focus on the overall picture of that distressing deprivation, to remind Gilad what lay at the root of the feeling.

Gilad canceled our meeting set for the coming week, because he was flying to Israel on business, and said he would make an appointment when he returned.

Katie's mother was at my door, in the Jacqueline Kennedy sunglasses, her long, colorful fingernails extended toward me in a placating gesture. She had come to get Katie. "We're on a flight to New York tomorrow, and this evening we're saying good-bye to Katie's little brother and stepfather, who are going to live in Oregon," she explained. "Katie and I will be traveling back and forth between the coasts." I sensed that she was not looking forward to this travel, but though I searched her face, I could not detect the slightest trace of sorrow. Rather, she seemed tired, and determined in her belief that there was no other way. She had called a couple of times over the past couple of weeks to speak with

Katie, and had sounded relieved and happy to hear that her daughter was holding up well, but she hadn't showed up to see her. Now, she would be separating from her little boy very soon. I honestly could not picture myself in her shoes.

Katie was clinging to Ayelet as if the sentence had been passed and the executioner awaited her at the gallows. Both girls looked at us with bloodshot, teary eyes. I mused that modern times, the changing world, and globalization were hard on this generation of children. I did not remember such difficult partings from my own childhood. When my friends moved, it was to a new house within walking distance. I remembered Gabi and the painful parting that loomed ahead.

"I've had a hard week. So much running around and working out details. But finally, it's all arranged," the woman said with a sigh and with no thanks to me for taking care of her superfluous child, who would certainly be a nuisance to her in her New York adventures. Perhaps I was wrong. It could have been that I was just picking up Katie's resentment at leaving California and identifying with her aggravation too deeply. I could feel the tension between Katie and her mom lying heavily beneath their unspoken words. I remembered the gift I'd carried for Gabi all the way from Paris to show her my deepest gratitude for taking care of Alon while I'd been traveling with Yoel. But Katie's mom lacked that feeling of gratitude. In fact, there was something entitled about her demeanor that made me feel I ought to thank her for letting me care for her daughter. And indeed, I said, "It was my pleasure to have Katie here with us," and I meant it. I gave Katie a hug, held her in my arms for a long moment. "We will miss you, Katie," I told her. "You are always welcome to visit us."

"I've got a few heavy suitcases. Do you think Yoel could give me a ride to the airport tomorrow and give me a hand with them?"

The tough lawyer wanted to borrow the chauvinist's muscles. Refusal mixed with derision was on the tip of my tongue, when Yoel suddenly turned up, as though he'd been standing by, waiting for a signal from Jackie O.

"With pleasure," he said politely. "With pleasure."

Ayelet looked delighted to have another chance to be with Katie before the flight. The girls clung to each other in a close embrace, which was broken only when our visitor gripped Katie's arm and forcibly pulled her away, while sweetly instructing Ayelet and me to pack Katie's things in a suitcase for Yoel to put in his car for tomorrow's trip to the airport. They had to hurry now, because they had dinner reservations and she was already late.

When the door closed, I turned to Yoel. "Why were you in such a hurry to help her?" I scolded. "She thinks Israeli men are all male chauvinists! So let her manage without their help!"

"Poor thing," he said pityingly. "Would you want to be in her place?"

"She is not a poor thing. She's an exploiter. Why should she have it both ways—throw off the ties of marriage, and use men who aren't free to be used by her?" I fumed. "I hope she's not planning to try to borrow another group of your muscles to achieve her personal happiness."

"Daniela, this isn't like you," Yoel teased. "As a psychologist, you should understand her distress. You've looked after her daughter for two weeks without a peep, and all of a sudden, a ride to the airport is too much?"

He knew that the phrase "as a psychologist" drove me crazy. As if a license to practice psychology automatically turned me into a Mother Teresa—a woman with no ego. I kept quiet. I was angry.

I came to terms with Katie's mother's triumph and my defeat in front of her and my husband: the chauvinist determined to help the weaker sex. At the moment, I didn't know which of us was the weak one. Could it really be the arrogant, taunting one who so easily got her way through flattery? Yoel would never understand my anger. Only a woman could understand me. Oscar, the faithful dog, was looking at me with sad eyes. He gazed at me as if he understood, even though he didn't have a uterus. His eyes told me that he'd seen how my husband jumped to attention in front of Jackie O., whose cloying scent of pheromones had called him to the flag and captivated him, leaving me overcome with jealousy at the small betrayal that had occurred right before my eyes. And he, Oscar, was my witness.

PART TWO

——

WINTER

Chapter 6

Yaron emerged before Mika and flung a scrap of paper at her, but it blew away before she could catch it. She looked into his flashing eyes, which wordlessly conveyed, "Get out of my sight, and don't ever come near me again." Mika tossed and turned as she awoke from the familiar recurring dream that had troubled her for years. "At least I managed to get some sleep," she consoled herself.

Nine in the morning. Shaul had already left and taken the twins to school. Mika thanked him in her heart for granting her a few hours of the sleep her weary body needed so badly. After a shower and a cup of strong coffee, she dragged herself to the piano and struggled with Chopin's Étude opus 10. She had been playing these études for years to warm her fingers, but over the last few weeks, her fingers had not been responding: like her feverish brain, they suddenly possessed a life of their own.

She didn't recognize this rebelliousness in herself. As if in a dream, stubbornly, for the tenth time, she started to play Étude 3 and got stuck on the ninth bar on the second page. Again and again, her fingers lost coordination and stumbled over the keys. They forgot the distance between one key and the next and even the correct hand movements for chords. Her focus gave way to a flow of compulsive, absolutely pointless thoughts.

For the past two weeks, the greeting card she'd sent Yaron kept flashing in her mind. She had read it countless times before sending it. She remembered the exact words:

> Shalom Yaron, I've tried to find your email address but couldn't find it anywhere, so I've resorted to this less direct route. Last month, I visited Israel and happened to attend a small, moving reunion of our

high school class. I hadn't seen most of the people since I left school, but Eddie and Pinni were there, and they told me you were married to Dikla from Ra'anana and that you have three sons. Pinni was just glowing when he told me that you won an award for excellence from the American College of Cardiology and a three-year study grant to specialize in heart transplants at U. of Washington. I imagine that this is no small achievement, and I congratulate you, albeit somewhat belatedly. My husband Shaul and I plan to be in Seattle next month, between the 14th and the 17th. I thought it might be nice if you and your wife would be free to get together with us. I'd like to hear from you.

With a shaky hand that no longer retained the muscle memory of her maiden signature, she signed *Mika Kaplan* and added her telephone number and email address.

Mika reminded herself that there was a chance he would not answer and that if he didn't, she would get over it. She was a big girl, after all. Promising herself to take things in stride and not to make a fuss over what could not be changed, she sent the card.

From that moment on, she was haunted: the words she'd written danced in front of her and came to her mind unwanted, uninvited, and troubling. *Shalom Yaron...I happened to attend...I congratulate you...last month I visited Israel...no small achievement...it might be nice...Pinni was just glowing...you have three sons...I'd like to hear from you...*and so on. Just like CNN headlines or the ads in Times Square flashing automatically on and off.

"Shaul, do you remember how I told you about Yaron?" she asked her husband. "The one who was in my class in elementary and high school? He's in Seattle. Do you mind meeting him and his wife, Dikla?"

"Is he the doctor that got a grant?"

"Yes."

"Could be nice."

How pleased she was to hear his voice on the answering machine. She recognized it at once. A voice from the distant past. He had been pleased to get the sweet card, what a surprise. He'd sent an email with his phone number. Shaul saw the blush on her cheeks as she listened to Yaron's voice. He hadn't seen her blush like that for a long time.

"An admirer!" he remarked.

"It's Yaron, from my class. Don't worry," she said in a placating, embarrassed voice.

Yaron apologized in the email. He was sorry, but he couldn't make it on the suggested dates; he and his family would be out of town.

She sent her reply the next day, in English, because she didn't have a Hebrew keyboard. She described her life and family. And Shaul's achievements, his start-up company in the solar industry that had turned into a great success. How proud she was of Shaul, how they'd come to Hillsborough, in Silicon Valley. She described the touching meeting with their classmates, how she'd discovered a whole world that had been sealed off for over twenty years and that now, suddenly, was open again. She was so surprised. The shiest guy in their class had five children who were not at all shy. The most attractive girl had never married. She'd spoken with their classmate who had made a fortune in the building trade and his friend, Eddie, who'd sat next to her all evening without saying a word except, in response to prodding, "Things are cool." She was happy to hear that he, Yaron, was successful. Not that she was surprised. Finally, she asked, "Who's this Dikla, the lucky woman who won your heart? Has she heard about all the hearts that were breaking over you in Haifa, while she was quietly growing up in Ra'anana?"

She reread the last sentence a few dozen times, debating whether to remove it, but left it, hoping it would make him smile. Many years had passed, after all. She sent it and immediately regretted having done so.

After a few days with no reply, she thought, he's probably decided I'm nuts. A woman of my age bringing up old things from the past as if thirty-five years had not gone by since our shared childhood. Anyway, who am I, for him? We hardly exchanged three words in high school. He's probably sitting in front of the screen wondering what to do about this pathetic woman. What does she want of him? How should he answer such an email?

What she had written on the greeting card and what she had written in the email became compulsively jumbled in her mind. A flood of incoherent sentences penetrated her consciousness and erased reality. Her mind was full of a babble of incomplete phrases such as *I've tried to find your email...happened to attend...moving reunion of our* *high school class…no small achievement…who's this Dikla…lucky woman…Pinni was just glowing…you won an award…I hadn't seen most of the people since I left school…*and so on.

"I'm sorry, what did you say?" she would ask, in desperate hope of blocking the echoing intrusions and understanding what people were saying to her.

"Would you mind repeating that?" she'd say, as though she were hard of hearing. And worse than that, she stopped functioning; she forgot to buy food and forgot to cook. She left bills unpaid and didn't return phone calls. One day she forgot to pick the girls up from school, and one afternoon she forgot to attend a directors' meeting at the conservatory where she worked. Music lessons she was supposed to give dropped out of her schedule, something that had never happened in her twenty years of teaching. During the lessons, the intrusions came with even more staggering intensity, and she had to fight to prevent herself from being engulfed in the tumult of words that were dragging her into an unreal world.

"They pay a lot of money for every lesson, and I can't even pretend to be listening to them. When will this all come to an end? This nightmare must stop," she thought in despair.

The nights were the hardest. Invasive, obsessive thoughts that never let go and drove away sleep. Mika tossed and turned and tried in vain to fall asleep. In the quiet of the night, the jumbled sentences were louder than ever. She tried to lower the sound, to turn off her internal broadcast, but she could not control it.

Between lessons and her playing obligations, Mika got lost. She was invited by a prestigious northern California musicians' association to play the prelude of Maurice Ravel's suite for solo piano, *Le tombeau de Couperin*, and Chopin's Fourth Ballade—two very difficult works that demanded much preparation. There was also a recital, with her violinist friend Karen, including the César Franck Violin Sonata and the Brahms Violin Sonata no. 3, due to take place at the San Francisco JCC, and rehearsals had to begin soon.

She tried to talk some sense into herself: "Mika, rest. Go to sleep, Mika. Your life is full of contentment and activity. Go to sleep, Mika, so that you can function, concentrate, work," she pleaded with herself. But logic was useless. Huge waves of obsession tore her logical thoughts to shreds, and she woke up in the morning, bleary-eyed, to face another torturous day.

After an especially long and difficult sleepless night, she decided to send Yaron another message. If he replied, she thought, she'd calm down.

"I'm sorry if I my email dredged up ancient history. Many years have passed, and I don't actually know you. Should you find yourselves in the San Francisco area, you and your family are welcome to get in touch." She pressed send.

That day there was a message on her answering machine. "Shalom Mika, Yaron Zelig speaking. I tried to reach you without success. All the best, 'bye."

Mika was disappointed. How was she supposed to answer such a laconic message, when she was expecting a long explanatory letter? "He simply doesn't want to talk to me," she told herself.

The compulsive need to talk to Yaron grew more demanding. She sat in front of the computer, struggling to refrain from sending him a message. She held herself back from sending him even a message as laconic as his. Trying to calm herself, she read and reread the mail she'd sent him as well as his answer. "Wake up, Mika, you're not thirteen. Get moving. Make dinner for your family. You're forgetting yourself," her inner voice scolded. She obeyed it, weakly.

Shaul asked, "Are you okay?"

"Awfully tired. Not sleeping well. Maybe it's menopause. I don't know what's happening to me," she said, hoping the craziness would stop soon.

Two weeks went by. Mika assumed that Yaron and his family were back from their holiday. The obsession had not subsided. On the contrary. It was more intense. Mika felt like a prisoner in her fantasizing mind, afraid she was becoming unbalanced. The feeling reminded her of a visit, with Gabi and Gila, to a multimedia exhibition in the San Francisco Museum of Modern Art. Unrelated scenes of landscapes, people, and objects were projected onto the four walls of the hall. The clutter of pictures and meaningless sounds had made her feel claustrophobic. She had wanted to get out quickly, to escape from the foolishness and unreality, just as she now wanted to escape from her fantasies into a saner frame of mind. Luckily, this torture was invading her mind after she had made a life for herself, completed her studies, and raised her children. What would have become of her had she been haunted by this madness all her life?

I have to find a way to relieve this pressure, she thought. She called her childhood friend Alona. Alona had gone with Mika to the class reunion in Haifa and knew the whole list of characters. She was now listening to Mika on the phone: "You know Yaron Zelig? Well, for the last three weeks, I've had some crazy thoughts about him. I need to talk to somebody about it," she said and revealed that she had been trying to reach him. "Do you have any idea what could be happening to me?" she said in a pleading voice.

Oceans away, on the other end of the telephone, a disturbing silence reigned.

"I cannot believe you sent him a greeting card!" said Alona. "And dear Lord, don't you dare contact him. He could cause you some real, deep harm." Alona remembered Yaron as a violent kid. "Leave that one alone."

"But why doesn't he answer me?" Mika persisted.

"Everyone gives only what they can," was Alona's reply. "Delete those emails," she advised in a commanding voice. "Try to forget. Shove the memories into a drawer, and return to the present. Get on with your daily life. Get a hobby," she said in a pitying tone, implying that Mika's madness was the result of boredom, as though her life weren't already overscheduled to its limits.

"Remind me what he was like when he was a boy," Mika pleaded, wanting an anchor in reality.

"A hostile boy, unpleasant. He could have ripped people apart with one angry glance. It was scary to be near him. He had these crazy eyes that made it seem as if he were about to attack at any minute."

"That's not how I remember him at all," Mika replied. "He was a smart and capable kid. Boys and girls loved him. He was very generous and protective of me in earlier years." She refused to be consoled.

"Well, that's what I remember," Alona asserted. "Whenever you have the obsessive need to contact him, call me. I'm here for you at all times." Her voice was steady and soothing.

Mika called her a number of times that week. Through long conversations that transcended their physical distance, the two friends tried to examine the bizarre phenomenon and understand it. Alona was as upset as Mika and worried about her.

"You need help, Mika. Perhaps you should see a psychologist."

"I'm not ready to admit that I have a problem. I'm hoping it will pass, that I'll forget about it. Nothing like this has ever happened to me. But if this current keeps electrifying me, I'll get help."

The next day, she decided to talk to Shaul. Her beloved Shaul, the person closest to her, her husband, her friend, the man who loved her. Maybe Shaul would understand and help her.

In the evening, when they took their walk around the neighborhood, she said she had something very embarrassing to tell him and didn't know where to begin. Shaul looked at her in suspense.

"Do you remember that I sent Yaron Zelig a greeting card and asked if we could get together with him and his wife in Seattle?"

"The doctor?"

"Yes, the doctor," Mika said, almost in a whisper. "After he left a message to say that they'd be on vacation when we planned to be in Seattle, I wrote him a long, detailed email. I told him about you and the children, a bit about myself, and mainly about the class reunion. I told him about the people who were in our class and sent him photographs. A few days later, I got a very brief message from him on the answering machine. I was very disappointed by his brusque reply. But what's even harder for me to understand is how much this whole thing is bothering me and how stressed I am because of it."

Mika paused to see how Shaul was reacting to what she was saying. He was listening quietly, and she felt she could proceed. "The nights are hardest. I can hardly get any sleep." She downplayed the situation, but gave Shaul enough information for him to understand her distress. "Why doesn't he answer me, in your opinion?"

"He's a cardiologist who performs heart transplants, right?"

Mika nodded.

"So he doesn't have time for you. Grow up, kid." Shaul gave her a critical look. "Anyhow, why did you write a long letter to someone you haven't seen for so many years?"

Mika was silent. He was right. She was thoroughly ashamed.

"What's missing in your life?" he asked accusingly.

"Nothing," she said and sought comfort in his arms. "The man has nothing to do with the present," she added, "only with my childhood, the distant past. He also didn't answer me when I was thirteen. Something happened between us when we were kids. One day he just stopped talking to me. The hurt I'm feeling now belongs to the past."

Mika and Shaul didn't raise the subject again. Not even on the evening she fainted.

She had put immense effort into practicing for the prestigious concert held by the local musicians' association. Wearing a black evening dress that revealed her shapely back, Mika walked toward the piano at the center of the stage. She seated herself on the lacquered stool and tried to concentrate on the work by Ravel. The audience was completely silent; all eyes were on the woman in black.

Mika's mind was in turmoil, with incoherent sentences spinning through her every thought. She took a deep breath as she struggled with herself and tried to subdue her inner noise, so that she could focus on the music. It was all in vain. She tried to remember the prelude, the scale, the opening notes. She knew that if she could remember the first few notes, the music would take control. Just the first bar, she pleaded. But the commotion in her head was intensified by the dramatic chords of the third movement of Beethoven's Seventh Symphony, which became the background to the nonsensical sentences.

The external silence and the internal noise seemed to continue for an eternity. Mika tried to raise her arms into the correct position for playing, but they remained heavy and unresponsive. She felt hot. The blood flowed from her head to her feet, and she felt as if her body could not withstand its own weight. She was panting and felt nauseated. Then all at once, her body lost its strength, and her hollow head sank to the piano keys and struck a harsh, resounding chord.

Cries of panic came from the audience. People in the first row jumped onto the stage and stretched Mika onto the floor. Someone sprinkled her face with water. She opened bewildered eyes, and out of the depths, asked, "What happened?"

"You fainted," said her friend Karen, the violinist.

Shaul lifted Mika into his strong arms, carried her to their car, and drove to the hospital.

Blood tests. CT scans. A brain tumor was ruled out. "You lack iron," the doctor said and sent her to a gynecologist, who suggested hormone therapy, saying that menopause begins long before menstruation stops, with symptoms of anemia and insomnia. Mika was somewhat reassured. She didn't like the idea that the brain evaporated in menopause, but what could she do about it? Maybe the obsession with Yaron was also part of her menopause, related to the hormonal changes that took place in the early years.

Mika tried to come to terms with her awkward obsession. But the incoherent sentences had now become infused with fury. She composed letters to Yaron steeped in anger, but didn't send them. She wanted to write, "Why is it so hard for you to answer? I invested time and effort to find your address, I sent you a greeting card, I wrote you an email and told you my life story. I attached photographs, and still you can't trouble yourself to send a simple answer."

Logic told her this was not the way. He didn't owe her an answer. Alona was right. Everyone gives only what they can. She had to come to terms with reality, but she couldn't. Her brain could not cope with a letter from the past, a different sort of letter. "Then, too, when we were kids, you ignored me, you didn't answer. One can forgive a childish reaction that stems from insecurity or immaturity, but today there's no justification and no room for forgiveness." Mika boiled with anger, as if decades had not passed since then.

A week before Pesach, she received an email from Eddie, who had once sat behind her in the classroom, and told her jokes that made her laugh during boring lessons. However, his main attraction in her eyes was his friendship with Yaron. She used to imagine that whatever she said to Eddie was automatically relayed to Yaron. Her internal antennae were tuned solely to the Yaron Zelig channel, and Eddie sometimes provided her with eagerly awaited reports about him. From Eddie, she heard about Yaron's life at home, the music he liked listening to in his room, the jokes they swapped, his opinions about girls. She hoped their biting remarks weren't directed at her, but she couldn't be sure.

Eddie sent her an old photograph taken at the Sa'hne pool, on the annual class trip when they were in twelfth grade: Alona and Mika, with their youth bursting out of their bikinis, hugging skinny Eddie. Yaron was in the background, looking away from the camera. A loner, aloof, he liked being different from the rest of the group.

Mika decided to take the opportunity to forward the photo to Yaron. To ease the obsession, she thought. She added, "Pity we didn't get to talk," signed, and pressed the send key. One day, two. No response from Seattle.

It was more than she could take. Mika exploded. She couldn't help but send him a furious message, accusing him of being indifferent and inconsiderate:

> You don't care that I made the effort to find you and took the trouble to send you the card as well as a detailed account of my life plus photographs. I merely wanted to know how you are, how the years have treated you, what your wife does, and how you feel about Seattle. Don't do me any favors. You don't have to answer. All the best.

She signed and sent it, certain she'd never hear from him. That was the end of the story, and the obsession would fade. It was only a matter of time.

Two weeks later, while they were entertaining Gabi and Danny and their kids for dinner, the phone rang, and Shaul answered.

"Yaron Zelig speaking. You don't know me, but I know your wife from our youth. May I speak to Mika?"

Shaul handed the phone to Mika with a broad, fatherly smile.

Taking the receiver, she heard gales of rather embarrassed laughter.

"Am I about to get chewed out?" she asked nervously.

"Not at all!" he laughed.

She relaxed. "Sorry about the melodrama," she said.

"No worries. It spices life up a bit."

They spoke about the reunion in Haifa, who was there, and so on.

"It's a pity I wasn't there," Yaron said.

"It's okay, they meet often. There'll be other times," Mika assured him.

"Is this a convenient time for me to call?"

"Not really. We have guests, and we're about to have dinner."

"Okay. So we'll talk some other time?"

"Promise?" she asked coyly.

"Yes, yes, I promise. I sent you an email. I was at a conference in Europe and couldn't reply when you sent the photo."

Mika was abashed.

She calmed down after the conversation, and the obsessions loosened their hold on her.

They exchanged emails under the heading of "We Finally Connect," chosen by Yaron. Her heart fluttering, Mika's eyes paused on "Finally." Was it possible that he had also eagerly looked forward to connecting with her? Since when? Since the last message, or the card, or maybe for thirty-five years? The emails that began with the here and now slid into memories of the past. They compared memories and wrote about those who were killed and two who had committed suicide. She reminded him how, in seventh grade, he had rescued her from the cruel hands of Shlomi Halfon who was pulling her hair just because she was standing in his way. Yaron had leaped to the rescue when he heard her cries. "You never hurt girls," he'd scolded, and Mika never forgot.

She told him about her two brothers. He told her that what he remembered most from their infrequent contact during their youth was a sense of shyness and awkwardness. It took him a long time to get over his shyness with girls. He asked if she remembered his brother and sister.

You ask if I remember your brother and sister as though we lived on different planets. You forget that my parents' house was situated such that from our backyard I could see exactly what was happening at your house, who was home from school, who finished their homework and went out to the basketball court, and who was sent to the corner store to buy a loaf of bread that she nearly devoured by the time she made it back home. Later on, I could see who came home with a new girlfriend on his hip. I remember your father crossing the road to have a look at the notice board opposite my house to see what movie was showing in the cinema in Ahuza and your mother walking up the road with the dog (Brownie, was it?). Your family was an integral part of my childhood landscape. You said you don't remember much interaction between us, but you must mean the time after our adolescence, because that's when you stopped talking to me for some unknown reason.

I remember the stories you would tell when we sat on benches during class breaks. Once you taught us how to work out our average mark for the semester, as your big brother Gidi had taught you and, because it was then beyond my understanding, you took my report card and quickly worked out that my average was 9.5. I understood from your consoling look that although my achievements were nowhere near as high as yours, there was room for a certain degree of satisfaction. Yes, you introduced a competitive standard when you joined our sleepy classroom, something you no doubt got from Gidi. I remember he was your hero. You once told me that he had started to play the violin at the age of six but stopped quite soon, and the violin ended up useless in the attic. And another story I recall. Gidi annoyed your mother one day, and she slapped him with an open palm before noticing that he had a fork in his mouth. It hurt, but your hero Gidi didn't make a sound. All this you told us, a herd of admirers, your classmates.

In high school Gidi became an icon. Not only were the girls interested in him, the boys ran after him, too. When my friend Dina dated him, her shares skyrocketed, and her ego inflated tremendously. (By the way, I was never interested in Gidi, only his younger brother…)

I'll sign off now, hope to hear from you, Mika.

Two weeks later, Mika received a line from Yaron: "Finally, I'm back at my private computer. I need to tell you that you blew my mind. I can't believe you remember all those details. I have to talk to you. I'm phoning right now."

Ring, ring. Yaron.

"How do you remember all that?" he asked in amazement. "Even the dog's name."

Mika laughed. "This is all a sort of journey back into my own childhood," she explained apologetically.

"Yes, yes. So, tell me, did you have a crush on me?"

"Yes, I did," she giggled.

"You, the unattainable hottie?" he persisted.

"Let's not exaggerate wildly," she answered, pleased. "Why did you stop talking to me?"

"As you said, adolescence, fear of rejection."

"Ah," she sighed, understanding. "But something happened there..." she added, without going into detail.

They glided from the past back to the present. He told her about life in Seattle, his wife Dikla, who was a successful interior designer, and his three children who each played a different instrument. He said he had also returned to playing the piano, as he had then, when they were children. He reminded her that she once said to him, in high school, "I didn't know you could play so beautifully," and he had mumbled thanks and turned away to hide his red face. He didn't know how much courage it had taken for her to say those words and they had embarrassed her, too. His retreat had confirmed to her that he was unattainable.

She told him about her eldest daughter who was studying at the Sorbonne, about the son in the army and the twins. She told him about jumping from continent to continent, about her life full of concerts and students.

In her mind, she envisaged him as he'd been at twenty-eight, when they'd met at the class reunion at Café Atara on Mount Carmel. She'd already been married, a young mother; he'd been stunning. He'd come over and asked about her husband: "Where's he from, what does he do, how old is he?"

"A kibbutznik, from Nahal Oz, a cool guy. You'd like him," she had replied.

"What makes you think so?" He'd focused his blue gaze on her.

She'd shrugged, thinking for the first time that, after all, maybe he didn't hate her even though he had stopped talking to her many years ago. And even though this was the first time they had talked since eighth grade.

Now, on the phone, he told her how hard it had been to adapt to Seattle, the dreary weather. During the first months, they had wanted to pack up and go back to Israel, to the sun. In time, they'd gotten used to the place and had even learned to make the most of it.

"Is there a chance you'll ever come to California?"

"Sure," he said.

"Will you come for a visit?"

"Of course! We'd love to."

As they spoke, Mika heard the garage door opening and the sound of Shaul's car. Shaul came up the stairs, calling her name. He found her leaning on the railing of the bedroom balcony, phone in hand, with her back to him.

"Shaul's home," she told Yaron, "say a few words to him," she added, wanting to include Shaul in their conversation.

"It's Yaron Zelig, from Seattle," she said, handing the receiver to Shaul. "Say hello," she urged her husband, unaware of the terrible mistake she was making.

Shaul took the receiver reluctantly and said dryly, "What fun you're having!" He mumbled a few more words and then cut the conversation short. With an angry look, he said to Mika, "I don't want anything to do with him."

"What?"

"You heard me."

"What's going on here?" she asked in amazement.

"That relationship isn't healthy," he said coldly.

"There's no relationship," she defended herself angrily. "I haven't seen him for almost twenty years. What are you talking about?"

"You don't sleep at night, because of him. Not long ago, you fainted, stopped functioning," he accused her. "Nothing like that has ever happened to you before. That relationship must end. It could be dangerous."

"Dangerous? What are you talking about?" Mika was shocked. She had not expected such a reaction. She looked at him as if she did not know her husband anymore. How could he not see that she was exploring her past? What was it that made him so restless? So uneasy? She had never seen him appear so threatened before. Never.

Chapter 7

The elegant elevator rose swiftly to the twenty-fourth floor of the Bank of America building in downtown San Francisco. Yoel checked the latest emails on his PalmPilot, and I surveyed my reflection in the mirror, not pleased.

"What are you thinking about?" Yoel asked.

The question running through my mind was whether the Ann Taylor suit I was wearing wasn't conspicuous in its simplicity in comparison to the fabulous examples from top Italian fashion houses I had already seen in the lobby. However, since Yoel did not understand such qualms, I dismissed his question with, "Nothing in particular"—my usual response when I knew he wouldn't understand.

The spacious hall was filled with distinguished members of the San Francisco and Silicon Valley Israeli community. Huge paintings decorated the interior walls, and beyond the exterior glass walls, the city was displayed like a sparkling stage set. The rooftops of the illuminated skyscrapers twinkled at eye level. The Bay Bridge connecting San Francisco and Oakland and the Golden Gate Bridge between San Francisco and Marin glittered to the east and north, like fully lit Chanukah menorahs.

The guests at the cocktail party Gabi had organized here in Luigi Fracassini's art gallery were grouped as usual—men in one corner and women in another, as though Orthodox synagogue guidelines were in enforcement.

Gabi had worked tirelessly to arrange the evening in honor of Fracassini and his art collection. She'd compiled a guest list, printed and sent invitations, seen to the catering, and invited the consul to address the gathering. The refreshments from Gabi's epicurean kitchen were supplemented by caterers and two waitresses bearing trays of appetizers. The centerpiece on the buffet was an installation by Gabi: a broken, burnt-out toy bus, a few modeling clay dolls holding Israeli and Palestinian flags, and two multistory structures of burnt Lego blocks, reminiscent of the Twin Towers. The work was entitled *Sorrows of the World*. Gabi explained to the women that she thought it right to remind the guests of the relationship between suffering and hedonism.

Unobtrusively, with my head slightly inclined, I joined the group of men on the other side of the room, where I was received with a few polite kisses on the cheek before they resumed their manly conversation.

"Well done! Excellent work!" they exclaimed, slapping Ami Mandovsky, one of the gang, another Israeli CEO of a high-performing company, on the shoulder. His photograph was on the cover of the previous week's *Globes*, the Israeli business newspaper, following an internationally acclaimed business success, which he'd pulled off in spite of the recession. The men climbed on the bandwagon of his success, proud that one of them had "made it big."

Ami had indeed made it. Nevertheless, some others also had reason to boast, and they took the opportunity to do so. Danny reported a second round of investments of sixty million dollars that boosted his share. He was keeping an eye on a new business development that, he promised, would "do wonders in the coming months."

Ido told them that his new company was going public after having done very well in the last three quarters. He did not mention the second start-up, where Gilad worked, that was about to crash and lose tens of millions of dollars of his own money that could never be recouped; failures were not discussed in those circles. Stories of failures, like juicy gossip about infidelity, spread like wildfire, but nobody volunteered to repeat them in public. He pointed out that nowadays it was harder than ever to find good, loyal employees who weren't greedy for money, because the bubble had spoiled people and taught them to make unrealistic demands. Ido, whose own bank account had swelled by hundreds of millions of dollars in the years of the bubble, enjoyed the silent agreement of his captive audience.

Rami told them he was in the process of acquiring a competing company from San Diego. If all went well, he said, he was planning an exit worth an estimated two hundred million in the coming year. Yoel, who always attenuated Rami's enthusiasm, said that it was still a long way to the exit. However, on a note of personal optimism, he added, "But there are signs of recovery in the market," meaning a light at the end of the tunnel after the bubble burst.

Yossi Giladi, whose company had sold for half a billion dollars two years prior, complained that his private capital had dropped together with the stock exchange, by dozens of points. So he'd had to tighten his belt and sell his private jet. Since then, he'd had to make do with a single-engine plane. Ido advised him to buy a race car instead, and I shed a tear for Yossi's tragic loss and returned to the women's side of things because, really, what did I have to contribute to male reconnoitering? I certainly didn't have the biggest one to whip out.

Anita, in a stunning taffeta gown slit from ankle to thigh, created by a renowned Israeli designer to suit her perfect figure, was holding court in the middle of the women's circle. Luigi Fracassini's wife was hovering on the fringe of the gathering, and some of the women made an effort to converse in English. Fracassini's wife, who looked like a restored mummy, was careful not to smile. If even a tiny smile were to appear, her taut cheeks would be in danger of splitting. After a few awkward sentences, she moved away from our ethnic circle and joined her husband, who was chatting with the consul's wife. With a sigh of relief, we lapsed into our mother tongue.

Anita told us about her latest trip to Davos, Switzerland, as a delegate from the Jewish Federation by virtue of being one of the "Rubies," a group of women who each contributed over a hundred thousand dollars a year. As a token of appreciation for their generosity, they were entitled to wear a diamond-and-ruby pin shaped like a lion. The number of diamonds indicated the amount of their donations. Needless to say, the Rubies wore their badges as would army officers proud to display their ranks.

The aim of the Davos conference, Anita reported, had been to create a bridge between the Rubies and the delegation of leading women in the Arab world, including Jehan Sadat, Queen Noor of Jordan, and even Suha Arafat.

"The Swiss are anti-Semites," Anita raged, waving her finger at us. "They subjected us, the Jewish women delegation, to a painstaking security check, as if we were the terrorists!" She also complained that the Arabs had been given the better suites in the hotel, those reserved for VIPs, whereas the Rubies had had to make do with regular tourist accommodations. "But the Swiss cuisine is out of this world! I ate so much foie gras I couldn't believe it. I actually stuffed my face so much that I spent two days in bed with an upset stomach!"

"And what was said at the conference, what were the conclusions?" asked Gila, wearing a flattering black Prada dress.

"Honestly," Anita said, "I have no idea. I spent most of the time squirming in pain until they brought me some doctor who didn't understand English. I had to gesture to him that I was running to the toilet all the time, and he finally gave me a pill for diarrhea. But I was told that I didn't miss anything. Nothing new. The Arabs accused Israel of child murder, and the Jews said their suicide bombers murdered children and innocent people and they would gain nothing from the bombing. Apart from which, our hosts gave the Arab women extra time to lecture in French, without simultaneous translation. So what could I understand?" Her face twisted right and left with disbelief.

"How did they expect you to understand without translation?" Mika wanted to know.

"They distributed an outline of the lectures, translated into English. But who had the patience to read? We had a few high-caliber speakers on our side, but our lectures were translated into French and printed in advance."

"Meaning," Mika said, "that the next conference must be held in a country that's actually neutral and that will give an equal platform to the Jewish and Arab participants."

"The problem is that there aren't any such countries in Europe. They all hate us, even if they don't say so outright," said Anita, and we sighed.

We turned to Gabi, who, in a red extra-large Max Mara dress, was inviting everyone to be seated on the folding chairs that had been arranged in rows. The men took their seats briskly and reserved seats for their wives, who graciously sat beside them. Two by two, as in Noah's ark.

Gabi opened the evening in English. She thanked the audience warmly and invited the Israeli consul to the podium.

"These are hard times for the State of Israel," the consul opened, without words of grace. He was a heavy man in his midforties. His balding temples and face were already red, the white shirt under his gray suit stretched tight over his round belly. "We all know that we're in a war for survival. We have enemies all over the world. Israel's name has been trampled in the mud in Europe and America as if we have no right to defend innocent civilians, children on the way to school. You, the Israeli community in the USA, have an important duty. You are Israel's emissaries wherever you happen to be. We have to make ourselves heard. I am asking each of you to contact the radio networks personally and express your support for Israel during this difficult period.

"Every week we hear about suicide bombers who blow up buses in Tel Aviv and Jerusalem. We hear about civilians, women and children and the elderly, who are being murdered without mercy in the streets. Last week, the consulate organized a demonstration of support on the Stanford University campus. The poor Israeli turnout compared to the Palestinian crowd was disgraceful. Where were you? You were probably enjoying your lunch. I suggest that now and then you forgo your sumptuous lunch and join a demonstration in support of your homeland."

The consul was flushed with rage, and we bent our heads, overcome with shame after the blunt reproof. The consul's wife glared reproachfully at us, her hair dyed red and cropped in what seemed to be the Israeli national hairstyle. Her paratrooper boots put the finishing touch on her militant appearance. The expression of contempt on her face clearly conveyed that she was unimpressed by the local bourgeoisie.

Yuval Avrahami rose from his chair and announced a mass pro-Israel demonstration that was being planned in San Francisco. He would send invitations by email and hoped for full participation. Gabi, afraid the evening would overflow into politics, quickly presented Luigi Fracassini, the host and main speaker. She spoke about her long acquaintance with the professor, who had tutored her at the San Francisco Academy of Art. She observed that he was a graduate of the arts academy in Rome, named after the three greats—Michelangelo, Leonardo, and Raphael— and we were greatly impressed. She thanked the professor for consenting to host her friends at his successful gallery, kissed his cheeks, and made way for him on the improvised stage that her children had constructed out of boxes and a carpet.

Fracassini, a lean, handsome man with graying hair and a pleasant expression, looked for words to calm the audience after the forceful speech of the consul. In an Italian accent as musical as a mandolin, he explained that visual art was based on four principles: line, color, form, and texture. The known artist's characteristic field became his recognizable signature: Picasso was the artist of line; after a signal from the professor, his assistant Marco presented a framed serigraph with Picasso's signature. "Look at the simplicity of Picasso's line, his virtuosity. With one sweeping line, he has portrayed an expressive figure with perfect posture." He gazed at the picture with awe.

"Chagall," he continued, as Marco displayed a Chagall reproduction, "is considered the artist of color. He is unequaled in the power and balance of his colors on the canvas. Matisse and Picasso are also considered to be colorists, but there's no one like Chagall who, with a dash of paint, can depict a whole world."

I was excited. Moved. In a moment I had understood more than ever before. And this was just the beginning.

"Dalí was considered the greatest artist of form," he continued, flooding the room with precise, simple truths. "The utmost detail is to be found in his paintings and, at times, a story within a story." Fracassini did not stop at Dalí. "Take the French Impressionist Georges Seurat, for example. With small points of color, he was able to portray a minutely detailed scene, as in the painting called *A Sunday Afternoon on the Island of La Grande Jatte*. See?"

Finally, he presented Bruno Bernoulli, artist of color and texture. With great care, Marco handed the framed originals to Fracassini as if they were fragile. "Bernoulli uses a unique technique of his own. He starts by spreading a base of sand on the canvas and then adds a few layers of paint, achieving a three-dimensional effect," Fracassini explained, stroking a painting and gazing at it like a lovesick boy.

I had to admit that I didn't know of Bernoulli's work. Fracassini exhibited a few samples, all of which seemed much alike: an array of colorful geometric frames with an indistinct, differently colored figure at the center of each picture.

Like artists, Fracassini explained, viewers responded to different stimuli. Some were drawn to line, others to color, form, or texture. As an art dealer, he said, he had developed specific senses that helped him identify the taste of a collector and match them to the art they preferred.

Hearing this, I mused that the Rorschach test was based on similar principles, meaning that Fracassini had developed his own Rorschach test for art. Suddenly forgetting the occasion and the audience, I spoke as if Fracassini and I were alone in the room.

"According to the Rorschach test," I said, "most people who are considered to be normal notice form first. Then they notice color, because color speaks to emotion. Emotionally less stable people respond first to color—that is, emotion."

Fracassini listened attentively.

"That's not quite right," Irit Brown remarked from the row behind me. A psychologist, like me, she was always ready to show her professional superiority. "If there's no indication of a response to color in the Rorschach, it's usually a sign of limited intelligence."

The blood rushed to my temples as I swallowed the insult.

Yossi Giladi's third wife, Haleli Bat-Ami, who had taken an art class once, also had to have her say in the conversation. "What about modern art? What's the meaning of a frame around an empty, flat plane? And why is Francine Kahn's framed shopping list included in an exhibition at MOMA?"

"Good question. Good question." Fracassini swayed from one foot to the other in search of a brief answer regarding conceptual art. "That kind of art," he said, "assumes that the concept is more important than the visual presentation."

His answer didn't satisfy Haleli Bat-Ami Giladi, who persisted, "Anyway, why was Francine Kahn's shopping list accepted as an exhibit in the San Francisco museum, whereas my shopping list, for example, is not on exhibit in a museum?"

The professor was looking pale and exhausted. Haleli's husband Yossi was slumped in his chair, and the audience had also lost patience. The professor finally evaded Haleli's questions by inviting the lady to pursue the matter more thoroughly in his office at the university.

Rami, who was known for his matter of fact approach to life, asked, "What's the difference between an original work and a lithograph or a serigraph? After all, in the latter two, the product looks identical."

The professor smiled happily, as if this technical question had been planted. A lithograph was stamped on the paper, whereas the serigraph was made in stages, during which the paint was applied in layers according to the artist's directions. With both techniques, the images were printed in numbered copies, so that the value of the print declined as the number of reproductions increased. However, nothing equaled an original work, which was most suitable as an investment, from a financial point of view.

The men in the audience perked up, maybe because they now saw that there was more than line and texture in a painting—there was the color of money. Fracassini, now as an art dealer, addressed the financial aspect of art and suggested that his listeners consider paintings as investments whose value increased with time. For example, he said, they should look into contemporary painters, and referred to Bruno Bernoulli again. Lovingly stroking and praising the artist's paintings, he explained that although anyone in Silicon Valley could afford to buy one today, it would not be long before their value skyrocketed. "Like Miró and Chagall. I predict sensation and greatness for Bernoulli."

Nevertheless, he gave Gabi an original, exemplary work by Bernoulli, a gift from the gallery, then hugged and kissed her and showered her with compliments for her initiative in arranging the evening. The audience applauded.

At the dessert and coffee table, Haleli Bat-Ami Giladi, encased in a skintight Donatella Versace suit, told me that she was not going to invest in Western artists anymore. "Only exotic third-world artists," she said, puffing cigarette smoke in my face and running her diamond-studded fingers through her platinum-dyed hair. "This summer, I have to finish my world art tour. I'm planning trips to Nepal and Somalia, where I'll buy some marvelous art for next to nothing. The problem is, of course, how to fly them to California." She took a drag on her cigarette. "The freight alone will eat up my budget. But that's another story." She sighed and moved on, as if I weren't there, as if I had dissolved like the smoke of her cigarette.

Fracassini's endeavors paid off. Almost everyone who was at the gallery that evening ended up with a Bernoulli original on the wall. The zealous ended up with two.

I confess that the magic also worked on me, and I nagged Yoel for a small Bernoulli original. As for Yoel, he said as far as he was concerned, he'd be willing to hire Fracassini for a marketing and sales position at his and Rami's start-up.

Chapter 8

Eventually, I learned Mika's secret. I waited for her in Café Borrone, in Menlo Park, as we'd arranged by phone. The café was crowded with people sitting at round tables under green awnings. Mika arrived looking tired, as if several years had unexpectedly passed. Smiling nervously, she joined me at the table and slowly returned her key ring to her purse, pushed her sunglasses above her hairline, and tried to find a comfortable position, but mostly she was trying to buy herself some time.

Over coffee and a bowl of salad, shared to watch the calories, I started to grow worried.

"So, what's going on?"

"Oh, Daniela," she sighed, "I'm going to tell you an embarrassing and weird story. If it didn't concern me, I'd be able to giggle and move on. But the sad truth is that it keeps me awake all night. It all began with my class reunion in Haifa. Imagine," she said, stressing each word, "thirty years flash before me in an instant, distorting memory, erasing it, adjusting the past to suit the present. Has anything of the sort happened to you?" she asked wearily, with a big question mark on her face.

"No. It's been years since I went to one of those meetings, even though everyone around me seems to be busy playing with their past." I thought of Gila and her beloved, of Gilad who had rediscovered his high school girlfriend online, and of my husband Yoel, who'd informed me that, according to Orly Bergman, he had been the class heartthrob.

Mika sank into a detailed, lengthy narrative to which I listened, hypnotized. Uncharacteristically, I did not interrupt her with a single question as she revealed the story of her obsession with Yaron Zelig from start to finish.

"What has happened since then?" I asked when she stopped talking and put down the fork she had been waving like a weapon.

"Shaul refuses to discuss the subject with me. He's convinced I've lost my mind and that I'm liable to do things I'll regret. He thinks it's his duty to restrain me."

"Is he right?"

"No way! From the beginning, I've had no romantic intentions. The obsession consumes me mysteriously, from inside myself. It's inexplicable. It has nothing to do with the present; it's connected to the past. I don't understand why this is happening to me now; I just don't have the answer." Her eyes darted nervously from the fork to the glass as if in her frustration she were looking for something to throw. "I'm troubled by events that took place when I was younger than my twins. It's hard to understand."

"And what's going on now with Yaron?"

"After my talk with Shaul, I sent him an email and apologized with all my heart. I told him Shaul wasn't happy about my phone calls and I didn't want to hurt my husband, because he is dear to me."

"Did he answer?"

"Of course not."

"And Shaul?"

"Shaul is acting like some rooster that has defeated an opponent in a cockfight over his beloved. He showers me with love, as if it's just been reborn. He kisses me and hugs me all the time, and I can't forgive him for his brutality."

"Were you in love with Yaron?"

"Many years ago, when I was thirteen. But there was no romance."

"Thirteen's a sensitive age," I answered. "That's when all great loves begin. Juliet was fourteen."

"But why has the obsession come now?" Mika asked. "Do you have an answer for that, Daniela?"

"It seems to me that your obsession is the result of an outburst of emotions and memories. The whole story with Yaron lay dormant for many years until a little troublesome bit of dopamine woke up and caused the obsession. Unfulfilled romantic love is a phenomenon similar to temporary mental instability."

"Temporary mental instability…What are you talking about?" Mika asked anxiously.

I told Mika about the lecture by Helen Fisher that Yoel and I had attended in San Diego. Fisher, I explained, had described romantic love as a nonclinical, minimal state of depressive psychosis. It distorted reality, since everything concerning the love object became enchanted and much more ideal than it actually was.

"So you're saying that I'm unbalanced over a person, actually a boy, that I was in love with more than thirty years ago. That doesn't make sense."

"No. I'm saying that something was triggered in your brain. The memories revived emotions from way back."

Mika nodded. The explanation sounded reasonable. "So what do I do to get back to normality?"

"It's not a terrible situation," I said. "It can be treated."

"Are you suggesting I need therapy?" Mika sounded alarmed. Maybe she was expecting a different response from me.

"There's nothing wrong with therapy, Mika. In fact, in mid-life it can be a very enjoyable experience. At our age, we no longer need pretexts in order to impress anybody, and we can reach depths we never knew we had in us." I gave her a level look, wanting to encourage her not to be afraid of herself.

"Can you recommend someone?"

"Yes. I'm thinking Dr. David Diamond. He's a psychiatrist who trained me in the past. He's a musician, like yourself, a talented violinist and a man of many accomplishments. I'm sure you'll enjoy working with him."

In my opinion, Dr. Diamond was an amazing therapist. Aptly named. For a moment, I was jealous of him, because he was about to get a wonderful patient whom I would have liked to keep for myself. But since she was my friend, Mika could not also be my patient.

Dr. Diamond, who had a pleasant expression and a gentle voice, received Mika with a warm handshake and led her to an armchair in a corner of the room. He sat opposite her and quietly observed her while she searched for opening words. She wore a pendant on a long chain, with which she nervously fiddled as she sat with her legs crossed, running her eyes over the loaded bookshelves on the walls.

"I'm here because of something strange that happened to me, an experience that has had an effect on me and that I don't understand." He waited patiently for her to continue and she unfolded the whole story, starting with the reunion in Haifa, the greeting card, the obsession, the insomnia, the fainting, the emails, the phone calls, and, finally, the anger she felt toward Shaul.

"The whole story is marked by skepticism," she concluded. "Yaron couldn't believe I remembered details from so long ago. My friend Alona couldn't believe I'd sent Yaron a greeting card, and I myself couldn't believe Shaul's brutal and jealous reaction." After a moment she added, looking directly at Dr. Diamond, "This is how things stand at the moment: Shaul's behavior deeply upset me, but he feels triumphant and refuses to discuss the matter, Yaron is silent in Seattle, and I'm in the middle, on the verge of losing my mind. I have nobody to talk to, I haven't had a decent night's sleep for over six months. I feel as if something has ruptured inside me, a sort of mental hernia."

"Mental hernia is a strong image," Dr. Diamond muttered. Then he asked for more details about Mika's life. She told him about her music career and about Shaul, who had succeeded beyond all expectations, about her daughter studying at the Sorbonne, her son in Israel, doing his military service, and about the twins in high school who still kept her busy in her daily routine. He asked her to describe her marriage. "Happy," Mika replied, adding that although there were ups and downs, they were in a golden era. Really. She had never felt such love and closeness to Shaul as she'd felt in the last few years.

Dr. Diamond smiled with satisfaction but continued to press: "You said you're angry with Shaul?"

"I never imagined he'd react like that. Through twenty-five years of marriage, neither he nor I had a jealous episode. Girlfriends from his past sometimes contacted him, but I never felt threatened. I thought our relationship was stable," she said bitterly. "In fact, I was hurt because he betrayed my trust. I always felt I could lean on him."

"What do you do with the anger?"

"He gives me no opportunity to express my anger, because he doesn't want to discuss the issue."

"What about couples' therapy?"

"No way. He won't come." Mika felt as if she were being pushed against yet another wall. She was annoyed with Dr. Diamond for insisting on prying into her married life instead of dealing with the obsession that had brought her to therapy and that was, in her opinion, the root of the whole problem.

She told him about her hospital tests, which had found that her levels of iron and hormones were low. She asked him if there was a connection between these findings and her symptoms. She also mentioned the possibility that she was suffering from a slight, temporary psychosis related to dopamine and serotonin and asked for his opinion.

After earnestly considering her questions, Dr. Diamond rubbed his beard, nodded his head, and said attentively that anything was possible. He told her that he felt hopeful about her condition and that he would be happy to help her, and he prescribed sleeping pills to ease the insomnia and enable her to function. They parted warmly, having arranged a session for the coming week. Mika left feeling that a weight had been lifted from her heart. She hoped that she would soon be freed from her obsession.

Their second session also began with broad smiles and a warm handshake. "How are you feeling this week?" Dr. Diamond asked.

"I slept peacefully the last few nights, thanks to the pills. The obsessive symptoms have also subsided a bit."

He asked her to describe them.

"They change with time. A few months ago, lines from the greeting card and emails I sent Yaron would ring in my ears. After talking to him on the phone, parts of our conversation would play in my head like a broken record. Now I'm having flashbacks of scenes from my childhood. They are as fresh as if they had happened a day ago."

"Describe what you see."

Mika was embarrassed. "There's nothing special about them. Just pictures of an ordinary childhood," she said evasively.

"What were you like as a child?"

"I had a good childhood, nothing really out of the ordinary. I grew up in Haifa, in a normal family, with two brothers and loving parents. We lived in a green wooden prefab with a red tiled roof, in a neighborhood that was built for Technion University faculty. My father taught in the mechanical engineering department, and my mother worked there as a part-time secretary. My parents were considered well-off because they owned a car. In the sixties in Israel, that was a real status symbol. We could see the Carmel forests from our living room—rolling hills, patches of red poppies on green fields. There was even a view of the sea, from a distance. There was a little corner store, which was the center of our lively social scene. We met up there as kids on the way home from school, talking for hours, eating ten-cent popsicles, from Yosef's kiosk. I was a good student, and I played the piano since I was quite young. I remember I used to spend hours looking at myself in the mirror from different angles, looking to see if there was any way to make myself resemble Brigitte Bardot, whom I just adored. My hair was golden, like hers, and I thought I had nice lips like her too—I just needed to push my little Jewish nose up a bit." Mika chuckled. "One day, a friend of my parents' came by, a big city lawyer, and he looked at me and asked if anyone had ever told me that I looked like Botticelli's Venus. I was curious, so I looked Botticelli up in the dictionary, and *The Birth of Venus* just happened to be there. I was so disappointed to find out that she looked nothing like Brigitte Bardot!" Mika laughed heartily, and Dr. Diamond joined her.

"And today? How do you look to yourself these days?"

"Today I see no trace of Brigitte Bardot, nor of Venus rising from the shell. I must have had pretty high self-esteem as a child!"

"At the time, was Yaron your boyfriend?"

"He was never my boyfriend."

"Are you saying you and he didn't have a romantic relationship? So, really, who is Yaron, for you?"

"Yaron was this kid I admired. He was one of those kids who was just good at everything—smart, handsome, cool. We all just looked up to him. Have you seen *The Princess Bride*?" Dr. Diamond visibly searched his memory and came up empty. "Never mind. I saw it with my girls when they were young. He was like the boy in that movie—all the girls wanted to become his princess. I can't believe at my age I still think this way." She laughed.

"But still, what happened between you? Last week I got the impression there had been passionate love between you."

"If there was passionate love, it was all in my head. Yaron was my classmate in both elementary school and high school. We were in the same places for years, but there was no close contact. We exchanged a few words. It's as he said in his last email: there was no interaction between us. Yet there was always a certain tension in the air, a kind of confusion I think we both felt."

"He never touched you?"

Mika shook her head. "His skin touched mine twice, and both times are seared in my memory. The first time was when I was twelve. All the kids from my class were playing some game. I remember he leaned his back against mine for maybe half a second and then jumped as if he had been shocked by electricity, as though my back was on fire," she smiled.

"Did you have breasts then?" Dr. Diamond cupped his hands in front of his chest, to illustrate his meaning.

"No. I was completely flat then." She was slightly embarrassed by his miming.

"Children usually find ways to touch one another during games or dancing. How is it that you didn't touch one another more than twice?"

"Yaron didn't dance and barely played with us. He was sort of separate, aloof."

Looking pensive, Dr. Diamond asked, "And the second time?"

Mika told him about seeing Yaron at their class reunion, when they were twenty-eight. "He asked about my husband. I told him Shaul was a great guy and that he'd definitely like him. And Yaron asked me why I thought so." Mika gave Dr. Diamond a direct look and said, "You can interpret that any way you like." Dr. Diamond smiled.

"When I said good-bye to him," Mika continued, "I touched his arm to get his attention, and he fixed his eyes on my fingers as if they were casting a spell on him. It was this electric moment, and he only raised his eyes to say good-bye to me once it had passed."

Dr. Diamond looked taken aback. "If so, was this an autistic love—in your head?"

"Yes, there probably was some element of autism. It was all in my head. I have never had a serious conversation with Yaron. Actually, I didn't really know him."

"And what do you remember?"

"Some of my memories of him are pleasant, others less so. When I was ten, I remember, Yaron came over to my house when we came back from school. He came with me into our yard and took an interest in my dog—she was just a little puppy then. He picked her up and brought her close to his face, and she licked his freckled cheeks and nose with her pink tongue. It made him laugh, and I stood by and looked at him with my puppy and also enjoyed it. I enjoyed watching her sweet tickles and laughed along with him, but mostly I remember feeling a slight tingle at how much love he was giving my puppy." She paused a moment and smiled at Dr. Diamond, who seemed enchanted by this memory. "A year or two later, he protected me when this punk from school started pulling my hair just to be a jerk. I was yelling in pain, and Yaron ran over and pushed him away, telling him you don't hurt girls. At that moment I was really thankful, but even more than that, I was mostly just smitten." She smiled, nostalgic. "Don't you think there's some element of valor there? Going out of his way to protect a girl?"

Dr. Diamond agreed.

"I have many mental images of him from back then, kind of shrouded in a sense of childhood anxiety. Mostly, I remember daydreams about one day being his girlfriend. I dreamed he'd hug me. I was convinced if it ever happened, I'd know true joy." She watched her younger self in her mind, perplexed.

"How old were you, then?"

"Less than thirteen, because when I was thirteen something happened that made Yaron stop talking to me."

"What happened?"

"The note." She sighed, bashful. "Child's play." She remembered that when she'd told Shaul about it, he'd been dismissive. "Why are you telling me this kiddie business?" he'd demanded.

Mika paused. She trusted Dr. Diamond. There was something quiet and reassuring about him. He wouldn't brush her aside with, "Grow up, kid." He wouldn't leave her abashed and pathetic, a menopausal woman preoccupied with childhood issues. She took a deep breath, dived into her memories, and, half mesmerized, told him the story of the note.

"If I'm not mistaken, it started on the first day I wore a bra, and one of the straps was showing. That day, Yaron sent a note to his best friend at the time, Eddie, who sat next to me. I remember Eddie read it and smiled, as if he'd just read the most scandalous gossip, and he passed it to me. Yaron was so angry. 'Give it back, don't let her read it.' I was so curious. God, I thought maybe there was some connection to my new bra, I wasn't sure. I took the note and shoved it into my bag. I thought I'd read it later, when I was alone. As soon as the bell rang, Yaron demanded that I give it back—he was so aggressive that I refused. He turned bright red, shoved me out of the way, and opened my bag. I begged him to stop, but he wouldn't. He went through all of my things—my papers, snacks, my notebooks, my pens, my menstrual pads...I asked—I begged—for him to stop, but he wouldn't. He just searched frantically until he found the note, then threw my bag on a bench and left, still so angry. And I was torn up—humiliated, hurt, angry about the violation. I was shaking and tearing up. I felt like I was bleeding."

"It almost sounds like you are describing a rape," Dr. Diamond replied sympathetically.

"It was a humiliating invasion. The insult stung mainly because I loved him and he hurt me." Mika felt the pain as if no time had passed.

"Do you have any idea what was in the note?"

"No. I can only assume."

"Apparently the contents were so shameful that Yaron was prepared to humiliate you to prevent his own embarrassment," Dr. Diamond explained.

Mika agreed. "The note appears in my dreams. I dream that Yaron sent me a note, and the wind carried it away. I look into his eyes, and it's like they're saying to me, 'Get away from me. Don't you dare come near me!' He stopped speaking to me from that day on. Our lives have taken separate paths, but my internal antennae have kept track of him on every available frequency." She returned to the present from her trancelike journey into the past when Dr. Diamond asked, "Did you speak about the note in your recent conversations with Yaron?"

"No. Only with Shaul, but he teased me for what he called my kiddie memories." She sighed.

"Why didn't you ask Yaron what was in the note?"

"How could I ask something like that in the first conversation with someone I hadn't seen in years?"

Dr. Diamond took a book from his bookshelf: *Lying on the Couch* by Dr. Irvin Yalom. He opened it to a chapter describing a woman's dream about her purse and read it to Mika: the purse symbolized female genitalia; research had shown that when women dreamed about their purses being violated, it symbolized rape.

"In Hebrew, the word *nartik* means both vagina and purse. Apparently there's a symbolic connection between the two," Mika thought aloud. "If so, if my experience was something like rape, I should be angry with Yaron and despise him. Why can't I get rid of my obsession?"

"The violation of the purse is in the nature of a presexual rape," Dr. Diamond elucidated. "It has all the elements of sexual rape, penetration, helplessness, pain, and shame. But there is no sexual act here. Yaron acted to protect himself, and you were hurt. The wound reopened when the memories stirred, and now you feel a need to help it form a scab and heal. One of the ways to deal with trauma is to talk about the experience, not to bury it, but to try to process it. In most cases, the victim of the trauma wants to hear that the aggressor regrets the act, is sorry, and wants to be forgiven. The desire to talk to Yaron could be part of your need to heal the wound."

"But why now? After all, so many years have gone by. Presexual rape is like a prehistoric event," Mika persisted.

"Maybe you're scared of drying up, of moving on to the next phase. Fear of menopause? Maybe the wish to return to childhood is strong in you because, as Nietzsche observed, childhood is the happiest age since it contains no past and no future."

Mika looked doubtfully at him. The explanation wasn't satisfactory.

At their next meeting, Mika told Dr. Diamond about a dream in which Shaul gave her a small plastic container, closed and sealed, like the ones they used in medical laboratories to examine stool. Shaul said that the container belonged to a girl Mika didn't know, and he asked her to return it to the girl. In the dream, Mika opened it and used the excrement like ink. She wrote a few smeared-excrement words on a card and planned to send it to the girl. As the dream progressed, the card began to stink.

Dr. Diamond listened intently. "The excrement relates to a shameful incident in your childhood. Shaul hands you the container and asks you to return it to the girl. He thinks there's something stinky from your childhood that should be sent back to where it belongs. In the dream, you open the sealed container—like your memories—and use the excrement to write on the card, which is like the card you sent to Yaron, which was really written to your inner child, whom you wanted to meet. The card is written with materials associated with childhood. The excrement could symbolize shame, as it's smelly, but it is also a very personal, internal substance that must naturally emerge."

"I feel the shame, mainly," Mika admitted. "I shouldn't have sent the card to Yaron. Look at the state I'm in because of it."

"But the card, like bodily excretion, had to come out," Dr. Diamond declared. "The shame is the bad smell that accompanies the excretion. But...we can't keep it inside, can we?"

"I can think of at least one historical figure who was as crazy as I am." Mika looked at Dr. Diamond ironically. "Hector Berlioz, a famous romantic who fell in love with one woman after another. When he was twelve, he fell desperately in love with a girl who was six years older than he and who obviously wasn't interested. But Berlioz was relentless—he kept loving her in secret, even when she didn't know about it anymore. He wrote the *Fantastic Symphony* for her, knowing she was in town and hoping she'd come to see him backstage after the premiere. And years later, after they'd both been married and separated, he still remembered her and found her when she was fifty-five and a grandmother several times over. And he confessed that he'd never stopped loving her—she was the true love of his life. Can you imagine? This grandma had no idea what to say to the hopeless lifelong romantic who ended up on her doorstep!"

Dr. Diamond smiled with pleasure. "What a story!" he said and proceeded to share his own version of lifelong infatuation, from *Love in the Time of Cholera*, by Gabriel García Márquez, in which Florentino Ariza waited fifty-one years, nine months, and four days for Fermina Daza. The count began on the day she first rejected him, and he kept careful track all his life, waiting for his unattainable beloved. At the end of the book, when they were both in their seventies, the old widow, Fermina Daza, submitted to Florentino Ariza's pleas and consented. The two of them went sailing on the rivers of Colombia, and as he was blissfully holding her gnarled hand, Fermina Daza breathed her last breath and sank into his arms. Nevertheless, his joy was endless: he had succeeded in being at her side when she died. Dr. Diamond concluded the tale with a sweet smile on his face. Mika listened to him, wondering if he himself, like Florentino Ariza, was a stubborn romantic.

Mika and Dr. Diamond laughed ironically.

"But the truth is that I never had the slightest wish to change my life, or Yaron's life. Really, I didn't."

"I know," Dr. Diamond conceded.

In the following sessions, they continued to discuss her dreams. Mika dreamed that she was sitting in the patient's chair in Yaron's clinic. Her legs were exposed, and she awaited his medical treatment of a gaping wound on her thigh. Her friend Alona was standing next to her, holding her hand, whispering that there was good in every evil. Yaron entered, wearing a doctor's gown and looking young and self-confident, as he had at their last meeting. With his back to her as he sterilized instruments and threaded surgical needles to stitch her wound, he reassured her, in English, with the words he had written in his email: "It's all good."

Dr. Diamond inquired as to the exact location of the open wounds. Mika shifted in her chair, embarrassed, and pointed to her inner thigh, near the crotch, aware of his eyes fixed on her. "I can't open my legs here," she said, blushing. And Dr. Diamond gave her an understanding smile.

"This is definitely a matter of presexuality," he said, confirming his first diagnosis. "In the dream, you are looking for a way to treat and heal your wound with Yaron's help. And in reality?"

"In reality, as in the dream, his words were soothing. The wound hurt because Yaron stopped speaking to me for years when he rejected me in disgust."

In the following weeks, Mika was inundated with dreams, as she had been previously by the obsession. The depths of her mind became chaotic, unrestrained, like a broken dam. She dreamed about excrement, about sitting on the toilet in public, for all to see. She wanted to hide, but could not. In another dream she sat on a transparent toilet bowl surrounded by a glass wall. She knew that her product, if it emerged, would be exposed to the world at large, but she could not restrain herself. In another dream, the outer walls of her beautiful house in Hillsborough were smeared with excrement, and she was ashamed because she couldn't get inside. In yet another dream, she was in a public restroom tiptoeing between piles of excrement that prevented her from relieving herself.

Dr. Diamond said, "Something has to emerge from you. Dreams about excrement are related to creativity, not only to shame."

Mika told me all of this in great detail as we sprawled on the velvet armchairs in her house, drinking tall mugs of coffee. In the end, she asked, "Listen, Daniela, Dr. Diamond says that my dreams about excrement are connected to creativity; have you heard that interpretation before?"

"Sure," I told her. "I was a bit surprised when I came across it for the first time. Who thinks of excrement in terms of creativity? But if you put aside the conventional idea that excrement is disgusting, the two elements have a common denominator. After all, both come from the inside, both result from a pressing need, and both represent something that comes exclusively from the maker."

I told Mika about a lecture I'd heard when I was in Zurich a few years ago, by a professor from the Jung Institute, who'd said that excrement in dreams indicated that something had to emerge. He'd shown his audience of professionals some impressive works created by patients after they'd dreamed about excrement. I also told her about a painter and a writer I treated at my clinic, both of whom were creative and had excrement dreams.

"You don't say! It would never have occurred to me. Do you know how many years I've been dreaming about excrement, and all I have is constipation."

We laughed. "How is Dr. Diamond?" I asked.

"He's sweet. Thanks for sending me to him. If he weren't seventy-five years old, I probably wouldn't be able to keep myself from falling in love with him. And then Shaul would really be in trouble!" She was joking, but I could tell from her tone that she was still angry with her husband.

Once Mika internalized Dr. Diamond's interpretation that there was something inside of her that needed to emerge, her obsession with the past turned into music. Since childhood, she had dreamed of composing thrilling music, like Chopin, Schumann, and Brahms, whom she admired. As a child, she had been a voracious reader of composers' autobiographies and longed to be like them. But she'd never dared. When she was studying composition at the Jerusalem Academy of Music and Dance, she tried her hand at composing a partitura and dared to submit it to Professor Edelstein together with the simple exercises in harmony that were part of the homework. Reverently, she knocked on the famous professor's door, hoping to hear his opinion of her first attempt at composition. Sitting in a chair that seemed too narrow to contain his flabby belly, the professor was casually tamping tobacco in his pipe. With a wave of his hand, he indicated that she might be seated. Condescendingly, he told her, "Composition is something exalted. Extremely few are capable of doing it. You should know that, in principle, writing music is not for women, and history has proven it."

With a patronizing smile intended to soften the blow, he dismissed her. She wanted to shout, "What about Clara Schumann? Fanny Mendelssohn? Cécile Chaminade?" But she knew that these exceptions were not the rule and, from that moment on, chose not to imagine otherwise. "Apart from an able few, writing is not for women." Mika was persuaded that what he had said was correct and dismissed herself in her own eyes.

But in the days that she was haunted by memories of her youth, she began to hear isolated notes accompanying the images, among them floating figures like those of Chagall. Slowly, the notes became melody.

Mika selected keys for her notes and played them in her head, dancing between scales. She produced a harmonic texture of chords and broke them into rising and falling arpeggios that accompanied the recurring motif. She composed variations on the theme and eventually penned a full sonata with a dramatic opening, a pastoral midsection, and a finale structured like a rondo.

The sonata never stopped playing in Mika's head, just like the words on the card to Yaron. In her heart of hearts she hoped, like Berlioz, that her music would reach the ears of her childhood love like a returned letter. She sat with her fingers on the piano and felt rushes of inspiration. The inner sounds accompanying the pictures became authentic. Mostly, she liked the sounds she heard, but at times she sensed inauthenticity, and it was like a stench that imbued her with shame for the crudeness of her notes. Mika wrote, erased, and wrote again, editing and expanding until her discomfort eased.

She continued in an interminable expulsion of melodies—written with the enthusiasm of someone freed from chronic constipation. In her heart, she thanked Dr. Diamond for unclogging the blockage.

Mika's outpouring soon produced two sonatas for piano; an opus for violin, piano, and flute; and a cantata for choir, soprano, and piano. She also wrote an opus for piano and orchestra, which she entered into a competition for beginner composers in California. To her surprise, she won first prize.

Upon receiving the letter informing her of her success, she phoned Shaul to share the happy news.

"We have to celebrate," he said and suggested a romantic dinner at Bellavista, a French-Italian restaurant that Mika loved. It had a magnificent view from the sky to the valley, from San Carlos to the horizon. They entered the restaurant hand in hand before sunset, when there was still visibility from the mountaintop, and watched giant aircrafts taking off and landing at San Francisco Airport. After the sunset, the valley became a glittering blanket of lights that spread to the bay, where they suddenly bordered darkness.

Mika and Shaul relished the Rockefeller oysters, chewed on frog legs, savored escargot, and nibbled on poulet à la Jerusalem while sipping red Bordeaux. Afterward, as Shaul kissed the Brigitte Bardot lips that had lost some of their softness over the years, tasting on them the Grand Marnier soufflé that had broken her resolve and her strict diet, he lingered on the aroma of the Boucheron perfume she'd dabbed behind her ears and whispered to her that he was so, so proud to be the husband of a celebrated composer. But Mika had not forgotten the anger that she still harbored, even in those intimate moments.

"Shaul," she said, "how could you hurt me like that?" With some hesitation, she reminded him of the telephone call with Yaron.

"I was afraid," he said, and she was amazed to see the frankness and pain in his eyes.

Mika couldn't believe her ears. Shaul, the successful man who never failed; the one whose every word was respected by all—including Mika; he who always managed to surprise her. Shaul, her man, father of her children, flesh of her flesh, afraid?

She took his hand, kissed it, and said, "Don't be afraid. There's no reason to be."

"How do you explain the connection between my obsession—my breakdown—and the burst of creativity?" Mika asked Dr. Diamond.

His words carried the weight of wisdom gained through a privileged view into countless lives: "Childhood is a sort of inexhaustible well of emotion. We draw strength from it throughout our lives. At times, we struggle to fill the cracks. At times, we struggle to fill the well with fresh water, so that it doesn't run dry. In your case, Mika, that well overflowed suddenly and powerfully one day in the middle of your life. You have to rejoice in this overflow…you have to savor it…"

PART THREE

—

SPRING

Chapter 9

Gabi and Danny traveled to Monterey for a romantic weekend. Thrilled at the idea of reviving the romantic side of their marriage, Gabi had booked an ocean-view suite at the Monterey Bay Inn. She had primped herself both physically and emotionally for the trip, with an electric massage deep-layer facial that promised to halt the ravages of time, at least momentarily, as well as a visit to the leg-waxing salon. Per my advice, she bought some lacy underwear for the occasion, although she wasn't sure at which stage of the evening lingerie would be expected to appear. She imagined herself in the hot panties, slowly undressing in front of Danny, revealing long slender legs that in reality she did not possess, dancing rhythmically, like Nicole Kidman in *Moulin Rouge*. Or maybe doing a seductive belly dance, wearing a bra with round cups that lifted and presented her quivering breasts. But she rejected the idea of this dance, too, because it was likely to make her belly, rather than her small breasts, quiver. Well, let it be. It remained to be seen whether the lace panties would arouse her dormant libido, she thought, doubting their power.

In the early evening, Gabi and Danny sat in the hotel restaurant, facing the wall-sized window from which they viewed a red sun setting into the waves of the Pacific. The sun's dying rays illuminated the rock formations that adorned the shore, whitened like snowcaps by the droppings of generations of seagulls. Gabi made a mental note to remember the details of the view in order to immortalize them in a painting. Danny asked if she would join him in a glass of wine before the meal. She refused, reminding him that she did not drink. He looked at her pleadingly and intensely, and she relented, not wanting to spoil the festive occasion, which she regarded as a nostalgic encounter with a past admirer—an encounter that might reignite their romance.

"Do you still love me?" she dared to ask, looking at him with trepidation over the rim of her wineglass. She felt her constant awareness of the layers of fat that surrounded her, and of the profound sense of betrayal that stemmed from years of Danny's unapologetic infidelity.

"Of course," Danny whispered, as if he were serenading her. "To me, you will always be the prettiest girl in class." He looked at her, and she knew that he was seeing a girl with blue eyes and black braids.

She looked into his eyes and, for that moment, believed him. She remembered Danny as the boy who had carried her backpack on their class field trip, who had helped her with her math homework, and who had been the best athlete and student in their class. She remembered the evening, during summer vacation at the end of ninth grade, when her parents were away at a wedding in Haifa, and she seized the opportunity to invite Danny into her bedroom. When she was twelve, her mother had, in a moment of unusual generosity, allowed her to choose the color of the curtains in her room. Gabi chose bubblegum pink. When she was older and asked if she could change the curtains, her mother refused and said, "It was your choice to begin with."

In the pink room, under the Auguste Renoir poster of the pianist and her little sister, they lost their virginity to one another. Tenderly, pleasurably, unhurriedly, they kissed, caressed, and embraced one another, like two cuddling kittens. Without exchanging many words, they found themselves naked, with Danny pounding on the narrow gates of her virginity. She opened herself wide, clutching him with both hands, helping him to penetrate her. When he was inside, her tears flowed.

"Does it hurt?" he asked in alarm.

"No, I'm crying because my heart is beating so fast."

He licked the tears and softly kissed her eyelids. "I love you, too," he murmured.

Breathing heavily, he withdrew and lay with his head on her small breasts that were still tender with growing pains. They lay entwined for a long time, moved by their powerful experience. If emotions were butterflies, she'd thought, the room would be full of them fluttering colorfully up and down, excited, filling the house, the street, the neighborhood, the whole country. She felt so much love for him.

Now, Gabi asked herself if she still felt those powerful emotions for Danny, but she found no answer. She was unable to overlook the thirty years that had passed and the hundreds of lovers she imagined he had taken to bed.

During the French-Vietnamese meal, they spoke about the children: about Roni's boyfriend, Nick the prick; Itai's learning disability; Gil's brilliance in algebra; Yaniv's karate lessons that left him no time for homework. They joked about little Keren's recently developed interests in God and death, and the guileless gems of wisdom she'd spoken on the matters. They also touched on Danny's attempts to find a replacement for himself at work. Gabi didn't raise the issue of their return to Israel. It was only after they returned to their room and renewed their love, after Danny withdrew from her body and kissed her beautiful eyes, as he had on their first night, only then did Gabi say, very softly, "Danny, I'm going back to Israel this summer. Do you understand?"

"Yes, yes," he whispered.

"We have to talk to the children and present a united front."

"We'll talk." He nodded.

"Promise?"

"Promise," he answered in a caressing voice.

Since he was in a tender mood, she didn't have to justify herself as she'd planned—not a single word about the sacrifices she'd made for him over the years, about how she'd never wanted to leave Jerusalem but had followed him without complaint. Not a word about how important it was for her conscience to live close to their parents now that they were old, how important it was to raise the children as Israelis, and not even about how it was finally her turn to navigate the direction of the family they'd built together. Apparently, Danny already knew. When he whispered his promise to stand by her, she felt the butterflies filling the room again. Her heart swelled for him. The tears flowed once more, and Danny licked them exactly as he had then, in her pink room, under the Renoir poster.

She gathered courage and asked, "Danny, are you still attracted to me, in spite of all the weight I've gained?"

Danny looked at her with authentic admiration and said again, "You have to understand that for me you have always been the prettiest girl in class, and now you are a wonderful woman. The more you weigh, the more Gabi I have to love."

Her heart skipped a beat, then melted. She at once felt she was his lover, his wife, the mother of his children, and, his friend; for the moment she was able to forget his wandering, his hunger for a taste of different flesh.

The following morning, Gabi opened her eyes, put on her glasses, and looked at the view beyond the window. Her breath stopped. She hurriedly donned the warm bathrobe, courtesy of the hotel, and stepped out onto the balcony. There was the smell of seaweed, and the icy morning air froze her cheeks. She unpacked her painting gear, which she always brought wherever she went, along with her toothbrush, body lotion, face cream, and makeup. As though hypnotized, she set up her easel, stretched the canvas onto it, arranged the oil paints and brushes on the wrought iron table that stood on the white marble-tiled balcony, and began painting. She drew the vast carpets of lawn on the golf course that spread as far as the water's edge in streaks of light and dark greens. Those rolling green hills resembled the nude back of a woman sprawled on her stomach, with well-raked sand dunes across her hips and the small of her back.

Gabi colored the ocean a deep greenish blue and marked the distant waves with short white brushstrokes, whereas the high, foam-crested breakers were highlighted with a blend of white and flashes of gold.

In the center of the course, she immortalized a golfer dressed in white, his torso twisted, his hands gripping the club, his right leg stretched behind him, his left leg bent, the moment after he had hit the ball. She painted the golf cart next to him, with a young caddy in the driver's seat.

Gabi examined the preliminary sketch with satisfaction; she would complete the painting in her studio at home, where she would be able to pay more attention to refining the details and mixing the paints.

In their room, Danny was plugged into the computer, checking the night's email.

"Good morning, Danny. You're missing the beautiful view, staring at that screen. Come, let's go for a walk before breakfast."

Gabi handed Danny his jeans and sweatshirt, leaving him no escape. He dressed, accepting the decree. "You win some, you lose some," he mumbled, thrusting his hairy legs into the jeans. Gabi dressed comfortably and wrapped herself in a windbreaker. They strolled hand in hand along the paved paths winding around the golf course and leading to the beach, while Danny explained the rules of golf, and she listened absentmindedly. Yes, she knew there were eighteen holes, and you had to hit the ball to get it into a hole with the minimum number of strokes; people spent hours on this boring activity, she mused.

The smell of seaweed grew stronger as they neared the shore, where the waves crashed onto the sharp gray rocks scattered along the waterline, and where white gulls and brown-winged pelicans gathered, crying their distinctive calls. Sleek, round sea lions reclined on two massive rocks protruding from the sea some distance from the shore, sunning themselves, and reminding Gabi of her youth.

Gabi and Danny sat on a flat, even rock. Waves broke all around them, nearly touching their feet and leaving bubbles of foam in their wake. Gabi's hand warmed in the clasp of his palm, and her heart swelled with bliss. Danny, however, was somewhat indifferent to the glories of nature and preferred an urban environment. He found the sea of people spilling onto Fifth Avenue during lunch hour thrilling—thousands of heads like a human cascade. He was amazed by the surging masses in the Tokyo underground, dressed mostly in dark colors, filing into the subways with exemplary, decorous obedience at the end of the workday. He preferred architectural towers and structures to these rocks, which he regarded as insipid despite the sunbathing sea lions. But that morning Danny accompanied Gabi and agreed to spend some time in nature, for her sake. He even refrained from complaining about how icy cold it was outdoors in comparison to the warm room awaiting them in the hotel, the earsplitting shrieks of the birds, and the rumbling of his empty stomach.

"Danny, what are we going to tell the children tomorrow?"

"Tell the children?" He pretended to have forgotten their talk of the night before.

"How are we going to present the subject of our return to Israel?" she persisted.

"We'll describe the situation as it is, without embellishing anything," he said dryly, like a boss dismissing a secretary with a wave of the hand.

"What do you mean?"

"We'll tell them you've decided to return to Israel this summer and I have to stay here and run the company until they find a replacement for me," he said plainly, as if talking to a stranger.

"Danny, they need to feel secure in knowing that you're coming with us, or they'll become anxious."

"I can't promise anything. I have no idea when we'll find a replacement, and I can't commit myself to a timetable. I'll join you when I manage to point the company in the right direction." He turned away from Gabi, checking his phone. His face was long and uninterested and he looked like he was going to lose his temper at any moment. Then he put his phone in his pocket and looked at her. "Gabi, I just raised sixty million dollars—I can't just get up and leave now. The company's in the process of changing direction. The market changed—the first product isn't selling. We suffered huge losses, and in order to recoup I need to work on a total paradigm shift and release a new product in an entirely different sphere. You know all this!"

"Yes, I know you raised funds in Japan. All those talks with Takagi San, the phone calls at four in the morning. Yes, I've heard you speaking about a change of direction lately, maybe in my dreams. But you're always raising funds and changing direction, so what else is new?" Gabi complained.

"Gabi, don't you remember how bad things were for the company, just a year ago?" Danny reminded her how the company had gone public, raised a fortune, then tanked. "The market can change directions in an instant, and whoever's not prepared to change with it dies out," he said. "Do you understand any of this? I carry tremendous responsibility—not only for *our* financial situation, but also for the finances of hundreds of my employees. Not to mention my reputation! I cannot get up and leave whenever I feel like it. The position of a CEO demands responsibility over and above what outsiders can see."

Gabi knew this tune by heart. She'd been hearing it her entire married life. Ever since Danny had announced that he was going to France to study at Fontainebleau, he had repeatedly hidden behind an armor of "facts," evading open, honest, face-to-face discussion. This time, she had decided that it was her turn to face him with the facts and, once and for all, find out where she and the children stood on his list of priorities. To her disappointment, she had been reminded that they would never come first. The company, the employees, and his professional reputation would always supersede them. As Danny understood it, this was the way it should be. As far as family obligations went, he regarded himself as responsible only for the family income. The rest was insignificant and dispensable.

Gabi withdrew her hand from his and sank under a wave of self-pity.

"I should have known," she accused him and herself, "that there was no real chance of you standing with me." In her heart, she knew that the previous night's acrobatic exercises between the sheets had neither moved Danny a millimeter away from his original plan nor really satisfied her. His sweet words now became hollow and infuriating.

"If you would at least give me and the children some idea of what to expect, at least an estimate, Danny," she said, on the verge of tears.

"Gabi, you need to stop with this unreasonable pressure. That's the situation as it stands at the moment. If you insist on talking to the children, that's what we'll say. If you were less stubborn, we could plan our return to Israel at a time that's convenient for all of us. I suggest you think twice before talking to the children and before we make decisions."

Danny sounded angry and impatient. As far as he was concerned, the conversation was over. Gabi felt rebuked, exactly as she had when Danny chastised her because she failed to understand the simplicity of the algebra equations he tried to help her solve when they were in high school.

Gabi rose heavily to her feet, Danny held out his hand to help her, but she recoiled. She suddenly missed the children. Their rekindled romance was over, on her part, at least for now. Back in the room, Gabi began to pack her canvases, paints, and brushes. The superb hotel breakfast was tasteless. The veggie omelet and the rich chocolate cake had lost their promised magic. Danny and Gabi chewed in silence, making no attempt to ease the tension, although both of them tried to act as if nothing had changed, while the waiter bounced from one to the other, suggesting, "More tea? Coffee?"

While Danny loaded the luggage into the trunk, Gabi waited in the passenger seat, eager to shorten the romantic weekend and return to the only pleasure that never disappointed her: her children. She changed her mind about the visit to see the elephant seals on the beach at Año

Nuevo, which she had planned in advance. Her aversion to Danny was like a tangible wall. It would be best if he took a plane and embarked on some journey, she thought. She no longer planned for her and Danny to gather the children and announce that they had agreed to return to Israel. She also gave up on the other option she'd envisioned—that they would hold a levelheaded family discussion and allow everyone to voice their concerns. She leaned her head against the passenger-side window of the Lamborghini, closing her eyes to signal to Danny her unwillingness to converse. Her mind drifted to the unused lacy panties packed away in the trunk. She'd return them to Victoria's Secret tomorrow.

Danny started the car, his mind on Gabi. Something had come over her, he thought. Probably something that would pass. The burning urge to return to Israel reminded him of her whims during her pregnancies. All of a sudden, she had to have something, an art nouveau table, or a designer kettle. In most cases, the urge passed sooner or later. One couldn't take Gabi too seriously, he reminded himself. In the end she calmed down, like the passing of a summer storm.

Danny's experience with women in general, and with Gabi in particular, had taught him that taking their wishes too seriously was a waste of time in the best of cases and, in the worst, could seriously knock him off course. And he, Danny, had not the slightest intention of changing direction at this stage of his life. Everything looked good and promising, so why spoil things? All the same, Gabi was dear to him, and he wanted to keep the peace with her. What was more, he'd have liked to do what was best for her, as long as it didn't mean altering his big life plans.

And Danny was Danny: when he had a problem, he boiled it down to its essence, looked for a practical solution, and took action.

The acute problem: what to do about Gabi.

The essence: how to please Gabi and make her happy.

The practical solution: a party!

A brilliant idea, indeed, Danny concluded. We'll throw an unforgettable party for Gabi that will make her give up the idea of going back to Israel. It'll give her something new to think about for many months after the party, and we'll all get back to a place of contentment. He silently applauded himself. Moments later, he was already in another world, thinking of his cut of the European market, recently acquired by his salespeople in Copenhagen, and his cut of the Japanese market, about to be acquired. He needed reinforcements in the sales ranks; he had to arm them with the sophisticated equipment developed by his R&D people and conduct the campaign with an astute sales strategy undreamed of by his competitors. Danny already saw himself as the victorious leader on horseback, brandishing his sword before a cheering crowd like Napoleon returning to his devoted masses after a victorious battle.

Chapter 10

Dr. Warner left a message on my voicemail informing me that Lori's condition was stable. She had been treated with Zoloft, an antidepressant, and a low dosage of an antipsychotic sometimes prescribed for patients with bipolar disorder. He said that there were no incidents of bulimia or self-mutilation and that in his opinion she was ready to be discharged. He also said he didn't think there was any connection between her guilt feelings and the death of her husband. He had discussed the accident with the chief of the local police station, who had told him that the husband's tragic death was an accident. Furthermore, he said, the insurance company had insisted on investigating the possibility of murder and what had emerged was that the deceased had been alone at the time of his death, on his way to the San Francisco Marina, where his private yacht was anchored. He was far from home or any other surroundings in which someone could have tampered with the car. If it had been a case of sabotage, said the policeman, the engine would have exploded soon after ignition and not two hours later. The file had been closed. Dr. Warner ended his message by saying that the ward nurse would be in touch to make an appointment for Lori's continued treatment.

Lori's appearance, when she came to my clinic a few days after her release from the hospital, suggested that she had wasted no time sitting idle. As befitted a new millionaire, she had gone on a spending spree in Union Square. She was wearing a sheer Stella McCartney dress, with her visible red bra leaving nothing to the imagination, Prada boots that reached well above her knees, and, slung on her shoulder, a leather Marc Jacobs bag like the one that had caught my eye two weeks earlier but remained on the shelf because my conscience rebelled against its exorbitant price. The false eyelashes were in place and on her colorful lips was a pampered smile. However, the huge plastic hoops in her ears bore witness to the fact that her expensive, ostentatious taste had not become more refined.

Lori sat facing me on the couch and, with a little sigh, began to describe the memorial service for her husband, the day before. "It was so beautiful and dignified"—she fluttered her eyelashes—"just as I had planned. Everyone was silent except the people who gave eulogies. Everyone was dressed so beautifully. My husband's friends from work and the yacht club were there. My sister sat next to me for support."

She gave me a thoughtful look. "After I sang my husband's favorite song, people came up to me and complimented me on my voice. I sang with all my heart. I gave it everything I had," she said on a low, drawn-out note. She placed her delicate hands with red nails over her heart, shed a little tear, and dried it with the tissue I offered her. "Some of the guests gave me their cards and invited me to get in touch if I needed any help. Some really nice men asked if they could come and see me soon. Since Steve and I broke up, I saw no reason not to. I'm meeting three of them next week."

I had to make an effort to keep a neutral expression on my face and not reveal my feelings. I remembered Lori's stories about her days as a star cheerleader for the high school football team, when she personally "cheered on" every one of the ten players in turn. And her penchant for promiscuous sex didn't end there. She used to hang around hotels in Los Angeles with her sister and friends, drinking and getting high, waking up to find herself naked in some nameless stranger's bed. Sometimes, she said, she remembered that there had been a few anonymous men in the room, who had likely all sampled her body. Only shame prevented her from disclosing how much she was paid for her services. It was nothing short of a miracle that she had never become involved with violent men. Actually, the miracle was that she had met her husband, who had saved her from a life of prostitution.

The danger that Lori might drag herself down again was obvious to me. I conceptualized her clinical picture: a young woman, with borderline personality disorder and severe disability in making emotional connections, who was unable to build normal relationships with people in her life, and who viewed others as instruments to meet her needs at any given moment, with no strings attached. She was incapable of basing a relationship on trust or on love, having never experienced such a relationship in her past—certainly not with her mother, who had thrown her out into the snow as a disciplinary act. No wonder Lori never perceived the possibility of any other kind of relationship. Just as a computer cannot recognize software that has not been installed, Lori's mind could not decode patterns of communication based on mutual love, trust, consideration, understanding, empathy, or the ability to give and take, and store the full range of emotions that comprised healthy communication. The therapeutic relationship would aim to install the missing software for Lori. Building trust is not a simple matter. The process takes time, patience, acceptance, and the ability to pass the many tests a patient sets for the therapist. I hesitated. What should I do right now to lay the foundations of trust and prove to Lori that I was on her side?

"Lori, do you remember our talk about the connection between love and sex? You used to go to bed with many men you didn't know, because you didn't believe anybody could love you in some other way. Remember how we talked about how you deserved to feel safe and loved by a man you're having intimate relations with?"

"Yes, yes, I remember." Lori nodded her head energetically, like a diligent student. "I'm not planning to sleep with them," she promised. "I'd just like to get to know a few of them. Maybe they're nice. Maybe one of them will help me develop my career as a singer."

I doubted both possibilities. My ability to protect Lori from herself was limited, I reminded myself. Part of the therapy was to enable her to experience the pain directly and to understand it during the therapy process. Lori was living a life disconnected from past and future. She must have totally repressed the past, for how was it possible to carry so much pain and still be smiling and sexy? As for the future, it seemed about as substantial to her as the skin of an onion. The only thing that hinted at any consideration of the future was her desire to become a singer. She was a typical example of living in the here and now, I mused; a perfect manifestation of existentialist philosophy. Yet something was missing: existentialism means using mindfulness to make responsible choices among alternatives, whereas it was definitely beyond Lori's intellectual ability to make self-aware, thoughtful decisions about steps to be taken. I estimated Lori's IQ to fall in the low average range and did not expect her to have meaningful insight with regard to understanding the connections between her urges and her emotions. Furthermore, in my opinion, Lori drifted through life like a leaf in the wind, oblivious to dangers and to her inability to cope with them. My therapeutic task in dealing with Lori was to provide professional intervention with the aim of helping her differentiate between good and bad in a way that would minimize the risks she faced.

I wondered about Steve, the man she was with a few months ago. I wanted to raise the subject so that I could encourage her to have an ongoing relationship.

"Lori, before you were hospitalized, you told me that you'd parted from Steve. Have you seen him since then?"

A long silence. Her eyes were fixed on the carpet. When she raised her head and looked straight at me, I noticed a tear on her cheek. I watched her intently. "I don't know if I was raped or not," she mumbled brokenly.

"What happened, Lori?"

She hesitated. "One evening, Steve turned up drunk and high. He'd had a cocktail of coke and ecstasy and offered me some. I said no. He couldn't fall asleep, but I was very tired and fell asleep immediately. A little later, he woke me up and before I realized what was going on, he shoved me back on the bed and stuck his dick in my mouth. He pushed and pushed deep into my throat, and he was holding my head so hard to stop me from moving that I thought he was going to break my neck. I was sure I was going to die. I couldn't breathe, or shout, or move. He just went on banging his dick into me. It hurt so much. I knew he was high, and I thought this craziness would go on forever. Then, he came in my mouth and left me there wanting to die. I was crying so hard."

She looked sadly at me. "But that wasn't the end. When it was over, he decided it was my turn. I was crying and begging him to leave me alone, but he started biting me...there. It was so painful. I yelled at him to stop and go away, but he just kept biting and biting until I bled." Lori wiped her tears.

I cringed in my chair and felt a shock of horror between my legs as I listened to her description. I wanted to put my arms around her, to stroke her, to soothe her, to protect her, to take her home and adopt her as a daughter. I felt helpless. I couldn't help but think about how one session a week was like a drop in her ocean, with no potential to truly affect anything in Lori's sorrowful condition.

My thoughts then wandered to my daughter, Ayelet. I prayed that she would never be exposed to such insane situations and consoled myself with the thought that her insight and wisdom made it unlikely. She would never mess around with addicts; the enduring love of her family would act as a safety net even when her parents were not physically nearby. *No!* That would not happen to my Ayelet. I pushed my anxiety aside.

I emerged from my reverie and looked worriedly at Lori. "Yes, Lori. That was rape. When a man has sexual relations with you against your will, it's rape. I suggest you contact the police and press charges for sexual assault, even though it involved a man you know. You should do this so that the police have a report on Steve."

"I don't want police, I don't want to see him or be reminded of him."

"Have you been examined by a doctor since the rape?"

"I don't want a doctor, I'm okay." She shook her head, stubbornly resisting.

"Was that the first time Steve sexually assaulted you?"

"He was never as high as he was that night."

"Drugs are dangerous, Lori. You have to keep away from drugs and people who use drugs. For your own safety. Looking after your health and making sure that nobody can harm you should be your first priority. You can't forget that personal rule."

I felt a bit like a scolding teacher, but I hoped that what I said would penetrate her awareness and be filed there as a defense.

Lori nodded again, like an obedient student, and I again asked myself if my words would have any effect. I didn't want to point an accusing finger at the victim. That was not my intention.

"You were right to part from Steve, Lori. Once a sadist, always a sadist. That behavior will repeat itself one of these days, so I recommend that you report him to the police. There are special therapy groups for sexual deviants and people who can't control their sex and violence drives. Only intensive therapy can change them."

"I told him to stay away from me, not only because of the rape, but also because he wants my money."

"Well done. About the money, I want to refer you to a consultant who will help you create a budget and advise you how to invest your money in a long-term savings plan, so that you can support yourself for a long time." I gave her the business card of an investment consultant named Carol Johnson, whose daughter was in Maya's class, and she thanked me.

The session was nearly over. Lori said she felt relieved after talking about the rape and left with the same sweet smile as before. It was as if the shocking story of the rape had been returned to the shelves of her heart where it was locked away, never to be retrieved again, much like other harrowing tales I'd heard from her in the past, which all sounded as if they had happened in another world, in another life, to another woman, and which never seemed to disturb Lori in the least.

Chapter 11

"Mom, Danny's on the phone," Alon shouted from the living room just as my hands were covered in egg yolk from making schnitzel for the kids. I rinsed and dried my hands and reached for the phone. Strange. Danny didn't usually phone to make weekend plans, or to coordinate the children's rides or activities. This was usually up to Gabi and me.

"Hi, Danny," I said. "To what do I owe the honor?"

"Can't I just call to hit on a beautiful woman?" Danny never missed an opportunity to flirt.

"I'm married," I answered with a laugh.

"So what? Can't you come up with a better excuse?"

I admit, I'd forgotten the rules of the game. I couldn't whip out a feisty wisecrack from my dormant archives. Danny couldn't resist the temptation to make yet another conquest, or at least make me giggle. And however ridiculous the occasion, I was flattered by the thought that Danny might regard me as a challenge.

"Daniela, sweetie, I need your help. I want to throw an out-of-this-world, unforgettable surprise party for Gabi at the end of June. I'm thinking of something really big. How do you feel about taking on the planning?"

"Give me a bit more info here, Danny. What do you want me to take on?"

"To be honest, all of it. Except the date, which is the last Saturday of June."

"And what do you mean by an 'unforgettable' party?" I persisted.

"Something like the party Haleli Bat-Ami gave for Yossi a year ago, or even bigger. The sky's the limit, Daniela. Whatever you want."

I immediately recalled the party for Yossi Giladi. The images flashed before my eyes: the exuberant dancing to the sound of the famous rock band flown specially from Israel for the occasion, the ecstatic dancers shouting the familiar lyrics at the top of their lungs, waving their arms toward the stage. It had been truly unforgettable.

"Danny, you're the best," I said, thinking nervously that these were probably the words he heard from countless women lying beneath him. "I'll call Gila, Nira, Mika, and Anita right away. We'll set up a marvelous production team. Don't worry!" This would be a really nice project. We, the girls, would show Danny what Gabi was worth.

I fried the schnitzel, prepared spaghetti for dinner, and sent emails to Mika, Nira, and Gila. I'd meet Anita tomorrow on the way to work. I told them about the surprise party and asked if they'd help. Mika said she was swamped with concerts and trips for the next two months, but that she'd be happy to volunteer her house and gardens for the event. Gila loved the idea, and we arranged to meet for lunch at Max's Opera Café next week, while Nira turned up at my house as if on cue.

No, she hadn't read the email, she said in reply to my question. "Is Yoel at home?" she interjected.

She was obviously disappointed to hear that he was not; the look in her eyes said this was not a social visit.

"Tell him I can't make our cycling trip this weekend." At Nira's urging, Yoel had recently begun training with her team. "I'm going to Israel. It's urgent."

"Did something happen, Nira?"

A heavy sigh. "I spoke to my sister on the phone. She heard from a friend of Tomer's that he doesn't have a warm army jacket. His kit bag was stolen on the first day of training, and since then the boy has been without a jacket and without a water bottle. Do you know what that means? Morning and night in the rain and cold without a jacket and out on patrol with no water bottle. Can you imagine? It's making me sick." She wiped her forehead. "How can I sleep at night under a warm blanket when Tomer doesn't have a jacket? Tell me!" She stared at me. I was speechless.

Finally I said, "Can't he get another jacket and water bottle?"

"Tomer's a nice boy from Palo Alto. He doesn't know how to work the system like the Israeli kids do. Rami said he should 'replace' his missing gear, but Tomer had no idea what Rami meant." The first thing boys in the Israeli army learned to do was steal from each other to avoid being punished for having a missing gear. Of course, a boy who'd grown up in Palo Alto would lack the necessary street smarts. "Until I see that boy with a jacket and with a water bottle on his belt, there's no way I can sleep," Nira declared. She shut her eyes and swallowed a tear.

"It's hard to be so far from Tomer," I said, and she, misinterpreting my unspoken subtext of disbelief as criticism of her decision to remain in the States while her son served overseas, continued, "I keep thinking of going back to Israel. To live there. Near him. But what about Rami? He won't leave the start-up. No way. And what about all of my cats? Who'll take care of them? It's not exactly possible to move seventy cats to an apartment in Ra'anana. I'm so torn. For months now, we've been looking for a house in the center of Israel—something that could house all of us—us and the cats." A stubborn tear rolled down to her chin, and Nira wiped it with the back of her hand, sniffling.

I hugged her. I understood that between her anxiety over Tomer's missing jacket and her preoccupation with feeding Rami and the cats, there was no use in mentioning Gabi's surprise party. And I knew that if there were a land bridge connecting America and Israel, Nira would have embarked on a cross-continental marathon in the wake of the missing-jacket-and-water-bottle crisis without a moment's delay.

"Have a good journey, and give Tomer a kiss from me."

Again, I looked at Nira as though she were a mirror of the future and imagined myself sleepless and dashing between continents in a panic over my own beloved son. Even the dog looked at me with a knowing, tortured expression, as if he foresaw the future drawing near.

Anita received me at the door of her beautiful home in the Los Altos Hills. It was a new house, built two years ago by a smart contractor who had invested his money in the right piece of land, and the Eitan family had purchased it for a fortune. She motioned me in, her cell phone stuck between her ear and shoulder while she murmured, "Yes, Yossi, no problem, we'll meet at Evvia at one o'clock." She ended the call and tucked a brunette curl into the heavy bun on her neck, explaining that Yossi Giladi had just called to say he would be late for their lunch appointment because he was going for a flight around the bay in his private plane first. Yossi liked eating at Evvia, the Greek restaurant that served the best moussaka in the Bay Area (apart from Gabi's which, of course, was unmatched).

Anita led me through the entrance hall, which had an arched ceiling and rounded walls. Alcoves along the walls held minimalist bronze statues by Bruno Bernoulli. In Anita's house, every feature and every ornament was like a living presence. It was impossible to ignore the pieces so painstakingly collected for the purpose of producing awe.

We arrived at the spacious salon, where Anita seated herself on a Louis XVI mustard velvet sofa, imported from Paris, which perfectly matched her vast cream-and-pistachio silk Tabrizi-style carpet. The sofa faced a low, square mahogany table with corners carved in antique French style. Three heavy leather armchairs on the other side of the table perfected the aristocratic, old-money effect.

The Tabrizi was in its second incarnation, a recycled variation of the earlier carpet, made in Isfahan and shipped to California in honor of the family's recent move into this mansion. However, it soon became clear that the carpet brought enjoyment not only to the members of the family but also to the family's golden retriever, who saw in it a spacious meadow—a bright and flowery field for his personal use. To relieve himself.

When Anita awoke one morning to find the dog's mess piled on the carpet, she shrieked and called the maid, who tirelessly rubbed the Isfahan. The stain had faded and Anita had just barely begun to calm down when—heaven help us!—the next day the dog returned to the lovely Isfahan meadow and deposited five disgusting yellow puddles that made Anita completely lose control. She screamed that she should kill the dog, because who the hell needed a dog in a house that had such beautiful, expensive Persian carpets anyway, and it was just a waste of money to clean up after such a stupid animal who failed to recognize the value of a silk rug.

On a phone call across oceans, Anita's father suggested that she strangle the dog—tie him to a tree, put a plastic bag over his head, and seal it. Then her mother piped in that, speaking of carpets, it would be nice if Anita would get around to furnishing the house that she'd bought for her sister Yaffa, because the house was still entirely empty. In the same breath, she mentioned that after all, Anita and Ido had invested a million dollars in Ido's brother Giora's start-up, according to the newspapers; so it was only right that they invest a similar amount in Yaffa's house, to balance things out. And, also speaking of money, her mother asked for the umpteenth time if Anita had made a will—what if something happened to her, God forbid? What if Ido took the whole lot for himself and completely forgot her side of the family? When Anita hung up from the call, she didn't know who annoyed her more—her idiot dog, or her gluttonous mother.

Poor Anita also sought advice from Gila, who suggested taking the dog to a psychologist she knew—a fantastic psychologist who specialized in dogs. Dog owners stayed on a waitlist for months to see her—she was really very much in demand. And Gila had heard that this woman achieved miracles and that two or three sessions would probably be enough to train the dog. This psychologist could probably prescribe the dog some antidepressants, Gila mused, because the core of the problem was no doubt that the dog was depressed.

In the end, the stained Isfahan was donated to a good cause and replaced by its smooth and shiny all-silk brother from Tabriz. As for the golden retriever, from that point on, he was sentenced to wear an electronic collar that issued him a strong electric shock if he even dared to dream of approaching the Tabrizi.

Anita was crazy about the collar—it was a brilliant idea; why hadn't she thought of it before? In all honesty, Anita thought to herself, if she could, she would have strapped similar collars on the children's necks as well and, even better, on Ido's, to prevent him from crossing lines whenever he felt like it. Too bad the collar couldn't be used on humans.

And so we arrive at my meeting with Anita. I sat facing her on the Parisian leather armchair and apologized that Rami and Nira couldn't participate in the WIZO fund-raising evening.

Anita, dressed in a slim pink workout suit for her daily training, looked at me with evident disappointment in my lack of fund-raising talent. She asked if I could think of anything to change their minds and was deeply disappointed when I said there was no way. In response, she whipped out her PalmPilot and noted on her digital to-do list that she'd need to speak to Ido about how to train her friends in sales promotion before assigning them any further philanthropic responsibilities.

Deciding to move on from the topic of my fruitless endeavor, she leaned over toward a photo album laid on the coffee table and explained that she was preparing for an interview with some journalist from Israel who was flying over to talk to her about her nonprofit organization, TechnoKid.

"I have to find a photograph for her that captures the right image," she said leafing through the album. "Last time, they photographed me in the kitchen." In that photograph, she had looked like a model advertising futuristic, high-tech kitchens. The caption had read, ANITA THE IDEAL HOSTESS. As the wife of a successful entrepreneur, she had found the description unbecoming.

"I don't want them to present me as some housewife looking to amuse herself. Anyone who knows me knows that's not me at all. I never cook. I have Raoul for cooking. I have to get the journalists and photographers out of the kitchen," she grumbled. "They photographed Ido sitting on the floor, under his office desk. Since when does Ido sit under his desk? You'd think he sits around under there running his company."

She surveyed the room, pausing to glance at the French table under the crystal chandelier in the dining nook, as if wondering how she would look seated there. She turned a page in the album and took out a photograph of herself bungee jumping in New Zealand and another one showing her free falling in tandem with an instructor in Brazil. Both of those photographs were options, but the one in which she was hugging the former Israeli prime minister by her swimming pool seemed the most suitable. It was at this meeting with the prime minister that she had conceived the idea of the nonprofit organization.

"He deserves credit." She smiled magnanimously. "He said the world is becoming homogeneous—a global village—and it wouldn't be long before people all over the world communicated on the Internet. Everyone would wear jeans and talk in tech lingo. But the problem is that computers haven't reached everywhere in the world just yet," Anita mused, "so part of the population is stuck in the Dark Ages. They all— every child in the world—deserve a computer. The day that computers are available to children in remote villages, children in Arab countries, Palestinian children, we'll be on our way to solving our conflicts—once those generations reach adulthood. That's the basic idea behind the nonprofit organization, and that is the idea I have to promote!" she said resolutely.

I could already imagine the headline: ANITA EITAN FIGHTS FOR THE CHILDREN OF THE WORLD. It would be accompanied by the photograph of Anita embracing the former prime minister, of course. Anita's mother, Marga, would lose no time in showing off to the neighbors. In my mind, I heard her voice with its distinctive Bucharest accent describing the first time she set foot in the Holy Land, wearing a white cashmere coat that soon turned black from the soot of the buses she took to her work as a seamstress in a workshop. And now, see? At last, she would have the satisfaction of waving around the photograph of her daughter in the newspaper—public proof that proletarian seed could indeed rub shoulders with the elite.

"On second thought, maybe it's better not to be associated with the former prime minister. Better not to take sides in the political arena," Anita wondered out loud. "Here's another possibility." She paged through the album and stopped at a photograph of herself standing with that famous *New York Times* columnist, the one who claimed the earth was flat. They had been photographed with his arm around her shoulder, seated on her couch underneath her original Bernoulli. The picture had been taken at the reception she'd held in the famous journalist's honor after he had given a speech at a TechnoKid benefit. He had spoken about strengthening ties and closing gaps between countries, and inspired a great deal of optimism in the crowd.

"But who reads the *Times* in Israel?" Perhaps the famous journalist would go unrecognized. "I need to find myself a PR person to help me brand my public image. Someone like that could advise me which photograph is best to include in the article. What I want is an image of a practical, energetic woman dedicated to worthy causes and who shares her good fortune with people in need. You have no idea how happy it makes me to have children come up to me, crying tears of joy, and thank me for their computers from TechnoKid." Her voice shook with emotion.

"Maybe you should contact Gila and ask her to find out if Talma knows a good PR person," I suggested, remembering that Talma was familiar with the marketing and advertising business in Israel, by virtue of her job as an event planner.

"Talma would probably land me with a lesbian," Anita muttered. "That's the last thing I need. My image would be ruined."

"What do you plan to say to the journalist?" I wanted to know.

"Very simple. That a philanthropic idea in itself is not enough to establish a nonprofit organization." Anita delivered her homily as if preparing for the big moment, and I heard Ido's voice emerging from her throat. "A successful nonprofit organization must be founded on a business model. 'A computer for every child in the Middle East' is a sublime goal that comes at a price and, therefore, I have to build a dynamic system that will reap generous donations. Like every successful, well-based company, this nonprofit organization must also be based on superb human resources. I'll explain to the journalist that the first step is finding the right people and that at the moment I'm selecting the team to lead the action."

I knew that Anita would not include me in the ranks of the chosen after my dismal failure on the Rami and Nira test.

"TechnoKid is built on contributions from top-level donors, of a different caliber," Anita continued her line of thought. "We aren't talking about small donors of a few hundred dollars, like the ones from WIZO fund-raising dinners. Not that I've forgotten where I came from, but here we're talking about an organization of a different kind. There are people who really care at TechnoKid—high-quality people who want to contribute wholeheartedly to the cause of true, not pseudo, world peace." She emphasized her point with a shake of her head and a long silence. Then she continued, "According to the model we've developed, the members of the organization are personally involved in the project. This isn't a case of throwing money at the problem and sticking one's head in the sand, as with other projects." She stopped again to breathe deeply. "With us, members are directly responsible for progress in the field. They fly all over the world, hold meetings, attend lectures, receive reports, vote on strategies and tactics, and decide where the money should go and what the next step should be." She was very pleased with her program.

"I manage them like a business company and demand real output the way Ido runs his company. When I tell the journalist that the goal is to raise ten million dollars from the fifty members of the organization, she'll understand the level of commitment we're talking about. On second thought, I shouldn't mention specific amounts. You never know where things will end up. Ido's good at this. He knows how to present ideas, what to say, and what not to say. With me, there's no bullshit. I say what I think." Anita paused for a moment, perplexed. "But it's best not to get too complex with journalists." Sigh. "In the end they write what they want, and you can't control them. I have to get a PR rep, someone who will train me to say things the right way; the way they train politicians for their election campaigns."

Raoul, the chef, shuffled in and asked demurely if we would like something to drink: Coffee, tea? I was about to ask for coffee when Anita waved him away, saying she was late for her lesson and had to rush off. After Raoul had left, she casually added that I was welcome to stay and drink with Raoul, if I wished. I declined.

She closed the album and reminded me about her lunch with Yossi Giladi. "Great guy—I can really count on him."

When Yossi sold his company for half a billion dollars, he retired and took on helping Anita to set up the organization. He was still her right-hand man. Anita ended the conversation, rose from the mustard sofa, waved good-bye, and started to leave for her daily session with her personal trainer, all before I could tell her about Gabi's surprise party.

"See you!" she flung my way as I attempted to convey the reason for my visit. "Send me an email!" she called from the Jaguar, leaving me standing there as if I were one of her servants. Imelda, who was the children's nanny in the afternoons, saw me to the door and coyly wished me good-bye.

When I arrived at Max's Opera Café in the Stanford Shopping Center the following week, Gila was waiting for me, with her Julia Roberts smile, at an outdoor table. She'd come straight from her voice lesson, which she attended twice a week in order to stay in shape should she be summoned back onto the stage.

"What's new, Gila?" I asked, eagerly anticipating news of whatever thrilling events had occurred in her life.

"Things are good. I just returned from a fabulous weekend in New York. Talma called, said she'd be in town for a few days, and asked if I wanted to join her. I booked us a fun hotel on Fifth Avenue, and we partied nonstop for three days. New Yorkers are kind of crazy, but they're amazing, and Talma knows everyone. We got invited to parties, two gallery openings, and an off-Broadway premiere. We hopped from one event to another and stopped only to eat and make love. Well, you know," she rattled off in one breath.

I searched for a way to relate to her load of novel experiences but decided that any remark from me would sound petty. Still, curiosity won. "What about Yigal? How does he react to all of this happening without him?"

"I invited him to join us, but he refused. He was under pressure at work but didn't object to my going. On the contrary, he said, 'Go and have a good time, sweetie.' That's Yigal, sweeter than honey."

I thought Yigal showed rare nobility of spirit. "But isn't your romantic relationship with Talma hard for him to swallow?"

"Listen," said Gila, her face almost touching mine, "between you and me?" I nodded. "Yigal likes to watch," she said. My blank face conveyed that I didn't get her meaning. "He...gets turned on when he watches me with another man, or another woman. To really get off, he needs to *see* that I'm having an affair. Sometimes he settles for listening to stories about what went on, but other times he needs to actually watch. So my affair with Talma really suits him." She beamed at me. "Everything's just great!"

I took a deep breath, a bit stunned. A quick memory search produced a similar case I'd heard in the clinic. Life was full of surprises; I began to comprehend the dynamics of Triangle Gila-Yigal-Talma, or, perhaps, Yigal-Gila-Talma. Uh-huh.

As I was catching my breath, Anita approached agitatedly, clutching an Israeli women's journal. Her body language conveyed rage. She opened the journal and pointed to the headline that had thrown her off balance: ANITA EITAN HEADS MILLIONAIRE COUNTRY CLUB IN SILICON VALLEY. The opening paragraph read, "If you want to become a member of the nonprofit organization Anita Eitan runs in the name of peace, you'll need to reach deep into your wallet and donate the equivalent of the price of a luxury apartment in Tel Aviv. In return, you'll get a suite of perks: guided tours, interesting lectures, biweekly meetings, and the chance to rub elbows with a roster of influential politicians."

She slammed the journal onto the table in disgust. Out of the corner of my eye, I caught a glimpse of the accompanying photograph. It showed Raoul serving her breakfast on the patio next to the pool.

Her hair and bathing suit were wet after her dip. Anita was in shock. She had tried to persuade the impertinent journalist to use the photograph of her with the former prime minister, or at least the one with the columnist. The picture of her with the servile chef Raoul, wearing an apron, certainly didn't help her image.

"How dare she!" Anita fumed. "After I opened my home to her, invited her to a directors' meeting, revealed our code of ethics to her, she calls us a country club for millionaires! She hardly mentions the big donations of computers and our immense contribution to the improvement of communications in the Middle East. She forgot the real story!" Anita stood in front of the table with her hands on her hips, ready to kick or lash out at her enemies. The enemy this time was hiding in small print beneath the article's outsized headline. Gila and I shoved our heads toward the open journal to discover the identity of the journalist and whatever else there was to see. "And poor Yossi Giladi gave her his time and took her for a spin in his private plane, and she shafted him too!" Anita continued forcefully. "She found it necessary to mention that his daughter from his second marriage just married a Chinese guy—a nice boy, an MIT graduate, who's done more for Israel than some of the local Jewish trash around here. Where is her journalistic integrity? From now on, not one of those women's weekly columnists will set foot in my house. From now on, I'm only giving interviews to The *New York Times*."

She slumped down into a chair. "Well, I'm not going to let some catty journalist break me." She sighed, glanced at the paper again as if it were poisonous, and proceeded to skim the detailed description of her ten-roomed house, her five cars, and her domestic staff of nannies, maids, gardeners, and chefs.

"Don't let an article discourage you from your big ideas, don't let it hurt you," I offered. I actually sympathized with Anita: I knew how hard she'd prepared for this interview, how much she'd hoped to be able to promote TechnoKid through this article, and how devastated she must feel about the awful put-down.

"It's hard to be in the limelight," Gila said, speaking from her own experience of being center stage. "You have to learn to live with negative as well as positive reviews. You have no choice. The main thing is to be at peace with yourself."

Anita nodded in agreement and said she was at peace with herself as she picked up her cell phone, which she had programed to ring with Mozart's *Jupiter*.

"Did you see that horrible article?" she yelled into the phone. "Okay, Mom, okay! Well, it's over now. Send me an email with the final list of people, with their names exactly as they appear on their passports, and I'll settle it with the travel agent. *Yalla*, 'bye."

She was paying for twenty-five people to fly from Israel to California for the Passover Seder, because her mother didn't feel up to having it at home, she informed us. She wiped the perspiration from her forehead, the result of two hours with her personal trainer. Her hair was plastered to her temples, and there were dark circles under her arms. Not an appealing sight. Or smell. But someone as sexy as Anita managed to attract attention under any circumstances—like the captivated gaze of the elderly man at the next table.

"I have to find caterers for the Seder," she continued. "Raoul doesn't understand Jewish cuisine. Daniela, do you know a good kosher Jewish caterer?"

"No." I told her I did all of my own cooking for the Seder. I received a sympathetic look in response, as if I were suffering from an incurable illness.

"No problem. We'll find you an Orthodox kosher caterer," said Gila, our resident expert in all fields, and offered to help with logistics.

When the waiter arrived, Anita, who had rigorously earned her calories for the day, ordered a jumbo hamburger with fries, coffee, and chocolate mousse for dessert. Gila and I made do with a Greek salad, which we shared. Gila pecked at three cubes of tomato. I counted.

"How's the WIZO fund-raising evening coming along?" Gila asked.

"There are some problems. The Israeli minister I was talking with has really let me down. I don't need him to do me any favors, he can go screw himself," Anita said dismissively, adding in the confident tone of an efficient manager, "I called the party secretary, and he immediately promised to send another minister."

I thought about Anita's flippant attitude toward ministers. With her self-confidence and her network of connections, I had no doubt she'd go far.

"In the meantime, I've got a new idea," she carried on. "I'm going to invite the Karmiel Dance Festival to the Valley. We can get a charter flight to San Francisco. A project like that could totally transform Israel's image in American eyes. What do you think?"

"Fabulous idea," I said, not sure what I was getting into.

"We have to contact a few families in the area and set up a fund of maybe only a few hundred thousand dollars to finance the project. Daniela, maybe you'll do this. I just don't have the time. I'm in way over my head."

I felt as though Anita had just drafted me into her army, given me a uniform and the rank of private, shoved a mop into my hand, and commanded me to clean the latrines.

"Maybe we should first concentrate on Gabi's birthday party." I sidestepped Anita's festival and took the opportunity to address the reason for our meeting. "Danny wants to throw a surprise party for Gabi. He's giving us an unlimited budget to do something big—bigger than the party Haleli gave for Yossi Giladi last year. Mika's volunteered her house," I concluded the opening stance.

"I like this unlimited budget idea," Gila reveled.

"Danny must have been spotted with another woman in San Francisco last week," Anita mocked, biting a fry off her fork. "Don't you think the party's meant to make up for his guilty conscience?" Like the boy in "The Emperor's New Clothes," Anita always said what everybody knew but didn't dare speak out loud.

"Okay. But that doesn't mean he doesn't love her," said Gila, with her flexible approach to married life.

"Every couple has its private kind of glue," I said, defending Danny from Anita's attack. I thought that he actually meant well, and I certainly believed that Gabi deserved his best intentions. And maybe the big party he was planning was also intended to serve as a farewell party, before she returned to Jerusalem. Still, I could not totally dismiss Anita's suspicion that Danny only wanted to clear his conscious. "What works for one couple doesn't necessarily work for another. Gabi and Danny have been attached to one another almost from the day they were born, almost like Siamese twins," I reminded my friends. I thought about what bound me to Yoel. His unwavering warmth, like a thick blanket in winter, like a nostalgic happy song in French.

"So maybe we could bring Rita and the Israel Philharmonic," Anita said, thinking big. Rita was an Israeli pop singer, a national superstar.

"That wouldn't be right for Gabi," Gila cut in. "We can save the Philharmonic for Mika's birthday. Something more personal would please Gabi, more conventional. We need a different concept, something she'll always remember, that she'll find touching." She mused in a burst of creativity. "I'm thinking more along the lines of a stage performance. Like *The Story of Your Life*. Maybe we can fly in some friends from school, the army, Bezalel, maybe teachers. We have to do some serious research into what really moves Gabi."

We agreed. We agreed that we had to do serious research, and we agreed that Gabi would be more enthusiastic about an intimate, modest event.

"Let me direct the creative program," Gila said. "Talma and I will produce an unforgettable event for her. I'll phone Talma immediately and get her started on the research, and we'll make a video and include some thoughtful words from everyone who knows Gabi and can tell us about her. This is going to be phenomenal!" Gila was full of enthusiasm.

"Lovely," I said, satisfied. "Gila and Talma will work on the artistic side. Music, too?" I asked Gila.

"Sure, sure, there's a fantastic group in Los Angeles; out of this world! I'll book them now. Consider it done!"

"In that case, we're left with the catering, waiters, tables and chairs, valet parking, guest list, a gift...Oh! And a cover story. You can't have a surprise party without a cover story," I said.

"Maybe we should hire a company to produce the event, like for bar mitzvah parties," Anita suggested.

"Oh, we're better than that." Gila grinned. "We can open our own production company and call it Valley Girls' Production."

We laughed.

Anita volunteered to hire a gourmet catering company that would include an open bar and waiters, as well as to take care of valet parking. I would see to the rest: renting tables and chairs, organizing a guest list, printing invitations and keeping track of RSVPs, collecting money for the birthday gift, and, of course, maintaining ongoing contact with

Danny, who would have to sign the checks. All that remained was the cover story.

"Maybe we should leave that to Danny," Anita said, then retracted the thought. "Actually, we can barely rely on him to turn up at the party...Maybe he'll be stuck with some sexy young thing that night." She laughed wickedly.

Gila said, "I suggest we take Gabi for a fun day in San Francisco. I know an excellent Japanese spa with a pool, massage, facials, mani-cure, pedicure, and all that stuff. In the evening, we'll pick her up for dinner with the girls."

We agreed.

"Yes!" I was happy. I knew this was a smooth team: expert organiz-ers, full of ideas and practical energy. Besides which, we all loved Gabi, all pitied her a little and thought she deserved a bit of gratification and attention beyond what Danny was able to give.

"Don't forget to specify informal dress on the invitation, but black and white," Gila laid down the rule for all the guests. I was already busy wording the invitation in my head, not forgetting our decision to enforce a black-and-white dress code. I could already imagine Mika's garden, the tables with black tablecloths and vases of white flowers, Gila and Talma's personal signature.

From a distance, Gabi looked like a pumpkin wearing a hat, a wide orange blot with dark curls drifting down her back. I approached her slowly with Maya and Oscar at my side and sat beside her on the park bench, where she had been waiting for me. Maya darted to Keren, who was bouncing up and down on the seesaw. Oscar followed the girls, happily wagging his white tail. Gabi, as usual, was equipped with a basket loaded with soft drinks, plastic cups, cakes in a Tupperware con-tainer, and a thermos of coffee. All of this despite the fact that her house was just around the corner. That's just the way she was, my good friend Gabi—a kind of huge, bountiful udder. Without a word, she handed me coffee and a slice of homemade cake. We drank and snacked.

"How was the weekend in Monterey?" I wanted to know, burning my tongue on the hot coffee. Gabi answered with a thumbs-down gesture.

Disappointment.

Her sadness touched me like an icy finger. I said nothing. I didn't know what to say to encourage her.

"You know, Daniela," she began after a long silence, "that weekend made me think about the nature of couplehood." She looked at me sorrowfully. "A young couple gets married. They're completely in love with one another, they promise to live together for eternity and sincerely believe that they will. Then the children are born. The couple takes on the burdens of making a living and building a home. Both work hard to establish the nest. One sits on the eggs, the other brings the food. But last weekend, it was like I finally shook off this little bird mentality. I took a step back from the day-to-day madness, looked at my partner, who's usually on some business trip and just happened to be there, and I suddenly thought: Who is this? How can it be that, although we began life together, we've turned into such different people? I saw a man whose whole life is devoted to a race for success, measured only by money, a kind of addiction that blurs the line between important and unimportant, because nothing is important enough in comparison to the success of his company. He sees me as a kind of necessary but secondary accessory in the big picture of his life. He takes it for granted that I'll always be there for him, like the car he turns on in the morning, like a full refrigerator, like a house. But what bothers me isn't Danny, it's me. Myself. I looked at him and thought, I don't want to spend the rest of my life in this superficial vacuum. There has to be something more stimulating in living together, something that connects a couple beyond belonging to a society that functions in pairs. Don't you think so, Daniela?"

"I'm not sure," I answered, wondering if there was anything particularly stimulating in my life with Yoel. "What do you mean by 'stimulating'? Dancing into the night, courtship, romance?"

"No, no," Gabi replied quickly. "I'm totally realistic. I don't want dancing and courtship. I'm thinking of Danny's personality. I asked myself a question. After all, Danny and I became attached to one another when we were children. If I had the choice today, would I choose Danny or someone like him? No. Today I would choose a refined, sensitive man, who would be truly interested in me, who would show his feelings, whose spheres of interest coincided with mine."

"You sound like a matchmaking advertisement," I couldn't resist saying.

Gabi looked angrily at me. My flippant remark had insulted her, and I regretted it.

"You're missing the point, Daniela. I'm talking about a process of estrangement in a couple. Something that happens gradually, not overnight. It's like two people rowing a boat for a long time, and one suddenly stops to ask who is this person with them in the boat? And if you had the opportunity to choose a new partner, would that promising young person you chose years before still be the right one to row the rest of the way with you, in the second half of your life?"

"As a rule, people grow together. Don't you feel that way?" I tried to lighten the picture. I wanted to be optimistic.

"Not in our case. I think we've developed separately. If Danny were here now, listening to me, he wouldn't understand what I'm talking about, because this sort of thing doesn't even come close to his way of thinking. It's a type of intelligence that he doesn't possess because it's not measured by tests. Tests, he gets. He passes tests with stunning success. All his degrees were summa cum laude." She rolled her eyes.

"Maybe he needs to be shaken up, Gabi? You know that he loves you in his own way." I was thinking about the surprise party he was planning for her and which, obviously, I could not mention. Danny, of course, wasn't making a personal effort to organize it, but he was certainly ready and willing to sign checks without limit.

"His love isn't enough, apparently. I need someone who likes to be with me, who would be interested in my inner world, what I think and feel. For Danny, dealing with emotions is a waste of time. I would choose someone entirely different today."

"Like?"

"Like Luigi Fracassini, for example."

In my mind's eye, I ran a film of slender, gray-haired Luigi Fracassini waving good-bye to his mummified wife and dancing over to Gabi, his face glowing as he offered her his arm, and Gabi staggering beside him, wide-hipped and fluttering with joy. The two of them slowly passed through the corridors of the Louvre, Fracassini stopping from time to time in front of this or that splendid work, to whisper in her ear the secrets of its creation. Gabi gazed at him in admiration and he responded, caressing her beautiful face with the same look of desire he had bestowed upon Bernoulli's paintings.

"What do you know about Luigi Fracassini? Not everything that looks perfect from a distance is perfect from up close," I said, knowing there was no such thing as a perfect partnership. There were only ups and downs, a sort of back-and-forth dance we all shared. My clinical experience had taught me that people who didn't dance in pairs were not prepared to accept this reality, so they sat on the fence waiting for a nonexistent ideal partner. Or else, there were the individualists who felt that their freedom was limited and their lives were constricted by a partner. Like Katie's mother. But Gabi was not like that.

"I'm not looking for perfection, Daniela, but I do want a partner. I just don't think Danny's built for it. He doesn't need one woman, he needs many," she said, with sadness clouding her eyes.

There was nothing I could say in response to her claim. I was worried. I saw her nest breaking apart, her children suffering in the ruins of the separation. I earnestly wanted to prevent this from happening.

"What are you thinking of doing, Gabi?" I asked.

"Yesterday Gil asked if we are Americans or Israelis. A question like that makes the reality immediate for me—we need to return to Israel as soon as possible. I'm raising Israeli children, not Americans. Most importantly, I have to get Roni away from her boyfriend before it's too late. The children will start the coming school year in Jerusalem. And what's going to happen with Danny? I don't have an answer yet."

I looked at Gabi sadly. I resisted the urge to protest that she was leaving me behind. Once more, I felt the upcoming void in my life—missing her, the pain of parting. I remembered my mother and the pain I saw in her eyes when I pulled her granddaughter from her and followed Yoel over the ocean. Only for a year or two, I had told her, and she'd clung to the words with high hopes.

That ocean…Whoever crossed it left broken hearts in their wake, because the rift hurt those who stayed much more than those who left.

For minutes on end, the two of us sat staring into space under a cloud of heavy silence, until Keren and Maya came huffing and puffing to ask Gabi for some juice and cake. Gabi briskly attended to them, as if their presence had breathed life into her.

Chapter 12

Since the meeting at Max's Opera Café, I couldn't stop pondering Gila's comment about her and Yigal. My curiosity drove me to her house to get the rest of the story that had been interrupted by Anita's arrival. It puzzled me, like an unresolved dissonance, when I realized that the angelic Yigal was actually no angel. He was a hedonist in his own way. Who would have guessed?

On second thought, what bothered me about Yigal's hedonism was my own voyeurism. I admit, I am prurient—who isn't, after all? What about the books, films, plays, and gossip almost all of us enjoy? Doesn't just about everybody want a peep at the juicy bits of other people's lives? My profession is almost completely based on voyeurism, because therapists have to probe into the lives of others. What motivates psychologists, psychiatrists, and other therapists to spend hours listening to their patients, if not at least partly their curiosity about patients' private lives? A kind of Peeping Tomism protected by law. If any of my colleagues don't agree, let them stand up.

Of course, there is a difference between professional prurience and sexual prurience or voyeurism. My prurience isn't regarded as a perversion. On the contrary, it is respected and demands years of training and the development of many skills. Psychologists study at length, after which we teach the secrets of the profession to succeeding generations.

Specializing in the therapeutic arts means learning and teaching how to peep into a patient's life in a way that makes it easier for him or her to cope. We try to change patients' ways of thinking, to help them develop their insight, to build their strength, to reinforce their ego, to correct early experiences, and to prevent them from falling into despair. That is what we are—providers of support and encouragement, using voyeurism in the most sublimated way.

Yigal's prurience, however, bore no relation to generosity, but was instead utterly devoted to a search for personal gratification via the invasion of privacy.

Having defined at least one significant difference between Yigal's voyeurism and my own, I felt my discomfort ease. I remembered the former patient I'd thought of when Gila first told me about Yigal—a pleasant, nonthreatening Peeping Tom who would record intimate videos of naked women through windows or holes in the wall and masturbate while viewing the tapes. He claimed that as long as the women were unaware of his invasion of their privacy, no harm was done. His sweet smile almost convinced me of his perspective. Except that in that case, there was clearly a great disparity between his voyeuristic activities and mine, which were preceded by signed consent. I reassured myself further: there was another difference between my professional voyeurism and Yigal's kink.

Yigal, a successful professor, was an amiable, sociable, witty, well-informed, and respected person. So much for outward appearances. Now I had learned that he was turned on by watching his wife have sex with other people. Unbelievable. I needed to understand this a bit better. So there I was, at Gila's door on my way to work, with the excuse that I had to pass a check from Danny to pay the musicians who had been hired for Gabi's surprise party.

Gila opened the door. She was wearing a black leotard, and a white towel was wrapped around her head like a turban. "I had a terrible migraine this morning," she complained, "but I'm okay now."

She pulled me inside and resumed what she'd apparently been doing when I arrived: polishing the pianos. "I get these migraine attacks every so often, and I know I can't give in to them. I take a pill immediately, rest for half an hour with a towel wrapped around my head. After that, I'm back on top again," she said, vigorously rubbing the surfaces of the grand piano, including the legs. "I have to clean these pianos every day. I can't stand any dust on them, and I can't wait for the maid who comes only twice a week," she explained, head down, arms working like windshield wipers. She polished with the hyperactivity of a perfectionist consoling herself by arranging her territory, the towel still wrapped around her head to forestall a migraine attack.

I walked to the kitchen. Carefully arranged on the scrubbed granite counter were a loaf of rye bread with sunflower seeds and raisins, baked by Gila that morning, three plates with fresh salad, and a quiche decorated with spring onions and cherry tomatoes. Gila, who kept a strictly vegetarian kitchen, was already prepared in the early morning to welcome her daughter and husband when they came home.

I sat on a high stool at the green granite island in the spacious kitchen designed in the postmodern style of Philippe Starck and dominated by cherrywood and copper tones.

"Have you seen Philippe Starck's luxury housing project in Tel Aviv?" Gila asked. "You have to do a tour of the place, but it's open only to potential clients, of course! If you say you're from Silicon Valley, you'll be welcome. But if you have any problem, tell me and I'll get in touch with the in-house architect, Naama, who is in charge of the tours. I've known her for years. Great girl. I heard that the luxury apartments are selling like crazy. We're also considering buying a penthouse; it would solve the problem of the distance from Talma."

Yes, I thought, I'd be happy to visit the luxury apartment project in Tel Aviv.

Gila offered me a latte from a sleek, copper-plated espresso machine that emerged from a cherrywood shelf concealed in a cupboard. We heard the whistle of steam jets, accompanied by the pleasant aroma of fresh coffee. Gila foamed low-fat milk and filled two cups the size of soup bowls, then sprinkled a fragrant mix of nutmeg and cinnamon on each. She bought the ground spices online from a company in Chicago. Everything arrived freshly packed. Lovely.

"It's too bad they don't carry za'atar," she said. "I love it on salad. Have you been to the new natural food store in Palo Alto?"

"No."

"You should really drop by. Their vegetables are unbelievable! I buy fresh organic vegetables and fruit there, every day. Food that isn't organic gives me migraines," she sighed. "You can find every kind of healthy, natural flour there. You know, I bake the bread myself, because you can't trust store-bought bread. You have no idea what disgusting stuff they put in it. It's a mix of chemicals baked with a bit of flour— that's what the supermarket sells you and calls it bread."

I consoled myself with the thought that my family members didn't suffer from migraines, so I didn't have to go looking for chemical-free organic food rich in natural ingredients. Also, I reminded myself that obsessive concern about food was a characteristic of people with eating disorders. For them, every meal became a complex puzzle based on intricate rules of what was permitted and what was forbidden.

"We had dinner with Yigal's boss last night," she continued. "His wife knows me and knows that I'm sensitive to chemical substances in food, so she bought organic vegetables especially for me. But there's no fooling my migraine. It immediately wakes up and protests any contaminants, and that's what happened this morning."

I sympathized with Gila, but I was burning with curiosity, and it was not about her migraine. I'm here about the voyeurism, I thought, but how can I get Gila to talk about it...?

Rummaging in my bag for Danny's check, I asked about Talma.

"She's doing well, getting ready to visit me soon," Gila told me. "I can't wait."

"So, tell me, Gila," I said casually, "how long have you known that Yigal likes to watch?"

She took the check and said, "Wonderful. The musicians want an advance to secure the arrangement." In the same casual tone, she said, "Always. Yigal's always liked to watch. But in the beginning of our relationship, I didn't quite get it; I thought he was kind of open-minded, like me. It was only later, over the years, that I realized he couldn't do it any other way."

Gila sat facing me, at ease, ignoring the migraine. Without any prompting from me, she generously opened her heart, as if she'd been expecting this meeting.

"My relationship with Yigal started the year my brother was killed in an air force training accident. It's hard to describe how hard it hit the family. My parents never recovered, never returned to a normal way of life. It was like an earthquake.

"I'll never forget that day, the seventeenth of October, twenty-five years ago. It began like any other day, even a beautiful day, ironically. I was on my way home, and I saw my brother's friend Eli standing in front of me, and his eyes were red and swollen. He held me tight and told me that Avishay had been killed. It's like it was yesterday...I remember just standing there, staring at him, waiting for him to tell me he was only joking. Because it couldn't be true. I wanted to scream, to erase the moment, to turn back the clock. My brain couldn't grasp it. My body had no place for such pain. None."

Her eyes were full of tears. "When I could finally speak, I asked Eli if my parents knew. He said they knew. I ran straight home. And our home had been destroyed. My parents still sit on those ruins." Gila dried her tears and I, also tearful, grieved with her over Avishay, whom I had never met.

"At first, I didn't really absorb the shock, because hundreds of people came to the funeral and to the *shiva* at our home. You have to understand, Avishay was a real prodigy. He was special. Everyone in Ramat Gan remembers him and still admires him from his high school days and his time in the army. Girls stood in line to go out with him. He was an outstanding student and an outstanding trainee pilot. Ask Ido. They were in the pilots' course together in the IDF. He'll tell you about Avishay. If he were alive today, he'd be at least as successful as Ido, if not more. He'd probably be making millions, like everyone else," she said, lifting her chin.

"The weeks following his death were just a frenzy of tears. I couldn't understand how the sun could continue to shine as if nothing had happened. His image was with me everywhere—when I was in bed, in the bathroom, outdoors—I couldn't get him out of my head. Can you imagine how it felt to have someone looking at you all the time? Even in the most intimate situations? His eyes followed me, I couldn't stop thinking about him rotting there, in the grave, with worms eating his soft skin, his beautiful eyes. I hoped his hair would remain silky. I wanted to open the grave and look. His eyes followed me all the time. It was madness. I thought I was going crazy, losing my mind.

"Two months after the tragedy, I couldn't bear my mother's weeping anymore. She stank in her bed, her hair was uncombed, her teeth unbrushed. She left her bed only to go to the bathroom, hardly ate or drank, held a photograph of Avishay in front of her eyes all day. My father wasn't doing any better—he also lay on the living room sofa all day, staring at an album of pictures of Avishay, at his certificates of excellence, at his pilot's cap on the shelf. He was also withering away.

"I was twenty-two at the time. I loved Avishay so much. I was his groupie, his constant admirer, but I wanted to live. I couldn't take the suffocation in the house, the grief in every corner, the oppressive darkness. Even the smell in the house was different: sour and sad. I had to fight on my own. I wanted to feel life, not death. I thought Avishay would also want me to live and not sit like my parents, staring at his picture, barely breathing. My way of uniting grief and life was sex. Pure and simple.

"I was a student at this actors' studio, Bet Zwi. I just slept with anything that moved: men, women, couples, threesomes. It was endless. I fled from grief, but not to the arms of anyone who loved me—that kind of love I was in no state to reciprocate. I escaped to anonymity. I slept with men and women in anger, in frustration, because Avishay wasn't there anymore, and my parents had vanished with him. I wasn't really all that different from my parents, who just obliviously stared at his pictures all day. I just fucked every set of private parts I came across, almost oblivious. Naively, I thought those games in bed brought me back to life, that this was some free and uninhibited way to really live, to feel that I existed, to feel a sort of warmth and belonging, but I wasn't aware of the cost. I didn't know that I was harming myself. Because you can't escape from grief, and all the anonymous fucking just leaves you with a bad smell and dirty sheets. And the wounds stay unhealed..."

Gila looked at me. I was breathing shallow breaths, gripped by her words, envisioning an ancient pagan rite that Gila had experienced so bestially.

After a moment, she continued with her story. By the end of her year at Bet Zwi, she said, the avant-garde Acre Theatre offered her a part, and she went for it. It seemed like a good reason to get away from her parents. She went to live in the north of Israel but she didn't change her way of life. She continued to participate in threesomes.

"You wouldn't believe how easy it is to find that kind of set up, if you want to," she told me.

She'd met Yigal in one of those threesomes. At the time, he was studying medicine at the Technion.

"Keep in mind, I had no interest in meeting people," she said. "Not really. What I remembered about Yigal was his impressive physiology, if you catch my drift. Nothing else." She laughed.

Yigal had pursued Gila slowly. He was consistent about visits, would come alone, without a third wheel. She told him she wasn't made for monogamy and had no interest in an exclusive relationship with a man, and he laughed. It didn't bother him. All he wanted was to hear about her sex life. And she told him, shamelessly, down to the last detail. He would listen, and they'd have sex that was so good that she felt it made it worthwhile to have given him all the graphic details.

She laughed again. "He wanted to know everything: what turned me on, where they touched me, what they did to me, what I did, how I came. Then it was his turn to sleep with me. At first, I didn't think there was anything special. You know, no big deal, just some deep conversations. Without realizing it, though, I became attached to him."

One day, Yigal had turned up at Gila's apartment with Assaf, his younger brother.

"What can I say, Daniela?" Gila asked. "I'd never, ever seen such a hot guy."

Built like a basketball player, Assaf was tall and blond with blue eyes and amazing teeth, a smile like Robert Redford's. Since Yigal and Gila weren't exclusive, she went to bed with him immediately. Yigal was in the next room over, and he acted as if he didn't care, but she could tell it had really wound him up. After his brother left, he came in to cross-examine Gila. As usual, she supplied the graphic details and, as usual, he was aroused, but this time, she told me, there was incredible intensity. Assaf began to visit her more and more often and, eventually, even though it was never the plan, Yigal joined them and they became a threesome. This arrangement lasted for a few years, sometimes as two, sometimes as three.

Apparently, my stare betrayed the fact that I had never heard of such a thing. Gila added that on one occasion Yigal had also brought his middle brother, but she wasn't attracted to him. She didn't like redheads. "Plus, the redhead had sadomasochistic tendencies. He chained me to the bed, and when Yigal saw it through the two-way mirror, he threw him out. He said he wouldn't tolerate such perverted behavior toward me."

"Uh-huh." I nodded, as if that explained everything.

"My relationship with Assaf was really special. Unforgettable. It was just purely sexual attraction, because we hardly spoke. He raised my...standards, if you know what I mean." She sighed. "Anyway, I didn't know he had a girlfriend, and when he told me he was getting married, I crashed. It turned out that I wasn't as tough as I had thought, and that, in the end, I did fall in love with men who slept with me. At first, I was in shock. And then, just unbearably heartbroken. I wanted him like a drug. I felt the pain of that breakup through my whole body. I felt like there was a knife stuck in my heart, like I was dying.

"It all happened before Netta was born. Thankfully, I haven't had thoughts like that since she was born. But even these days, when we see him at family events, children's birthdays and all that, I can feel Assaf's eyes on my body. It almost makes me come. He once told me I should have been a model. He really loved my body. I see how he looks at Netta, in the same way he once looked at me, with a look that could split her hymen. But, oh my God, he'd better not touch her! There are limits!"

Gila rubbed her face and shook her head side to side. I could not tell if she was crying. Then she lifted her face and gazed at me, continuing in an angry voice.

"Deep down, I hope it was at least as hard for Assaf to break up with me as it was for me to let him go. I hope he suffered, too, because he broke my heart. Such an arrogant type, unattainable. The kind who doesn't return phone calls or emails. Maybe he's scared his wife will catch him. Otherwise, I know he'd have reached out to me. I think about him sometimes and fantasize about what would have happened if I'd married him, such a sweet, strong man, a man who turned me on so intensely. He's not as kinky as Yigal. He's more vanilla, but he's not mine. He'll always be part of my life, though, one of the family." Gila stopped for a moment, with a deep, heartrending sigh. "I wrote poems to him; I've got whole notebooks full of poems I wrote after we parted. I still write, now and then, but less often. I've got Talma now, you know." She beamed at me, moving away from the deep anger she'd betrayed just a moment ago. I was astonished. Speechless. Did not know what to say.

"When Assaf got married, I pressured Yigal to marry me, and he didn't refuse. He also wanted to get married and have a child. For a while, I thought everything was working out, that we'd become a regular bourgeois family, a mommy and daddy raising a little baby. How nice, I thought. But I was naive. After Assaf was no longer part of our sex life, Yigal folded. When Netta was born, he started to become celibate, while I was still on fire. I needed him. I was young and demanding, if you get what I'm saying…But he didn't respond. It was like a fire that had burned out. I tried everything. My mouth, my hands; I tried massage. I told him stories that had worked in the past, but he stopped responding completely."

"Nothing?" I asked in amazement.

"Completely lifeless. He couldn't get it up. He said, 'If you want to sleep with me, go fuck someone else, and come back and tell me about it.' And me, with a newborn to take care of, when would I have time to find someone else to sleep with?" she said bitterly. "So he arranged it. He found a couple looking for a third wheel. They seemed nice, at first. I told myself that for the sake of a sex life with Yigal, I was willing to give it a try. The first few months were all right. Yigal installed a two-way mirror, and he'd watch from the other side. They didn't know he was watching; I don't think they would have agreed. If he wasn't home when they came over, he'd want a detailed description of the action, and then he'd sniff me like a dog. And then fuck me like I was in heat."

"It's a kind of abuse," I said, horrified. "You're an actress, after all. Couldn't you come up with some story?"

"You don't understand. He reads me like an open book. Games don't work with him. He looks into my eyes, smells me, and knows the truth." She had tears in her eyes.

"Smells you?"

"Yes. He has to. He has to watch or smell. His senses have to be stimulated for him to get turned on…"

I swallowed. I'd never heard of voyeurism via the sense of smell.

"After a few months of three-way sex, which at least brought my sex life with Yigal back somewhat, the woman suddenly said she didn't want her husband to come inside me, she liked him to come inside her, that's what was good for her. I told her, 'Honey, you can't expect to bring someone else into your bed and have everything stay the same.

After all, you're looking for variety, right? If it's not working for you, you can go.' And they went. What could I do? Yigal was angry with me, but I couldn't go on being everybody's doormat." She was tearful.

"Why didn't you leave him?"

"Yigal?" She gave me a piercing look. "You don't understand how much I love him. Yigal's an angel. A good soul."

I thought of the beaten wife syndrome, wherein a woman repeatedly returns to an abusive partner despite maltreatment, claiming that it's love that keeps her there. In reality, it is usually dependence or fear of ending the relationship that keeps her from leaving. I would never have guessed that Yigal had that side to him.

"Since things ended with that domineering woman and that particular threesome, I've had tons of lovers, all arranged by Yigal. I told him that if he needs to see me fucking, he should make an effort. In Strasbourg, we joined a swingers' group, and when we returned to Israel, he brought home his boss from Ichilov Hospital, who slept with me for a few years. I didn't like that man, and I was happy when we moved to California and that chapter ended. But…when I'm not having an affair, our sex life is dry.

"A few years passed like that until I met Talma. Can you imagine how happy it makes me to be in love with my childhood friend and, at the same time, have my husband back?"

I gave her an involuntary psychologist's nod, although I absolutely could not imagine it. Gila seemed to read my mind.

"Don't think I haven't always known it's deviant," she said. "I dragged Yigal to therapy with the best sexologists in the country. Who didn't we see? At first he was willing, but I eventually saw that nothing would come of the therapy—it was only a huge waste of money. All of those sex therapists just stared at us as if we were freaks. I guess they'd never heard anything like it. Most of them suggested that Yigal should use fantasy instead. They said fantasy could be stronger than watching or sniffing, and they encouraged him to fantasize about whatever came into his mind. A very nice notion. But it didn't work for Yigal. The therapists didn't even understand the sort of kinks we were talking about. Yigal is a rare case. Whenever I'm with Talma, I leave her smells on me…for him," she whispered. "Talma isn't always okay with him watching, so I rub her smell all over my body, including my face. It works."

For a moment, I felt Gila's Julia Roberts lips tenderly kissing my inner lips and a faint nausea flooded my body when I imagined my juices smeared on her face and Yigal sniffing at them like a dog. I excused myself to the lavatory, where I concentrated on the flow of my urine as if it were cleansing me of something poisonous. I washed and dried my hands and face. In the mirror, my face reflected back at me, paler than usual; I strongly felt a need to wash myself, to scrub, to wash my hair, brush my teeth. To repeat my morning ablutions from beginning to end. To start the day anew, to erase the last hour. I trudged back to the kitchen.

"You know, Daniela, my migraine's completely gone," Gila said happily, removing the towel from her head, letting her long hair fall to her shoulders.

"It's good to talk to a shrink now and then," she laughed, and I thought to myself that the migraine wasn't gone, but displaced from her to me. I went to the copper sink and poured myself a glass of water. I considered getting in touch with my patients and canceling today's sessions; I felt as if my strength had been squeezed out of me. I mentally reviewed the list of the day's appointments and realized that it was impossible, as I had appointments with two patients with borderline personality disorder; one was depressive, and possibly suicidal, and the other was hysterical. At the end of the day, I had to see a couple in a crisis. They were all suffering more than I was. Move on, I told myself, you've heard much worse stories. What's the big deal?

"And what do your parents say about all this?" I asked, wanting to know to what extent Gila's story was public knowledge.

"My parents don't know a thing about our sex life. They barely care what happens to me. They still sit staring at Avishay's picture, even though twenty-five years have passed since he was killed. But I don't judge those who are consumed by sorrow. I lived my childhood in Avishay's shadow. He was the popular, successful boy, and I was the other child, the one they were sometimes ashamed of and tried to hide. These days, my parents are proud of Netta and even find comfort in her musical accomplishments, but they still constantly talk about Avishay and the successful children he would have produced, if he were still alive."

I nodded, thinking that the source of Gila's problem was self-flagellation and profound loss. I was angry with Yigal for exploiting a lost, grieving girl and offering her a comforting shoulder while robbing her of her self-respect. He revolted me. Gila could try to sell me on the idea of what a kindhearted angel he was, but to me he was an abhorrent, manipulative demon now that I knew their secrets. Gila, on the other hand, seemed to me like a bumblebee with cupid wings, buzzing around and settling on Talma's colorful corona, gathering nectar, and flying back to spew it onto Yigal's honeycomb. A fastidious clean freak who fed her family only organic food and was prone to migraine attacks caused by chemicals but who, in total contrast, jumped into bed with strangers and wallowed in their juices in order to present their scents like frankincense and myrrh to Yigal's nostrils. A flight like that was sufficient in itself to cause a migraine.

The phone rang. "Talma. She's probably calling to update me about Gabi's film," said Gila. Part of the budget for Gabi's party had been used to hire Talma to interview all of Gabi's Israeli friends for a short film that would be screened at the party.

Gabi pressed the speaker button.

"Hi, baby. I miss you." Talma's voice caressed Gila from across the ocean.

"Hello, sweetheart." Gila returned the caress. "I miss you, too. I've been having dreams about our time in New York," she whispered.

"Me too. I can see you in my mind—dancing, laughing, with your arms around me," Talma whispered back.

"Daniela's here, on speaker. She sends her regards."

"Likewise."

"Any news about our project, beautiful?"

"I've begun the research. I found a few interesting things. Not too many. And I've also hit a serious obstacle."

"What's that?"

"It's like this. I began by looking into Gabi's elementary school. It turns out that Danny's mother was their teacher. She's still there, planning to retire next year. Such a great woman—and she just praises Gabi nonstop. She put me in touch with three childhood friends of Gabi's. I spoke to each of them separately, and we've arranged to have a joint meeting next week.

"Well, I couldn't find the slightest trace of anything about Gabi's army days; seems she was a clerk. Made a lot of coffee. Nobody remembers her. However, at Bezalel where she studied art, they remembered her. And how! There's a huge sculpture by Gabi now in the permanent exhibition of the school, and two of her collages are hanging at the entrance to the main hall. Her advisor, Professor Yehoshua Levin, was just going on and on with superlatives: highly artistic, unforgettable, supreme, creative imagination. When I told him about our film and her plan to return to Jerusalem, he said he'd be delighted to meet her and discuss the possibility of her returning to Bezalel as a teacher. He remembered she taught there years ago. Imagine Gabi's surprise when she sees him in the film, inviting her to return to Bezalel!"

"Wonderful. Great!" Gila exclaimed in excitement. "She'll fall off her chair! So what's the obstacle?"

"The interview with her parents was interesting, to put it mildly. Both were very suspicious. They asked, 'Why a birthday party for Gabi, all of a sudden? What is she, a little kid?' And her mother said she always hated organizing parties for Gabi, because she dreaded the kids coming in and making a mess in her house. I asked what Gabi was like as a child, and she said Gabi was lazy and a daydreamer. That she always had to keep reminding her to finish the chores that she started and forgot because she lost focus. A kind of sleepwalker. She didn't understand how Gabi had managed to raise five children without losing one of them somewhere, 'because her head's always in some painting somewhere, isn't it?' And then—God, I couldn't believe it—she said, totally without shame, 'Oh well…Gabi's children are all kind of savages, aren't they?' Then her husband joined in, adding that Gabi was a good girl, with a heart of gold, but that the luckiest thing in her life was Danny, 'because without Danny, she'd for sure be lost forever. A woman's nothing without a man.' That's that," Talma concluded.

"Oh, no," Gila sighed. "We can't let her be humiliated like that. The film's supposed to be a gift, not an open channel for the family's dirty laundry. That bit can't go in," she said. "Talma, go back there, tell them it needs to be redone, and you direct them. You know. Just a few nice words and happiness that Gabi's planning to go back to Israel."

"They've also got nothing positive to say about that. They say she must do what Danny wants."

"Okay, so without blessings. Go for the minimum." Gila frowned. "Will they come to the party?"

"No. They said they had enough of the Diaspora during the war. They won't board a plane or a ship. They're not going to leave Israel under any circumstances. And they are neither young nor healthy enough to fly to California."

"Maybe we should've invited Rita and the Israel Philharmonic, after all," Gila muttered to herself.

"What did you say?"

"Nothing, beautiful. I'm just wondering if I was wrong about the video. Maybe it would be better to do something more conventional and forget the personal baggage. No prying and no pain."

"Giloosh, it's better not to drop the project. After the interview with her friends, I'll have enough for a fifteen-minute film. When I'm in California next week, I'm bringing my cameraman, and we'll interview her friends there. Also her colleagues and teachers in the Bay Area. In the end, we'll have a fabulous little film, you'll see!"

"Fine. So we're seeing each other next week?"

"You bet, sweetie. Will you keep a few days open to spend with me?"

"What a question! I can't wait...Don't forget to bring me some za'atar and floor rags, and Amos Oz's latest book, something about love and hate, or light and darkness?"

"Amos Oz is already packed for you, and I'll throw in some za'atar and rags tomorrow. I'll see you very soon, sweetie!"

"'Bye, darling," Gila whispered.

Turning to me, she said, "So what's worse, parents like Gabi's, who treat her like a wandering child, or my kind of parents, who stopped functioning twenty-five years ago?"

"I don't know," I murmured. "As long as they've got their health." I got to my feet and gave her a warm hug. I looked at my watch and dashed to the door. "Gotta run!" I said, waving good-bye. She blew me a kiss and headed to the family room to begin her daily run on the treadmill. Gila had to stay in shape. She couldn't know when she might be called to perform, and she had to be prepared. Always.

As for me, I could not get Gila's story off my mind. There were too many contradictions to absorb. My sweet friend Gila, who was so sure of herself, could not protect herself from an abusive husband. The charming professor had turned out to be a sexual pervert. Just another story that exposed the shadow underlying a perfect persona, a shadow observers could not see. I wondered whether there was anything I could do for Gila, to help her extricate herself from this sick triangle. On second thought, I asked myself, if this triangle worked for her, preserving her marriage and her inner balance, why should I intervene?

PART FOUR

———

SUMMER

Chapter 13

I felt uneasy on the morning of Gabi's birthday. In order to play the surprise game to the end, I baked a cake and drove to Gabi's house, as if nothing out of the ordinary were going to happen.

She was waiting for me at the front door. I hugged her and wished her happy birthday. I also apologized for not joining the girls' day out in the city, owing to my work, but promised to come with Mika in the evening. I didn't like to lie. The surprise party hung between us.

Anita and Gila were taking Gabi to San Francisco, as planned, for a day of massages and other pleasures. I was staying behind to help Mika and Talma put the finishing touches on the party. When I arrived at Mika's, I easily identified Talma among the many people running back and forth in the backyard. She had long black hair and was dressed all in white. There was something about her, hard to pin down, that reminded me of Gila. Maybe it was her tenacious quality of movement. They both struck me as being persistent in a similar way.

I stopped Talma for a brief moment to introduce myself. She hugged me and said, "So glad to meet you finally. I've heard so much about you!" And off she went, back to her demanding chores. She checked the Los Angeles musical group's sound system, and the big screen Yoel had acquired for the film. She prepped the musicians and the two singers so that the music would come in at the right moments. She confidently supervised the professional lighting teams and directed all other personnel. Mika and I ran around breathlessly between black tablecloths and white flowers, making final arrangements with the help of the caterers. In three hours, two hundred guests would pour into Mika's garden, and we were still busy with last-minute preparations.

To compound my headache, three couples phoned with the happy news that they would be able to attend, after all; someone else notified us that he would be bringing his cousin, visiting from Tel Aviv at the moment. Of course, the joyous news meant that we had to add two tables and rearrange seating. By late afternoon, Mika and I were drenched in perspiration. On my way out to my car and then my shower, I encountered Danny—clean, polished, and redolent of after-shave. He wanted to hug me, but I warned him off with a shake of my head.

"Is everything okay?" he asked, like the big boss deigning to visit his factory workers.

"One hundred percent," I answered without anger, because Gabi was dear to me. At least Danny had gone to the trouble of coming before the guests arrived, for which I awarded him one small point.

"Where are the children?" I asked him.

"I dropped them off at the hotel, with my parents. They'll come with the bus that will be bringing the visitors from Israel. I've brought the high school soccer team and a few others from our class. In short, half a plane straight from Jerusalem." I remembered Danny giving me a list of guests I didn't recognize, but I hadn't realized they filled half a plane from Jerusalem.

After about two hours, I returned to the party arena, bathed, sham-pooed, and dressed in black and white, on the arm of Yoel, whom I'd convinced to submit to the dress code. I explained that we'd worked hard on the production of the event and that the final effect depended on everybody's cooperation; so why did he have to be the one to ruin it? I mustered all my powers of persuasion until he gave in, still lament-ing that it was a silly idea and that he'd never heard of wearing a uni-form to a party. In the end, he wore the black shirt I had bought him at Bloomingdale's and white jeans and looked satisfied, overall. Before we got into the car, I asked him how I looked. I twirled in front of him, in a slim black dress with white shoulder straps crossed on my back and stilettos. He observed me, like a student trying to recall the right answer and, proud to have remembered the exact word, said, "Wonderful!" The compliment I'd extracted from him elicited a smile from me.

The parking valets, in gleaming white jackets, met us at the gate of Mika's house. Yoel handed one of them the car keys and another one opened the door for me as if I were a celebrity.

Many guests had already crowded into Mika's salon. They were all in black and white, except the consul's wife, who had not relinquished her paratrooper boots, implying that there were red lines one did not cross, come hell or high water.

Everyone was there! Even Nira had given up a half-marathon training session and was there all in white, matched by Rami all in black. She looked happy and relaxed and I assumed she had managed to arrange a jacket and water bottle for Tomer before she returned to California. Professor Luigi Fracassini and his surgically enhanced wife were already there, nursing gin and tonics and politely nodding to acquaintances, most of whom were the professor's privileged clients.

The crowd was well versed in surprise parties. Everybody kept the secret. Everybody knew the routine: Arrive before the star of the event and crowd together in absolute silence in a closed room. When he or she arrives, emerge in a great wave, singing "Happy Birthday," and expect the subject to faint with joy.

And so it was. Minutes before Anita's Jaguar darted up the hill, Gila phoned Mika and, using the agreed-upon code, informed her that they were around the corner. Mika herded the flock of guests to the dining room opposite the entrance, where we stood huddled together, barely daring to breathe. Even the parking valets were ordered to hide behind the bushes. Gabi knocked on the door, Gila and Anita behind her like bodyguards. Mika, in a long white dress, flung the door wide open and invited them in, then immediately walked to the piano, giving the signal for the mob to emerge singing at the top of their lungs. Gabi, as was to be expected, was dumbstruck. I asked myself if this was supposed to make her happy. By the look on her face, I thought otherwise.

When it was all over, Gabi shared with me that at the moment the avalanche of guests rushed to embrace her, all she could think about was the exhausting argument she'd had with Gila on the subject of what to wear to dinner, and about the hints her children couldn't help but drop regarding the surprise that awaited her. Gabi had insisted on remaining comfortable in a pink floral print, which clashed considerably with the elegant dress code concept. She remembered how Gila and Anita had tried to convince her to go to the hairdresser after the spa, a suggestion she had rejected on the spot. Why should she? What for, and for whom? By tomorrow, the ornate hair tower would collapse, and the curls would return to their state of wild abandon, so what was the point?

Fine, she understood that we'd cooked up a surprise party for her. That was not unusual—maybe even predictable. But she was moved to her core upon seeing the loving, embracing crowd there, comprised of so many beloved and unexpected faces from Jerusalem. For long minutes at a time, she found herself at a loss for speech. First of all, she embraced Zwi and Yael Gonen, Danny's parents, who were surrounded by their five grandchildren. Then she saw the men who'd been on the high school soccer team and the friends from her childhood and youth. She made her way through the excited swarm one by one, exchanging kisses and hugs.

Danny followed behind her, beaming like a bridegroom, or like a happy father who had achieved his goal. As she was hugging the last few guests, the rest of them took their places at the tables according to my sociometrically organized seating plan. Gabi finally reached us, her friends. She embraced me, not without a loving rebuke. "You've got secrets, Daniela, and you don't share them with me…"

I spread my hands in a gesture of helplessness. "Sorry. I was forbidden to tell."

While the crowd was busy sampling the bounty of the catering, Danny mounted the improvised platform and welcomed the guests. In a voice filled with emotion, he continued, "I'm a lucky man. Life has given me far more than I anticipated." At which I was reminded of the superstitious warning against public declarations of happiness and success.

"I have five beautiful, talented children," he continued. "I run a successful company and have no financial problems. What more could a man wish for himself?" Without a pause, he answered his rhetorical question. "A man can wish himself lifelong love with his partner. This happiness, too, life has given me."

Continuing to boast, Danny said, "Luck has been on my side. When I was still a child, I met the love of my life: Gabi, my amazing wife, my best friend, who grows more wonderful as the years go by. I owe the success and happiness of my life to her. I love you, Gabi, and I wish both you and myself many more years of happiness and love."

The torrent of honey that gushed from the platform brought about a storm of applause. Talma then called the five Gonen children onto the platform. They stood side by side, half-turned to the audience like the Platters, and sang the tirelessly rehearsed words Gila had set to the tune of Neil Sedaka's "Oh Carol," which praised Gabi as a woman, a mother, an artist, an angel, admired from San Francisco to Jerusalem, their beloved, marvelous supermom.

The children ended their song to overwhelming applause. Gabi wiped away a tear and ran to embrace them, each separately and then all together. Yoel turned to me and whispered that the song was one long kitschy cliché, musing that we could have afforded to raise the bar a bit. But Gabi's tears assured me that our goal had been achieved.

Talma invited Professor Fracassini to say a few words. The professor mounted the platform, carrying the gift we had bought from him with the money we'd collected. He removed the wrapping and revealed a huge original painting by Bernoulli. To compound Gabi's surprise, he invited the artist himself to stand beside his painting. He had flown in from Milan especially for the occasion. Swaying like a man who had unloaded a whole barrel of Chianti into his rounded gut, Bernoulli rose onto the platform. His face flushed, he passed the gift to Gabi, wrote an inscription to her, kissed the honored guest, and congratulated her in his melodic Italian, which was translated by the professor. We understood that Bernoulli was very moved by the occasion, by the meeting with Gabi. News of her rare talent had reached him overseas, and he was excited to have her among the collectors of his work. Bernoulli explained that his work was steeped in the pastoral landscapes of Tuscany. He said that he had studied painting in Rome and Paris and was influenced by great painters such as Picasso, Giacometti, and Max Ernst. I noted to myself that I wouldn't have grouped those three artists together and wondered what they had to do with Bernoulli's work, but who was I to question the esteemed artist? Gabi received her present with much emotion, kissed the artist and the professor, and, in a trembling voice, thanked everyone for the precious gift.

Then, the time came for the film. The lights dimmed, and a series of pictures of Gabi in her youth appeared to a soundtrack of Hebrew songs from the seventies: Arik Einstein, Shalom Hanoch, Kaveret. A sweet, skinny little girl with black braids and tiny glasses appeared on the screen, crowned with a garland on her fourth birthday; with a basket of fruit on the holiday of Shavuot; in a Queen Esther costume on Purim; with three friends in eighth grade; with a backpack standing next to the shaggy-haired high-schooler Danny; and finally, in an army uniform. The camera then focused on people we had interviewed, who lovingly showered Gabi with praise. Professor Levin of Bezalel invited her with open arms to come back and visit. Everyone, including the San Francisco Israeli consul, Fracassini, and her classmates at Berkeley, spoke admiringly about her. Her parents were shown festively seated on a green-and-orange-striped sofa in their home in Beit Hakerem. In honor of the event, her mother had smeared her thin lips with blood-red lipstick, which had lain unused since the seventies in the first-aid drawer in the bathroom. In a much-rehearsed duet, her father and mother recited the congratulatory script composed for them by Talma.

Finally, Gabi's three friends from Jerusalem, Ilana, Orna, and Michal, appeared on the screen and spoke about their childhood. They spoke about coming to Gabi's house every afternoon to copy the math homework that Gabi had copied from Danny. They had the same arrangement on tests: Danny passed notes to Gabi, who passed them on to the friends. That was how the four friends had survived the horrors of algebra. Giggling youthfully, they proclaimed their bond of friendship to be unbreakable. With excitement, they recounted how difficult it had been to say good-bye to one another every day after school; Gabi would walk with all three until they reached Ilana's house, but then they'd walk to Orna's, and from there to Michal's. And then they'd all accompany Gabi halfway to her house, but when they got there, she'd accompany them halfway back to Ilana's, and so on and so forth. And once they did finally part, they'd just continue the conversation from home on the phone, because there was always something important to add, they recalled with joyful nostalgia.

Then, Orna looked directly at the camera and said, "Gabi, remember when we went to that palm reader that last summer? She promised that my girls would marry your boys. So move your butts back to Jerusalem, because my girls won't wait forever." The three of them broke into laughter as the image faded and refocused on the walls of the Old City. The soundtrack ended with Rita's voice singing "Jerusalem of Gold."

END.

"What schmaltz," Yoel couldn't resist whispering in my ear.

The lights came back up and Ilana, Orna, and Michal emerged from behind the screen. Until then, Gabi hadn't known they were present and as soon as she saw them, she dashed toward them like an excited young girl, just as in the past, in Beit Hakerem. Danny joined in on the group hug, and they clung to each other as if nothing could ever separate them.

Now it was Gabi's turn to speak, with Danny proudly at her side. In her wrinkled floral dress and with tousled hair, she began by saying she couldn't remember ever feeling such excitement before. She reviewed the events of the evening, starting with the elaborate cover story woven by her friends in the Valley, her surprise at the sight of the people flown in from Jerusalem, her pleasure at seeing both old and new friends among the guests. "And thank you from the bottom of my heart to my dear friends who invested so much effort in this unbelievable production."

She was silent for a moment before taking a deep breath and whispering into the microphone, "For me, this is not only a birthday party. It is a farewell to the dear friends who have accompanied me through the years of my life here, in the Valley. Because I'm returning to Jerusalem at the end of the summer."

A dramatic turn of events. Danny, who had been silently hoping that the party would make her forget her determination to return home, took the microphone from her hand and said jokingly, "Gabi plans to go home at the end of the summer, but she hasn't said which summer!"

The audience burst into laughter. Gabi shuddered and forced herself to keep her right hand by her side despite her impulse to issue a resounding slap to Danny's face; she didn't want to escalate the situation, to provoke a violent response from him. He had managed to ruin it all for her with one remark. She remained standing on the platform, her eyes clouded. I saw her swaying as if she were about to faint, but she found the strength to save face and join the gales of laughter, bitterly laughing at her own fate.

Talma's professional instincts told her that this was the right time to bring out the musicians and commence the dancing portion of the evening. The dance floor surrounding the pool was soon crowded with couples in black and white. Gabi tottered toward the table where her mother-in-law, Yael, was sitting. The look in her eyes pleaded for shelter from Danny's insensitivity toward her feelings. Yael understood her, and so did we, her girlfriends from the Valley as well as from Jerusalem. We surrounded her—Ilana, Michal, and Orna; Gila, Mika, Anita, and me—consoling, trying to dull the pain of her humiliation, to right what had been overturned, to help her out of her misery. We huddled around her like eight protective spirits and joined our voices in singing "Pretty Woman." Gabi forced a smile, claimed she was all right, and implored everyone to get on with the party.

I left Gabi in Yael's capable hands and walked toward the dance floor, where the guests were cavorting as if at a party hosted by Jay Gatsby. Untouched by his wife's distress, Danny floated cheerfully among the friends who had copied his math homework some thirty years earlier.

Yigal swayed to the music, gazing lovingly at his two queens, Gila and Talma—one black, one white; one on his left and one on his right—as he twirled them around the dance floor. Yoel was dancing enthusiastically with Nira, who was devouring him with her eyes, swaying her hips, clapping her hands rhythmically, and singing in loud voice, along with the song that was playing, "You are so great!"

I sipped some wine and caught sight of Gabi's daughter Roni and her Romeo entwined, sucking at each other's lips with urgency, as if the sun wouldn't rise in the morning. I hastily looked away, feeling as if I'd trespassed.

My embarrassed glance fell on Mika and Shaul on the dance floor. Her thin hips twisted in his firm grip, as if he were scared a fresh partner would step forward and steal his love from him. Then he wrapped his arms around her neck and whispered something into her ear, and she kissed his earlobe. Near them, Anita and Ido moved with the heat of a rare meeting outside of the bedroom, their movements remarkably harmonized, like two candle flames in the wind.

While I was absorbed in watching the dancing couples, someone took my glass of wine from me, placed it on a table, and pulled me onto the dance floor. Before I had time to understand what was happening, I found myself turning and spinning on the dance floor in Danny's confident lead, scrambling to match his steps to prevent myself from losing my balance. "You've thrown us a great party, Daniela," said he, without thanks.

"Thank you." I nodded. "Gila, Anita, and Mika also contributed." He spun me once more, and when I returned to my spot facing him again, he cupped the side of my left breast in his hand without a trace of self-consciousness. I looked at him in disbelief. "Sorry," he said, his blue eyes revealing no regret, and only a juvenile and mischievous smile across his face.

Yoel liberated me from Danny's hold. "May I?" he asked, and Danny politely withdrew. Yoel took me in his arms, and I felt I was back on safe ground. I held him tight, letting him sway me in time with the stormy beat.

Our dancing was like the courtship dance of the Galapagos albatrosses. The birds would extend their long beaks to each other and tap out a kind of rhythm, as if kissing, all the while turning and pacing in an untiring dance. On our trip last winter, I could have stood for hours as if hypnotized, watching the birds' love dance. Our tour guide had explained that before mating, the albatrosses would choose a partner through their dance. Sometimes the females danced for four whole months with their intended mate, in order to decide whether he was suitable. Now and then, if they were not sure after dancing for some time, they would take a different partner. This was because they mated for life. They would fly to the Japanese islands every year and return to the Galapagos to mate, nest, and hatch one chick, which they raised with devoted care. Every year, before mating, they would dance again in order to renew their love and to rekindle their relationship.

Toward the end of the evening, the Jerusalem friends carried Gabi to the dance floor on a chair, with the enthusiasm of a soccer team hoisting their captain after a victory. They wound among the tables, gleefully singing and cheering, and Danny, happy and lighthearted, was among them.

The exuberant dance ended. Gabi returned to the platform cautiously, her face red and her voice shaky as she reached for the microphone. "Danny," she said, "I want to tell you something, from this stage, and it's important for everyone to hear." She paused, waiting for silence. "I have a surprise for you, too. In spite of your denial, there are no secrets here. E-e-e-verybody knows"—she circled her arms broadly and pointed a scolding finger—"that while I'm busy raising our five children, you have also been busy, jumping from bed to bed, all over the

Valley, and also overseas. Now it's my turn to take my freedom into my own hands and do as I please. Listen to me, Danny, and listen good. Let everyone here bear witness: I know exactly where I'm going and when. I'm going back to Jerusalem in two months, at the end of this summer. This time with no arguments and no compromises, and nobody will stop me."

Shock. Silence. Then one person clapped, followed by another, and soon a full crowd of applause and cheers as if she were Leontyne Price after the performance of a magnificent aria: "Bravo Gabi! Good for you!"

Caught off-guard, Danny swallowed in frustration. His usually sharp tongue had been silenced. His lips tightened, and his eyes glinted with fury. He was not accustomed to someone else getting the last word. Least of all Gabi. He'd show her what a mistake she had just made. Would he ever!

"And I have another surprise for you," Gabi continued. "I'm going up to the mountains with my girlfriends, until further notice."

And like a bride after the wedding ceremony, Gabi disappeared with her three bridesmaids from Jerusalem into a waiting limousine. At the last moment, I decided to leap in after them. Luckily, it was a long weekend. My patients were on vacation, and Yoel had planned a camping trip with the children. They'd get by without me. Mika handed Gabi the keys, and the limousine sailed like a cruise ship to Mika's cabin in the Sierra Mountains. There'd be plenty of toiletries there and clothes in her closet; Mika told us we were welcome to use her things, no need to waste time on packing. With an insincere smile on his face, Danny agreed to join the soccer team from Jerusalem for some manly fun in Las Vegas.

Gabi and Danny's five children returned home from the party with their grandparents, Yael and Zwi Gonen. The guests scattered until the next social event, when they would get together and discuss the evening's happenings. Drama like the sort experienced that evening was unlikely to happen again: a thrilling performance, beyond any creative program that Gila and Talma could ever have conceived. In the following days, the Valley rustled and whispered with the gossip about Gabi and Danny, which gained more and more momentum and continued to echo for months after the stage curtain had fallen and life's routine had resumed.

Chapter 14

Danny's blood was boiling. At the end of his Las Vegas trip, he parted from his Jerusalem friends with mighty pats on the back, as they boarded the plane for the flight home. Gabi was still in the Sierra Mountains with her friends and, unlike her usual self, did not return his calls. She did phone the children, however.

She was avoiding him, obviously angry, Danny told himself. But she was in the wrong. He was infuriated by her refusal to communicate with him, which revived his anger about his wife's audacious declaration of independence at the party.

In the first place, he fumed, she had no right to announce her intention to return to Israel in front of the guests. The matter was unresolved between them. He had been right to shut her up; the last thing he needed right now was for his board of directors to start asking questions. The Valley would cackle with malicious delight at hearing that Danny Gonen was leaving, which he was not. The last thing he needed was that kind of rumor circulating. There was no way of knowing what conclusions would be drawn. Buzz like that on its own could cause the share price to drop. It was close to the end of the quarter, and this just wasn't the time for this nonsense. He would lose face if he were forced to apologize and explain his wife's announcement to the board of directors and the shareholders. He'd be accused of withholding information, and she had no idea how much trouble she was causing him.

Secondly, what was she blabbering about "jumping from bed to bed"? Where did she get that mouth on her, all of a sudden? After all, she had always known her place in the past—always behaved appropriately. Poor thing, she'd completely lost it. So she got a bit of condescending applause at his expense. Instead of being properly appreciative of his efforts, she embarrassed him. He didn't have to throw that party for her, his ungrateful wife. Who did she think he was working for, if not her and the children? She didn't even begin to appreciate his efforts. Took everything for granted. Everything came to her much too easily. It wouldn't be a bad idea to make sure things weren't quite so easy for her anymore.

The budget for Gabi's personal expenses could be cut, to teach her to appreciate what she had. He had to keep her on a short leash; that's what he had to do, and that's what he would do from now on.

That's how it was with women: offer them a hand, and they wanted the whole arm.

Thirdly (Danny was conducting a rational mental list), deciding to go with her friends to Mika's cabin instead of to Las Vegas with him was in poor taste. That was no way to lead a family life. He rehearsed a few words to say to her about the matter when she got back. Where was her loyalty to him? And she dared talk about jumping between beds, shamelessly humiliating him. In the end, people would laugh at her, not him. She was too stupid to see how pathetic she was. And those friends she was with, a bunch of real winners, too. He remembered them back in school, pouncing like starving beggars on the notes he tossed to Gabi during math exams. They were probably brainwashing her right now. Knowing her, she'd come home completely lost.

Danny was familiar with this scenario. Even when they were children, he had found himself having to neutralize her against her friends. They were always full of stupid ideas stemming from their heart-to-heart talks, the thought of which made his eyes roll. Afterward, he'd have to work hard to eradicate their nonsense from her mind, and this was occasionally a rift between him and Gabi. Nowadays, too, from time to time, she came back with all sorts of advice that he had to talk her out of. For all he cared, her friends could run around as much as they pleased, from one workshop to another on how to improve their marital relations. But couldn't they leave Gabi, and more importantly him, out of it? They babbled on and on about active listening, quality time, empathy, communication, cooperation. For God's sake...what was he supposed to share with her? After all, she couldn't help him with the quarterly reports, present strategies to the board of directors, face customers, handle hundreds of employees, demand progress from the developers, give the salesmen a kick in the pants, keep an eye on forecasts, raise funds, see to it that his shares and the employees' shares didn't deteriorate after each investment. Her thinking couldn't reach those levels.

He would have to straighten her out the moment she got back, to show her what real life was all about. All those prattling, middle-aged women, her friends, should grow up and stop playing with workshops. He would definitely have to enforce some order and help her regain the appropriate perspective. And she owed him an apology for embarrassing him. A hell of an apology, at that.

Meanwhile, he had to attend to an urgent matter, something much more serious. The previous week, Mike Jacobs, the VP of marketing and sales, announced that he was having domestic problems. His wife was threatening divorce, and therefore Jacobs had to lower his profile for a few weeks until things were sorted out. Danny couldn't understand why Mike Jacobs wasn't able to handle this hiccup at home without letting it affect his work—why some men who were so successful in their working lives didn't have things under quite the same control on the domestic front, why they couldn't assert themselves with their wives. He, Danny, could handle Gabi without taking leave from work. As for Mike Jacobs, Danny had no alternative but to fill in for him, for the time being. It would use up a lot of his time and distract him from his main task, which was to run operations while at the same time plan the long-term strategy. Because of Jacobs, Danny would have to handle sales, deal with customers, and nag about orders, all of which was not on his usual agenda. He had grown far beyond the job of salesman, and he didn't have the patience to go back there. With a sigh, he remembered that on his upcoming trip to Copenhagen, he wouldn't even have time for Margot, at least not for the next few weeks. In short, things were not going his way. And where was Gabi gallivanting off to in the middle of all this? His leg jerked forward; he was ready to kick anything that got in his way.

Danny tried Gabi's mobile number again. Nothing. A recorded message. He was about to hurl his impotent phone into the wastepaper basket, when he suddenly remembered that Daniela was in the Sierra Mountains with Gabi and her friends from Jerusalem, enjoying Mika's cabin. Irritated, he dialed Daniela's cell.

᳇

Gabi used the days at the cabin to gather her thoughts and plan her next steps. We were in Mika's Jacuzzi surrounded by the Sierra Mountains, which were dark green and glinting in the friendly late June sun.

"I can't bear the insult anymore, Danny's insensitivity and lack of respect," Gabi said to her captive audience, without any unnecessary preamble. "Our relationship has been a mess for a while, and now we're at the end of the road. I'm not prepared to let him go on humiliating me. I don't want a man who *manages* me. I don't want him to look down on me, as if I'm helplessly dependent on him and have no choice. I do have a choice. I can live my life without him. Actually, I live without him most of the time anyway. I live only parallel to him. He makes home visits now and then, pays a little attention to the children, and moves on to some hot deal or hot girl. Maybe the separation will be good for him too, in the end. He'll be free to have his love affairs." Gabi delivered the monologue with evident effort aimed at maintaining her conviction.

"How could you bear his unfaithfulness all these years? I would have kicked him the hell out a long time ago." Orna supported Gabi.

Gabi hesitated for a moment. "Well, you know, Orna, there are much worse betrayals than being unfaithful. When someone humiliates you in public, talks to you as if you're a child, and doesn't even understand how much he's hurting you, the wound is much more serious than the kind from affairs. At least the affairs don't humiliate me in front of an audience."

We agreed in silence.

"That aggression," Michal added, "was always there in him. I remember him in high school. Danny always scared me. It was a terrifying combination—so smart but so angry. I never knew on any given day if he'd be pleasant or nasty. I never understood how you tolerated him."

"I don't always feel his aggression. You know, he's become part of me. Part of my life. Sometimes people around me raise an eyebrow, because they don't understand how I restrain myself when he's so dominating, when he plays the role of boss with everybody around him as servants. He's certain that nobody's smarter than he, and I don't even always notice how much he condescends. When I do notice and point it out to him, he has no idea what I'm talking about."

"A real emotional cripple," Orna observed.

"Tell me, Daniela, is there such a condition, where people are unable to understand others?" Gabi asked me.

"Yes. Narcissistic personality disorder is characterized by lack of empathy. The narcissistic personality is the center of his own world and views other people in his life only as extensions of the self, the 'I.' Narcissists can't understand or respect differences. Anyone who does not behave according to their expectations is invalidated."

"I wonder if that characteristic is a basic requirement for running a high-tech company," Gabi remarked.

Her comment had some validity. I reflected that discontentment with the self and others was also a characteristic of the narcissistic personality, and that was one of the traits that made people ambitious. Success and ambition went hand in hand, so yes, there was a degree of narcissism in all successful, ambitious people. Of course, there were different levels of narcissistic disorder; most people in the West suffered from some of the symptoms. And some characteristics, like striving for achievement, self-esteem, and self-love, were regarded as healthy narcissism. However, in people with extreme narcissistic personality disorder, these characteristics were maximally exaggerated. They were at the other end of the scale. Such people were prepared to trample others to achieve personal goals, because others didn't matter or even really exist for them. They lacked empathy.

"Apparently, I have no narcissism in me at all, because I have no ambition," said Gabi, after I had acknowledged the connection between narcissism and leadership.

"But you're also not satisfied with yourself," Michal remarked. "You constantly negate yourself, and that's what allowed you to be dragged overseas by Danny. Who knows what you might have achieved had you remained in Jerusalem!"

"Aha, maybe the time has come for me to develop some narcissism," Gabi laughed. "To put myself first. I can imagine myself walking around Jerusalem, returning to familiar scenes from my childhood, to my language, to the family, people who remember me, perhaps. Ah, it feels good. Going back to Israel will be a narcissistic gift to myself."

"And the children?" Ilana asked. "What about them?"

"They'll adapt. The separation will be hard, especially for the boys, but it won't be so bad. Their lives won't change completely, because they don't see Danny that often anyway. Maybe the separation will get Danny to make an effort to visit more regularly, and we'll all actually benefit from it." She looked at us as if pleading for approval, and we all nodded encouragingly.

"Yes," Gabi continued to persuade herself, "instead of flying to Copenhagen every two weeks, he'll shift the business model, to use his phrase, and fly to Israel to spend some time with his children for once." She mentally planned his itinerary, not without resentment.

"What about his parents and yours?" Michal wondered.

"Yael will understand," Gabi said. "She also thinks that Danny's behavior is immature and, as she says, he's made his bed, so now he can lie in it. And my parents will blame me, as always, and remind me that 'marriage is not a picnic.' They will also inform me," she added with evident growing bitterness, "that things aren't easy for them either, and that's life. Nor will they forget to accuse me of being unable to hold on to a man; tell me that if only I looked after myself and watched my weight he wouldn't be looking elsewhere. Divorce will be a sign of my personal failure and, while on the subject of failure, I'm sure they will be happy to point out a few more signs: after all, I don't have a profession, because what's the use of a degree from Bezalel and some talent for painting? 'You think you can make a living with that?'" Her voice became shrill. "They'll go back to what they've been telling me for thirty years, that I should go back to school and study accounting. And then they'll take great pleasure in declaring my children uneducated and badly mannered. Tell me that my kids talk to me as if I were one of their friends and that a spanking here and there wouldn't be such a bad idea."

We roared with laughter, which encouraged Gabi to present further dramatizations of her parents. "I can actually hear her scolding me," she said, holding up an admonishing finger and imitating their nasal whine. "'Where is your head? Now Danny will find a new woman, and all his money will go to *her* children!' She'll say that Danny was a choice I made, as if we were talking about the color of curtains. She's been feeding me that poisoned apple my whole life—telling me how worthless I am. But there's no hope that my parents will change," she concluded. "There's no doubt that part of this painful transition will be enduring their abuse. It will hurt, of course, but it's nothing I'm not familiar with from those two. I've survived the pain of five childbirths—I'll survive that too."

Her phone played the theme from Bizet's *Carmen*. She glanced at the screen. "Danny," she said, "looking for me, again. Let him look." She put the phone on the rim of the Jacuzzi.

A moment later, my phone rang with Rossini's *William Tell* overture. I stepped out of the Jacuzzi, wrapped a towel around my waist, and took the phone out of my bag. The call was from an unfamiliar number; I answered.

Danny.

"Hi, sweetie," he flirted. "How are things in the Sierras?"

"Fine, Danny," I said, emphasizing his name for Gabi to hear. She waved her arms frantically to signal that she wasn't interested.

"Everything's okay here; you're probably looking for Gabi, but she's not available at the moment. Do you want to leave a message for her?"

"Tell her to contact me right away. I've been trying to reach her for two days; she doesn't answer my calls. She can't just disappear like this. She's got five children. She caused me enough embarrassment in public, and now she's hiding and ignoring my calls. Explain to her that this behavior isn't acceptable by any standard." There was a strong threat in his voice. As if four hundred years had not passed since *The Taming of the Shrew* was written.

"Should I tell her that you love her?" I snapped.

"If you insist," he said, and hung up.

"That's what you get when you get involved in couples' quarrels," I mumbled to myself. Then I told Gabi, "He's desperately looking for you."

"So what are we having for dinner tonight?" she said, changing the subject.

Dripping wet and wrapped in towels, we thought about the meal we would make together, for ourselves for once, and not for a gang of children and husbands who relied on our cooking. We silently thought of our families, who took for granted and devoured the meals we prepared in our function as nurturing mothers and wives, worthy of the crown of an archetypal she-wolf goddess with multiple teats. Now and then, they rewarded us with a few words of thanks or compliments on the food, making us profoundly happy, captive women that we were.

The next morning, Gabi and Danny met again in their kitchen. Gabi had bid a tearful good-bye to her Jerusalem friends at San Francisco Airport, promising that they would soon meet again. Now, Gabi and Danny faced one another like two boxers before a decisive match. Flexing their muscles, stretching, tensely sizing up their opponent, waiting for the bell. Gabi knew that Danny had a smooth, practiced tongue and encouraged herself like a seasoned coach to stand up to him, not to break, not to be afraid, because she had nothing to lose.

The tension mounted. They were ready, each focused on anticipating the opponent's opening move, their blue gazes measuring one another up like two precise laser beams. Danny, who believed that offense was the best form of defense, didn't hesitate to attack first.

"You disappeared without even thanking me for the party I organized for you," he said, sending out a feeler.

Gabi wasn't perturbed and answered with icy resolve, "Thanks for the party, Danny, but it doesn't seem like you were the one who organized it." She knew. "Gila told me she tried to find you, to interview you for the film and include you in the rehearsals for the children's song, but you were busy with your flights to Copenhagen, and if the smells you brought back with you are any indication, you had a really nice time there."

Danny dodged the direct blow with a familiar tactic.

"What smells? There were urgent matters to attend to in Copenhagen. Jacobs had family problems, and I had to fill in for him this past month—you know that. I couldn't allow our share of the European market to fall out of my hands."

Gabi knew that this was the stance in which Danny had the upper hand. When he spoke about running his company, he assumed the pose of the breadwinner, wrapping himself in a self-righteous cloak of irreproachability that exonerated him from all other obligations. She was silent. Encouraged by his temporary advantage in the fight, he continued the attack with carefully chosen words. "You could have joined me in Las Vegas instead of going off to the mountains with your friends. You've forgotten the meaning of family loyalty."

"What right do you have to lecture me about family loyalty, Danny?" Gabi lost her composure. "And I didn't have the slightest wish to be with you after what you did."

"You're talking about what I did without thinking about what you did." Danny hit back, raising his voice. "You stood on the platform and said things that should not be said in public. We never reached a decision about your return to Israel, and you shouldn't have made an announcement regarding something that was still undecided between us. And what's all this nonsense about me jumping from bed to bed, have you gone crazy?" Danny flashed frightening looks at her, like a big boss furious with a lowly employee who had to explain her actions.

Accusatory words intended to hurt had always caused Gabi to withdraw, to fold, to be pushed into a corner in defeat. Not this time.

"Only a blind liar like you doesn't see what he's doing. You're convinced that everyone around you is stupid. I've always known about your unfaithfulness, Danny, and I decided to ignore it. But this time you pulled the rope too tight. I'm sick of your betrayals, your lies, and most of all, I'm tired of getting slaps on the wrist in front of everybody. You've humiliated me, insulted me, spoken disrespectfully to me in front of everyone, and I'm not going to accept that contempt from you anymore. This time you've gone too far, as your mother used to say." Gabi's upper lip trembled, and she wanted to take the frying pan that was on the kitchen counter and throw it at him.

"What did I say at the party that hurt you so much? You should have thought before you spoke. Nothing was decided, so who do you think is so interested in your deliberations?" Danny continued to lash out at her, ignoring what she was saying.

"You don't even understand how much you humiliated me, you idiot. Everybody laughed at the joke you made at my expense," she boiled.

"You had no reason to be hurt. You spoke without thinking. It's you who hurt me," he answered.

"That's just the point, Danny. You are incapable of understanding me. You're preoccupied with yourself and see only your side of things. You can't even imagine what I'm feeling. I asked Daniela if there's a sickness like that, when a person can't understand someone else. She told me that the condition is called narcissistic personality disorder. You remember that legend? Narcissus looks at his reflection in the water and is so intoxicated by his own beauty that he freezes there? Then the gods punish him by turning him into a flower that constantly gazes at its own reflection and sees nothing else. That's your problem, Danny. You haven't got even a drop of empathy in you." Gabi shouted the whole speech almost in one breath, surprised by her own courage and strength.

"Daniela must have brainwashed you," Danny muttered, as if Gabi were incapable of independent thought, as though she'd said nothing that referred to him personally.

"Daniela did not brainwash me. She described a condition that fits you like a glove. You are a true Narcissus!" she shouted. "You don't notice the people around you, and you ignore me constantly. My feelings don't even register on your radar, and that's why I've decided to leave you, Danny. I'm sick of this artificial relationship with a childish narcissist. I need a real man. Someone who can understand my feelings and truly love me." Gabi stared straight at him, enjoying every word.

"You've gone completely nuts." Danny looked at her in amazement, unprepared for the blow that had landed on him.

"No, Danny. For once, I'm as clear as the waters of the Caribbean," Gabi answered triumphantly. "I'm going back to Jerusalem without you. We're separating. You may as well get it into your head. Record it on the hard disc and press save," she said, speaking his language.

"Your friends have confused you." His arrogant expression gave way to one of despair. Gabi looked at him without compassion and counted to ten.

KO. Danny was out for the count. She walked out of the kitchen, leaving him to wallow in his pain.

"Think very carefully about what you're saying." Danny threw the last word at her, in a desperate attempt at a threat. But Gabi didn't hear him—she was out of his range.

Chapter 15

Lori arrived for her appointment shrouded by a cloud of perfume and carrying a huge, colorful bouquet. Although I was accustomed to her dramatic entrances, the flowers came as a surprise.

"I'm going to live with my sister in Las Vegas," she announced happily. "My house is up for sale, and I'm busy with the final arrangements. The flowers are for you, to thank you for all your help. I'll always remember the things you told me. You are unforgettable." With a self-indulgent smile, Lori fluttered the long lashes that created the impression of an Asian Snow White.

I hadn't expected this abrupt parting. I wanted to understand why she was making such an extreme change in her life, what she was actually planning to do. I again felt a strong need to protect her from making impulsive, hasty decisions.

"What made you decide to do that?"

"Loneliness. The men I met last week weren't anything special. Just as we thought, all they wanted was to get into bed with me."

None of the men had any connections in the entertainment world, Lori said; they couldn't help her in her singing career.

"On the other hand," she continued, "I spoke to my sister, who's now a dancer in a cabaret. She told me they're looking for a singer, and auditions are starting in a day or two. I'm going to fly to Las Vegas for the audition."

"Sounds exciting. Isn't it a bit soon, though, to decide to leave everything behind, sell the house, and cut all ties?"

But then I paused and thought, actually, what connections does Lori have here? Apart from me as her therapist, she had Dr. Warner from the psychiatric ward and Carol Johnson, her financial advisor.

"My sister said that if they don't take me, I can go to tons of different auditions until I find the right role." She sounded as if she'd downed something that was giving her a bit too much confidence, maybe alcohol or drugs.

"There's something else. But you have to swear to keep it a secret." As she said this, she looked at me seriously and piercingly.

"You know that everything that is said in here is strictly confidential except information about child or elderly abuse, or threats of harm to you or someone else."

She nodded. "This time, I'm not giving you permission to tell Dr. Warner, my sister, the police, or anyone else," she commanded, rather strangely, sounding like someone who was well acquainted with the limits of the laws of confidentiality.

I nodded my consent, tensely waiting to hear what she would say.

"Steve won't stop bothering me. He wants my money, and he's making threats. I'm scared he's going to harm me, so I have to disappear, and I don't want to involve the police."

"That's a criminal matter. You must inform the police. Running to Las Vegas is not going to solve the problem." This was the obvious logical move, and I was amazed at Lori's refusal to turn to law enforcement.

"Yesterday, Steve turned up again, this time with his brother. They threatened to ruin my life if I didn't give them the money."

"What's his brother got to do with it? And why do you owe them money?"

"They claim that his brother knew my husband and that my husband owed him money."

"How did Steve's brother know your late husband?"

"He's a mechanic at the gas station near the marina where my husband's yacht is anchored. He sometimes did repairs on the yacht," Lori said dryly.

"Do the police know about the connection between your husband and Steve's brother?"

"The police closed the investigation." Lori sounded more adamant than usual, adding, "and I definitely don't want to reopen the case. Now I have to go. I've got an appointment; for safety's sake, I'm transferring the money to another bank. Thanks for everything." She stood up and smilingly handed me a check before opening her arms wide for a hug. I returned the hug and wished her well, still dumbstruck by her words and her determination.

"You're always welcome to get in touch with me," I mumbled. "When you settle down in Las Vegas, I suggest that you continue therapy, and I would be pleased to be in contact with your new therapist."

As soon as the door closed behind her, I sank onto the couch in my usual manner after a session with Lori. The big bouquet on the coffee table glowed in vibrant colors. I closed my eyes and tried to analyze the situation.

I was shocked by the idea that Steve's brother was possibly the last person to have seen Lori's husband when he stopped to refuel at the gas station. It was quite possible that the brother had sabotaged the car and caused the accident. Presumably, if that were the case, then Steve and Lori were accessories to the crime. Lori had received a handsome sum from the insurance company. She'd fooled all of us: me, Dr. Warner, and the police inspector. Which of us—Lori or me—has the lower IQ? I chided myself. Lori's sudden cunning baffled me. Never before had I heard her speak with such sharp-mindedness; her IQ appeared to have risen by at least thirty points.

Could it be a clinical case of split personality? There was an ongoing professional debate on the subject. According to the diagnosis, such a patient had absolutely diverse character traits. In some cases, the patient was aware of the other personality, while in others, there was no connection between the first personality and the second or third. There were psychologists and psychiatrists who said they had met hundreds of such patients in the course of their work. Others said there was no such condition. According to those who negated the phenomenon, the other so-called personality was created as a result of dissociation, which served as a defense mechanism against unbearable pain. I tended to agree with the clinical approach that said there was no such thing as split personality.

Lori had simply deceived everyone: a superb actress on life's stage, who knew how to present herself as an innocent and helpless victim and, in the end, grabbed the lot. I suddenly wondered which of her stories throughout the years were actually true. The father whose father was also his grandfather? The mother who threw her into the snow?

The wandering around Las Vegas with her sister? The rape? It was impossible to tell. Sometimes real life exceeded imagination. "Here's one more story to keep to yourself," I thought.

I sat at my desk to write my session notes:

> Lori arrived for the last session carrying a bouquet. She said she had decided to move to Las Vegas to pursue a career as a singer. She claimed that Steve and his brother were threatening her and were interested in her money, which was why she was moving away. Her mood was balanced, her thinking was clear, and she sounded decisive and confident. There were no signs of depression or impulsivity behind her decision, which was based mainly on her wish to put distance between herself and Steve and his brother.

I put the notes in the folder with her name and filed it under "Past Patients." Then I dragged myself, still in a state of shock, to the Starbucks around the corner to revive my spirits with a double espresso.

The thoughts of Lori continued to disturb me on the way home. I imagined being summoned to appear in court. The judge would look accusingly at me and ask, "How do you manage to live so calmly with the knowledge that your patient was misleading the police?" And I, writhing like a fish in a net, would reply that I was bound by the law of patient confidentiality. The judge would declare that I was a passive accessory to withholding information from the police and must be severely penalized.

I felt a strong urge to share the day's events with Yoel, to be comforted, to hear a soothing voice promising that I wouldn't be penalized, that this wasn't a criminal matter. I was about to call him on my mobile phone when I saw his car parked in front of our house. In broad daylight? A rare occurrence. I knew the children would come home later, thanks to Gabi, whose turn it was to pick them up from school and drop them at their after-school activities. I quietly entered the study, where Yoel was sitting at the computer with his back to me.

I blew a little cool air on his neck to startle him, and spoke his name. "Yoel!" He jumped like someone caught red-handed and shut his laptop. His haste clearly indicated that he had something to hide.

"What's up?" I asked.

"Nothing special." His answer raised my suspicion further. I didn't know he had secrets, nor had I ever suspected him of it until that moment.

"What were you up to?" I prodded.

A blush crossed his face. Was he furtively watching pornography, like one of my patients? Nah…So what made him jump?

"Remember I told you about Orly Bergman?"

I nodded. How could I forget?

"She wrote me an email saying that she's coming on a visit to San Francisco and asked if I'd like to meet her."

"How nice for you." This was the second time I'd used this phrase with regard to Orly Bergman.

"Do you want to come with me?"

"I wouldn't want to spoil the meeting for you," I said sourly.

"Do you object to my meeting her?"

Of course I did. Yoel, crowned Class Hunk, was going to meet the blonde with the boobs who had turned his head in high school. What did he expect? That I'd jump up and down and clap in excitement?

"No, I don't object," I answered, drawing on what remained of my graciousness.

The chutzpah of the woman! How dare she reach out to a married man with children, just to stir some romantic nostalgia, brushing me aside as if I didn't exist? I was already on my way to the kitchen to prepare dinner when I turned around and walked back into his study, feeling uneasy. This time, too, he seemed to jump and close the screen when he sensed my presence.

"When did you hear about Orly's visit?" I asked casually.

"She sent me an email today. Are you sure you don't want to join us? I'd be happier if you came." He'd noticed my uneasiness and was trying to reassure me.

"When are you meeting her?"

"Next Tuesday. She's coming to a conference at Berkeley with a delegation of special education teachers and will be free to meet me in San Francisco. Come with me," he coaxed, "it'll be fun."

I wasn't sure if the look in his eyes indicated that he wanted me to accept or refuse. I opted to refuse. I didn't want to leave him the slightest leeway to feel that I was in favor of this nostalgic meeting. His jumpiness in front of the computer gave him away: he had something to hide. I was profoundly offended, but didn't dare to reveal my true feelings. Just like a schoolgirl. I couldn't have him know that I was offended; it would be a sign of weakness, and I did not have a weak character, or so I thought.

Then I remembered why I'd come into his study. "Yoel," I said, "I think one of my patients is involved in a murder."

"You're kidding!" he said in an indifferent voice, barely looking up at me. He seemed to respond only to be polite.

In an instant, my world had been turned upside down. I totally forgot Lori and the possible murder of her husband. Orly Bergman pushed Lori aside and took the leading role in the feverish drama in my head. I left the room.

That night we said nothing more about Orly Bergman. Nor about Lori. Yoel had rattled my nerves, and I avoided him like a wildfire. Yet Orly Bergman continued to flicker in my imagination. My memories then drifted to Dalia Givon, a stunningly beautiful girl in my class; her hordes of admirers had never quite satisfied her, and she'd made it her mission to attract any guy who took the slightest interest in one of her friends. According to some unwritten law, Dalia Givon had a sort of prerogative to check out every male. If she liked him, she kept him at her side briefly, and when she got bored, she handed him over to the public, as if running a consignment sale. And the rest of us? Boys and girls alike meekly obeyed the unwritten law.

The boys all yearned for Dalia. She was breathtaking in her bikini on the beach. Men followed her as she paced the seashore, each one trying to catch her attention with jokes and rowdiness. Whenever one actually caught her eye, he dutifully presented himself for her assessment. The moment he was dropped, usually because he didn't meet her high requirements, he became available merchandise for the rest of us girls. Even my boyfriend in high school, the one who for three years tightly circled in my orbit like a planet, making sure that no foreign body collided with mine, even taking my virginity, was one of her rejects. Over the years, a little nagging voice whispered to me from time to time that had he passed her stringent inspection, I would never have had him. Even the letters he sent me, threatening suicide when I told him I wanted to break up with him in order to enlarge my social circle, did not erase the feeling that he viewed me as a consolation prize for the much desired Dalia.

And that evening I, who had regressed suddenly to my adolescence right along with the blushing Yoel, asked myself whether Orly Bergman represented merely a middle-aged reincarnation of Dalia Givon, calling my husband up to be inspected before deciding whether to release him back to me. What if she were to enter his life, arouse memories, even reignite the passion of his youth? What if he became addicted to her voice, the way Gilad was addicted to the telephone conversations with Nirit? The way Mika's mind was addled by a thirteen-year-old boy from the past, and the way Gila found her childhood love and placed her at the apex of a sex threesome? I couldn't soothe my nerves.

Outwardly, I was serene. Life went on as usual. The dinner I made was chewed and swallowed by my family. I gave Maya her bath, checked Alon's homework, read a bedtime story. Then I restlessly got into bed with a book. I deliberately refrained from going to Yoel's study, not wanting to risk seeing him suddenly shut his screen and blush again.

Later that evening, Yoel came into the bedroom and shut the door, signifying what was to come. He sent the book flying out of my hand and threw himself onto me. Everything felt different than usual. The familiar minuet—two steps forward, one step back, a turn or two, a bow and it was over—was replaced by a frantic samba. His muscles taut, he clamped my body to his, fondled my skin as if he'd never touched it before, and galloped in ecstasy to the beat of thousands of unseen drums. My head banged against the headboard. My wide eyes were fixed on the ceiling, from which Orly Bergman was peeping at me, blond and full-breasted, but faceless. Since none of my friends' faces matched the few details available to me, I tried to draw on my imagination. I thought of Meg Ryan, but rejected her because of her flat chest; then I imagined Michelle Pfeiffer. I couldn't imagine such refined beauty in the neighborhood of Holon, where Yoel had grown up. I recalled Sharon Stone's face on a magazine cover. The photographer had snapped her without makeup, her short blond hair unstyled, and wearing jeans and a T-shirt. Sharon Stone completed the puzzle.

"Yoel, who are you thinking of?" I asked.

"You, sweetheart. Who else?" But a few minutes after Yoel caught his breath and steadied his pulse, he wanted to sleep with Orly Bergman again. I refused. I had my reasons.

The image of Sharon Stone seeped into my dreams that night and remained with me the entire following day. I stared at every blonde who crossed my path.

Chapter 16

Most of my mornings were marked by routine and comfortable monotony. Not this one. On the morning of the day Yoel was scheduled to meet Orly Bergman, Gilad came to my clinic.

His words remained echoing in my head long after he left, and well into the night.

"Now is the winter of our discontent," he joked bitterly before he'd even seated himself in the armchair, before he removed his glasses and rubbed his eyes. "In short, my life's shit." He replaced his glasses. "Kimberly's taken the girls and left me. She's gone to her parents in Texas."

He confessed he'd seen Nirit while he was in Israel for business, and told me the details of their meeting.

He'd met Nirit on Tuesday at eight in the evening, as they had arranged. She chose a restaurant in the revamped Tel Aviv Port area and sent exact details that included nearby parking facilities. Gilad waited for her in the bar, keeping an eye on the entrance. He asked himself what he expected of the evening. No, the meeting with Nirit was not related to his anger toward his wife. He did not intend to break up his marriage. Not yet.

Nirit walked down the dim passage leading to the hostess, ignoring the bespectacled fellow staring at her from the bar. She doesn't recognize me, Gilad thought as he walked toward her, calling her name. Nirit turned toward him, looking surprised.

Almost twenty years had passed since they last met. He knew his hair was going gray, and his hairline had shifted. Her hair was also shorter and thinner; he didn't remember her with hair only down past her ears. Her clothes were too tight, as if she had not yet come to terms with the current dimensions of her body. Three children, long shifts at work, a mortgage, and life in general had left their mark. Gilad graded her "average" on his personal scale. Kimberly passed the test of time with a higher grade, he decided.

"Gilad," Nirit exclaimed in delight, clasping his neck with her right hand while planting a kiss on his cheek. Gilad returned the kiss and held her hand for a long moment before releasing it to pay for his drink at the bar.

"Back soon," he said.

When he returned, she looked at him intensely. "I'm sure I've changed," she said nervously, while also scanning the changes in him. He nodded, and she bit her lip.

"Hey, Gilad wears glasses!" She smiled in disbelief.

"You've never seen me in glasses before?"

She shook her head, and he obligingly removed the glasses, although she said they suited him. She said he looked more mature and more handsome than the boy she remembered.

A few more deep breaths and sentimental smiles later, they sat facing one another at a table overlooking the sea. They soon found themselves deep in a conversation that was wrapped in nostalgia and punctuated by youthful sexual tension. Their intense phone conversations had already bridged the gap of twenty years, and they found themselves feeling as though they were eighteen years old again, silly and giggling. She mentioned Vered Talmon, his girlfriend in eleventh grade, and recalled the day when Vered turned up wearing a see-through blouse and no bra. Even the math teacher froze in the middle of solving an equation on the board, his gaze glued to Vered's exposed breasts as he exclaimed in amazement: "Vered, is that a school uniform you are wearing?" They laughed. Their conversation veered from amusement to deep sympathies, too, such as when they remembered their mutual friend Ophira, whose husband had died of cancer; fate had not been kind to her. Eventually, they returned to the present.

Nirit told him about the unforgettable party that her friends had thrown on her last birthday. The men performed a striptease like the one in *The Full Monty*, which culminated in a full-frontal reveal, uncovering the parts that they had been concealing with hats. "I'd never seen so much male nudity at once, and all in my honor!" she told him.

Gilad withdrew a little, asking himself if she was playing the ingénue, or purposely trying to arouse him with erotic stories. He decided to steer the conversation toward less intimate topics and asked about her job and children. Before she could answer, they were approached by a waitress dressed in black, with one ring in her eyebrow and another peeping from her navel. He ordered a bottle of wine and an array of appetizers to share.

Nirit shared the pain of her marital crisis. She told him about her last fight with her husband, Uri, which had led her to think about the meaning of life and the relationship between spouses.

"Don't you think it's hard to maintain a romantic relationship with only one man for so many years?" she asked, and he wondered what she was implying.

"What does your psychologist have to say about it, and what's the alternative?" he said, putting the ball back into her court.

"My psychologist thinks my husband has a problem with intimacy. He loves me in his own way, but he can't give what he doesn't have. He has no patience for my needs," she concluded sadly and looked expectantly at Gilad. He was silent. "If I had known that his ability to give was so limited, I would have thought a lot more before marrying him," she added, imbibing her wine and immediately refilling the glass. Gilad summoned the waitress and ordered another bottle, pointing to the empty one on the table.

"Our sex life is also not what it used to be. He makes weak excuses and does his best to come to bed only after I fall asleep. He even suggested we have separate rooms. It's hard to accept that I'm not even forty, and everything is already behind me. It's all over." Her frankness was touching.

Gilad was unsettled. Her words over the telephone echoed in his mind: "I'm also married, and I'm not interested in breaking up my family." He remembered her demanding nature, her restlessness, and her chronic dissatisfaction and wondered what she wanted of him.

Nirit continued drinking, and the more she drank, the more severely she criticized Uri. She gazed at Gilad with a yearning sadness, and he felt like an ascetic monk, tortured by a tempting morsel that had invited him to take just one little bite. She laid one hand on his arm in a tentative caress while the other hand poured another glass of wine. He shrank in his chair, mortified. This was not how he had imagined the meeting. He was annoyed that she had foisted onto him the full responsibility for setting limits. He couldn't depend on her to behave appropriately; her cloying behavior made it impossible. Her backbone was like the stem of a wilted flower. There was no evidence of the connection he'd felt during their phone conversations, which had led him to imagine that Nirit understood the history of his parents and himself, that she could read his innermost experiences as she would a book. She wasn't entertaining him with imitations of his mother's strong, guttural South American accent, as she had over the phone. He had expected a provocative, exciting encounter and was disappointed to find that Nirit was even more troubled than he was, and that her intentions were completely different.

Clearly tipsy, she asked, "Where are you staying?"

"At the Hilton," he replied hesitantly, wondering if she was planning a surprise visit to his room. He had never been in a situation in which it would be so easy to be unfaithful to Kimberly. The seduction was blatant and supposed to be provocative, but Gilad wasn't carried away by temptation. He was overcome with pity and distaste when he looked at Nirit, drunk, with a partnership even more miserable than his. He considered whether to drive her home or call a cab. He chose the latter to avoid unpleasantness should she try to put a drunken hand down his pants in the confines of the car.

"It's late," he said. "I've got a long day of business meetings tomorrow. Can I call a cab for you?"

"Yes. Time for Cinderella to go home," she declared.

He accompanied her to the cab, gallantly paid the driver, and gave Nirit a farewell peck on the cheek. On the way back to his rental car in the restaurant parking lot, he became aware that he was angry with Nirit for forcing him to be the sole responsible adult. He thought about Kimberly and reassured himself that his conscience was clear. He had not been unfaithful and remained hers in both his body and soul. He had toyed with the possibility of inviting Nirit to his room at the Hilton, even allowed himself to fantasize about stormy sex. But she wasn't attractive enough, he told himself, and it wasn't worth it to complicate his relations with Kimberly for a totally unnecessary, superfluous fling with Nirit.

In the plane above the Atlantic Ocean, Gilad daydreamed about Nirit and Kimberly becoming as close as sisters. He imagined them meeting and falling in love with each other. Saw them laughing, exchanging recipes, standing in the kitchen chatting about children and husbands. For him, a friendship between them would be a kind of wish fulfillment. They would kindle something inside him that would revive his sapped inner strength. Nirit's grown children would tend to his little girls, and the two couples would enjoy a safe, noninvasive intimacy, full of children's stories and laughter. Kimberly would have the opportunity to see him in a new light—from a feminine, Israeli perspective. She would get to know the boy he was, through Nirit's admiring eyes, and love him the way Nirit once loved him. Yes, he decided, he would tell Kimberly about Nirit and suggest that they meet. There was no reason for Kimberly to object. After all, it was only the renewal of an old friendship. It was all going to turn out for the best. He fell asleep after a glass of vodka and dreamed of Nirit and Kimberly sitting with a newspaper spread in front of them, looking for neighboring houses.

Gilad came home at ten in the evening, took his bags from the trunk of the car, and opened the door quietly, so as not to wake the children. He went to the bedroom where Kimberly was sitting at the computer with her back to him, her eyes fixed on the screen as usual. He hugged her.

She shoved him away and turned her furious face to him, her eyes gleaming.

"Don't you dare put your dirty hands on me!" she roared.

"What's happened?"

"You ask what's happened, like some innocent lamb?" She pointed to the emails to and from Nirit.

"If I thought I had something to hide, I wouldn't have left the correspondence for you to see," he said quietly.

"Did you meet her?" she attacked.

"Yes," he said, looking her in the eye.

"Then I have nothing to say to you. If you have anything to say, you can tell my lawyer." She was adamant, leaving him no room to explain. "Tonight you sleep in the living room, and tomorrow I'm flying to Texas with the girls. I've been waiting to see you face to face to hear it from your mouth before I go. And by the way, regarding our 'dancing,' you can tell your psychologist that I say you have no idea how to 'dance.' You're clumsy and awkward, you step on my feet, your grip is like sandpaper, and all I want is for you to leave me alone, in peace. That's why I ever even bother to fake it—to make it end sooner. But believe me, 'dancing' with you is something I haven't wanted to do for quite some time. And now that you have lied to me, there's no chance that I ever will again. So spare me your bullshit, and get out! Now."

She pointed to the door. Gilad hesitated for a moment, hurt. He considered standing up for himself, but her words had cut him too deeply. He felt as if blood and tears were flowing together as he crept out in search of a corner where he could lick his wounds, away from Kimberly's hurtful words.

He arranged the cushions of the sofa in his den and wrapped himself in a light blanket. This was not how he had imagined his homecoming. Kimberly had never been so cold, distant, and wounding. She had not given him a moment to explain himself. She didn't know how seriously he'd been tested and still remained faithful to her, how much effort and willpower he had put into preserving the sanctity of their marriage. What an idiot he'd been. At least, if he had taken the opportunity to fool around, he could have accepted the cold shower from Kimberly as fair. But no. He didn't deserve this. He had been good; he had not been unfaithful to Kimberly. Gilad felt his hurt turning into anger, which turned into fear for his disintegrating family. The history of his childhood was repeating itself. His wife had banished him from the bedroom just as his mother had banished his father; she, too, couldn't find forgiveness for a sin that could not be atoned.

Morning brought no relief. Kimberly was busy with last-minute preparations for the flight. She flatly refused Gilad's offer to drive her and the girls to the airport and ordered a limousine. The girls sensed the tension and hostility and clung anxiously to Gilad. They felt that there was going to be a painful separation despite his promises to visit them in Texas. He took his daughters in his arms and held them close, fighting back tears for their sake.

"I'm going to miss you," he whispered, meaning every word. His heart pounded in his chest. He thought, my life's falling apart in front of my eyes, and there's nothing I can do about it. Not guilty, Your Honor. I wasn't unfaithful, I'm innocent. I don't deserve this humiliation. She doesn't want to dance with me? She doesn't have to. I won't beg.

He walked the girls to the limousine, where Kimberly was sitting next to the driver, not batting an eyelid. In vain, Gilad tried to catch her eye. No good-bye. Nothing. With a heavy heart, he waved to the girls and returned to the empty house to huddle under the blanket on the sofa. The silence grated worse than nails on a chalkboard, and the emptiness cut into him like a saw.

His cell phone rang. Nirit. Gilad was relieved that someone was thinking of him and was happy to answer. Nirit's voice sounded sweet and inviting. She whispered that she'd had a great time seeing him again. The years had been good to him. He looked just as sexy and handsome as always. Since their meeting, she hadn't been able to stop thinking about him.

Gilad was a bit embarrassed by the flood of compliments and the open declaration of intent. Nirit sounded as if she had opened wide the gates to an affair. Here's a woman who is interested in me, he thought, who is courting me, who wants to dance with me, whereas my wife has discarded me like an old rag. What does one do with such an open invitation? The memory in his body of his young daughters clinging to him so recently was compounding his miserable state. Gilad didn't want to respond to Nirit with the same frankness. He was silent for a while, then sighed and said he needed time. He considered telling her about Kimberly leaving, but decided against it. He was wary of involving Nirit, whose advances mainly alarmed and disconcerted him.

"Nirit, I have an important meeting in five minutes," he said, ending the conversation apologetically.

Indeed, he had to convene with himself. Gilad meditated on his situation, asking himself what was happening to him. His life was disintegrating. How had he allowed himself to deteriorate to the point of losing control like this? What could he do?

That's when he'd decided to call me. I knew him and his history. He thought I would help him to see the light—that I would lead him to a better place. I knew he hadn't been unfaithful to Kimberly. I would believe him. He dialed my number and left a message.

"Daniela, I'm back from a business trip to Israel. Can I have an appointment as soon as possible?"

After Gilad finished his story, he added, looking straight at me, "What hurts me most is that Kimberly didn't believe that I wasn't unfaithful to her. "Do you believe me when I say I wasn't unfaithful to my wife?"

"I believe you," I said with no hesitation.

"I'm sick of running after her and begging. She doesn't give me a chance," he said with tears in his eyes. "With my own hands I ruined the possibility of a happy family life. She'll never forgive me. I've lost everything."

He was restless, speaking in an agitated voice and shuffling his feet as if his body wanted to get up and chase after the words. I sensed that the tissue of Gilad's soul, so patiently and laboriously mended through our therapy, was about to be torn once more to shreds. I wanted to take him in my arms, gather the fragments, and bind them, to bandage his wounds. I wanted to be a soothing, uncondemning mother.

"Gilad, you're blaming yourself and forgetting that Kimberly barely gave you any chances to speak to her in the last few months." I paused. "Paradoxically, a crisis can actually improve a couple's relationship. Apparently she is also hurt. You regarded the meeting with Nirit as a meeting between childhood friends, whereas she saw it as romantic. It's a misunderstanding that can be corrected by simple communication," I told Gilad and myself. Maybe the meeting between Yoel and Orly was also creating a misunderstanding that could be corrected by simple communication. I looked at Gilad as if looking in a mirror.

"In all misunderstandings," I continued, "both sides have to explain themselves. What would you wish to explain to Kimberly?"

After thinking for a long time, he said, switching from Hebrew to English, "I overreacted."

"Meaning?"

"I shouldn't have acted suspicious when Kimberly was absorbed in endless conversations with her boss. And at the same time, I was drawn into a whirlpool with Nirit, for which I'm sorry."

I thought about Gilad's choice of words. He had chosen to explain himself with an English phrase that had no close Hebrew equivalent. *Overreaction* correctly defines a situation when one superfluous reaction, one faulty judgment, one step beyond the correct step, can alter the whole picture. I thought about Yoel and his anticipated meeting with Orly, about my jealousy, my fear that my world was about to collapse.

With an unspoken thank you to Gilad for enlightening me, I told myself, in English, "Do not overreact."

"If you could turn back time, how would you have responded?" I asked him.

"In retrospect, if I'd been wiser, I would have ignored Kimberly's pre-occupation with her boss, and I should never have let myself be dragged into the contact with Nirit; it was a costly mistake."

Correct. I should also let the Yoel-Orly storm blow over without overreacting.

I thought about Gilad's feelings of helplessness concerning Kimberly. He had always been afraid that his life was doomed to failure from the start, cursed by his mother's dire prophecies. He had been expecting this failure for a long time, since his wedding day, when he couldn't believe that the universe had granted him such great happiness. He did not feel like a master of his own destiny; it was this that I had to correct.

"Assuming that all possibilities were open to you, how would you choose to improve the way you feel?"

"I don't have many possibilities." He smiled for the first time that morning, albeit sadly. "I have to get on a plane and meet Kimberly and the children. I'm planning it out as we speak. There's no point in carrying on in Silicon Valley without my family. And anyway, Ido's start-up is at the point of folding; it's a matter of days before they announce that they're closing. Even the timing of the move to Texas is good. Kimberly's refusing to talk to me on the phone, but I hope she'll agree to meet me face to face. I miss the girls. Even if the crisis with Kimberly doesn't sort itself out quickly and even if we part in the end, I prefer to live near them. I feel homeless and alone here in the Valley."

"So, we're parting?" I couldn't hide my sadness.

"So it seems. I'll settle the terms with Ido today, and I'll try to be on a plane tomorrow. I hope Kimberly lets me into her parents' house and doesn't leave me standing at the door like a bum. Thank you, Daniela, for everything. I promise to stay in touch."

We parted with a handshake. In my heart, I didn't foresee a rosy future for Gilad. The glue that had once joined him to Kimberly wasn't strong enough to weather change, and had apparently already dried up.

Chapter 17

That evening, I drove home in a car loaded with children and groceries. Once again, I was surprised to find Yoel's car parked in the driveway, because he was usually the last one home. Orly Bergman has changed all our routines, I thought bitterly. Alon and Maya dashed toward the house, and I dragged after them with grocery bags and question marks.

I was met by the sound of the stereo. In the living room, Yoel was swaying, arms outspread, his deep voice joining the singer Noa's in her rendition of a Leah Goldberg poem: "And crashing waves / rise in their weeping / to the heights of my love…" He spun Ayelet and concluded with the sentimental refrain, "Come, my bride, come my bride, come…"!

"Do not overreact," I murmured to myself, biting my lips. I gave Yoel a meek smile that failed to match his euphoria. He was wearing his most flattering jeans, the ones that gave him a "tight ass," to quote Nira. I noticed that he had found time to drop in on his hairdresser. When the song ended, he apologized for having to leave in a hurry, but Orly was waiting for him in San Francisco.

Donning a wool coat that lent him a distinguished air, he murmured, as if I had become transparent, "I wonder if she still looks the same as in high school."

Then he turned to me and asked, "How do I look?"

"Great," I said, like a kindly, sexless nun.

"Sure you don't want to come along?" he asked offhandedly.

I answered politely, "No, thank you."

The moment he left, I decided I also deserved to have some fun. Me too. The neglected wife. I certainly deserved a little pleasure in life. I spared myself the task of whipping up omelets and salad for dinner and ordered pizza to the children's delight. We devoured huge quantities, and for a change I allowed myself two slices loaded with calories and dripping with fat and cholesterol.

I decided to take some shortcuts that night. I told Alon to walk Oscar and quickly loaded the dishwasher. Ayelet, with her fine sense of intuition, realized something was up with her mother and volunteered to put Maya to bed and read her a story. Alon returned from his short walk with the dog, and I finished cleaning the kitchen to the soundtrack of his guitar.

By now, I knew, Yoel was with Orly in San Francisco, but I didn't quite know where I was, myself. Piles of papers awaited my devoted attention in the study. Not tonight, I told them, accepting the fact that my patients' session notes and the month's billing would just have to wait. I went to bed with my current book, but although my eyes ran along the lines, my mind was elsewhere. I flipped the pages impatiently and absentmindedly skipped chapters. I closed the book. Not tonight. I turned on the TV and quickly turned it off again.

What advice would I give myself if I were a patient in my own clinic? What solution would I offer an uneasy woman? Deep breathing was one, although not sufficiently substantial. Guided imagery—another possibility. I nixed that one immediately, because my imagination couldn't distance itself by so much as an inch from my husband, who I feared was receiving some special education at that very moment. I consoled myself and my wounded pride by opting for a hot, bubbly bath. A blue package in the bathroom trash bin gave Yoel away: he'd finally opened the new Hugo Boss cologne I had given him on his birthday for the special occasion. I then frowned upon seeing another, more worrisome bit of packaging with the image of a pair of Calvin Klein boxer-briefs stretched on the body of an exceptionally muscular young model. I undressed and filled the tub with boiling-hot water and added scented bath salts. Very slowly, I tested the water with the tip of a toe and gradually immersed my whole foot.

The distraction of the heat didn't ease my restlessness. My mind was locked on the question of whether Israel's own Sharon Stone had worn sandals and whether my husband's eyes were fixed on her feet at that very moment. I'd always thought that Yoel's attraction to feminine feet was something unusual, idiosyncratic. I held this view until I came across *The Key*, by Junichiro Tanizaki. The book revealed that Yoel had a twin soul in twentieth-century Japan, who also had a sexual weakness for women's feet. Tanizaki's fixation, it turned out, was referred to as a foot fetish. While Tanizaki's character's obsession bordered a perversion, I didn't think of Yoel's fervor as a perversion, given that Yoel was also enthusiastic about other erotic zones of a woman's body. Nevertheless, his attraction to my feet had emerged on our first date, when we were students, a few million years earlier.

It happened like this: one spring day, when I was a second-year student in the humanities department at Tel Aviv University, I made my way to the sciences building to give my cousin Noam an important envelope from our grandmother, who used me as a courier. I knew Noam was urgently in need of money. My wanderings in those corridors where female feet seldom trod drew a few tortured souls from their alcoves in hopes that their seductive communications—"turn right, straight to the end of the hall, then take a left"—might lead to romance.

"Can I help you?" asked a curly-headed, broad-shouldered young fellow who resembled Michelangelo's David.

"I'm looking for Noam."

"Noam isn't here yet."

"I have to give him something."

"Can I do anything? Do you want me to give him the envelope?"

"Tell me," I heard myself asking, just to talk, "can you explain all these pipes?" I pointed at the serpentine arrangement of pumps and flashing lights. He gladly delved into comprehensive explanations, seizing the opportunity to demonstrate his expertise, and all the while his gaze was focused toward the floor, concentrating on the area around my sandaled feet.

In my naivety, I thought the man with the curls and broad shoulders suffered from shyness. Blatantly false.

"You want to meet up sometime?" he asked, flashing his piercing green eyes.

"How about the university pool?" I suggested. I might as well put my goods on full display and gauge the reaction, I thought to myself.

In time, I discovered that Yoel had used his lengthy explanation about the pipes and lights to buy himself ample time to get a good look at my feet; he confessed that he had never seen feet so narrow and delicate, such marvelously shaped toes, like dots on a perfectly slanted line. To his great disappointment, however, he found a flaw in the length of the toenails. It baffled him that such an obviously refined girl would sink to such a sordid state of pedicure. He wanted to find a nail clipper and get to work on them right there and then. As for me, I couldn't have cared less about the length of my toenails on that day. I had finals and term papers to finish and hardly had time to breathe. And on top of that, to trim my toenails? Give me a break…It didn't occur to me that anyone would ever pay attention to something so trivial. But here too I was utterly wrong.

So what if, at this very moment, Yoel was staring at Orly Bergman's feet in the heart of romantic San Francisco? And what if he was finding that they were the very feet his heart desired?

Yoel, whose youthful curls had long since vanished from his forehead, might get tangled in the web of his memories, which was sprawled out before him. No doubt, the two of them were reminiscing, giggling and laughing, eating and drinking, maybe getting turned on.

Yoel and I did meet at the pool after our initial encounter. He sat by me for a while, taking an interest in the textbook I was using to study for my upcoming psychology final. He even demonstrated considerable knowledge about the behavioral sciences. Apparently, he had some ex-girlfriends in the field. He suddenly rose to his feet and walked away; Michelangelo's David would not have been ashamed of such legs. I watched him as he walked the length of the diving board with Olympic style.

I learned later that the stylish bikini covering only tiny patches of my skin had yielded the desired effect. My untrimmed toenails, on the other hand, continued to bother him. The final conquest, the collapsing of the walls and the bursting of the dams, didn't happen until he invited me into his modest student apartment a few days later, for a light dinner. Yoel seated me in the kitchenette, between the wall and the little Formica table. He made me a toasted cheese pita sprinkled with a pinch of *za'atar* and served it with a cup of instant coffee. A taste of heaven. My husband won my heart with toasted cheese and a pinch of *za'atar*. After feeding me, he took a nail clipper and with my permission gave me an exceptionally moving pedicure. The rest, as they say, is history, recorded in the Oren family annals.

So what would happen if Orly seduced him with her charms? What would he grant her in return, these days, as a respected adult member of society? He could feed her expensive delicacies, whisper poetry in her ears, embrace her on exotic mountaintops, fly her over the oceans and dive with her into the seas, sail with her across mighty rivers, dance with her in glamorous metropolises, build her a home, give her a child. Oh, stop it! I silently chastised myself. He's not giving her any children, she's his age. She's lost her chance, passed the childbearing years.

I was carried away.

Enough self-torture.

I pulled myself out of the cooling water and wrapped my body in a huge towel. I dried my short hair. The face peering back at me in the mirror looked like a rose that had reached the peak of its bloom the week before. Its petals spread, leaves tipped with delicate wrinkles announcing time's passing, the stem straining nobly to bear the load. Tomorrow it would bend and droop its head. Its leaves would wither and leave behind a dry stem. And as though to complete the image of yesterday's blooming, my eyes drifted south and met two deflated balloons that had lost half of their volume and swayed sadly between the heavens and the earth, as mementos of a fabulous party that had once raged. Farther down, close to the navel, the two slices of pizza I had devoured bulged in my stomach, no doubt padding its walls with a lush layer of fresh fat. I remembered Jane Fonda's words, when she was going through menopause; she said that whenever she looked in the mirror she took comfort, because she knew that she would never look better than she did at that very moment—tomorrow would not bring lovelier images.

Looking in the mirror is a recurring motif in women's literature. I recalled a heroine I'd recently come upon, who conducted the pencil test on herself in front of the mirror. She placed a pencil under the fold of her breast, and if the pencil dropped, the perkiness of her breasts passed the test. If the pencil remained in the fold, her drooping breasts had failed the test. It was shameful that all I remembered of the book, which poignantly explored trauma, loss, divorce, eroticism, and hope, was the pencil test. Oh, and an irritating psychologist character named, if I remembered correctly, Davida.

For weeks after reading the book, I had argued with the writer in my mind. First of all, I told her, it's a pity that you didn't write about the pencil test a few decades ago. If I'd conducted it then, I might have had a chance of passing. Secondly, I told her in my heart, the breast size of the heroine, who passed the test, was not revealed. It's a fact that the organs and limbs of different people come in a wide range of sizes. So, is it fair to apply this rigorous test to pancake breasts not built to secure a pencil? In other words, I suggested that she standardize the test—verify its statistical validity—so that her readers might know what to expect. Why, I only wanted to save her readers, like me, from unnecessary frustration. Women's literature must be precise, I muttered to myself. Either way, I failed the pencil test miserably. Maybe my breasts would withstand the hammer test instead, but at the cost of my toes, whose importance I have already highlighted.

Amused by the idea of a hammer test, I stepped out of the tub, buttoned myself into my pajamas, and laid my head on the soft pillow. Images of Yoel and Orly flickered on my closed eyelids. He opened his arms to her and galloped with frenzied desire to the beat of a thousand drums: "Come, my bride, come my bride, come!"

It was ten o'clock. Yoel had left the house at six and arrived in San Francisco at the latest at seven o'clock. By now they had been sitting together for three hours. When would he be back? Maybe never. Maybe he had decided to change the course of his life after one meeting with the unrivaled Orly, as had happened to Anita's divorced sister Yaffa. Once happily married for years, she had been informed one day by her husband that he had reunited with his first love, the one he still adored with all his heart without knowing that she also still held a torch for him. As soon as he met her again, as an adult, and learned that their passion was mutual, he left his home, wife, and three children and moved on to live the life he was always meant to have lived. As if he had a self-correcting program, a sort of GPS—even after an accidental wrong turn, the program rerouted him back to the right track.

Yes, I reminded myself morosely, such things do happen, and I'd better be prepared for the worst. The hands of the clock moved slowly. The last time I'd sat with my eyes helplessly glued to a clock had been three years ago in a narrow little room in the cancer ward at Stanford Hospital, wearing a shapeless polka-dot hospital gown that was open down the back. I'd been waiting for the results of a second mammogram, two days after they had flattened my breasts in the quiet clinic across the street. In the minutes before they finished checking the new tests, my life passed before my eyes. I said good-bye to my loved ones, Yoel and the children. I saw my children raising the grandchildren I would never know, would never shower with all my love. I would leave things unfinished, and I didn't even know what I still had to finish.

Fear flooded me. I longed to call Yoel on my mobile, but the battery was dead. I also didn't know what to say to him. I wondered if I could drive home with cancer in my breast. I could. I thought about my childhood best friend, Chami, how a few years earlier she must have sat, waiting for results, exactly as I was sitting now; when the results came, they were merciless.

I reminded myself that it was possible to survive the worst of circumstances. I knew I'd get through it. The nurse knocked on the door. I gave her a probing look, which turned into a sigh of relief when she gestured with an upturned thumb and a smile that everything was okay. "See you next year," she said, and I wanted to fly away and never return.

Apparently having exhausted myself with thoughts of horror scenarios, I was on the verge of falling into a deep, sweet sleep. It was better that way. Better that Yoel wouldn't find me up waiting for him. Better that he thought I had no strong feelings about his date with Orly Bergman. It really wasn't such a big deal. Me? I do not overreact.

When Yoel returned, I heard his steps along the hallways and up the stairs to the bedroom. I shut my eyes. He crawled to my side of the bed where I lay curled, leaned over me, and pulled my eyelids open, the way the children used to do when they were little.

"Daniela, are you asleep?" he asked, with his face against mine. I smelled the unfamiliar mist of Hugo Boss, and the spicy fragrance of Italian cuisine mixed with wine and coffee on his breath. I stubbornly went on pretending to sleep. I didn't want to open my eyes and see proof of his happiness. I didn't want to hear his stories, as if I were his roommate. I didn't want to hear about the exciting date. I didn't want to. Really didn't. Yoel left me in peace and went to check emails late into the night. I tossed and turned for another long hour.

⚘

The next morning, a disquieting cup of coffee awaited me beside the bed. It looked like the coffee he made me every morning, but this time it was cold. Yoel had awakened early and had left the house already. Now he was elsewhere.

Was this a sign? I wondered. This morning there was no kiss on my forehead, no cheerful "Good morning!" I concluded that he must be in some kind of emotional tangle. Orly had mixed his mind. I stumbled from my bed and into the new day that guaranteed nothing but trouble. Gilad's magical words from the day before were forgotten like an expired mantra.

The day was indeed gloriously bad. After my shower, I stood in front of the closet, trying to choose an outfit that would lift my mood, something refreshing. I went from hanger to hanger in search of a garment that would let me feel that my life wasn't over—a garment demonstrating a simple fact: I was neither transparent nor invisible. In a moment of unrestrained yearning, I was seduced by a red silk dress that fell softly over my curves and emphasized my feminine outlines. I wore it with the addition of a white brocade top, a double string of pearls, and satin heels. One look in the mirror left no doubt that I'd gone overboard. I looked like someone dressed for a meeting with the Queen of England. After all, I was only going to meet some patients this morning, and then have lunch with a psychiatrist colleague, Dr. Don Waksberg; there was no need to get all dressed up. However, Alon was calling from downstairs, "Mom, I'm late!" so instead of changing into something more comfortable, I had to hurry down to get the children ready for school and leave the house on time.

"Do you have an important meeting today?" Alon asked.

"Uh-huh," I muttered. I thought of Don Waksberg, who was not in the least important but rather quite ordinary; how kind of me to elevate him to VIP status merely for being a man who might notice my changed appearance and compliment my femininity.

At the clinic, each and every therapist asked me in turn if I was headed to an important meeting. "Yes," I said, without expounding. I was hoping Yoel would phone and suggest that we meet for lunch, as he did on rare occasions. I would have gladly canceled my monthly meeting with my colleague.

"I'm sorry," I'd say on the phone, "something very important has come up. Really. Sorry!" And he would forgive me. And when Yoel saw the red dress, he would also ask if I had an important meeting, and I would answer mysteriously, "Yes," without elaborating. But the dream remained a fantasy. Close to noon, I dialed his number thinking that if I pushed my luck a little the wish might come true. Nothing—just the voicemail message announcing his unavailability.

I waited for Don at California Café, which, at noon, swarmed with doctors, psychologists, and other professionals with offices in the vicinity of Stanford Hospital. I felt at ease among the women in diamonds and pearls and the men in expensive suits and ties, authentic Rolex watches peeping from their cuffs.

From my corner table, I saw Don Waksberg's ungainly approach, his eyes on the ground, his body bent as if his briefcase were too heavy. We met once a month to discuss medication for my patients.

Like everyone else, he wanted to know if I was dressed for something special. I acknowledged this with a smile. Apparently it was clear to both of us that he, Dr. Don Waksberg, was not in that category. In contrast to me, he came to the meeting looking as if he had just left a rumpled bed. His hair was disheveled, his cheeks were unshaven, his checkered jacket was creased and in need of cleaning, and his breath was foul.

He sat down heavily across from me, glanced at the menu, and ordered pasta marinara and a bottle of wine. I ordered a salad. We made it through the caseload quickly and moved on to the second part of our lunch meeting as Don polished off the bottle of wine. As his second bottle arrived, he changed the subject to his third wife, who was threatening divorce. It was fortunate, he said, that they had no children. There was no point in bringing children into such an unstable world. He'd been through this before and he knew what to expect, but whenever he faced a new divorce, the pain hit him hard and drove him back to the bottle. He'd tried to quit a few times in the past and had a few successes to his credit, but in times of crisis, the bitter drop always won.

I asked if he'd considered speaking to someone, perhaps a colleague; maybe he could prescribe an antidepressant for himself, or attend some

AA meetings. In response, he sneezed, spraying a mix of saliva and chewed pasta and tomato sauce on my party dress. As if that were not bad enough, he blew his nose loudly into the table napkin and, while mumbling apologies, attempted to use it to remove the pasta shrapnel stuck to my dress. I recoiled, said there was no need! Not to worry! Dry cleaning would take care of it! Everything was okay!

Was this a sign from above, I wondered, that as a married, if somewhat neglected woman, I should not run around in fancy clothes to fish for compliments? Don Waksberg allowed me to pay for the meal when I offered. He said that he was working on changing his habits, and was trying to learn to accept gifts from people—especially women. Until now, women had only demanded that he give, give, give, and now he was learning to take, as well. And anyway, he might soon be back on the singles market, so it was best that he learn to demand good treatment. I nodded in understanding, and handed my credit card to the waitress. Hey, I said to myself, there's something to be learned from this meeting, too; I promised myself that for our next lunch, I'd wear a raincoat resistant to unpleasant showers of all kinds.

At the end of the day, after apologizing to everyone I met for the stains on my clothing, I was glad to take off the silk dress and the now multicolored brocade top and change into jeans and clogs. The problems of the day would soon be fixed by a visit to the dry cleaner, and everything would return to normal. I phoned the unavailable Yoel again and wished that the day that had begun so badly would end calmly. After dinner, the phone rang. It was Gabi, who said in a choked voice, "Daniela, come over, Roni's in trouble."

I dashed to the Toyota and sped down the road to Gabi's house. The dark living room was alarmingly silent, as if I'd come to a house where someone was on her deathbed. Gabi was there, with little Keren clinging to her wide thighs and the startled boys staring at Roni who was pacing like a caged animal, her hand on her heart, panting, her eyes downcast.

Gabi whispered that Roni's heart was racing madly, she felt as if she were going to faint, she was dizzy, her whole body was shaking, and she had waves of heat and cold. She felt as if she were dying. The bright lights nauseated her, and she'd asked for them to be dimmed. They had just come from the doctor, who had examined Roni and said there was nothing wrong with her and, no, she was not pregnant.

"What can I do, Daniela? What's wrong with her?" Gabi asked, deeply concerned.

"Looks like a panic attack." I approached Roni and looked into her eyes, which were darting from side to side, bulging from the sockets. I kicked off my clogs and stood face to face with her, holding her shaking hands.

"Listen to me, Roni, you're having a panic attack. Do what I do, copy my movements, and you'll get over it, you'll see."

I took her hands in mine and spread her arms. Feet apart, I jumped up and down; Roni copied me. I increased the rhythm and we jumped and waved our arms in jumping jacks. When I became tired, I stopped, but Roni carried on. After five minutes, I ordered her to stop. That was it. Her nausea and dizziness passed, she stopped shaking, and her pulse returned to normal. She no longer felt a looming heart attack.

"What happened to me?" she asked. I told her that her body had reacted in an extremely physical way to anxiety. I used Robert Sapolsky's explanation: Roni's brain had sent a danger alarm to her autonomous nervous system, as if she were a zebra confronted by a lion and had to run for her life. In fact, it was a false alarm. There was no lion, and she didn't need to run anywhere. But her brain continued to prepare for flight, because it had not received the message that the danger had passed. The jumping conveyed to the brain that the survival action was complete, and it could calm down. Roni listened to me with a distressed look in her eyes.

"What's worrying you, Roni? Something's making you feel as if you're being chased by a lion," I said, and she burst into tears. She had good reason to feel threatened. Her parents were separating, and her world was collapsing.

Her brother Gil read my mind and explained the simple but menacing truth. "Roni is worried because our parents aren't talking to each other, and Mom wants to go back to Israel." His words echoed in the room where the five children huddled in silence. Only Keren sobbed for her family's sorrow, tears flowing down her nose.

Gabi took Roni in her arms and whispered that everything would be all right, that they were only going through a hard time that would soon be over. That there was nothing to worry about.

"Daniela, will I also meet a lion like that?" Yaniv asked anxiously.

"Not necessarily—only a few people, less than five percent, panic when they are very anxious. It's got something to do with biology," I said, stroking his hair to reassure him.

Turning to Roni, I explained that one of the main problems with a panic attack was the fear that it might happen again. The best thing she could do was to teach herself to remain calm by doing breathing exercises and by changing her way of thinking. But she could also consider keeping medication with her in case of need—it calmed the autonomous nervous system and worked like the jumping, I told her. I suggested that Gabi talk to Roni's doctor about prescribing it.

Gabi invited me to stay for dinner, but I was in a hurry to get back to my children, who were alone at home. I hugged Gabi and her children and left them to deal with the invisible lion that had entered their house. I headed home, where my own lion, who had only recently sneaked into my life, was waiting.

Yoel wasn't home yet. He was back to his usual routine and would turn up only after sundown—if at all, I worried. It was Orly Bergman who had caused an upheaval in his usual schedule last night—only for her had he come home so early. As I walked toward the front door of my home, my fears returned more forcefully. Look! they called to me, don't ignore the signs! All the families around you are breaking up. It's a fact. Roni was attacked by an invisible lion in Gabi's living room; Gilad flew to Texas to knock on his in-laws' closed door; even Don Waksberg's third marriage had come to an end. And what was going to happen to my home? Who would guard me against that threat? Before I went inside, I called Yoel for the third time. He was not available.

I found Alon at the computer, chatting with his classmates. He looked up for a moment and asked, "How was your important appointment, today?" I gave him a tired smile.

"Nice of you to remember," I said.

"Well, you don't see your mom looking so dressy and pretty every day," he said.

There, I told myself. This is the compliment you've been waiting for all day.

"I'm glad you think so. Good night, kiddo."

I looked in on Ayelet, who was on the phone to Katie in New York. Maya, in the living room, was watching television. "Mom, why didn't you take me to visit Keren?"

"Because Roni wasn't feeling well, and Gabi asked me to come and help."

"What's wrong with Roni?"

"She was very scared, and I helped her to feel better," I answered.

"I was also scared today." Her long, light brown hair fell softly on her shoulders and her eyes, the one pure green and the other mixed with brown, gazed at me questioningly. "It happened at school. I thought there was a lion on the playground, and I ran and hid in the classroom."

I stared at her in disbelief. Again, I asked myself if this was a sign.

I sat on the sofa next to her, stroking her soft hair. "You know, Maya," I said, in the most reassuring tone I could find, "lions don't run free in Palo Alto, you don't have to worry."

"Yes they do. A mountain lion climbed up a tree in someone's yard last week, remember?"

She was right. I remembered the TV news report from the previous week, in which the reporter had interviewed terrified neighbors about a lion that had come down from the hills to wander through their streets. All of the pure-spirited former hippies demonstrated against shooting the predator down, because "it's so rare and beautiful." They cared little about the fact that the hungry animal could catch and eat a child for a snack.

"Right," I told Maya, "people sometimes do really meet a lion, but it doesn't happen often." To myself, I noted that this was a sign.

Later I read her a bedtime story and went to my room, to be alone with my distress. I missed Yoel. I buttoned myself into my pajamas and tried to read a book I'd started two days earlier, eons ago. I paged through it without interest. The prolific author had rushed to release it after her first book became a bestseller. Silly me, I fell into the trap and bought it.

And then, in came the lion himself, pacing on soft flexible paws into my bedroom. He smiled at me, the predator, as if nothing had happened, unaware that my soul was in turmoil. I could feel the dull worry turning into a stinging insult.

"You look familiar." I opted for sarcasm. "Remind me who you are again?"

"What's up, Daniela?" he asked, startled by the attack.

"Is it hard for you to return my calls? Maybe I'm passé, old history, wallpaper, nonexistent? What if your house was on fire? Or a lion ate your wife and children?"

He looked at me in silence, understanding that something was indeed going on with me; he knew he needed to pause, understand what I was going through, and that under no circumstance should he just carry on as usual. Perhaps it was my piercing expression that warned him against carrying on as usual.

"I've had a crazy day," he said. "The board of directors' meeting started at seven this morning and ended only an hour ago. Then I drove the chairman to the airport, and I only had a chance to check my calls a little while ago, on the way home. I had thirty. Three from you. Has something happened, Daniela?" He came closer and sat on the bed.

"Nothing. I just missed you," I said evasively. "So what happened at the meeting?"

"Problems. The Japanese who promised to invest got cold feet. Without their investment, we don't have enough money to buy Jenkins. The situation's lousy."

"So what needs to be done?"

"We spent the whole day looking for ways to raise money. The VCs are vultures and getting involved with them may change the dynamics among investors, the management, and the employees. On the other hand, we don't have too many options. If we don't find private investors like the Japanese company, we'll have to turn to venture capital funds."

I listened, trying to work it out and realizing that my worries were pointless. While Yoel was busy with the company's existential problems, I had been busy with fears of abandonment.

"I haven't seen you for ages," I said.

"Are you referring to the meeting with Orly?" The penny finally dropped.

"How was it?"

"Great. Too bad you didn't come. Orly sends her regards. She wanted to meet you."

"Lovely," I said dryly, but I couldn't help asking, "What's she like?"

"Used up. You've got nothing to worry about."

"I wasn't worried," I lied.

"You weren't?" He moved his two emerald lakes close to my brown pools, while his fingers threatened to tickle me in the exact spot that always made me jump sky high.

"Okay. A little," I confessed, to avoid the punishment. "More used up than me?" I had to ask.

"You're jealous!" he crowed. "In your case, I'm the happy user, and I have no complaints," he said, generously paying me a small compliment.

"What did you two talk about?"

"She reminded me that in twelfth grade, when we got our drivers' licenses, we arranged with Zevik and Shmulik to go to a movie at the Armon Cinema. She came down the stairs when we said we'd meet, and found all three of our cars parked in front of her house. Not a single one of us was prepared to give up the right to drive his father's car, that night."

"Who did she choose?"

"She admitted that it was a difficult choice. In the end, she got in next to Zevik."

"Poor you..." I stroked his head. "What else?"

"Stories about her family, her husband, the children, work, renovations to her kitchen, and her husband complaining about how expensive it all was. And I thought about you and me and the kitchen you want to change and me not understanding why you want to change it. And I thought that all families probably live pretty similar lives on parallel planes."

I smiled in solidarity with Orly.

"We talked a bit about some of the guys I haven't seen for years. Orly said she'd organize a get-together next time in Israel. Will you come with me?" He caressed me with his eyes. His body language and his voice told me that he was mine again. He was home from a decades-deep journey that had ended with a soft landing in my bed.

I mused that the lions had suddenly vanished; the menace standing between us had evaporated like mist at sunrise. Orly Bergman, the Japanese, and Tom Jenkins had vanished along with the lions.

"You know," he said as he gently unbuttoned my pajamas, as if he were opening an expensive gift, "I've always regretted having never learned to play an instrument. But there's one instrument on which I can make music." He moved a finger over the bones of my chest, slid it across my hips and thighs: "This cello."

PART FIVE

SUMMER'S END

Chapter 18

Mika

Months after Mika's composition for piano and orchestra won first prize in the California competition for beginner composers, she received another surprise. The secretary of the San Francisco Symphony called with the good news that the orchestra's conductor and musical director, Michael Tilson Thomas, had invited her to perform her concerto in a tour of appearances beginning in San Francisco, moving on to San Diego, and ending in Seattle.

Mika was out of her mind with joy. She placed the receiver down, drew her knees into her chest, and covered her face with her hands. She heard her inner voice saying, "Wake up, Mika. You're dreaming. You're a little girl from Haifa, the mother of four...Shaul's wife...You're going to perform with Michael Tilson Thomas? That's not possible! Your piano teacher in Haifa would turn in her grave if she knew how far you've come."

She roused herself from her momentary paralysis and phoned Shaul, then the Sorbonne, then she left a message for her son in Israel, and she still couldn't wait to pick up the twins from school to tell them the news. Shaul suggested flying their kids, Yuval and Noa, to San Francisco for the occasion. Everyone was overwhelmed with excitement.

The newspaper ads as well as a billboard near the San Francisco exit on the 101 printed Mika Navon's name alongside the venerated Tilson Thomas's. The grandeur of it all was breathtaking. Mika's phone didn't stop ringing during that time, and she knew that the hall would be packed with her relatives and with the Israeli community. In anticipation of the big opening, her house filled with flowers sent by proud family, friends, colleagues, and members of the community. In the weeks before the concerts, she practiced tirelessly, afraid that although she knew the pieces in the cells of her body, she would freeze again, as she had once before. Dr. Diamond prescribed a mild sedative in case she became overwrought. "Take one pill twenty minutes before the concert. There are no side effects," he said and reassured her that he took the pill before his own violin performances.

"It'll be okay," he promised.

Indeed, the first concert, at the Davies Hall in San Francisco, was roundly applauded. Many familiar faces smiled at her and demanded an encore. Mika acquiesced with Chopin's *Fantasie* in F minor.

The tension subsided in her following performances, and Mika came to regard the concerts as a pleasurable routine. Dr. Diamond's pills also helped.

A few days before the last one, in Seattle, she remembered Yaron and wondered what he was doing that very moment. She tried to put him out of her mind, fearing that her mental hernia would reopen.

Benaroya Hall was filled to capacity. As usual, for the performance Mika wore the backless black dress that was as comfortable as her housecoat. Even the session with the makeup artist had become a pleasant routine.

Michael Tilson Thomas raised his baton and gave the opening beat; Mika erupted confidently and enthusiastically into her playing, enjoying the dialogue between the piano and the orchestra's harmonious response. At the end of the concert, the audience's applause squeezed an encore from her. This time she dared to play Chopin's Ballade no. 3, although she had not managed to practice it night and day.

When she eventually left the stage, drained as if she'd lifted enormous weights, she wiped her perspiring forehead and quenched her thirst with the big bottle of water in the dressing room. There was a soft tap on the door and the stage manager appeared, saying that Mr. Zelig wished to see the star of the evening. Her heart skipped a beat. She stepped out and was confronted by Yaron in all his glory. As if her thoughts had conjured him up for her. No longer a boy. Looking like a respectable doctor in his fine jacket. Still handsome, even though his hairline had receded considerably. She hugged him.

"What a surprise," she murmured, her hand on her chest, to steady her racing heart. When she met his eyes, they twinkled at her with the magical blue she knew from twenty years ago.

Mika looked at Yaron, suddenly aware of the wrinkles on her forehead and at the corners of her eyes. She knew that the Botticelli glow that had once framed her face in her youth had been erased by now.

"Your hair is so short," he said as if reading her mind, touching the back of his neck to indicate where her long locks had once been.

Mika shrugged, comforted by the thought that he'd had the opportunity to observe her from the audience, and hoped that catching the more distant view had softened the blow of the changes the years had wrought.

"I didn't know you played so beautifully." He repeated what she had said to him an eternity ago.

Mika smiled in gratitude. "How did you hear about the concert?"

"Your name was everywhere, I couldn't miss it. My sons are here, come and meet them." With evident pride, he pulled her to a corner, where three adolescent boys were waiting. "Yoni, Nadav, and Ran," he introduced them. "Ran plays the piano, Nadav the clarinet, and Yoni the guitar."

Mika shook their hands, thinking that they looked like clones of Yaron: Freckled Ran looked exactly as Yaron had while holding her puppy in the yard. Nadav was the replica of Yaron saving her from Shlomi Halfon's punches, and she could almost hear Yaron's voice coming from his son's mouth: "You never hurt girls." Whereas Yoni, with a youthful flush on his cheeks, looked just like Yaron looked when she'd told him, "I didn't know you played so beautifully."

"When are you going back to Jerusalem?" Mika asked politely, looking for something to say that would bring her mind back into the present.

"At the end of summer," Yaron said. "There's a job waiting for me as the chief of the department. Can't pass up that kind of opportunity." Then, rather apologetically, he added, "I have to take the boys home, they've got school tomorrow. I just wanted to say hi, after the concert."

She nodded in understanding. Then she took his arm and drew him aside. She boldly enquired, "May I ask you something that has to do with an old memory of mine?"

Yaron tensed up. "Sure, what is it?"

"Do you remember the note?" She watched as he searched his memory. "The note you sent to Eddie, who sat next to me. The note I put in my bag and that you demanded back. The note you took out of my bag without my permission. Do you remember?"

"*Me?* I opened your bag?"

"Yes, you."

"I don't remember. What grade were we in?"

"Eighth."

"Don't remember."

"If you don't remember, you can't tell me what was written in the note." She smiled.

"No." He stuck to his story.

"That note appeared over and over in my dreams," she said, looking straight at him. "I dreamed you threw it to me, not to Eddie, and it blew away." Yaron smiled. She continued, "From the look you gave me in the dream, I knew that the note said, 'Get out of my sight, and don't you dare come near me, ever.'" Yaron's smile vanished.

"Mika, you have to understand. For me, you were the prettiest girl in class and everyone loved you, and I was just a nobody..."

Mika shook her head in denial. He was not a nobody. Not at all. She shook her head again, sadly, regretting the missed opportunity, an opportunity that had now passed irreversibly.

"I'm sorry about the choices I made at the time, when I was growing up." He had read her thought again.

Out of the depths of the years, a smile rose to her lips. The circle was closed. Dr. Diamond was right. She had wanted to hear that he was sorry, and she believed him.

She had so many things she wanted to tell Yaron. She wanted to tell him that the note had cut a wound in her that had been buried under deep emotional strata—forcibly pushed from her heart and removed from her consciousness. And that the day she sent him the card, an uncontrollable flow of obsessions had burst forth from inside of her and addled her mind. She wanted to tell him that she was in Seattle, play-ing beside Michael Tilson Thomas, because of that note he'd thrown, but then she realized that Yaron wouldn't understand. As far as he was concerned, it was just a note that he'd rescued from a girl who could have done some damage had she read it—something immediately for-gettable. Mika understood that the story of the note belonged to the girl she used to be, the one who loved him with an autistic love that was interred deep in her soul and that erupted one day accompanied by a stream of obsessions, a profusion of dreams, a profusion of creativity. Instead of all of these words dancing on the tip of her tongue, she said, not sure of why she was saying it in English and not Hebrew, "It was really nice to see you. I hope to see you again sometime."

And he also reverted to their Internet language and replied, "Same here, we'll keep in touch." And he left.

Mika contacted Shaul and told him about the brief meeting with Yaron and his sons. Shaul replied with matter-of-fact politeness, as if she'd told him about something casual that had happened on her way to the concert, such as a traffic jam. For the rest of the evening, Mika's cell phone rang constantly; Shaul called every half hour.

"How was the concert?" he asked, because he'd forgotten to ask before. Then he called to ask where and with whom she was going to have dinner. And again, he called to say good night. Then once more, just to ask if she was asleep yet. Early in the morning, he called to ask if she'd slept well. Mika was happy about those calls, but a little suspicion nibbled at her. Did Shaul doubt her faithfulness? No. Couldn't be.

Gabi

Gabi and Danny spent the days after their quarrel like two strangers, exchanging only brief and necessary words. The children sensed the tension and kept their heads down to avoid being hit by stray shots, like soldiers in the line of fire, avoiding eye contact with the antagonists so as not to fan the flames of battle. Both Gabi and Danny slept in the double bed that had known happier times, neither of them wishing to relinquish their claim to the territory. They slept parallel to one another, coldly conscious of each other's presence, while grieving over the destruction of their family.

On the seventh morning after the devastation, Danny lay beside her in the bed. He hadn't slept much, either the last night or any of the previous ones. He lay there reviewing the storm that had arisen between them over and over in his mind and, for the first time in his life, tried to understand where he had gone wrong. He had expected the talk between them upon her return from the mountains to make

Gabi cringe and surrender, and he couldn't understand how things got turned upside down. A new Gabi had confronted him in the kitchen. A stranger. Unfamiliar. Different. As if she were possessed by a demon. There was something strong, even violent, about her that didn't suit her. She wants to leave me, Danny reminded himself; it was unbelievable. What could he possibly do?

He tried to imagine his life as a divorced man, without the enfolding warmth and sense of family. Without the domestic turmoil that always awaited him on his return from his travels, without the wonderful dinners Gabi made, without the weekend festivity of children around the family table, family vacations, birthdays and other celebrations, without the presence of Gabi, her voice, her stories, her jokes. To strike at the essence of the matter, life without Gabi's cream cake was tasteless. Meaningless.

He couldn't remember any time in his life without Gabi. They'd grown up together, as if she were one of his ribs. Hand in hand they'd skipped through the years, growing from grade to grade, from childhood to maturity, from couple to family. Gabi was with him in whatever he did—his quiet, efficient teammate. She complemented him like the disciplined gunner in a tank crew, like a copilot, like the right marker on the field. Danny knew that if he looked for her, she'd always be there for him. That was the essence of being a couple, in his opinion, an ongoing connection that expressed itself in the solid presence of the one in the other's life, without the expenditure of too many words. Being a couple meant a man and a woman living together, sharing tasks and guarding the nest. How could she think of living apart? Danny was stunned. He'd thought he was immune to this sort of trouble. But apparently, just like Jacobs, Danny had not been careful enough and had stepped on a mine.

Maybe Gabi was having regrets; he clung to this faint hope. He leaned over her in the bed, silently pleading, trying to catch her eye, searching for a sign of conciliation. But she pushed him away in contempt, brushing him aside like a troublesome fly. Her mind was made up. As far as she was concerned, the matter was settled.

Danny returned to his side of the bed, dull-eyed, his tail between his legs, depressed and humiliated. She doesn't want me, he faced the thunderous truth. She said I'm not a man, but a childish Narcissus. He repeated her words to himself and, for the first time, considered their meaning.

All of a sudden, he wondered if he'd hurt her. How could it be? He'd found a perfect balance in his life. His life was full of interest and achievement and lacked nothing. Nor did Gabi lack anything, in his opinion. She had a good, comfortable life. She'd always wanted a large family, and he'd given her five beautiful, happy, successful children. Sure, she raised them, but she was not short on money, she had as much help as she needed, and she had enough time and resources to paint, to meet her friends, and to shop for whatever she wanted.

Burning anger arose in him again. He met his obligations as the breadwinner, and his ungrateful wife did not appreciate his efforts. For whom did he run around the world, if not for her and the children? What was she talking about, what did she lack? Danny stirred his rusty memory for matters of an emotional nature, like he was searching a computer for old, unused folders. He found nothing.

Gabi says she doesn't have a loving partner. He recalled her words in amazement. Meaning what? Again for the first time in his life, he asked himself what it was that she needed. What did she mean when she said she wanted a man who would love her innermost soul? He didn't understand. Danny was reasonably confident he loved her innermost soul and didn't know what she wanted. He scratched his clever, businesslike head—the head that left everybody in the dust when it came to far-reaching strategic planning. The head that propelled him to the front and enabled him to launch projects and lead companies. The head with the healthy intuition, which understood which way the market was flowing, which way the wind was blowing. The head that made thousands of decisions a day and handled budgets of millions of dollars.

Could this be the head that didn't understand what Gabi needed?

Danny sank into profound sadness. He was overcome with a sense of helplessness. Most of all, he was distressed by the frustration that came from failing to understand, like an honor-roll student who had never before failed a test. Danny did not like failure and was not prepared to accept Gabi's rejection. He was not a defeatist. It couldn't be that Gabi was actually hurt by his little affairs on the side, could it? The question flickered in his mind, marginally. From the platform, at her party, she had said something about him jumping from bed to bed in the Valley and overseas. But where had she gotten that idea? She knew nothing about his one-night stands. He was always so careful; in fact, he could think of no incidence she might have caught wind of, he convinced himself, ready to dismiss the matter. But...maybe someone had hinted to her about his indiscretions? Who could it be? After all, nobody knew. He had always been so guarded with his privacy. Apart from which, he reminded himself, Gabi had really been the one who pushed him into the arms of other women.

He never refused on the rare occasions when she approached him sexually. Most times, he had to knock on other doors, because Gabi's desire was fading with the years. She turned her back on him, chronically tired, night after night. It had been years since she had even placed a hand on him down there, he remembered, with a twinge in his heart. The fury he'd felt when she stood up and spoke from the platform at the party turned to sorrow. And that sorrow evolved into amazement at Gabi's determination to abandon him.

Danny wasn't familiar with the helplessness he felt, and his inner voice urged him to fight. But fight what? It seemed he couldn't budge Gabi from her stance and had to come to terms with the new reality. But she had no right to dismantle the home they had worked together to build for decades! She had no right to shake him off like this, like a stranger! That was not part of their agreement, he thought bitterly. In any case, she couldn't manage without me, he thought, trying to draw encouragement from his deep knowledge of her dependent personality. He looked at her from across the pillow and realized otherwise. She was different now. Maybe she'd received encouragement and strength from her friends in the Sierra Mountains? He should never have flown them here. Or maybe it was one of the lesbians' ideas, Gila or Talma. His anger returned.

And what about the children? For the past week, they'd been hiding in their rooms as if their world had come to a standstill. How would they decide who would get whom? How would the children feel if he suggested they stay with him in in Palo Alto when Gabi returned to Israel? He felt a strong desire to fight Gabi for custody, but knew he didn't stand a chance. He was constantly traveling for business. It was best for the children to stay together under one roof with Gabi to take care of them. They should be with their mother and not with some nanny. Gabi was an outstanding mother, he knew, finding himself at a dead end, again. So, fight for what? He felt like a samurai preparing to fight a mysterious and unknowable opponent.

Hot tears rose from his throat to his eyes. He hadn't cried for a long time. Actually, he didn't remember ever crying. "Men don't cry" was a rule he'd internalized when he was just a boy. He had always bravely borne the blows he received from other children, soldiers, and bullies. Later, emotional blows from competitors, clients, and colleagues; blows that strengthened him. No. Danny would not cry. Not even Gabi would wring a tear from him. But here it came rolling down, the bastard...

He rose and dragged himself to the bathroom, to refresh himself. Heaven forbid that Gabi should notice the tears. On the way, he mentally divided their possessions. She would get the house in Jerusalem, and he would keep the one in Palo Alto. She probably wouldn't even know that their value differed by millions of dollars.

While Danny was conversing with himself, Gabi lay open-eyed beside him, still angry. A moment earlier, Danny had looked at her as if nothing had happened. He thought she'd forgotten. That look infuriated her. He was still treating her dismissively, as if his conscience was not affected by what she had said. Typical of Danny, always thinking he was right. For all she cared he could remain righteous, and lonely. This time she'd been able to stand up to him without fear, hadn't become confused even once, and had issued him a knockout blow. And boy did he have it coming!

And now that he'd been defeated, she had to plan her next steps. She had to think of herself as an independent woman, no longer part of a couple—making decisions and running her own life. It was all new to her; she'd never had to think like this before. Danny and the children had always come first, while she'd dragged along behind them as a matter of course. A shot of healthy narcissism straight into a vein would do her no harm, she thought. It was high time. It was *her* turn to live her own life.

"How are you going to handle life on your own, a daydreamer like you?" As long as she could remember, her parents had hammered this into her head, and she had internalized it. She'd believed she couldn't manage on her own and had better find someone who knew how to make it. Someone like Danny. He always knew what he wanted and where he was going. But from now on, she decided, she would count herself among the people who knew how to make it in life. The first thing she needed to do was to move out of Palo Alto and go back to Jerusalem with no arguments. She wasn't going to plead, consider, or persuade. Rina, the travel agent, would book the tickets. Afterward she would tell the children that the time had come to part from their friends, that the long visit to California was over. In their hearts, the children also knew where they belonged and the return to Israel would lessen their confusion. It would do them good. Gabi was firm. What a relief.

As an independent woman coping with life, she would get organized in Jerusalem. She'd enroll the children in school, renovate the house, buy a car, find a job...no problem, no big deal.

She envisaged her pleasant, warm house in Jerusalem, which she would organize and furnish as she pleased; oil paintings and carpets that would suit the high-ceilinged stone house with the French windows. She would ship the contents of this house. After all, Danny wasn't interested in design and certainly wouldn't argue over paintings and carpets. Then, when everything was nice and orderly, she would invite Luigi Fracassini, the sensitive soul, to visit and encourage her. She pictured them sitting in a café in Emek Refaim in Jerusalem, drinking something hot and sweet as they discussed life, art, emotions...In her fantasy, his hand covered hers. His eyes regarded her with true, mute admiration, and she blushed like a schoolgirl. She imagined them strolling along the promenade overlooking the Valley of the Cross, the wind ruffling her hair, Luigi Fracassini gazing deep into her blue eyes and telling her that she had a rare combination of beauty: her body was round, like Renoir's women, her eyes were elongated, like Modigliani's women, and her soft, curly hair reminded him of Gustav Klimt's magnificent women. She imagined him kissing her tenderly on the lips and although nobody apart from Danny had ever touched her lips, Gabi knew that this kiss would be a gate to heaven.

At the thought, a pleasant shudder went through her, but she quickly snapped back to reality: Luigi Fracassini would not visit Jerusalem. "What am I thinking?" She looked at Danny, hunched beside her like a hippo; she knew every inch of his skin, every hair on his body. She tried to imagine Danny sitting opposite her in the café in Emek Refaim and knew that Luigi Fracassini's pleasurable words would never roll out of Danny's mouth. She remembered their romantic moment in Monterey, when he'd promised to be at her side and support their return to Jerusalem. She'd believed him then, only a few months ago, and look where they were now.

She looked at him, across the pillow. In spite of her anger, she felt a flicker of longing for the touch of his hand, for the warmth of his arms. To bring him back to her. But she rejected the idea once and for all. After finding the strength to come this far, she wouldn't turn the wheel back. This time she wouldn't break, wouldn't plead with him. There was a life without Danny on this globe, she encouraged herself, and she would find the strength to create it.

Nevertheless, despair settled on her heart like the cloud over a volcano after an eruption. She thought about the destruction of her home. She remembered Roni running breathlessly in circles, almost fainting as the children watched her with stunned eyes. Profound anxiety flooded through her when she confronted the disintegration of the family. Perhaps a shot of healthy narcissism wasn't such a good idea after all.

She suddenly pictured Danny, the children, and herself abandoning their home; the children led helplessly into the oblivion she had imposed on them, the nonexistence of their family. She pictured them shackled by their ankles, walking in a chain, like Rodin's *Burghers of Calais*. And like those seven burghers, who had sacrificed their lives to save their town from the onslaught of the invaders, Gabi too felt like she was sacrificing precious lives. And for a moment, she asked herself, "Wait, why, what for?" Her mind was addled.

Danny rose from his side of the bed and shut himself in the bathroom. Gabi looked at the closed door that was like a barrier between strangers. Not so long ago, yet eons ago, Danny would leave the door open, and she would quite naturally come and go while he showered, shaved, or urinated. No more. Gabi sat up in bed and stared at the door that now precluded intimacy and declared their new alienation, the approaching separation. She sat for a long time, frozen, mute, gawping.

When the door opened, Gabi stepped toward the bathroom, keeping her eyes lowered. Danny emerged, full of grief, and without thinking fell at her feet. He got to his knees, wrapped his arms around her hips, and pressed his face against her stomach. He inhaled her, breathed in the aroma of her nightgown and the faint smell of menstrual blood that clung to her. A woman's scent. A mother's scent. The scent of a womb that had carried five children, of the wife who had grown up in his arms. The smell of home, of the life Danny was clinging to with all his might.

"Gabi, I'm sorry." He whispered the unfamiliar words. She wanted to push him away, but her hands wouldn't obey her. Slowly her fingers started to move. As if her fingers had a will of their own, they gently touched, stroked, traced thin furrows and tiny flowers in his hair and automatically caressed his earlobes, as if to say, "You're somewhat welcome under my roof; your hair and the tips of your ears are wanted here."

Danny, whose blood was surging through his body feverishly, as if her fingers had flicked a hidden switch, said, "I want to learn to love you deep, deep inside your soul."

Except for her fingers, which seemed to have a life of their own, Gabi stood frozen, shocked. A shudder crossed her shoulders, breasts, hips. Her tear ducts opened and great streams of tears flowed from her to him, wetting his forehead where it pressed into the cushion of her belly. Danny stood up, put his arms around her shuddering shoulders, and tenderly kissed away her tears. Her outburst continued, and she stifled a wail; a swarm of butterflies fluttered forth from her heart to form a colorful blanket, like a wedding canopy.

They stood for several minutes, huddled against one another, releasing tensions with their long embrace while great transparent cords of oxytocin bound them as one. The children, sensing the sweetness in the air, came to the parents' room, drawn like bees to spring blossoms. Keren came first, pushing herself between them, her head against Gabi's thigh, her hands clasping her parents' legs.

"Mommy, are you done being angry at Daddy?" she asked, and Gabi responded with a caress.

The three boys also dashed in, shouting, "Me, too! Me, too!" Even Roni, hearing the joyful cries, dragged herself away from the Internet and joined the family hug. Parents and five children, they stood clasping one another under Gabi's imagined butterfly blanket, incomparably happy.

"Let's make mommy a breakfast fit for a queen." Danny led the children to the kitchen, and they flew after him like a flock of swallows. Gabi was left by herself. She went to the toilet to empty her bladder and, with the flow, the remains of the argument drained out of her. What had made her so angry? She couldn't remember. What had the upheaval been about? The drama? The memory dimmed, melted as if it had never existed.

After the royal breakfast and after Danny and the children loaded the dishwasher, Gabi and Danny continued to caress each other like a pair of lovebirds. They held hands, gazing passionately at one another as though they had been separated for a long time by uncontrollable forces and, at last, here they were—a couple joined in renewed love.

"Danny, are you coming back to Jerusalem with me?" she asked.

He assured her, "Yes, I'll keep you close to me. Always."

Gabi said, "To keep me close, you have to learn not to hurt me."

Danny looked at her. "You also shouldn't have spoken like you did on that stage," he said.

She looked at him in despair, and recalled Yaacov, their high school math teacher. Twenty years earlier, she had stood at the blackboard attempting over and over again to solve an equation with two unknowns until the frustrated teacher cried out in a heavy Iraqi accent: "Take a dog's tail, place it among the reeds for forty days and forty nights, and it will still never straighten out!"

So it was with Danny. In spite of his best intentions, he couldn't straighten out.

She said, "If you really want to learn to love me, deep, deep inside my soul, you first have to learn to accept me as an independent woman, with an opinion of her own, who has the right to express her opinions without criticism from her husband."

She gave him a meaningful look, and Danny looked back at her, rebuked. "Yes...of course, you have your own opinions," he said, enunciating each word, "and you certainly have the right to them, but you don't have to run around and advertise them, certainly not from a platform."

Gabi sighed, shook her head right and left in amazement, and muttered her parents' words: "It is what it is."

୶

Anita

Anita was in a fighting mood. She was under pressure because Elinor, the evening and weekend nanny, had asked to leave early that evening to attend a family event. Elinor supplemented the hours of the full-time nanny, Imelda. Anita answered my casual phone call in her workroom that overlooked the mahogany deck, designed in the style of Ben-Simon, the Israeli architect who had designed the New York City penthouses of several celebrities. She glanced at the backyard, where her two daughters and their friends were happily splashing in the pool under Elinor's watchful eyes. In about half an hour, Elinor would fetch Elad from his basketball game in San Jose, and in the evening she would drive him to his school party.

"I've got a weekend full of board meetings, events, and two cocktail parties in the city. I can't be running around driving the children, making their dinner, and looking for babysitters," she complained. "If I have no other choice, I'll get Imelda to come; it's not like she does anything on the weekends, and she could use a few extra dollars. Which reminds me," she added, "I need a ride to the city this evening, because Ido's coming straight from the airport, and I don't want to drive home in two cars. And as for Elinor," she carried on, "I should have told her I don't give pay for time away from the job. I can't employ a woman who's busy with family affairs during work hours when she's supposed to be with my children. This isn't going to work. This time I gave in, but she'll hear from me if it happens again."

She didn't have much time, she explained. Jackie, her personal shopper, was due in an hour for consultation about an event next month.

"I'm going to the Women for Peace conference in Washington, DC. You know, Daniela, I'll be introducing the main speaker, which means I have to prepare a short biography of the woman. She was this well-known fighter for women's rights in the sixties."

I felt obliged to be filled with awe.

"I mean, they don't give that honor to just anybody," Anita went on. "And what's more, Hillary Clinton will be sitting in the first row. Hillary will be back in the White House before long, and it's important to make a good impression on her. You never know how things will turn out."

I envisioned Hillary Clinton approaching Anita between speeches, introducing herself, and telling Anita how moved she was by her impressive presentation. Hillary might want to know more about her, her activities and so on. Anita would eagerly tell her about the projects she was promoting and the nonprofit organizations that she headed. And one of these days, when Hillary was president, Anita might be invited to the White House to represent Israel and the world's leading women at the Clintons' receptions, where she would address them with simple familiarity, as Hillary and Bill.

Anita would breathe in the clean mountain air of high society, and her mother would be happy. She'd always believed in her. She'd always said she had two daughters, one successful and one miserable. But Anita liked to say that Yaffa wasn't miserable, just dumb. Okay, maybe not actually dumb, she amended, but one of those daydreamers. Anita took her to parties and receptions in the company of mayors, tycoons, journalists, and politicians. What better connections would her sister need to succeed? At every one of these events, Yaffa stood to the side, at most speaking with the wives about their kids or exchanging jokes with the waiters. That way, you got nowhere, Anita complained. She had to learn to reach out and grab. Nobody was going to shove a job into her hand if she didn't try, didn't even attempt to prove herself. Meanwhile, Yaffa sat at home, raising her children on Anita and Ido's bill. What would she do without their support? God only knew.

In life, you had to take what was available and optimize. This was Anita's credo. She always aspired to get ahead, move upward. Ever since she was a child, she'd understood what was important and what not, where to invest and where not. Of course, she knew that one also had to give. All her projects were based on giving, plenty of giving. She donated a lot of money in the belief that her way was the right way. What goes around comes around. Money went, money came, but the relationships she built would last well into the future. She already had excellent contacts with key people in the community. One hand washed the other. You had to know how to be seen in the right places, how to meet the people who could open the right doors, and then the sky was the limit. They said her success stemmed from the money Ido made.

What nonsense, she thought. "Ido's an exceptionally successful guy, and I love him with all my heart, but if I hadn't met him, I'd have met someone else and still be myself."

"I'll send Jackie to buy me some suits for the conference and match some jewelry and accessories," Anita told me over the phone. "I really want to be in top form on that stage. Oh, and when she arrives, I also need to remember to remind her to get me some silverware and tablecloths from Milan."

Anita considered her acquaintance Kiki Sanders a personality worth emulating, because she had a personal assistant to take care of phone calls, invitations, and correspondence. That's why Kiki was so well organized. Every morning, the assistant gave Kiki a list of things that required her attention, including birthdays that must not be forgotten and important people to whom she must send greetings. Anita wanted to hire a personal assistant for the same reason. An assistant who would write speeches for her in sparkling English, a girl with superb organization skills, and with the ability to react quickly. Anita had ideas, and she had to run ahead with them. She had no time for details and hoped that an outstanding assistant would tie up the loose ends. Maybe she'd find someone with experience in company management. She'd get in touch with Ido's headhunter tomorrow; he'd attend to it. There was no point in spreading the word among her friends, because she had no plans to interview bored housewives who lacked the right qualifications.

Only after I'd heard all of Anita's urgent problems was I able to inform her that I'd called in order to invite her to lunch at Sausalito, to say good-bye to Gabi, who was boarding a plane to Israel the following day.

"Who's coming?" she asked, to ensure that she wouldn't miss anything important, should she be too busy to attend.

"Only Mika and me, so far. Gila's in Tel Aviv and Nira's running a marathon in Honolulu."

"You know what, Daniela, I'm looking in my calendar, and I see that it's at exactly the same time as the community center's board of directors' meeting. Sorry. I'll say good-bye to her before she leaves, and I'm sure I'll see her in Jerusalem. After all, I'm often in Israel on short visits."

"No problem. We'll tell Gabi you can't make it."

"Will you be at Kiki Sanders's cocktail party this evening?"

"No. We weren't invited."

"Too bad. I need a ride. Okay, 'bye."

Anita ended the conversation feeling a bit torn. If she really wanted to join her friends for lunch, she could leave the meeting early, like everyone else did. Gabi was a wonderful woman, a good soul. Anita owed her a lot, after all. Gabi had welcomed Anita and Ido with open arms when they'd come to Palo Alto. She'd helped them to get settled, to enroll the children in school, to find a nanny, to find a house. There were no words to describe her kindness. But, with all due respect, Anita shouldered heavy responsibilities, and she was sure Gabi would understand. Besides which, Daniela, Gabi, and Mika were no longer part of Anita's social circle. They were all good women, but they hadn't come very far. Gabi was a defeatist—she thought the world was run by men, and had relinquished her right to run her own life; she wasn't made for running projects. At most, she was capable of organizing the catering for parties. Mika was too involved in music, and Daniela only knew how to talk. She made her living by talking. Some profession! "I threw her a line," Anita reminded herself. "I wanted to see how she'd do with arranging the Israeli folk dancing festival, but she didn't bite. She doesn't have what it takes. She can't get things going. She's not made for action."

However, Anita was a practical person. No bullshit. She needed to find new blood for her social circle. People with style, like Kiki Sanders, were the right people for her. Anita could learn a lot from Kiki. To succeed in life, one had to cut out excess baggage and people who were of no use. There was no alternative.

A knock at the door interrupted Anita's train of thought. Jackie, her personal shopper, was there with a big smile and a briefcase full of elegant catalogues. A short hug and they sat down to page through the catalogues containing details of designers who couldn't be found on the hangers of even the most exclusive stores. They meticulously selected the suit that would never be forgotten by Hillary Clinton, sitting in the first row while Anita presented the curriculum vitae of the main speaker in her brief but impressive moment on stage.

❧

Daniela

I'm awakened every morning by the radio, set for seven o'clock. I drink the coffee Yoel has brought me and put next to my bed, I listen to the news on NPR, concentrating on the announcer's first sentence. If it does not include the words "terrorist attack in Israel," I breathe in relief and start the day with a smile.

Today started with a sigh. A terrorist attack in Jerusalem. The bus on Route 18 went up in flames. Twenty-two dead, including the suicide bomber, described as a "Palestinian militant."

We hear that in Israel people have become inured to the horrors of terrorism. In California, we've developed a cautious routine. We phone everybody we know in the area of the latest attack, to offer comfort, demonstrate solidarity, and find out if anyone we know has been hurt. We're glued to the Internet, reading Israeli newspapers, somehow carrying on with our everyday routine. I read that the bus was taking children to school. On one of the bus benches, a seven-year-old boy and his grandmother died holding hands.

The image of the boy and the grandmother remained with me as I got the children ready for school; I thought that the boy had probably been scared to go alone on the bus and the grandmother had promised to protect him. I hugged Maya tightly, and she skipped to the car where Yoel was waiting to drive her to school. She was also seven.

I recalled scenes from the mass demonstration in support of Israel, the week before. Yoel and the children made a huge sign with the Hebrew inscription ISRAELIS FOR PEACE, and we headed for San Francisco, wearing T-shirts with the logo WE STAND WITH ISRAEL. In the elevator taking us from the underground parking lot to the square, we crowded against an elderly woman with grocery bags. She looked and sounded like George's mother on *Seinfeld*. She fixed her beady eyes on us, looked us up and down with revulsion, and I thought our sign was at least as threatening to her as a machine gun and our T-shirts as menacing as camouflage guerilla uniforms. After a moment of thunderous silence, she said in a nasal voice, "Do you think this is going to help you?" And Yoel answered with a smile, "Maybe it won't help, but it certainly won't hurt."

The contemptuous look in her eyes conveyed that she was not convinced.

The square was packed with a crowd of expatriate Israelis. They were all there because they felt the pressing need to express support for Israel.

The good atmosphere went some way toward dulling the evil eye of George's mother from the elevator.

Later, as I drove to the office, I listened to the nine o'clock news. The number of casualties on the bus had risen. I parked in the lot near my office and closed my eyes for a moment. How does an Israeli psychologist working in Israel feel, from where does she derive the strength to treat, to support, to encourage?

I locked the car and walked heavily up the stairs. I collected my mail from the mailbox on my door, went in, and put the letters on my desk. I had fifteen minutes before the first patient was due. Curious, I opened an envelope postmarked Las Vegas and addressed in Lori's handwriting. The envelope contained a photograph of Lori and a note in her childish handwriting:

> Dear Dr. Oren,
> I'm doing great in Las Vegas. Recently I auditioned for a part in a musical with Leonardo DiCaprio, which will be on in New York next year. I got parts as a dancer and choirgirl. I get to dance solo with Leonardo. I'm moving to New York. I have never been happier. Come and see me in New York next fall.
> Yours, love, Lori.

The photo was of Lori and DiCaprio in each other's arms. I looked closer. Indeed, it was Leonardo with his blond mop, the famed actor hugging Lori. I felt an oppressive hot flash. I pictured Lori unbuttoning another button on her blouse, fluttering her eyelashes, and rolling with her legs spread from bed to bed until she reached the station where she received the ticket to an audition with Leonardo.

My glance fell on the patients' armchair, seeking Lori, but a different image was sitting there, a sort of combination of my likeness and Lori's; a kind of Daniela with false eyelashes and a mane of long, streaked hair growing out of my own cropped hairstyle. She was wearing a leather miniskirt, her crossed legs in fishnet stockings with the top leg wiggling with youthful audacity. On her feet, spike-heeled shoes. The top button of her blouse was undone.

"Jealous?" she asked with pouting red lips.

"Look at you!" I said. "This isn't a circus."

"Bet you'd also like to dance with Leonardo DiCaprio," she said with a cheeky smile, still swinging her leg.

"Leonardo DiCaprio could be my son, and I don't want to dance with him."

"Okay. So what about Richard Gere? You always wanted to dance with him. He's not so flexible anymore either. I saw him dance in *Chicago*, and the way he dances, so can you. Might be nicer than sitting in this room all day, living through the stories of your patients." She winked at me.

"Richard Gere's worth considering," I admitted. "But what about my responsibilities? Yoel, the children, work, life?"

"Honestly, Daniela, live a little!" she said to me, toying sensuously with her hair. "You've forgotten that you've got sex appeal."

"What am I supposed to do with you?" I rolled my eyes at her. "I don't have time for you—you're a ridiculous distraction."

"Daniela, you don't know what's waiting for you in this life," she fluttered. "Think of Lori dancing with Leonardo DiCaprio and what's awaiting her."

"I know exactly what's waiting for me: Jacob Starr will be here in a few minutes."

I tucked Daniela-Lori back into my mind, the way you tuck a shirt into pants to look tidy. Jacob Starr would soon be knocking at my door, wearing an expensive tie and exuding grave solemnity, as well as striking loneliness. Nearing fifty, he had found the love of his life at last. A woman after his own heart: a serious, successful lawyer like himself. But there was a fly in the ointment. His beloved had undergone a hysterectomy some years ago and could never bear children. Jacob found it difficult to choose between the almost perfect love he had found after so many years and his powerful desire for a family with a woman whose uterus could bear his children.

And so we seesawed from week to week between the two possibilities that were tearing his heart apart. If Jacob knew who had been sitting in the hot chair before he arrived, if he were even to peep at Daniela-Lori and perceive that I, too, had an irrational side, he would surely report me to the Board of Psychology for improper professional behavior and suggest that my license be revoked.

A knock on the door. I assumed my warmest, most empathetic smile. A smile that shoved Daniela-Lori, the terrorist attack in Jerusalem, the grandmother and the boy, and George's mother, the woman in the elevator, deep down inside myself, and welcomed Jacob Starr with a handshake.

Sausalito

Gabi's house underwent a metamorphosis: bare walls, rolled carpets, cardboard boxes everywhere. Men loading everything into the big truck in front of the house. The Gonen family would soon have moved out. Roni took her little siblings on a farewell outing to Great America, their favorite amusement park. Danny directed the movers, while Gabi met the girls for a good-bye lunch. She was flying to Israel the following morning, leaving me behind. The next time I passed Gabi and Danny's house, I would not be able to stop by to say "Hi," pick up or drop off the children, smell the inviting aroma of Gabi's cooking, warm myself a little in her warmth.

Gabi got into my car, thinking out loud, updating me on her shopping spree, and sharing with me the whole experience of moving. She had cleared the shelves at a number of local stores in order to fill her house in Jerusalem with essential American appliances and household goods that were unavailable in Israel. Sets of cutlery for two dozen diners; pots; coffee and espresso machines; bargain-price bed and table linens that would be a pity to leave on the shelves of Bloomingdale's; cartloads of pajamas and underwear, jeans, and sneakers for the whole family. Everything from the leading designers and manufacturers.

It would all be packed and sent that afternoon in the freight container bearing the address: GONEN FAMILY, REHAVIA, JERUSALEM.

Gabi was upset; she couldn't remember the measurements of the dining room in the Rehavia house, so she hadn't bought the splendid Italian dining table and chairs that seated twelve diners; she didn't want to ship it around the world. Instead, she'd decided to send a marvelous two-hundred-year-old French carved wooden cabinet with glass doors, that she had found in a second-hand store. It would hold her Italian serving dishes with the Tuscan decorations. That set, Gabi told me, would be in the dining room, to match the Persian carpet and low window overlooking the garden. She had already packed and sent the Italian living room furniture and Roni's piano, hoping that the room would not be crammed too full.

She'd been worried about Itai's drum set, because she couldn't find any place to pack it. She'd already given up on the American beds, which were too wide for Israeli bedrooms, and decided with a heavy heart to leave the drums behind also, and donate them instead to a worthy cause.

While Gabi was making her mental rounds of the house in Rehavia, I said good-bye, for her, to the green hills and the blue lakes flashing past us on Interstate 280, on which we made our way toward the Golden Gate Bridge. As we crossed the bridge, which was not golden but terra-cotta, Gabi's attention turned to her Jerusalem garden. I felt a twinge in my heart, thinking of the family we once were and that was now disintegrating. About the holidays we had celebrated together, the family outings, the children now parting from their best friends and about Danny, who wouldn't flirt with me anymore. And about Gabi.

Gabi who had taught me so much. The correct way to set a table: matching tablecloth to dishes, flowers to tablecloth, and candles to flowers. She had introduced me to Greek cuisine—how to stuff eggplant with meat, how to make fish in agristada sauce, how to make artichoke and squash pickles, how to bake five kinds of borekas and many other recipes. I'd never succeeded in making moussaka, however hard she tried to teach me. She'd even tried to teach me to paint. But most of all, I was going to miss her voice: warm, honest, humane, sympathetic—all the qualities that made her a true friend. A proven recipe.

Gabi described the house in Rehavia. It had only four bedrooms, compared to the five here. The children were already arguing over rooms. Yaniv was willing to share with Keren, whereas Roni said she would under no circumstance agree to live with Keren. Perhaps the balcony overlooking the garden could be closed in to create a small fifth bedroom, Gabi continued, adding that the house was in need of renovations. It hadn't really been occupied for ages. The pipes were rusty. The kitchen cabinets were very small. There was not enough space for two cars. The neighbors were too close and peered in through the windows. Gabi sighed.

We approached Sausalito from the north end of the Bay. A mosaic of colorful houses decorated the green slopes of the hills that tumbled almost to the waterline. On the right, the road followed the coastline, and we finally came to the Spinnaker, the seafood restaurant on stilts in the water of the Bay. After I parked the car, we strolled leisurely to the restaurant, taking our time. I wanted to stretch out Gabi's last day in California as far as possible.

Mika was waiting for us on the deck of the restaurant. The glow had returned to her face, thanks to Tilson Thomas, apparently.

"How's the maestro?" I asked her with a hug.

"Knight in shining armor. He kissed my hand in front of the audience every night, but I'm not sure he would recognize me on the street. Do you know how many pianists' hands he must have kissed in his lifetime?" Mika laughed, then turned her attention to Gabi. "Gabi, you're going away, just like that? Leaving us behind? What are we going to do without you in Palo Alto? For Israelis, your home here is like Mecca for the Muslims." Mika complained using words I didn't dare utter, not wanting to complain about my loneliness without Gabi in my life.

"It's okay, Mika, we'll transfer Mecca Palo Alto to Jerusalem," Gabi told her. "Will you come and visit me?"

"Do you really have to ask?" Mika opened her PalmPilot. "You're not getting rid of me so easily. I visit Israel every few months. Give me your Rehavia phone number."

As Gabi wrote the number on a piece of paper and handed to Mika, who entered it into her phone database, I caught them up on news of Gila, who'd just called me from Tel Aviv where she was spending time with Talma.

"She sounded very happy as usual," I told them. "They seem to be prolonging the party they started in New York. She's in Tel Aviv for only a few days, and then she'll be on her way to Berlin. She's looking for a place to live, to relocate her family in the spring."

I thought to myself that no one could really know the painful wound Gila carried under her happy persona.

"She said she'd be glad to help you settle down in Jerusalem when you arrive," I told Gabi. "You know Gila, she has connections everywhere—in Palo Alto, in Tel Aviv, and in Jerusalem. She said she'd be glad to introduce you to a few of her Jerusalem friends who can help with anything you need when you arrive. You never know…things may have changed, and you may not recognize the Jerusalem you left fifteen years ago."

Gabi nodded. "Yes, Gila is a sweetheart. It's comforting to know she'll be there when I arrive. It will be like a continuation of my life here in Palo Alto, only faster paced and more stressful."

The waiter proudly informed us that he'd worked in the restaurant for forty-five years. He made the dressing for the restaurant's special Caesar salad at our table, mixing the eggs and oil, mashing the anchovies, squeezing the lemon, grating the Parmesan cheese, grinding the salt and pepper and, finally, tossing the lettuce in the dressing before serving our portions from a huge salad bowl. We read the leather-bound menu hungrily and ordered fish. Our last feast with Gabi. The bay was blue and still. Scores of white sailboats floated around in chaotic patterns, and big ships sounded their warning blasts from time to time.

The visibility was perfect; not infrequently, haze covered San Francisco and blurred it, but today the sky was clear. Alcatraz Island and the prison stood gloomily in the center of the bay, and the skyscrapers of the Financial District could be seen in the distance, on the south bank.

The meal was a farewell to everything that had connected Gabi to us. While we tasted the sea bass baked in a crust of ground almonds, the bouillabaisse, the shrimp in butter and garlic sauce, I reminded them of our weekend at Mika's cabin.

"An unforgettable experience," said Gabi. "It's hard to believe that only nine months have gone by since then. I feel as if I've lived a whole lifetime, as if I've become a different person."

Mika nodded in agreement. She, too, had become a different woman. I thought about the upheaval in Gabi's life.

"Do you still have a cloud inside you? The one that hovered above your painting?" Mika wanted to know.

"No. Many things have become clear since then. Actually, when I painted the cloud above the island, I didn't even know what was troubling me. The cloud painted itself. Since then, things have changed in my life. I found the strength to stand up to Danny, something that I couldn't even imagine doing before, and to steer my life to the right place. Everything looks clearer, in retrospect. As if I've suddenly grown. As if I've been given a shot of healthy narcissism that has helped me to come to terms with Danny and myself." Gabi smiled happily at us, and I thought that she had even grown a little taller, as if a vertebra had been added to her spine.

"What about the floating couple in your painting—are they still hovering?" Gabi asked Mika.

A slight flush of embarrassment appeared on Mika's face, and a mysterious smile touched her lips. She said she remembered the hovering couple when she wrote music. Their floating inspired her, like a fantasy that carried her to a distant yet internal world from which she drew melodies she never knew she had in her.

"I've reached the age of conciliation," Mika said. "Conciliation with myself, my past, and everything I feared would stand in my way. I experienced a kind of inner coming-to-terms with things."

I looked at my two friends, Mika and Gabi—women in midlife, radiant with mature beauty, the plump beauty of menopause. Neither defiant nor conspicuous like the beauty of firm-bodied, smooth-skinned young women. A beauty steeped in serenity. A friendly, appeasing beauty.

"And you, Daniela, what about the boldness you expressed in your painting? Has anything come of it?" Gabi inquired like an experienced art therapist, and Mika also fixed a pair of curious eyes on me.

I considered that boldness. I could recall only one moment of boldness in my life, when I had asked Yoel about the pipes and flickering lights in the university hallway, decades ago. A momentary inspiration. A one-time spark that died almost immediately. I unreeled my memories, as if rewinding a video tape, until I arrived at the earliest one. A foundational memory. I looked at the bold blue of the bay's water, a blue that conjured before me the memory of another blue—that of the Mediterranean Sea.

I must have been about three years old. I was able to roughly estimate my age at the time because it had been autumn, close to my birthday, and my brother, who was three and a half years younger than I, hadn't yet been born. I was walking with my parents on a deserted beach that, years later, I grew to associate with an Impressionist painting by Boudin. We walked through quiet stretches of sand and sea with no people, caressed by the autumn sun with a light wind carrying the salty smell of the sea. A wide band of seashells covered the fine sand, and lacy collars of tar from the ships at the pier marked the waterline. The little girl that had been me was hopping among the sharp shells, careful to avoid stepping on them, although she was delighted to stomp on the soft clumps of tar that stuck to her toes. In the background, my father was telling my horrified mother to "calm down with the hysteria about the tar, we've got turpentine at home." Thus, we slowly made our way along the beach until we came upon what first appeared to be a neutral, unemotional scene: fishermen had spread a net on the sand, relaxed and occupied with their work. As she approached them more closely, the girl in my memory noticed flecks of silver jumping in the dense net.

"What's that?" she asked her father.

"Fish."

"Why aren't they in the water?"

"The fishermen have pulled them out."

"They'll die. They need water, put them back!" the girl shouted, running toward the fishermen.

The girl in my memory cried, and the fisherman looked at her, amused. I ran back to my seemingly all-powerful father and begged him to order the fishermen to put the fish back in the sea, but he laughed and opted to pick me up and remove me from the scene, kicking and screaming in empathetic solidarity with the convulsing, condemned fish.

To this day, not much had changed. Inside of me, there was still a kicking little girl, concerned for safety and engulfed by the embrace of her family. The fishermen, whose images changed from time to time, still stood on the sidelines, chuckling.

And what if I did have boldness in me? What would I have done with it? I would have returned my complete "I" to myself solely. The "I" that had subdivided into five parts and now lacked a center. Like Katie's mother, I would have reclaimed it for my own. Dressed for a cocktail party like Anita, I would have also soared to the top. Like Lori, I would have shunned convention and danced on stages.

Gabi and Mika were staring at me, waiting to hear what I'd say, wanting to hear about my boldness, while inside my head a tall tale was unfolding. I imagined telling them that I was also leaving, moving to New York. I could already see them looking at me in amazement and asking, "What, really, you and the family are moving to New York?" And I would emphatically correct them: Not the family. Me. *I* am going to New York.

I wanted to find my new, complete "I." I wanted to dance as they danced in *Chicago*. I'd blow through my life like Daniela-Lori, I'd dress in Anita's glamorous outfits, I'd adorn myself in Katie's mother's cheeky sunglasses, I'd wrap myself in Gila's glowing aura, I'd arm myself with an extra vertebra like Gabi's, and with a sense of floating creativity like Mika's.

Just a little bit, I'd tell them. Only for a short time. Only in order to feel my true "I," to see if it still exists. When I find it, I'll happily come home. I promise. I'll come back to the "I" divided into five parts.

My friends would look at me with frank concern, thinking that the poor psychologist had gone crazy. And when I dared confide my secret wish to dance with Richard Gere, reminding them about how we had seen him in *Pretty Woman*, the perfect lover who was both handsome and a pianist, who spread Julia Roberts on top of the piano, their concern would collapse into giggles. In my mind's eye, I could already see their uncontrolled laughter, the same as the fishermen's laughter, which would confirm for me that, indeed, from the time of my first memory till now, nothing much had changed. Not the essence.

I turned my eyes away from the blue sea and looked at my friends' expectant faces.

"Boldness...?" I answered. "I don't think I have it in me. Maybe I'll enroll in a painting class where I can boldly scribble on the canvas to my heart's content." The same predictable Daniela. I hadn't impressed them, and they weren't falling out of their chairs in shock.

Hesitantly, I added, "Or...maybe I'll write a book."

I thought I saw Mika raise an eyebrow and Gabi, to change the subject, raised a festive glass of lemonade and said, "Next year in Rehavia, Daniela. That's also bold."

"Rehavia? Works for me," I said clinking glasses with them. But to be honest, I didn't even remember the last time I had visited the upscale

Jerusalem neighborhood. For someone like myself, who had grown up on the Mediterranean coast, and who now lived in a different coastal city that had come to feel much like home, Rehavia was like another country.

PALO ALTO, 2002–03

Epilogue

Copenhagen. The end of summer. Danny boarded the plane. On his way to grab a newspaper, he caught a glimpse of the seat in the last row of first class, the seat he had been occupying some months before on the flight to San Francisco when the flight attendant had spilled the bowl of caviar and smoked salmon onto his head. A man was sitting there, resting blissfully, paging through the *New York Times*. You don't know me, Danny inwardly told the man, but I know you well enough. You are a winner at winning. Most people don't measure up to your kneecaps, could never dream of your accomplishments. I tip my hat to you—*chapeau!* as they say in French. But watch out, my friend, that in the end you don't eat your hat, if you get my meaning. You feel like you're on a high horse. Life's a thrill ride, and you take it as it comes. Nothing can stop you, because you're not built for restraint. You have a hunger for money, women, and success, and that's fine, because only the hungry succeed. Every baby knows that; it's chapter one, the first lesson in Business Administration 101. I know you. You don't like to be managed. You have to be in control, and you have to pull the strings. You've got life by the balls, because nobody's cleverer than you. You smooth-talk everyone with your slickness, but believe me—and I am not just being paranoid—not everything is acceptable, not everything works out in the end. There are claims that don't hold water when you stand before yourself on Judgment Day, and you'll get what's coming to you big time. Remember what I'm telling you, my friend. Allow me to address you as my friend, because I've been in your place and in your situation, and I understand you very well. Your wife will make you see straight. Believe me. She'll come up with proof by a reverse twist. You try to manipulate her so that she won't catch you. But even though you've never appreciated her sharp mind, to put it mildly, she'll confront you, and you won't even know where it's coming from. You've always tried to cover your tracks and hide evidence, as if nothing ever happened. I know you think she's no rocket scientist; I know you think that you've known her from a very early age, and she's never been the brightest one around. You think she would only ever find the most trivial and unconvincing arguments to prove your sins. And you're right: she'll never catch you in a lie; that she knows. You're too smart. But in the end, she'll tell you she needs someone to love and understand her deep down. And that's a claim you can't weaken. Between you and me, even with your high IQ, that's an argument you can barely understand. So after your wife has you by the balls, you'll suddenly begin to think. And all of a sudden, you'll sort out what you really want from life. You'll conclude of your own accord that your sexual history is overspent. You forget the names of girls you've nailed. So what's the big deal? One more, one less? That's not going to sour the cabbage, as your mother used to say. So cool it, friend. Start thinking about what matters in life. Don't be ashamed to think like old Morrie, even if you haven't read his book, about the things you'll remember on your deathbed. And you don't have to be ashamed of admitting that your family is the most important thing in your life. The wife and children. The simple things that life is really made of. Your wife's cream cake, for example: How would your life look without it? Have you ever thought about that? So what if your wife quickly loses interest in anything to do with your business? Yes, she gives you that blank look when you try to include her in what's going on. You rush ahead, and she remains light years behind you. So what? Make an effort. Invest a little. Use your head, and learn to communicate with her. That's also a crucial skill. So there you have it, my friend, if you'll still allow me to call you *friend*. Without meaning to, I've drilled the doctrine into your head. Sorry. I don't like getting lectured on morality either. I wish you well, and I'll be seeing you on the NASDAQ board.

About the Author

Noga Niv is a clinical psychologist in a private practice in Palo Alto, CA. She holds an MA in psychology from Tel Aviv University and a PhD in psychology from PGSP, now Palo Alto University. She was trained in clinical psychology at Stanford University and in psychoanalytic psychotherapy. Inside the Bubble is her first novel. It was previously published in Israel in 2008.

Inside the Bubble was made possible in part by the following people who preordered a copy on Inkshares.com.
Thank you.

ALLEN CALVIN

BARTON J. FREEDMAN

BRENDAN CURRAN

CARMELA PASTERNAK

CHAYA HIRSCH

CLAYTON A. SMITH

CURT F WITTIG

DENNIS TEIFELD

DOROTHY V. CALVIN

DR. A. MORAG

DR. GLORIA GOLDEN

EHUD CHATOW

FRACASSINI LUISA

GILI ASPITZ

GUY PAILLET

HANNA REISLER

ISAAC AGAM

ITA MORDETSKY

JANET SPRAGGINS MD

JEAN WONG

JENNA ELLIS

KEVIN JORGENSEN

MICHAL SHALON

NATHAN ZOMMER

ORLI RINAT

PAUL WITKAY

ROBERT M. BRILL

RUSSELL ELLIS

SHARON ASHKENAZI

SHARON NASH

SHARON NIV

TALYA RONEN

YUVAL BRISKER

INKSHARES

Inkshares is a crowdfunded publisher. We democratize publishing by letting readers select the books we publish—we edit, design, print, distribute and market any book that meets a pre-order threshold. Interested in making a book idea come to life? Visit inkshares.com to find new projects or start your own.